FIREPROOF

Raj Kamal Jha is Chief Editor of *The Indian Express* which has won the International Press Institute's India Award for Excellence in Journalism three times. His novels include *The Blue Bedspread,* shortlisted for the Guardian First Book Award, winner of the 2000 Commonwealth Writers' Prize for Best First Book (Eurasia) and a New York Times Notable Book of the Year; *If You Are Afraid of Heights,* a finalist for the Hutch–Crossword Book Award in 2003; and *She Will Build Him a City. Fireproof* was rated first in CNN–IBN's list of best books published in India in 2006. His novels have been translated into more than a dozen languages. Raj works in New Delhi and lives in Gurgaon.

Also by Raj Kamal Jha

THE BLUE BEDSPREAD

IF YOU ARE AFRAID OF HEIGHTS

SHE WILL BUILD HIM A CITY

Raj Kamal Jha

FIREPROOF

PICADOR

First published in India in 2006 and in Great Britain 2007 by Picador

First published in paperback 2008 by Picador
an imprint of Pan Macmillan Ltd
Pan Macmillan, 20 New Wharf Road, London N1 9RR
Basingstoke and Oxford
Associated companies throughout the world
www.panmacmillan.com

ISBN 978-0-330-49377-2

3 5 7 9 8 6 4

A cip catalogue record for this book is available from the British Library.

Typeset by Intype Libra Ltd
Printed and bound in India by
Manipal Technologies Ltd, Manipal

For my parents Munishwar Jha and Ranjana Jha

In memory of C.R. Irani (1930–2005)

◆◆◆

WHAT'S left about two months after an apartment complex is set on fire? After many of those who live there have been killed? And those who haven't, have flown away on wings of fear, never to return?

Not much.

Just four policemen at the entrance, one fast asleep.

The shells of houses where parents and children, husbands and wives, brothers and sisters, friends and strangers, once lived.

Blackbrown streaks on walls.

Lines, short and long.

Stains, big and small.

Windows, their bars twisted. Their molten metal congealed in bursts of black iron rash.

The ribs of what was a car. Still parked in a driveway.

And debris all around. Like a tonne of black flower petals strewn in the yard to welcome ghosts.

And so it is, on an afternoon in the month of May in the year 2002 in Gulbarga Housing Society in the city of Ahmedabad. It's touching 40 degrees, there is fire in the sky.

It was here, on the last day of the February gone by, that a mob had stood and set the buildings on fire, burnt alive 38 residents – 12 are missing to this day. The Gulbarga massacre, as it came to be called in newspapers and on TV, was one of a series across the state of Gujarat that killed over 1,000 men, women and children, 70 per cent of them Muslim, ostensibly as revenge for the death of 59 Hindu passengers in an attack on a train by a Muslim mob the previous morning.

◆

This afternoon, in the scant puddle of a shadow in the yard, half-covered by shreds of charred cloth, scraps of burnt paper, there lies a child's book. It's called *Learning to Communicate* (published by Oxford University Press, New Delhi).

A brown patch in the top left-hand corner – possibly the work of fire and water, sun and shine – has seeped into each of its 124 pages. It's a junior-school English workbook, its leaves marked by what's clearly a child's handwriting and sketches. All in pencil. The fly leaf where the child would have been most likely to write his or her name, address, maybe phone number, is gone. Torn off.

On page 43, there is a poem called 'The Town Child' that has been underlined. Line by line, paragraph by paragraph.

This is how the poem begins:

FIREPROOF

I live in the town on the street,
It is crowded with traffic and feet.
The houses all wait in a row,
There is smoke everywhere I go.

There is only one thing that I love,
And that is the sky far above.
There is plenty of room in the blue,
For castles of clouds and me, too.

The child's last entry in the book is on page 84.

How many children were killed in Gulbarga isn't known – police say the bodies were too badly burnt to be identified.

All of the above is fact.

All of what follows is fiction.

◆◆◆

PROLOGUE

(THE OPENING STATEMENT)

We, the undersigned, do solemnly affirm in this, our opening statement to you, the reader, the following:

1 That we regret to inform you we shall not tell you our names.

2 That if you insist on at least one piece of identification, you may call us by the roles we play, mentioned at the end of this statement.

3 That alternatively, you may refer to us, at any time, by one or more of any of the following: bird beast, black blue, Hindu Muslim, Muslim Hindu, fire ice, cock cunt, song dance, sickness health, bridge river, radio TV, cat dog, night day. So on and so on.

4 That we could keep providing you with more such options. Endlessly and tirelessly. Until the hours go by, until night uncoils into day. Weeks

slide, months fold, seasons shift. Until the city swells, the streets crumble, the earth moves.

5 That one reason we can do this is because we have all the time in the world.

6 **That this is because we are all dead.**

7 That beginning the morning of February 28, 2002, we were killed in ones and twos, sometimes in groups of three, four. Sometimes thirty, forty, fifty, sixty, seventy, eighty. At one time, even ninety.

8 **That some of us had our throats slit, some were stabbed in the back, some in the front. Most of us, however, were set on fire.**

9 That we were killed in our homes and on our streets. At work and at play. In our sleep and in our waking, in the darkness and in the shining. And in the dim, half-lit spaces that lie in between.

10 **That there are, as of one count, a thousand of us. Not that many, not that few. If each of us were even just over a foot tall, stacked one on top of the other, we would reach almost as high in the sky as either of the twin towers of the World Trade Center. Perhaps, then, we could restore the skyline of a damaged city three oceans, three continents away. A tower of flesh**

and blood. (By the way, that's just a thought meant to illustrate. It should by no means be construed as an intention. For we do not want controversy.)

11 That once dead, we have discovered gifts we never knew we had. We have found a home in the sky far above, where, as the poet says in the child's book, there is plenty of room in the blue. We can ride across the city curled around wisps of smoke. We can climb up drops of rain to reach the castles of clouds, paint them red, yellow, any colour we choose. And while we are up there, we can even scrub the moon clean, stoke the sun if it begins to cool. Our children can dance underwater on the tips of leaves, our fish can fly, our birds can swim. In short, we can do anything. Except coming back to life, of course.

12 That during the hours we were killed, the world was a busy place. Girls in bikinis were barred from a Commonwealth summit in Australia to respect 'religious and cultural sensibilities'. An institute in Chicago revealed, in a medical first, that a thirty-three-year-old American woman had conceived a baby girl 'scientifically selected' to ensure she was free of Alzheimer's.

13 That closer to home, the nation celebrated Pandit Ravi Shankar's third Grammy and the

first-ever nomination of a Hindi film for the 74th Academy Awards. Government officials seized fourteen tonnes of fresh, endangered marine wildlife, illegally removed from the Andaman and Nicobar Islands. Work continued on the four-lane highways of our Prime Minister's dream, on sealing the glass atrium of the new mall. The point we are trying to make is this: our killing was certainly not the end of the world. Because elsewhere there was fun, there was frolic, there was the promise of a better future.

14 **That considering all of the above, we decided death should not be an excuse for inaction, grief should not become a substitute for sloth. That instead of trying to fight the fire with our tears, perhaps the time had come for us to give ourselves the promise of a better future, maybe some justice as well.**

15 That this is the story of how we went about it.

16 **That its narrator, though, is not one of us but one of the living. He is a man waiting for news of the birth of his first child, his wife in the operating theatre. In a hospital that night where we lay dead and dying in the city on fire.**

Signed (in rough order of our appearance in the pages that follow)

Head Nurse **Doctor 1**
Doctor 2 **Ward Guard**
Miss Glass **Lobby Guard**
Ambulance Driver **Old Bird**
The Book **The Watch**
The Towel **Taxidriver**
TV Body **Fruitseller**
Manhole Man . . .

17 We won't list everyone. Doesn't really matter because you will anyways meet us in the pages that follow. Some of us will walk in, walk out of the margins, lose our way between the lines, reappear to speak in footnotes. Where we will whisper in small type, dispense with full stops, not even pause for breath. For there's no time to waste.

So let's get started right away, let's get started with that night.

PART ONE

THAT NIGHT

1. *The Birth and the Delivery*

DON'T listen to the dead, please do not listen to the dead – whatever they tell you, whatever fancy name or un-name they wish to go by, howsoever lyrical they may wax, because once you lend them your ears, they will nibble at your guilt, feed on your pity, swallow you whole, from head to toe, make no mistake. That's why I need to tell you, right in the beginning, there's only one thing in this story about which there's not much doubt, in fact, there's no doubt, none at all. And it's this: it was, as they say in their opening statement, that night when it all started.

That night it was that night.

All the rest of it, everything else that follows, ninety-nine point nine nine per cent of it, doubt dispute distort deny.

Bury.

Cover with gravel, dead leaves, shrivelled, dry and rotting. Pat the earth flat, slap your palms against the hips of your trousers, let the dirt fly, then walk away not to look back. Never ever.

Or if you aren't the physical type, round up the little boys who at traffic lights knock on your car windows between red and green, get them to pile it all up, then fetch some kerosene, the poor man's fuel – only nine rupees per litre –

sprinkle it all over from a jerry can. Light a match, set the whole thing on fire. And blow.

Blow, blow, blow.

Like the North Wind blows in the children's tale.

Or if you want the exact opposite, if you want to preserve it so you may come back to it later, forget fire, use ice.

Freeze it. Cold, hard, solid, white.

Find a spot like they showed on TV that night. Under a glacier north of Himachal Pradesh. Which for twenty-three years preserved the bodies of a woman called Marin Bjornhaden, resident of the Swedish city of Göteborg, and of Lars, her fiancé. Both were tourists, trekkers, who had lost their way, but neither was damaged nor defaced. (Their golden hair was streaked with ice, like sunlight caught in the snow. Even their clothes were untouched, the fabric turned hard and brittle but perfectly in place, the white and blue checks on Marin's blouse not one bit discoloured. Ditto the fringes on her red scarf. The lapels of the fur-lined jacket that Lars wore.)

In short, do whatever you want.

Because it doesn't matter, the dead are going to get me in the end. Come what may, any which way.

And that's why it's the beginning there should be no getting away from. The beginning of the night, when they told me my wife had given birth to our first child.

A baby, severely deformed.

The only part of the baby's ten-point-two-inch frame left absolutely untouched by Strange, Mysterious Forces, seen or unseen, that cause such things to happen, were his eyes. (In a while, even the doctors at the hospital will stumble as they pull out *Gray's Anatomy*, 36th edition, turn to chapter title *Embryology*, page 178, run down the paragraphs they highlighted in medical college, first year, try to refresh their memory on which foetal organ is formed when . . . but let's leave that for later.) Each eye of the baby was perfectly shaped, fully functional. His eyebrows were perfect, too. As if drawn by an artist, talented and tender, who had all the time in the world and only two things to pour his life's purpose into: these two lines.

The rest of the baby was a mess.

So much so that if all the parts of all the world's babies, black, brown, yellow, white – choose your colour, mix a little bit of this a little bit of that – if all the babies conceived, imagined, all those about-to-be born or born, the half-made, the half-unmade, the aborted, the dead, through the present, the past and the future, down the ages of Baby History, were letters of an alphabet of a Baby Language and each normal baby a sentence making perfect sense, ours would have read:

Zd^hjd srty!lks. op*fhT)

Maybe shorter, maybe fewer words. But unreadable, nevertheless.

Twisted full stops, varying types, incomplete parentheses, dotted commas, fused colons, lost asterisks. The letters, of varying sizes, welded and split in the wrong places, the words mangled and missing.

So had it not been for those eyes and those eyebrows, the staff at the Maternity Ward of the Holy Angel Nursing & Graduate Hospital at 1607 Mahatma Gandhi Road, would have put him down as a 'growth'. Or they would have called it a mass. A lump. Or whatever the medical term is for a Mess. They would have then dropped him into a container, cold and glinting, so that his parents, my wife and I, could see for ourselves, if we so wished. Confirm the news that, sorry, there was no baby, only a growth. There was an *it*, there was no *him*. And after we had left the hospital for home, they would have incinerated it*him* in the hospital furnace. Or if there was a power cut and the generator wasn't working, they would have left it*him* on the floor. In the corridor of the ward, a bundle leaning against the wall. Wrapped in cotton gauze and bandages so thick you would have mistaken it*him* for soiled linen waiting to be picked up for laundry. Or to be sniffed, nuzzled, by a stray dog that might walk in from the street outside. Drawn in by the smell of a newborn, a newdead.

But it*him* had eyes and they were alive.

It*him* had eyelashes. It*him* had eyebrows and they moved.

Ithim (let's do away with the two types, roman and itals) was my baby. And my baby could see.

No, that won't do, that's evading, that's fudging with words.

For there's no running away from the sum, no hiding from the substance.

Indeed, the harder I try to avoid mentioning the baby's details, the harder I try to pass them off in a couple of paragraphs or slip them in between phrases deceptively roundabout, the more these details push at the walls of my reticence. And before they break through, come tumbling out in a headlong footlong rush – along with countless other details that are not relevant now, that will only clutter things up – I need to describe the baby. In terms as specific as I can. As the cliché goes: Cold & Clinical.

Just like the hospital that night.

To do this, I will need the unrelenting light of reason. Which means I should switch off all the adjectival neons, the Soft Yellows and the Harsh Whites, the Cold Blues and the Warm Reds.

Switch them off. Click, click. Click, click.

Mere switching off won't do, let me yank the wires out, wear heavy shoes, ankle-length, thick rubber soles to insulate my feet, let me smash these lamps, stomp hard on the shards until there is glass dust on the floor, dust so fine it reflects nothing. There, I have killed the lights, banished the shadows they cast. Of grief or pity. Tragedy or terror. Leaving behind only reason. No emotion, none at all.

So that when you read, hear or listen, no muscle in your face should twitch. No eyebrow arch, no eyes water, no face frown. So, here goes, following is A Brief Description Of Ithim, My Baby Boy:

ABOVE Ithim's perfect eyes and perfect eyebrows, his forehead was a narrow strip of flesh, less than a finger wide, wrinkled and dark in several places, as if charred, projecting half an inch or so beyond the level of his face. Like the narrow brim of a tiny hat made of human skin, discoloured and damaged beyond any possible repair. This forehead set off Ithim's head, a tiny sphere flattened at the top, its surface uneven, dented where the bones of his skull had not, and would, perhaps, never fuse. If you put your hand on it, you could feel, under the jagged edges, a movement inside: a grating, a buzzing, a fluttering. As if insects and worms, creatures with hard shells and scaly wings, had fallen into the spaces between his bones and were trapped inside, thrashing, waiting for a crack through which they could all come wriggling out, piercing my baby's skin.

To crawl and fly away.

For his nose, Ithim had a minute bump in the centre of his face with two holes. A membranous mound pierced twice with a pin but the mound so small you had to strain your eyes to make it out. Where his lips should have been, there was only a slit. Like a knife-cut, a nick. His right ear was missing. Leaving no trace, just the skin there stretched taut, merging with his noseless, mouthless face and the back of his head. His left ear was there but this was nothing like an ear, it was a very small flap of skin resembling a funnel, more in spirit than in flesh. For it was essentially shapeless and almost translucent. Folded upon itself, more than once, like the whorls of some alien pink flower. Diseased, waiting to fall off its fleshy stalk.

My baby had neither arms nor legs. None of the four, not one, neither left nor right. Not even stumps. Just four dark stains to mark what he should have had, no rough edges, no hollows. Making it seem that there was nothing amiss, that even looking for his arms and his legs was not only stupid but insensitive, too, an act of extreme prejudice. That it was absolutely normal to be born this way, that Ithim either heralded the birth of an entirely new generation, armless and legless. Or that he had countless such siblings, across the world, who had been born exactly like him and were now living happily ever after. Maybe in an apartment in Mumbai facing the Arabian Sea, in a cottage in Tierra del Fuego washed by the Atlantic, in a bedroom in Greenland, the Aurora Borealis dappling his body. Or in a house in Kabul, its windows and doors blown away by the war.

Like all newborns, Ithim did not have much of a neck but he had no chin either because in the absence of a defined mouth or nose, his face had little shape. Under the overhang, the weight of his forehead, it fell, listless, right down to his chest.

The chest itself was straight and, like his eyes and his eyebrows, it could have been unblemished had it not been for the way it ended. Imagine a garden path, neatly laid out, soft grass and freshly opened flowers on either side, the path itself smooth and clear, and then all of a sudden it stops and vanishes. Falls into a gorge, the bottom of which you cannot see through the dense foliage on either side. This is what happened at Ithim's waist.

There his chest disappeared and instead of a baby abdomen, that soft little swell, there was another strip of wrinkled skin mirroring the one on his forehead. But thicker and darker. It ran right around him, a string tied around his midriff, a belt welded to his waist. Like a skin-rod had been melted under a blowtorch and then allowed to drip onto his frame, congeal and then harden.

Below it was the penis, no longer than the nail on my little finger, two folds of flesh below it, drooped over the anus, which was, in turn, covered by a stretch of skin – little more than a flap that could be lifted or lowered, by the slightest of touches.

All this, in this much detail and more, I saw later when I

got to hold Ithim for the first time, when we boarded the taxi and when I brought him home. My first view of Ithim, however, was nothing . . .

. . . but just a white bundle carried by a large woman, also in white.

Her blue plastic name tag read HEAD N RSE, the U rubbed away leaving just a little white dot. Although I had been waiting in the Maternity Ward's lobby the entire evening and I knew my wife was the only one scheduled to deliver that night – her name written in chalk on the blackboard outside, her patient number 110742 – although I knew the next baby brought out of the Operating Theatre would be mine, I didn't see Head Nurse when she emerged with the bundle. I lost her in the shuffle of the crowd, in the cautious hurry of patients, their relatives and the hospital staff, in the scramble of those running to take the lift or walking up and down the stairs that led to the main entrance below. I lost her in the shapes of those on the floor, lying down, curled up, those still waiting for beds with their names and their numbers.

And it was only when I looked hard, when the crowd dissolved under my stare, that I saw Head Nurse walking, almost running, carrying my baby, wrapped from invisible head to invisible toe. As if he had been delivered stillborn and she was rushing him to the Morgue downstairs. Before other dead babies and dead adults took up the place that the hospital had assigned to him.

The end of the white sheet that covered him was tucked firmly between Head Nurse's left arm and left breast, she trying hard to ensure it didn't slip off, show even a bit of the baby's face. Afraid it would frighten those she passed along her way.

Like the solitary security guard. His plastic name tag, red in colour, read WARD GUARD, all the letters this time in place. Beyond Ward Guard, in the staircase landing, near the lift, there was a child fast asleep on a sheet spread out on the floor, his leg in a cast. There was a couple who sat on a wooden bench in one corner, the wife sleeping, leaning her head on her husband's shoulder, a white plastic bag by his side, crumpled, supported between his feet. The wife's eyes, half-closed, were fixed on the ceiling where there was nothing to see. Except the hooks and the fans and the paint, hard, hospital blue-white. If I try hard, I can recall others, I can remember what exactly they were doing the precise moment Head Nurse walked past them holding the bundle. But suffice to say, they couldn't care less, they had their own bundles to worry about.

Surely Head Nurse had no reason to walk so fast.

'You don't have to see him right away,' Head Nurse said, her back turned towards me as she pressed the button to call the lift.

I had ploughed, rather rudely, through the crowd, so fast she was moving and I didn't want to lose her. My feet had brushed against many sleeping on the floor, their sleep so deep there wasn't the faintest stir. Without even knowing, I had elbowed people, including patients, pushed them aside, charted my own way. And was now standing barely three feet behind Head Nurse, near the lift.

'Is he dead?' I asked, not courageous enough to walk up to her, claim the baby, pull the sheet off his face.

I didn't know what else to say, I didn't know what to ask.

There was a long pause as if she needed to think of the answer to this question, as if there were several ways to answer it, several options between yes and no.

'No, no,' she said, 'mister, how can you talk like this? Yes, it's an abnormal delivery, there's a problem with the way he looks but that's because of the way he has been born, the way he came out into this world. It doesn't sound nice, such words from your mouth.'

And she said this without once looking me in the eye, her eyes fixed on the display panel above the lift on the wall that showed the numbers rising; the lift was moving up.

'What's the problem with the way he looks?' I asked.

'Just wait for a while, I need to clean him up.'

It doesn't sound nice, she said. *Such words from your mouth.*

There's a problem with the way he looks, she said, *just wait for a while.* And I took all of this with not a word of protest.

For, obviously, this woman called Head Nurse thought that because she held the baby, *my* baby, in her arms, she wielded at that moment more power over me than anyone in this world. A power that had made it possible for her to climb from the hospital's Dettol-swiped marble floor to some astronomical moral high ground and stand there, a ground so high I should be struck speechless. That I should go down on my knees and gaze at her, not only at her huge feet trapped in tight black leather shoes, men's shoes with laces, but at her thick calves that draped over the rims of her white socks, up past her starched white skirt as well. Past the yellow half-moons under its buttons caused by an over-heated iron. Up her legs, into the darkness of her thighs, across the planets and the stars that lay inside and, in between, the whole of space. Head Nurse was God. And I, less than a mere mortal.

Hold it, why do I sound so bitter?

Head Nurse had nothing to do with the baby.

It was *my* sperm, it was *my* wife's egg, it was *my* wife's womb, it was *our* nine months and Head Nurse was just a hard-working woman trying to do her job and maybe she wasn't standing there in judgement, she was only being considerate and her words and gestures were innocent and well-meaning. Which my eyes had seen and my ears had heard, but which I had persuaded myself to turn and twist to sound harsh and brutal. Maybe because it was *I* who was the bitter one. The half-crazed father, frightened and insecure.

I didn't hear the lift reach the floor, I didn't hear it open, I didn't hear it as it began to swallow Head Nurse. With my baby. With at least ten more people. As she walked into it, she turned to look at me and smiled her first smile of that night: 'You don't need to get us any sweets to celebrate. I will clean the baby, then you can fill out the registration form, get the discharge slip.'

I heard the lift close with a creak, I heard it shudder in its shaft.

Up ahead, at the end of the corridor that led to the Operating Theatre where my wife was, beyond the glass door where someone had carefully painted a sign without caring about either spelling or grammar, NO ENTRY EXPECT FOR AUTHORISED PERSONAL, I saw two doctors in surgical scrubs, their masks still on, come out, look in my direction, say something to each other and then hurriedly walk in. They did this twice, thrice. As if someone had both of them on invisible strings and was playing with them. Like they were life-sized puppets, in doctor costumes. Gowns, caps, stethoscopes, androgynous. And someone was pushing them out and then pulling them back in. Pushing them out, pulling them back in. Maybe as part of a game called Doctors Come Out to Watch the Waiting Father of the Deformed Baby And Go Back In Without Breaking the Bad News.

'That's the first time I have heard her say that,' said Ward Guard, who, sitting in a red plastic chair, had seen it all, had seen Head Nurse, had seen the bundle go down the elevator, had even seen the Doctor Game, seen them come out, go back in, come out, go back in.

'Say what? Heard her say what?' I asked.

'That you don't have to get her any sweets. She never says that, never. Even when the baby's dead, she doesn't say that. She must be in one of her moods, don't take her seriously. She's had a very busy day, she has been here since morning. In the evening, she left for a while saying she was going to check on her children to see if they were safe, she had heard about some fire in her neighbourhood. Then she must have come back later in the night. Ask me, I have been watching her for five years. She has a good heart.'

'So why did she say that?'

My fifth sentence that evening, my fifth question.

The guard didn't want to answer, maybe he thought I wasn't ready to hear. Hear what? Perhaps this?

'You know why Head Nurse said that, you know why Head Nurse smiled at you and said you needn't bring sweets for her or for the hospital staff because and listen carefully she knows that your baby isn't dead in fact he's worse than dead Mister he's grotesque he's frightening he is ugly he scared the hell out of the doctors and the attendants and the nurses when they pulled him out they first thought it was a tumour that there was no baby and it was only when they saw the head and that's when they all said as in a chorus cover the monster is this human or is this an animal and Mister if I were you I wouldn't even take him home I would pray he dies that his internal organs twist and turn and fold upon themselves so that they choke him to death I would pray and wish that his perfect eyes close and never open again that his perfect eyebrows lie still and you don't ever have to answer your wife when she asks you what happened what's the fruit of my nine months of labour where is the pleasure of all my pain you can just tell her that he is dead let's go home rather than show her that fucking freak.'

No, Ward Guard didn't say anything like this.

Instead, he said: 'The baby must be sick, very sick.

'But don't worry,' he continued, 'there are very good doctors here. This may not be among the city's top hospitals but there are some very good doctors. And there's a temple near the parking lot. It's open until midnight after which the priest locks the main door to the room where the idols are kept but he keeps the courtyard open. It's very clean and quiet, it has a white marble floor where you can sit and pray. I do that, once in a while, just like that. Who knows – prayer may work.'

Sensing that I wasn't listening, Ward Guard fidgeted in his chair and I waited, my back now turned to him, my eyes fixed on the hallway that led to my wife, the row of windows on my left.

Another cluster of patients and relatives had collected, once again waiting for the lift that hadn't returned since it took Head Nurse and my baby downstairs. I passed them by as I walked to the nearest window. And that's when it happened, that's when I saw it.

And like a wind that rises on a still afternoon from a place unknown and keeps rising until it grows to a gale to a storm, making the tops of trees tremble, snapping branches, clapping doors and windows, toppling things in its way, it made me forget, blank out, erase, why I was there at the hospital, it made me forget the doctors, it made me forget Head Nurse, Ward Guard, the ward, the patients, the crowd, the child in a cast, the couple sleeping, the plastic bag between the man's feet, the display panel above the lift.

Above all, it even made me forget my baby, my wife, my baby, my wife.

It was a face by a window.

AT first, I think I missed it. For, as I stood there, by the window, looking straight ahead into the night, into the first wisps of fog that had started swirling above the ground like smoke from small, invisible fires, my mind had already taken flight, propelled by Head Nurse's words, by Ward Guard's words, by questions to which I had no answers. I had begun to wonder how come, of all the babies born at that moment in the world, it was ours that had to go wrong.

Like most parents-in-the-making, we had followed all the advice prescribed by the gynaecologist, who had returned from Riyadh after the First Gulf War, was herself a mother of two and a grandmother of three, and who kept telling us, as proof of her competence, that all five were among the healthiest men and women in the country, if not the world. Besides the four hundred rupees she charged every visit, she got us to dip into our shallow pool of savings as well and pour whatever we had into nuchal scans to look for genetic defects, intrauterine procedures, amniocentesis, fetal blood sampling to ultrasounds and tests and scans so specialized I can't even recall their abbreviated forms. None of these tests, the doctor said, revealed anything that warranted concern.

Still, at a cybercafe, just down the street from where we lived, every evening of my weekly day off from work, my wife and I would Google child disorders + disabilities, congenital + abnormalities, early + warning + signs + deformities + childbirth + India. We would trawl the sites of the world's best hospitals and nursing homes, look at each list of FAQs trying to find out if there was anything the doctor had missed.

*

(The cybercafe owner was a man in his forties, a man called Saxel Meeko, who, maybe because of its oddness, had printed his name out in several fonts on A4 paper and pasted the sheet on a board behind his chair.

Saxel Meeko

Saxel Meeko

Saxel Meeko

Saxel Meeko

He kept the cybercafe open until late in the night, his own computer screen split into frames, each showing a landmark of a different city live from across the world. One day it would be Times Square in New York, the Eiffel Tower in Paris, another day it would be Trafalgar Square in London, Darling Harbour in Sydney, the flower market in Amsterdam. One window that never changed, however, was the one linked to the webcam outside the cybercafe, mounted high up on the wall and trained on the pavement below.

The rest were fuzzy, sights familiar from magazines and picture postcards, the movement in them barely perceptible except over long periods of time, of the sky changing colours or like once in the case of Darling Harbour a sea-gull flying into and out of the frame. And in New York, a man running to board a bus. But Mr Meeko's pavement scene was where the image was clearest, where you could see people walking in and out of his shop. You could even see the occasional street dog sniffing the water in the drain.

Ordinarily, Mr Meeko kept the screen turned in such a way that no one but he could see this image. I got to see it only after my wife and I had made what would have been our tenth or eleventh visit, and that evening there was no one in the cybercafe except the three of us. 'I am happy to inform you,' Mr Meeko said, 'that now I can share what I keep very private, very confidential, but you are nice people who avoid any unpleasant situations. So I have decided to do this, thank you, please.' He had never spoken so many words to us at one go but he made the offer seem like a privilege so rare that we were struck more by the warmth of his gesture than the oddity of its manner, the singsong lilt of his voice. I don't recall what we said in response other than making polite exclamations on his idea of bringing the world to our neighbourhood, but from that day on, Mr Meeko would always smile at us and even began giving us the printouts for free. He became a friend, in fact, the only friend I had in the city, and I am going to meet him later, there is much to tell about him, but now, back to the baby.)

My wife and I would read all the printouts at night, she on her back, her legs raised on a pillow. And everything we read pointed to only one conclusion: that we had nothing to worry about: my wife was only twenty-six, this was by no means a late pregnancy. And there was no record of any congenital abnormality in either her family or mine. Her father, a businessman in Calcutta, had suffered one heart attack and her mother wore glasses – hardly a recipe for a gene scarred irreversibly. As for me, both my parents had died early, my father first, not because of any long-drawn-out illness but a rash bus driver who ran him over, in the morning, right in front of the school where he had taught for more than twenty years (a street intersection which he had boasted he could cross blindfold at any time of the day or night). My mother followed him, dragged down more by grief and loneliness than any specific ailment. So, yes, child-birth, like everything else, was a roll of the dice. But as far as we were concerned, the doctor from Riyadh told us, we could uncross our fingers and roll.

So as my wife slipped into her last trimester, into her last few weeks, she began to exhibit, instead of jitters, a resolve that grew more pronounced by the day. She told her parents not to visit her until the child was born – thank you very much, she said, I can take care of myself, I have my husband and I have my home – and when I asked if she wouldn't, like all first mothers, feel more comfortable with her mother around, she turned to me and replied: 'My mother isn't a doctor so is there anything I can show or tell her that I can't show or tell you?'

She began talking about redoing the second room of our three-room rented house. She told me she had lined up a carpenter to make a bunk bed, the kind they have in newspaper advertisements every Saturday in the Home and Décor section. She even, one afternoon when I was at work, called to say that she had hired a taxi and gone around the city looking for stars and planets to fix on the walls because she had read in some novel, in its first few pages, about a nursery painted blue, the sky on the ceiling, because the parents wanted to give the child a 'hand-made heaven'. That was what she wanted for our child, she said. A hand-made heaven at home.

If all this recalling appears detailed, even sentimental, blame it on the kind, gentle gaze of hindsight. For, of course, that night, standing at the window, I didn't remember it in so logical a fashion, just as scraps of images, fragments of sound.

The gynaecologist, the ultrasound, the cybercafe, the gynaecologist, the bed, the printouts, the swell of my wife's stomach.

And while my mind raced through this, my eyes kept looking through the window of the Maternity Ward on the sixth floor. And it was then that I saw the face.

The Face.

⬩◆⬩

FIREPROOF

I am Ward Guard, I am the first one to slip into the footnotes to whisper my story which, to be frank, wouldn't have been much of a story if I hadn't been killed the way I was because I was no different from the hundreds, the thousands who arrive in this city from outside the state looking for work as I did five years ago, when I was twenty-three years old, when I came from a village near Udaipur, Rajasthan, and after knocking on all kinds of doors for more than three months, I got a job at Holy Angel as a security guard doing the night shift every day, seven days a week, only one day off every three weeks, even that off day spent washing my uniform, doing household chores, writing letters home, all at a salary of Rs 3200 per month, a salary not enough to bring my wife and three children – two daughters and one son, ages four, two and one – to live with me in the city so I left them in the village where they live with my parents to whom I sent Rs 1500 every month by money order, Rs 500 to my wife separately, and lived on the remaining Rs 1200, not so difficult since I had found a room-mate, a friend who works as a driver for a businessman, both of us rented one room in a slum for Rs 450 per month, it had a light bulb and a table fan, and while my friend worked the morning shift, it was my job to cook dinner every evening before leaving for the hospital and in return, my friend let me pay only Rs 150 towards rent, a convenient arrangement which helped me save a few extra rupees for my family, rupees that will be of great help now that I am gone which brings me to the last thing I recall which is the window of the house, someone standing there not allowing me to climb out, the heat and the pain, like boiling oil splashed into my eyes and all I could see then was the image of my wife, she is only twenty-two years old, she should not be a widow for the rest of her life, I hope a good man agrees to marry her, doesn't behave like a stepfather with my children and then, who knows, maybe my wife will have more children from her new husband, I hope he has a good job and can provide for her and my parents too because my money is going to run out, tomorrow, March 1, is payment day for February, the hospital does have the permanent address of my village and I hope they directly send the money order to my parents along with the lump sum, as compensation, about Rs 1 lakh, I think, for those who were killed plus my Provident Fund which should be around Rs 15,000 and if that happens, it will help my parents pay off their debts although I worry most about my mother because she won't eat anything for days, she will sit up at night, crying, she will keep telling everyone that no, my son hasn't been killed, he is safe, he is just busy and hasn't called, he will return by the morning train but then days and nights and weeks and months will pass, her grandchildren, my children, will grow and maybe, one day, looking at them, all grown up, adults, my mother will realize that I am not going to come by the morning train, she isn't going to see me ever except those nights when I happen to slip into her dreams.

2. *Face By Window, Letters On Glass*

THE Face The Face The Face, that's the only way I can refer to it right now, using the common noun, capping the T and the F, repeating the words for effect, because how else do I illustrate that, in a setting so commonplace – the view from an ordinary window of an ordinary hospital building – I saw something so extraordinary.

For consider this:

There was a lawn downstairs, less of a lawn, more of an empty space not used, draped in darkness, except its edge skirted the main building where the EMERGENCY neon cast a narrow flood of harsh white light, softened somewhat by the fine fog rolling in from across the main road. There was nothing to see down below, just the covered heads of a crowd of patients and visitors walking in and walking out, the black bodies and the pale yellow tops of several auto-rickshaws, parked in one messy tangle, like insects huddling in the rain. Right in front, across the lawn, was the other wing of the hospital building, rows and rows of windows, the ones in the middle, third to sixth, all lit; these were the patients' rooms. The first two floors were dark; this was the administrative block, which closed at five in the evening. My eyes moved over the heads of the people below, up the lampposts, until they stopped at another window, a rectangle of light, greyed by the curtains.

To this day, I cannot say what happened first, what followed what. Did my eyes take in this window in their aimless, desultory sweep? Or did something in the glass pane draw them there? Either way, there it was: a woman's face looking down, peering out, a bit of her shoulder visible.

How do I describe it without sounding fictional?

It was not a face that you see every day in this city. Perhaps it was her hair, dishevelled, the strands splayed across her forehead, the face itself small and angular. Perhaps it was the way her hair was cut, short, setting off her face that made it appear so striking. Almost involuntarily, I pulled myself back. Had she seen me? Was I intruding? I looked again and there she was. I tried to follow her eyes by drawing an imaginary line from her window at the angle I thought her gaze was but in the darkness even that was difficult. Still, I tried. My imaginary line led to an ambulance that until a moment ago wasn't there, a white van, dented, streaked with mud, parked just in front of the Emergency Ward, its engine still running. Two hospital attendants, in uniform, stood next to it, holding a stretcher. I think I could hear Ambulance Driver say something but that may just have been my ears playing games given the muffled chatter from the Maternity Ward, from the corridor behind me. And the voices floating from the lawn below, the sputtering of the auto-rickshaws, the idling of the van, the shout of the hospital staff.

When I looked up again, back to that window, the woman had gone. The light inside was still on, the curtains slightly parted and through the glass, I could see a bit of something against the wall, a bedside lamp maybe, a cupboard perhaps. But what was that?

On the window itself, a distinct smudge.

It could have been the warmth of her breath, its vapour condensed on the glass but, if so, this smudge was unusually large in size. As if she had breathed six or seven times onto the glass, moving her lips from one end of the window to the other until enough of her warm breath had condensed to stain the glass. And in this condensation, she had written two words with her fingers:

HELP ME

All upper case, a gap between the two words. The size large enough for me to read clearly, even from so considerable a distance.

Yes, I know, I know what this sounds like, what this appears to be: a lie, a cheap shot at a cheap thrill, the fevered outpourings of a male imagination, fired by the fact that he's just been shown the price of fatherhood, that the baby will now be the centre of his wife's universe in which he, his yearnings and his desires, will take a permanent back seat while the baby enjoys the ride. Wife gone, welcome Mother. And this realization frustrates this Male, this New Father, making him see things that are not there. A woman, of all things. Her face, a bit of her shoulder. And this woman asking him for help, when his wife is yet to recover from labour? Give me a break, even a pre-pubescent schoolboy could come up with a fantasy more delicate, more nuanced.

Yes, I know, I know, I know.

And that's why my first impulse was one of disbelief – I

turned to look away, look the other way. The van was still there, its doors still closed and Ambulance Driver was gesticulating furiously, telling the two attendants to go open the door. I looked up, again, at that window; The Face wasn't there. But the words were.

Maybe, and this was my first thought, these were words in my head that my eyes had tricked me into believing were imprinted on the window so I blinked once, twice, and looked again but, no, These Were Words Written On The Glass. As sharp and as legible as a moment ago, although I wasn't sure how long these would stay this way given the creeping fog of that February night. I found myself breathing onto the window where *I* stood and drawing lines with my fingers. I was tempted to reply but checked myself; there were patients waiting, sitting and standing behind me, and although not one of them was looking my way, I didn't want to be seen doing something as silly as writing on glass. And what would I write?

A reply to something scribbled on a window by someone I had only vaguely seen?

What if the streaks and the strokes that looked like HELP ME were just that: streaks and strokes, appearing not by design but by chance, by the accidental brush of the curtain against the cold glass?

Or several brushes, more like it?

A dozen or more, one by one, the first drawing the straight line of the H, the second bisecting it in the middle, the third an upward stroke completing the letter; then the fourth marking out the stem of the E, the fifth, the sixth and the seventh its three branches, the eighth and the ninth laying down the *L*, the tenth the downward stroke of the *P*, the eleventh its curve – and so on and so on?

But, surely, that was improbable, a curtain writing in the glass.

That night, however, even this explanation, bizarre it may have seemed, appeared more plausible, easier to understand and grasp, than the straightforward one staring me in the face: there was a woman in that hospital room who had seen me watching her and there was something else in the room or something outside she was perhaps afraid of, needed help with. And maybe because there was no other way she could get her message across – perhaps the nurse had been uncooperative or there was no phone in her room – she had chosen this option. Or there was no one she could send her message to and standing at her window, looking down, she had chanced on me looking at her. And when I pulled back, she had sensed my discomfort, my getting self-conscious, which must have come to her as confirmation that there was someone, this man standing by another window, who would see what she wrote on the glass, in her breath with her fingers.

HELP ME

She wanted me to read that.

I looked at the window again. The words had begun to fade as the room inside must have got colder. All I could see now was *E P ME*, the *E* of the *ME* disappearing, and as I focused on the remaining letters there was the blur of a movement inside, I saw a form pass by the window, a hand reach out to wipe the glass clean, draw the curtains closed.

I saw the lights switch off turning the window into a rectangle of darkness.

So that I didn't lose the window now there was nothing to make it stand out, I kept my gaze fixed. I needed to map this window's coordinates, remember them, if I were to look at it again: five floors from below, I counted, the thirteenth window from the left. Fifth floor, and then maybe the thirteenth room from one end (assuming the inside was a faithful reflection of the outside, that there were no hidden rooms and alcoves).

Fifth from below, thirteenth from the side.

Should I go there right now? I thought.

'MISTER Jay, excuse me, can we talk to you for a minute?' The doctor was behind me, Ward Guard standing so close it looked as if his job was to protect the doctor from me, as if I would, any time now, lunge at him, tear his gown off, strangle him with the rubber tubing of the stethoscope.

I followed the doctor to his room.

There was another man there, sitting by his side. Perhaps another doctor; he didn't look like an attendant because he was well dressed, had shoes on, his shirt was tucked into his trousers, he wore glasses. When we entered, he was writing something without looking up, as if he had begun taking notes even before we had started our 'talk for a minute'.

'Mr Jay, the baby has arrived prematurely, he didn't get time to be fully formed,' said Doctor 1. 'The good news is he is alive, how long he will live – that I can't tell you.'

I sat there, listening. *How long he will live – that I can't tell you*, the words seemed to float across the room to me.

I wanted to swat them down, as if they were flies, but all I could do was watch them fall to the floor, word by word, until they had all gathered there, in a heap. Adjusted themselves, on their own, to spell out the two words I had just seen on glass: *help me*.

'The bad news,' Doctor 1 said, 'is that he will not change.'

He will not change.

'What do you mean he will not change?' I asked.

'Whatever you see today, Mr Jay, you will see tomorrow, you will see as long as he lives. He will neither speak nor hear. He doesn't have arms or legs. All he can do is to watch since his eyes are functional, we have checked. That's a miracle given the state in which he is in. We have never seen something like this.'

'How come there's nothing wrong with his eyes?'

'That's what we have been asking ourselves.' Doctor 1 pointed to an oversized book on Doctor 2's desk. 'We have even been reading. That's *Gray's Anatomy*, that's our Bible, we even checked it again in case we thought we had got it wrong. The eyes and the eyelids form some time in the third month while the limb buds, that's the word we use for the small elevations which grow to become arms and legs, these buds sprout at the end of the first month. Four to six weeks, maximum. How did this happen, how did the limbs not form but the eyes did? How did the ultrasound miss this? We have no answer, the book has no explanation.'

'He can't speak, he can't hear?'

'He can't speak,' Doctor 1 said. 'He will make no noise. Normally, children who can't speak do make a noise, when they cry. This child can't even do that. He will be silent, for ever. We shall, of course, keep checking him regularly.'

'What about my wife?' I asked.

'Yes, that's what we were coming to. She is fine but she has bled a lot, we have put her under sedation. It will take her a few days to recover.'

'When can she come home?'

'We have to do some tests,' he said, 'keep her under constant supervision. She needs rest. If I can suggest this, it's better that you don't tell her anything, nothing about this baby until she's back on her feet, until she returns home.'

'When can I take the baby home?'

'Mr Jay, ideally, we should keep the baby here for at least twenty-four hours, if not forty-eight, under observation, that's standard hospital procedure. But I am very sorry, it's a busy night at the hospital and it seems it will get busier. We don't have too many beds so the best course of action, in our opinion, and I have discussed this with Head Nurse, is that you wait for a few hours until she cleans him up, finishes the paperwork, and then you can take him home.'

'But how do I take care of the baby? I have never done this before.'

'You can rest easy, this baby won't need much, just regular feeds and cleaning. Even the feeds, we will have to do it differently. With a tube, like a dropper. Head Nurse will show you how, it's easy. She's the best we have. And as we said earlier, this baby won't cry. So no disturbance,' Doctor 2 smiled. 'Look at the bright side, Mr Jay, many new parents will envy you, a baby that doesn't make a noise while crying. Won't bother you in your sleep.'

Perhaps, it struck him as soon as he had completed this

sentence, that what he had just said, in an attempt to give me some comfort, had ended up being insensitive, almost callous. He instantly checked himself. The smile disappeared, he was back to being polite and formal: 'I didn't mean it that way, I am sorry. In the meantime, I have to go and check on your wife. Why don't you come and take a look, we will be in there for only about five minutes.'

To get into the room where they had wheeled in my wife from the Operating Theatre, I had to take my shoes off, get into a green, disinfected gown, blue rubber slippers that had been used by someone very recently, were still warm.

My wife was covered up to her neck, her face as if she had slipped into a sleep she would never wake up from. Several thick sheets were draped over her, rising almost a foot so that I couldn't see the shape of her body. Tubes punctured her wrists. I thought I heard her move, let out a breath, but no, it was one of the machines in the room, its whirring like the sound of her breath. Her own breathing was so slow, so light, that I had to bring the back of my hand below her nose to feel the air. Had it not been for this, she would have passed as lifeless so still and silent was she, both her arms by her side, pressed close to her body, hands outstretched, palms up, fingers frozen in an unnatural curl, the time-tested, time-honoured position of the dead. I touched my wife's fingers, their tips were cold, there was a bit of translucent tape on her thin wrist, smooth, wrinkled in just one spot where the needle from the tube pierced it.

I touched her there.

*

THIS had been our first touch, almost four years ago, my hand against her fingers and her wrist. It had been purely accidental and I would be lying if I said the touch was what started it all, no it wasn't, no it didn't. It was a brush with a stranger, one of those brushes that happen every day in any city in this world. And even if it had showed up on Mr Meeko's webcam window, I doubt he would have noticed.

We were sitting in the reception area of a recruitment agent's office, on the second floor of a three-storey building, a restaurant below and a shop selling bathroom tiles above, the two of us among twenty or so college graduates who had come to be tested and interviewed. For five openings with a company that claimed to provide 'research services' for foreign trading firms investing in Indian stocks.

What had brought me and, I guess, her and the others there as well, was the advertisement:

Join the Business Process Outsourcing boom but no night shifts, no calls, no need to learn neutral globalized accents. We need graduates with analytical skills but no specialized knowledge, just a meticulous disposition, a desire to find out facts and details, research, an ability to work well with others, meet deadlines, attractive commission and bonus. Work for the movers and shakers on Wall Street.

Rewritten for accuracy, this should have been: *If you don't have a fancy degree, if you don't know what you are good at, if you have no place better to go, if you are young and starting off as a loser, come to us and try your luck for we don't need any better. We need you to collect facts and figures.*

And although we sat there, with our CVs in plastic

folders, looking as if we were ready, as if we had been brought into this world only to take it on, we were united by the tacit awareness of our desperation. For, frankly, other than two commerce courses which I had somehow scraped through in college, I knew little of stocks and shares, of the ups and downs of the market. (The previous night, in what I had thought would be a preparation for the interview, I had stayed up watching business channels on TV, the ticker tape at the bottom of the screen, the stock abbreviations tagged with electronic arrowheads pointing up or down. But all I could think of was how the arrows pointed right into the necks of the women anchors, between their black shirts, over their firm breasts, under their chins, to their painted lips from which rolled words like futures and options and derivatives and equity and yields. And all I could think of was how some arrows pointed down to where their legs would have been, their feet. And how irrelevant and ignorant I was, how hopelessly unprepared for the next day's interview.)

But that afternoon, sitting in the reception for about half an hour, looking at the worn-out sofa and the scuffed chairs, at the three interviewers walking in and out, each looking more washed out than the other – the most energetic one was a short man in glasses, with wavy hair, who rolled his r's in what seemed to be an American accent – I wasn't even sure if getting the job would be in any way better than leaving the room with nothing to show except a couple of hours killed. And maybe the memory of the unusually thin woman sitting beside me. A woman in black trousers, close-fitting, and a red sweater, long-sleeved.

She had picked up an old magazine from the centre table

and was reading it, her wrists resting above her knee. It was a film magazine, more suited for a dentist's or a doctor's waiting room than a place where they were looking for the next generation to keep the wheels of the markets going round and round. I could smell the jasmine perfume she was wearing, I heard the rustle of glossy, printed paper, her movements as she flipped the magazine. Our chairs were so close that our knees could have touched and no one would have even noticed. Not that I felt any urge to do so. I was waiting for my fifth interview in as many months, too tired to try a sixth, and the couple of inches my knee needed to move to the left to touch hers was not going to do anything for me. I needed something less fleeting, more tangible.

Her hair was cut in such a way that with her head bent over the magazine pages, it covered the half of her face that was towards me. I did look sideways but more out of boredom from staring at the wall than any genuine sense of curiosity. Her arm was painfully slender, the skin sheer and pale, stretched taut over her entire frame, so tight that near her elbow there were no wrinkles. I saw her foot in red sandals, again so thin, the nails translucent, almost unnatural, that it was difficult to look at her and not conjure up the image of a skeleton, covered with just one layer of skin instead of the fat and the tissues and the veins and the nerves and everything else that go to make it human.

They called my name and when I got up from the chair, almost instinctively she drew herself closer, to avoid our knees touching. My chair moved, she got up to let me pass but the moment I turned to walk towards where I had been called, her magazine fell. Feeling partly responsible for this predicament and, all the while, her thinness playing on my mind like a frailty, almost an ailment, that called for understanding, if not pity, I stopped. She was already on her knees, about to pick up the magazine, but it was too late for me to backtrack. What could have turned into a very silly, very awkward situation was saved by the fact that I beat her to the magazine (although later she told me that she had deliberately given me that extra couple of seconds) and when I handed it to her, my hand brushed against the tips of her fingers and her wrist.

Our first touch.

But because she was down on the floor and the entire sequence lasted for less than ten seconds or so, I still couldn't see her face, her hair had once again kept it out of bounds.

At the interview, the questioners, it seemed, couldn't care less.

They saw a man, Me, sitting across the table and perhaps that's all they needed, a human being with two arms and two legs who knew how to write his name, who needed a job. (And I had, I think, impressed them with factoids I had gathered, like how India's nominal GDP was expected to exceed one trillion US dollars by the end of 2007, how the Communist government in West Bengal was re-thinking its ideology to attract investment, how the Prime Minister's highway project was going to connect the length and breadth of the country, how Dalian in China was being prepared as the next outsourcing centre to rival Bangalore, how I wanted this job ever since both my parents had died. And how I would never even think of leaving, I am not the kind of person who can handle two things at the same time, like working at one place and applying to another. Stuff like that. Self-pitying nonsense. But, I guess, it worked.)

On the way out, assured that an appointment letter was on its way, I smiled at the woman with the magazine. 'I will wait, you finish your interview,' I said as she was called in.

She didn't get the job but she got me.

And her face, which only then I could see clearly, would, in a just under a month, make me forget everything, make me tell her that I wanted to wake up every morning for the rest of my life, looking at it.

Yes, I am digressing.

But see how naturally this digression happened, how the recollection of the first meeting I had with the woman I married and who is the mother of my child comes within moments of recalling The Face by the window, the other woman? For, in a way, doesn't this show the integrity of my intentions? Doesn't it confirm that when my eyes fixed on to The Face, it was of their own accord, not any premeditated design on my part?

HEAD NURSE stood in the doctors' room, with the bundle. 'Fill out the form,' she said. 'You have a name for the child?' My wife had, indeed, chosen a name. So confident and assured she was that it would be a daughter that she had chosen only one name: *Baaraan*. She had checked, she said, in Persian, it means the sound of rain falling.

I could have gone with it, so what if it was a boy, the name was apt since hadn't the doctor said watch out for his eyes, that his eyes were the only things perfect? And that if he cried, there was no way you could hear him so you had to be careful, you had to keep watching his eyes because the only way you could hear him cry was if you could listen to the sound of his tears falling. Tears and raindrops. Both, in essence, the same.

But, no, I had already made up my mind, my baby boy would be Ithim.

And so I wrote: *Ithim*.

'Just go with Head Nurse, Mr Jay, she's the best we have, she will take very good care of you,' said Doctor 1, stepping aside to let Head Nurse pass, showing her a respect, almost an unusual deference, that struck me as odd if not misplaced. (*She's the best we have*, that's what Doctor 2 had also said just a little while ago.)

'What kind of a name is that?' Head Nurse asked, staring over my shoulder at the form I had filled out, handing it to Doctor 1, who took one look at it, smiled, then passed it to Doctor 2, who read it, laughed.

'Ithim,' Doctor 2 said, pronouncing it as *e-dim*. 'Does it mean anything?'

Before I could reply, Doctor 1 stepped in: 'Sure it does. It must. Let the father decide, what's your problem?'

'Thank you,' I said.

Whatever name I gave my baby boy, it would anyways have been without his consent, entirely self-serving, so why not this name, this word that when split, divided the world in two, into those who would look at him and see an object and those who would look at him and see my son, my baby. Now when I think of it, I realize it wasn't anything profound like that, it was more my way of distracting myself that night from all that had happened, the birth, the face by the window, my unconscious wife, my despair and my dread. And not just a distraction, I would like to think that it was also my act of defiant assertion that none of this had thrown me off balance. That if I could call him Ithim, if I could still play around with words, that meant I wasn't all gone. That I had it in me to take it all in my stride because, in the heaviness of that night that was threatening to crush me under its overwhelming weight, hadn't I just fashioned a little lightness?

Ithim.

It and *him.*

Hadn't I just signalled to my baby, in whichever language babies a few hours old understand, formed or deformed, that he was my necessary accomplice? That his condition at birth may have thrown the natural order of things into complete disarray but his subsequent naming by me, by his father, had brought back some sense into this chaos?

How wrong I was.

⬩◆⬩

FIREPROOF

I am Doctor 2, I was twenty-eight, I was born in this city, I did my MBBS from Osmania University in Hyderabad and I wanted to do an MD but I couldn't make it despite two attempts although the second time I did get into Biochemistry but I didn't want that subject so I joined Holy Angel and although private practice wasn't allowed, I saw about twenty patients every week in my neighbourhood because that way, I made about Rs 6000 extra, I needed that because my father died five years ago, I lived with my mother and my sister who is twenty-two, she's just completed her architecture course – she is very bright, after the Republic Day earthquake in this city, she explained to my mother, drawing on a piece of paper, why cracks had formed in our house and how she would have designed it better – and it was her day off today, my mother told me not to go to work this morning because she had heard on TV the news of the attack on the train and how everyone said they feared trouble but the hospital had arranged for a van to drop us off home that night and I thought that would be very safe but it didn't work out that way, the last thing I remember is Doctor 1 telling me to be quiet, a dozen people stopping the van, asking the driver our names, then letting the driver run away, I remember trying to open the van but they broke the windscreen, I could smell the kerosene being poured in, my glasses were the first to catch the heat, I could smell my hair get singed, I felt the skin peel and then it was all over, pretty fast, and now all I think of is what happens to my sister and my mother, the only hope I have is my uncle, he's my mother's younger brother, he lives in Mumbai, runs a restaurant and a taxi service and I think my mother and my sister will move there to live with him because we have good memories of that place, when we were in school, my sister and I, we would visit Uncle every summer vacation and, on Sundays, he would give us a taxi with a driver who would take us to show filmstars' houses facing the sea, his wife – my aunt – and my mother also get along very well, only last month, my aunt sent my mother two pictures of some girl in Mumbai saying in two years I will be thirty so I should get married, the girl was attractive but I wasn't so keen, I wanted to firm up my practice, my sister joined the chorus, she said look at the picture, you won't get someone more beautiful than this girl, but all that's in the past, I worry about the future although I am sure Mumbai will be a better city for my sister, workwise, there are many more opportunities there for an architect, new cities with high-rise apartment complexes are coming up in the suburbs, she will miss her friends but she will make new ones, Mumbai is also safer, there are many more people there like us, there is strength in numbers when they single you out.

3. *The Empty Room, The First Picture*

STRANGE, how a hospital should go to sleep at night just like the healthy when, in fact, disease sits in each room, on the bed and in between the sheets, when death stands behind many a door, pressed flat against the wall, ready to walk in unannounced. But come night, the hospital has to sleep. So its eyes, all the doors to its rooms, close. Its limbs, the long flanks of its corridors, fall still and quiet. And the only thing you hear is its breath, the hum of the tubelights, the buzz of the machines.

Soft and steady, soft and steady.

So it was with Holy Angel that night when I stepped out of the doctors' room and followed Head Nurse as she walked towards the paediatric Intensive Care Unit to deposit – that's the word the doctors used, *deposit* – Ithim for a few hours.

As if he were *it*, not *him*.

'Mr Jay, you may stand outside the room and look through the window,' said Head Nurse, walking briskly, each word thrown like a ball, travelling down the deserted hallway in front, bouncing back from the wall, grazing her shoulder, then grating my ears. 'Hurry up, because you will get only a couple of minutes,' she said, 'then I will have to draw the curtains. My shift is over, I can't stay here for ever. I am not even supposed to be here right now.'

The walk to the ICU was long.

And it was the sight of the floor, bare and glistening, stretching on either side as far as my eye could see, catching Head Nurse's reflection as if it were glass, showing a certain cleanliness and order less evident earlier on in the evening, that made me realize how the hours had clocked by since I had first rushed into the hospital with my wife. Because except for a sweeper wiping a table and one male orderly, his eyes half-closed as he sleepwalked by, there was no one. As if during the time I was with Doctors 1 and 2, listening to their diagnosis of what had afflicted my child, a wind had blown.

A wind so strong it had swept the crowd away, along with the trash and the litter, even sent flying the dogs that had strayed in, leaving the floor looking as if it had been just now washed with water and Dettol. And then mopped dry with clean towels.

This sudden absence of clutter and noise, its suddenness more than its absence, seemed to have set off a kind of spring cleaning inside me as well. The rooms inside my head that were, the entire evening, flooded with the detritus of images and fears, imagined and feared, had also been swept clean. So while I followed Head Nurse, I couldn't help feeling a sense of purpose, a spring in my step although I have to confess that I had little idea what that purpose was. Or where that step was leading me.

'Wait here.' Head Nurse had stopped in front of a hydraulic door marked RESTRICTED ENTRY; she was pointing to a tall, vertical glass window to her right, a window sunk so deep into the wall that I could not see it from where I stood and, therefore, had to walk right up to it.

Through this window, I saw five glass cots in a row on one side. Three of them were occupied by babies, all asleep, all with tubes attached to their tiny chests. The room was dark except for lamps that glowed over each cot. Like table lamps, softer, more yellow. A nurse, much younger than Head Nurse, sat on a chair, her head leaning to one side, perhaps asleep. There were monitors all along the wall behind her where I saw the dancing points of light in their oscilloscopes, I heard their beeps. And, of course, there was no getting away from the constant hum of the hospital's electric sleep.

I watched Head Nurse enter the room, walk right up to the glass and wave at me as she put Ithim in the glass cot next to the window.

Ithim was still covered and I waited for Head Nurse to remove the sheet so I could see my baby exactly as he was but she only reached out and pulled the curtains close. I tapped at the glass, at first gently, trying to draw her attention, then tapped again, this time louder, my fingers more insistent, the noise echoing in the hallway, magnified by the silence and the stillness.

The curtains Head Nurse had drawn were not the window's exact size, they were smaller in width, leaving a gap between their edge and the frame, a narrow chink through which I could see a strip of Ithim's cot. I stood there, hoping the fan inside would blow the curtains aside, make them flap, widen that strip so I could see more of my son, maybe the whole, but that didn't happen, the curtains moved so lightly I could have waited there for hours and hours. And seen nothing.

'Why don't you go catch some sleep?' Head Nurse was now out of the ICU and standing behind me, in the hallway.

I was taken aback. For a moment, I didn't recognize her because she had changed from the starched white of the hospital uniform, the skirt and the blouse, to a blue sari, a white shawl draped around her shoulders. She had loosened her hair as well, the bun on her head stretched tight was gone, the hair now fell straight to her shoulders in a wave that showed she had put more than cursory care into its grooming. She looked shorter but softer, the change of clothes had smoothened the edges, the shawl had rounded her hard angles.

'Why don't you let me see him?' I asked.

'Just wait for a couple of hours,' she said, 'we need to do some tests and then you can take him home. You will get all the time you have to see him, you will get twenty-four hours. You will be his father, after all, won't you?' And with that she turned to walk away.

The hallway was empty, no one to my left, to my right, up front or behind, and for the second time that evening, I felt like running up to Head Nurse, grabbing her by the shoulder, the arm, forcing her to open the ICU door and let me see my son. I wanted to say something, anything, words that would sound like I was putting my foot down rather than going down on my knees, surrendering so meekly. But before I could even start arranging these thoughts into some kind of concerted action, Head Nurse was already at the end of the hallway and I was still rooted to my spot, near the window. Where the curtain had hardly moved, where the visible strip of glass was still as narrow as when I had first looked.

Head Nurse had now disappeared, I heard her go down the stairs and it was then that I ran.

I ran to stop her, I ran down the hallway, past the rooms on the left and the right, all closed. I ran down the stairs, two, sometimes even three, steps at a time. A couple of people coming up the stairs stopped, pressed themselves against the wall to let me pass, one I had to push aside although he was carrying a child in his arms, the child I had seen earlier on in the evening on the floor, his leg stretched in front, in a fresh cast. But I didn't care, I had enough, I had to see Ithim come what may and I had to get Head Nurse to walk back to that ICU, change into her whites if she had to. I wouldn't let her get away.

But Head Nurse was gone.

And I was at the end of the staircase, the ground floor, right near the main entrance to the hospital. I had run six floors.

But Head Nurse was gone.

'Sir, what are you doing, why are you running?' asked a guard who had walked right up to me and was standing so close I could smell his sweat through the hospital's blue regulation pullover. Mixing with his breath, the smell of his sleep, half-broken. His tag read: LOBBY GUARD.

'Have you seen Head Nurse?' I asked.

'Who is Head Nurse?'

'The nurse, she had my baby, she put him in the ICU and she has just gone home.'

'I haven't seen anyone, mister, and I have been here all this while,' he said.

'How could she have vanished? I saw her only minutes ago and I came running down.'

'Then she must have gone,' the guard said, this time not even looking at me. 'If she hadn't, she would have been here.'

The lobby where I stood was empty. From above the reception counter, the row of wooden boards stared at me, telling me the names of doctors and their degrees and their departments. Paediatrics, Urology, Gastroenterology, ENT, General Surgery, Obstetrics & Gynaecology, Cardiology, Orthopaedics, Ophthalmology, X-Ray, MRI, Pathology.

Ithim needed them all.

I was breathing hard, my heart was racing and in the cold air that slipped into the lobby beneath the main glass door I felt sweat on my neck and forehead. Outside, the fog had thickened, scattering the light from the Emergency neon across a far wider area than earlier in the evening. The logical next step was through the door. And when I had taken that, as soon as I had stepped out, I turned my head to try to see through the fog – to maybe catch Head Nurse walking to where the auto-rickshaws and taxis were – but I found myself looking skywards to the building in front, its fifth floor, the thirteenth room.

Fifth floor from below. Thirteenth room from the corner.

That's where I had seen The Face by the window. But the window was now dark and shuttered, the curtains drawn, exactly like all the rooms to the left and to the right, above and below, no trace of The Face. Once I had seen this room again, once I had a fix on its coordinates, I forgot Head

Nurse, I ignored Lobby Guard. I was seized with the need to get into that room.

Why?

Again and again, over and over, I have gone back, in my head, to find out what made me do what I did that night, what made me search out that room and enter it. And, in effect, change everything in my life, perhaps for ever.

Why did I decide to go there?

As with every question, here, too, there must be a simple, straightforward answer that covers the surface and, then, there must be an answer that comes from the depths. I have neither so I can only speculate, conjecture. Perhaps, as I said earlier, it was my anger at Head Nurse, my helplessness after running down the stairs and finding her gone, my frustration mixed with my disappointment mixed with growing despair. Perhaps the events of that evening, Ithim's birth, the condition of my wife, the realization that I could do nothing to change a thing, all these, like floodwater, had threatened to submerge me. And I needed something to clutch on to so I could keep my head afloat and that something had to be more tangible, something that should not only serve as a mere foothold but anchor my entire body from head to toe. In short, what I needed was a sense of purpose, the tug of a cause. Or maybe it was just curiosity, plain and simple: I knew I had nothing to do that night other than to kill a few hours before I could take Ithim home and exploring that room seemed more inviting a prospect than sitting in the lobby.

Maybe.

But then who knows, does anybody care? It's now too late to look for reasons.

So there I was, right in front of the entrance, the fog now so thick that in the glare of the white lights I could see its changing shapes, could see how it was creeping up the glass door, how it had blanketed the E M E and R of the EMERGENCY and was about to swallow the G as well. I checked my destination once again, fifth and thirteenth, as if afraid it might have disappeared when I was not looking. The fog had reached there, too, but because it was higher up, it wasn't so thick and had left uncovered a small sign, black lettering on a yellow wooden board that caught whatever light reached it from the lamps below, a sign I had certainly missed when looking at the window earlier that evening: BURNS WARD.

I had to go to the Burns Ward.

FIFTEEN minutes and twenty rupees later, I was there. At the entrance to that room on the fifth floor, the thirteenth door from the corner, the four five-rupee notes slipped into the hands of a thin, old woman, wearing lenses so thick in her glasses that her eyes were two giant smudges, white, black and grey, filling each frame. She squatted on her haunches, wiping the floor, a mop in one hand, the other holding on to a red plastic bucket filled with water, milky with some sweet-smelling antiseptic. So frail and small was the woman at first glance, she appeared like an old, oversized bird which had flapped across the city that night and got lost. Strayed into the hospital ward to rest until daybreak. And would, any time now, hop from the floor to perch on the rim of the bucket, maybe even bend down to drink the water.

'You have to wait for Sister,' Old Bird said when I told her I needed to get into that room.

It was then that I handed her the money. 'Keep this,' I said, 'it's already so late and I can't wait, I will take only ten minutes.'

'Why do you want to go there?'

'A relative was in that room, the patient left something . . . a bag . . . I am here to check.'

I knew she knew that this was a lie. And if not my weak answer, my twenty rupees had given it away. It was a bribe and barely looking at the money, let alone counting it, she slipped it into her blouse over her breastless chest. 'Don't step on the wet floor,' she said, 'I just scrubbed it clean.'

She got up, her knees clicked, a sound soon replaced by the slap of her slippers against the floor as she led me, her shoulders hunched forward, her back bent at the waist, into the room. Holding the door open, she gestured to me to walk in. I had put one foot inside when she reached out and with her free hand switched the light on in the room. She took one look around and seeing the emptiness inside was sure if I meant any harm it would be the harmless kind that would neither endanger her job nor compromise her position. Relieved, she walked out, closing the door behind her.

'Hurry up,' she called, from outside.

Old Bird.

There was nothing there.

The Face had left nothing.

Surely there should have been something, some clue, something to show The Face had been in the room earlier that evening? To establish, beyond reasonable doubt, that I was not imagining. If just hours ago there had been a patient in here, there must be a chart, a bit of a shiny wrapper left after the pill was swallowed? Or even a pill left untouched. A cup or a glass left there by accident? Some thread from her dress where it caught a nail? A dent on the mattress where she sat, slept? A hollow, even temporary, in the pillow where she rested her head? A puddle of water, yet to evaporate, something she spilled? But, there was nothing.

So I walked to the window, stood where she had stood, looked at what she would have looked at. But nothing again.

Just the black of the night, the grey of the fog mixing with the cold winter wind that through the windowpane lit by the soft white from the lights below looked like one huge shapeless smudge. I tried to write what she had written, those two words, *help* and *me*, but the windowpane was cold to the touch, there was a chill in the room – the heater must have been switched off – and hence no vapour had condensed on the glass for me to write in. Instead, like a child playing a memory game, in which you set a lavish spread on the table and tell the child to look carefully before you cover it all with a sheet or a towel and ask her to recall the objects one by one, I began looking around, trying to register whatever I could see.

The bed was not made, there was no linen, no bed sheets, just the mattress and two pillows, all three bare and cold.

I sat on the bed.

A mattress, off-white. A sticker: *Sleepwell, Foam.*

The floor beneath the bed, also off-white, was tiled, each tile a large square, the grout painted white.

The door, the window, the windowsill, the curtains, the cupboard in the room.

Old Bird knocked. 'You are done? I have to lock the room now.'

'Just five to ten minutes,' I said. 'I will tell you.'

'Please hurry up.' I heard her shuffle, her feet drag her slippers along the floor she had just wiped clean.

For a moment, I closed my eyes and when I opened them again, nothing had changed: the swirling dark outside the window, the haze in the fog, the chill in the room. But I did have the impression that I had been dreaming, no not even a full dream, more a fragment, a dreamlet, torn and twisted, a piece that had perhaps fallen off from something larger because it had neither a beginning nor an end. And then I realized it wasn't a dream, I had seen a photograph lying wedged in the narrow space between the mattress and the bed's headboard.

It was a photograph that may have slipped there by accident. And it was still lying there after the room had been cleaned so it meant the cleaners, possibly Old Bird, had not noticed it. And because it was the only thing in the room that I could pick up and take away with me, like a souvenir, I did:

The photograph shows a pavement. A street in a city, perhaps this city itself because look at the rubble lining it, covering it completely, not even leaving a space for pedestrians to walk.

There is a sapling that grows beside the pavement, you can see it in the bottom left-hand corner of the picture, and another a bit to the right, both stunted because their roots are trapped in cement, their leaves breathe in the fumes of petrol, diesel and kerosene of vehicles, their stems are drenched with the spit of strangers.

In the foreground, that's where I would like to draw your attention, in the pile of garbage, are three things lying on the street.

Near the top edge of the picture, to the right of the half-way mark, you can see two stones, one on top of the other, the pair looking a bit like a hat dropped onto the pavement. Right in front of this are three things that don't seem to be visible in the photograph: a book, a wristwatch. And then a piece of cloth, more like a towel since I could see the threading on the fabric, the curls that give it its furry feel. The book is open, almost halfway. The watch is lying, face down, its strap unfastened, maybe its dial face has broken, maybe it fell. The towel lies inches away from the book and the watch in a tiny crumpled heap.

What you definitely don't see in the picture is what I saw in the dream: a wind blowing, rustling the pages of the book and making the towel lift, at its edge. Not forceful enough for the towel to flip over but strong enough to run its fingers over my face, in my hair.

How do I remember all this in such precise detail? It's odd, I am not sure now, looking back, how much was in the picture and how much in the dream, where did one end and the other begin. I do still have the photograph, of course. It lay crumpled in my hand, imprinted on my eyes when there was a sudden, insistent knocking on the door.

It was Old Bird.

'Get out, now,' she whispered. 'You have to leave,' she said, entering the room, mop in hand. 'There's someone here looking for you.'

Seeing that her words had scarcely registered with me, she patted her chest with one hand. 'Don't worry,' she said, her voice falling several notches until I had to strain my ears to hear. 'I have given you your money's worth. There was a call from the ICU, they were looking for you all over the hospital. I told them you were walking down the corridor and you looked tired as if you would trip, fall down any time, so I told you to rest for a while in an empty room. I told them it wasn't your fault, it was my idea and although I shouldn't have done that, what could I do? I saw you and felt sorry.'

Old Bird smiled.

By now I was up, off the bed and near the door, the picture in my pocket, folded, I could feel its edges press against my legs.

'Who called, who was looking for me?' I asked.

'Head Nurse,' she said.

I was back in the hospital lawn, the Burns Ward behind me, the night's fog still there, thicker than when I saw it last. I shivered as a blast of wind much stronger than the one in my dream, much sharper and more bracing, slapped me in the face. Head Nurse was waiting for me at the entrance, charged, refreshed. Where did she get her energy from? However much I detest admitting it, I couldn't but feel a grudging respect for this woman. We retraced our steps, up the stairs, down the hallway to the ICU, to its narrow glass window, to the drapes beyond which I knew Ithim lay.

Ready to come home with me.

'You stay here, I will be back with him in a few minutes.'

There it was, the moment, when the child is handed over to the father. There should have been a celebratory warmth in the corridor and in my heart; there should have been smiles all around. Maybe a picture being taken. But there was nothing except for the taste of unfinished sleep in my mouth, that shred of a picture of a city street, the trash on the pavement, the book, the watch and the towel, the image as if stuck, thumbtacked to my eyes. I could feel the winter in the hands that I shoved into the pockets of my jacket trying to warm them in the couple of minutes I had to wait: I didn't want Ithim's first touch with his father to be cold.

'Here, hold it like this. Sorry, hold him like this,' said Head Nurse, as she emerged from the room, the hydraulic door closing behind her with a whine almost as loud as her voice.

'He's a bit different from the other babies, so you have to be a bit careful,' her voice now surprisingly soft. Gone was the harsh, matter-of-fact tone, in its place almost a whisper, soft and reassuring. 'Cover him with one side of your jacket, hold him close to your chest, he needs all the warmth he can get as what he's been through no one can imagine. But we know you will take good care of him.'

Ithim was with me now, his father.

Father and son.

Once or twice, I have held newborn babies, a few days old, in a room crowded with branches of the baby's family tree, all the leaves and all the fruits, rustling with joy. The mother and the father right next to me, telling me to do this do that, don't do this don't do that, hold her gently, support his neck, let her rest in the cradle of your arms, sit down, be gentle, look how his eyes open, crinkle, how she stares at your face, at the ceiling, at the light, at the black spot on the wall, how he likes black and white, can't understand colour yet, look how small she is and look how good you look with the baby in your arms, so natural, so perfect.

So I cradled my arms, my left palm underneath my right elbow, the fingers of my right hand outstretched to support his head but this was no baby I had ever held before. At first, I thought Head Nurse had given me an empty towel – like the one in the picture – wrapped into a roll and crumpled at either end, making it seem that it held something rather than nothing. But no, Ithim *was* there. I could feel him against my chest, through my shirt, even through my sweater and my jacket, through the towel.

But where was the head, the back, the neck, the legs, the hands?

I could feel nothing, no movement either, howsoever small, and Head Nurse had wrapped Ithim so well to guard him from the cold that I was scared it would smother him, not let him breathe.

'Here, let me open this a bit,' she said, as if reading my

fears and, without moving from where she stood, as if for the first time she was afraid of coming anywhere near the baby, she reached forward and opened one end of the towel, like peeling a petal from a flower.

And that was my first glimpse of Ithim, my son.

'You can take him home now,' said Head Nurse, 'ask the guard downstairs, he will call for a taxi. Keep the windows rolled up, it will shut out the cold and it will be safer.'

'Safer, what do you mean?' I asked.

'What, haven't you heard? The city is on fire, has been all night,' she said.

'Fire?'

'All across the city, that's what I heard.'

'What did you hear?'

'I don't know the details, all I know is that just an hour or so ago, when you were in the Burns Ward, fifteen bodies came here. They are all in the Morgue, all are badly burnt. There are men, women and children. Someone said there are many other bodies too, taken to other hospitals.'

'What's happened?'

'I don't know, but be careful. You have a baby.'

That was the first time it registered. Ward Guard had told me about a fire, about Head Nurse going to check on her house, but this was the first time, the very first time I heard the whole city was on fire.

WHEN a city is on fire, they say, everyone says when a city is on fire, there should be sights and sounds and smells. There should be flames all around, yellow and blue. There should be smoke, grey and black, against the sky, the sun and the moon. There should be fire engines, red and ringing. Bystanders, witnesses, men and boys on the streets, women and girls at doors and windows, all their faces upturned, specks of light flickering in the black of their eyes. Maybe there should be, even in winter, heat and sweat as well, a line on the neck or the back, beads under chins, above lips. And to complete the picture, there should be a child being rescued, no, make that a baby, with a rattle in his hand, brought down a steel ladder, then wrapped in a clean towel to be photographed for the next day's newspaper. Or for that night on TV. Tiny eyes closed, little head against the brave fireman's chest. But when we stepped out that night, Ithim and I, forget the fire, it was as if the city was on ice.

So cold it was.

And in the darkness, the only fires we could see, as the taxi drove us home, the taxi that Lobby Guard had called for us – the driver, an old man with white hair and glasses, who drove slow and steady – were those by the side of the street, lit by men and women whose tarpaulin sheets or asbestos roofs could keep neither the fog nor the wind from their children fast asleep.

Only once during the journey, when Taxidriver pulled up into a petrol station to fill up, did I see any evidence of anything more disturbing: a glimpse of a group of men gathered at the pump, talking, pointing in the dark, filling plastic cans with fuel. It's then that Head Nurse's words came back to me: *Be careful, this is a city on fire. I have heard they are killing people, men, women and children. And you have a baby, newly born.*

'You heard something about a fire?' I asked Taxidriver.

'What fire?' he replied, looking straight ahead, as the

vehicle hit a pothole, lurched forward, and then began to swallow the night and the road, taking me and Ithim home.

The rest of the journey not once did I look out of the window – my eyes were fixed onto my child – but at the same time I was aware the space next to me on the seat was empty. Black leather, frayed, gleaming in the weak light that came from the taxi's dashboard, from the streetlamps and from the neons of the shops that streaked by. And although the doctor had said my wife should be fine in a few days, I could then bring her home, so we, father, mother and baby, could be all together, I couldn't help feeling an unbearable emptiness fill me up: my child was on his way, on his first night in this city, in this world, to only half of a home.

⬩◆⬩

FIREPROOF

I am Old Bird, I was very old, about sixty, seventy years old, I can never get these numbers right, I was born in this city, I worked as a sweeper in Holy Angel, part time, I had three children, one son and two daughters, both daughters are married and live in Surat where their husbands work in diamond shops as polishers and cutters, one of them has two children, the other has one, all of them are safe, nothing happened in Surat and it was only last month that I met my grandchildren – one of them is doing very well in school, he comes first or second in his class – who had come to visit me in this city where I lived with my son, his wife, and their daughter who is five years old and is to start school next month, my son had gone to work in the morning, he has a cycle-repair shop, the mob came in the afternoon and surrounded our neighbourhood in such a way that no one could escape without being seen, I heard them, I saw them, too, I told my granddaughter to run to Mr Shah's house where I worked as a maid-servant, they are nice people, they always treated me with respect although Mrs Shah told me I should not enter their kitchen because of my religion, she told me I should sweep the floors of all the three rooms, I should clean the bathroom and go home, never enter the kitchen for which she had another maid but the daughter of the house was very kind to me and many days, behind her mother's back, she would give me some of the food that had been cooked in one of their dishes and tell me to take it home, I would wash that dish with extra soap, bring it back, covered with my sari so that her mother didn't notice but the daughter is brave, she once even let me enter the kitchen, open the fridge, get her a glass of water and that's why I told my grand-daughter go to her, I told her, she will take care of you, and once the child had left, my daughter-in-law and I covered our faces with our saris, we poured water over our bodies but the fire was too strong and now that I am gone my only hope is that my son is safe, that my granddaughter still has her father, I hope they, too, move to Surat, I hope my son marries again, my daughter-in-law should not have died, she was very young, I am very old, I am almost blind, my time was up and that's why I don't feel sad that I was killed, the tragedy is that my daughter-in-law was killed, too, when she had just started her life as a mother, when she was waiting to see her daughter go to school.

4. *Ithim At Home, Call At Night*

BUT look at the bright side, Ithim and I were home. Now I didn't have to wait outside a glass door for Head Nurse to graciously condescend to brush the curtains aside so I could see my child, I didn't have to tail her like a dog does his master, I didn't have to run down the stairs like a man crazed, begging, imploring, pleading Her Excellency to show me my baby. Now I could look at him, undisturbed. And it was then, when we walked into the house, when I switched on the lights, that I noticed there was no escaping his eyes, there was no looking away.

Because these were the only part of my Ithim that moved, that betrayed life, newly born, when I placed him on the bed – still wrapped in Head Nurse's hospital towel – I was convinced that Ithim was *only* his eyes, that the eyes were only Ithim. And that the entire rest of him was a blur, a mere distraction, an unnecessary appendage that I could, at least for the time being, ignore. That my baby, severely deformed, began and ended with his two perfect eyes and their two sets of eyebrows and eyelashes. And that these performed, and would continue to perform, all the functions that were meant for his head, his neck, his hands, his arms, his legs, his feet, his stomach, his everything. Of course, this was nonsense.

But, at first glance, this seemed to be the path of least resistance that my mind took, telling myself that if I could tend to these eyes, if I did all I could to prevent even the slightest harm coming their way, I wouldn't need to worry about anything else. Ithim would be fine. For a while, even Ithim fooled me into believing this by his blink, his beautiful baby blink.

Sorry, I should take the last sentence back.

Why blame the child? That's unfair, if not cruel.

Because what could this baby, just a few hours old, without his mother, a baby that should have been kept in the warmth of the hospital nursery, under an infrared lamp, an attendant by his side full time, a baby who should have been taken out every hour, on the hour, to be placed on his mother's breasts so his heart could feel hers beat, who should have been feeding on his mother's milk, resting his tiny hands on her breasts, his soft head against her chin, but was, instead, now lying all by himself in a room with his clueless, bumbling father – what could this baby do?

What could this baby do other than look?

Other than just open and close his eyes, raise and lower his eyelashes? Which he began to do the moment I peeled the towel's edge from his eyes and switched off the harsh white tubelight in the room to cut out its glare.

Outside, the sky was beginning to stain the colour of ink, the purple blue that forms when night begins to grow old, a colour that softens the edges of this hard city, washes the washed-out yellows and the whites and the greys of the houses.

Letting my eyes adjust to the darkness in the room, this night light slipped in through the window and bathed Ithim so that when I held him, my palm cupped beneath the place where his neck should have been, and removed the towel, for one moment what should have been grotesque appeared only a little out of the ordinary. And even before I could start listing what was missing in my child, the night rushed in to cover his empty spaces with shadows, half-light and half-dark.

So what did I see?

There is no one answer, there cannot be one answer. I have already described him, at the beginning, cold and clinical, and yet that doesn't even begin to do justice to the original. For the Really New, the genuine original, defies all description because there is nothing in the old to compare it to. But then, because the number of words at our command is always limited, predetermined, we have no choice but to fall back on the old, on what has already been imagined, what has already been described. That's why I am going to take the easy way out.

As if we are all in school.

Imagine you are taking an examination, sitting in a class, with a piece of paper in front on the desk, and Ithim facing the entire class on a raised platform with the blackboard as his backdrop so all of you can see him clearly.

The question in the test is: *Please look at the child carefully (he will be placed on the desk for the entire duration of this examination). Please rank the following in order of likeness. Mark your rank in the box provided against each choice.*

- ☐ A small cylinder made up of flesh and skin, wrapped around bones and cartilage.

- ☐ A vegetable, gourd or pumpkin, more long than wide, that has been placed on a fire and quickly removed, leaving its two ends charred and its tip wrinkled.

- ☐ An oversized insect, its six legs and its two antennae torn out, leaving just the abdomen intact.

- ☐ A bird, its feathers plucked, its legs and its wings cut, skinned, its head distended.

- ☐ A piece of plastic tubing, sawed off, and then covered with a material, stretched tight, resembling skin.

- ☐ A caterpillar, without any serrations in its body, seen through a giant microscope, its tentacles clipped, its legs missing.

- ☐ A Thermos flask, the colour of skin, the kind they advertise for picnics, which keeps the water warm or cold depending on what you want.

- ☐ A child's toy, made of rubber, a broken toy, perhaps a train or a cargo truck to be dragged along with a piece of string, bits and pieces of it fallen off, lost while the child was at play.

- ☐ A bit of all of the above.

Without even taking this test, without even seeing any of your answers, I can speculate: most of you would have ticked the last box.

What should I have done? I, who had no luxury of taking tests or marking the order of likeness? I, the father, who had just brought his son home and now was looking at him, what about me? What should I have done? Should I have recoiled in horror? In fear or anger? Disgust, maybe even hate?

In fact, when I first looked at Ithim, I felt nothing.

Perhaps, the strangeness of what lay on my bed, this object, this creature, this toy, this flask, this rubber tubing, this bird plucked, this insect, this vegetable, this cylinder, this *all of the above*, was so overwhelming – along with the exhaustion of that evening and the night at the hospital, the shapeless blur of people and events – like a fuse that temporarily switches off some connections to save the entire house when there is a surge of electricity, something inside me had done the same. Shut me down.

So that the mere realization that I was back home, with my baby, had filled me with a flooding sense of achievement that had drowned all dread or foreboding that lay, I was sure, just below the surface.

I decided to touch him.

I sat down, on the bed, leaned close, brought one hand over his face. I stretched my fingers out, moved my palm four or five inches above his eyes. My hand must have blocked the ceiling fan and the plaster from his view but I could see no change in his eyes, he kept staring, blinking once or twice, as if nothing had happened. As if my hand hadn't even been there.

I touched him between the eyelashes with my little finger; even that had no effect, none at all. I touched him on the double-pierced, tiny mound that was his nose, I touched him on his knife-cut lips, on the thin funnel-flap of skin that was his left ear. I ran my little finger along the length of his body and all the while, kept looking at his eyes, for the faintest flicker of movement, for some change that could tell me that he was reacting, that the blinking wasn't only an involuntary impulse.

I moved the finger to where his waist was, over the strip of charred flesh that ran like a belt fused to his body, and the moment I touched him there, his eyes blinked hard, blinked again. His eyebrows moved closer to each other, as if he was furrowing his forehead, as if he was trying to understand something called pain, perhaps. I promptly pulled back my finger and his eyebrows returned to where they were before.

Life.

Yes, that was a sign of life.

A sudden wave of relief washing over me, like the warmth of a fire in winter, I lay on my side, next to Ithim on the bed, placed one hand just behind his head, my fingers resting against his scalp. And then there was the second sign, the sign I remember describing to you at the very beginning, the movement just below the surface of the skin, inside his head. Of tiny things flying and resting, a heaving and a churning, as if the bones inside had yet to form the skull and were, therefore, trying to lock themselves in to give his head a form, a solid shape. Life, once again, the second sign.

Two signs, both of pain, but I was the father, I was the beggar, I could not choose.

MY wife had downloaded pages at Mr Meeko's cybercafe from websites on how to take care of newborns and those sheets of paper, with their *urls* at the bottom, the page numbers, the dates – mocking me with their sense of a more hopeful past – lay on a table in the living room, in a blue folder my wife had marked BABY HOMEWORK, and that now seemed to carry within its folds missives from some other world at some other time.

If the baby is lying on its back, you need to slide one of your hands underneath the neck, splay out the fingers so that your hand acts as a prop for the whole head. Then bring your other hand, spread its fingers like a fan and slide this one under the lower back. Then bend down, if you have a problem with your own back bend the legs at the knees, come close to the baby and lift it gently. Don't let the baby's arms or legs flail around and keep the head a little higher than the rest of the body. While you are holding the baby, you always have to make sure you are supporting its head. It can be in your hand, above the spread-out fingers, it can be in the crook of your arm. What is important is that the baby's head shouldn't be flopping around because the neck of a newborn isn't very strong, the head is big compared to the rest of the body, you will need to help it support its large head until it can manage itself.

There was no head to flop around, neither were there arms nor legs to get in the way. In fact, Ithim seemed to be a quiet baby, as Doctor 2 had said, he just lay on the bed, exactly as he was when I had first put him there.

Hold the baby in your lap with one arm around him so that his neck is in the crook of your arm. Brush a finger across the baby's cheek closest to your body and the baby should turn his face towards you and his lips should part slightly. Gently push the nipple of the bottle into the baby's open mouth, keeping his head and upper body raised at a slight angle so that it's easier for the baby to swallow. Tip the end of the bottle up as you are feeding so that the baby doesn't swallow air as the formula disappears. To burp the baby, hold him with his head over your shoulder and rub his back softly until he lets out a satisfied little belch.

Ithim's mouth was such a tiny slit that no nipple, no bottle would serve the purpose. But before I could work out how, I needed to first arrange the feed. My wife had kept all the provisions in the second room of our two-room flat, which she had half-converted into a nursery.

I should not have entered that room.

Desecrated that shrine my wife had so painstakingly built to her hopes and expectations, to our future as a family, this eight-by-ten-feet rectangle of space with four walls and one ceiling and a floor. It was the room my wife had always kept locked, telling me, whenever I asked (and even if I didn't), that it was a surprise she had in store for me and the baby and for all of us, as a unit. But clearly, this was no time for me to dwell on abstract commitments when our child was lying on the bed in the next room and I was clueless.

The ceiling had been painted blue. My wife had pasted stars on it, tiny white specks, not stars that razzle and dazzle in cheap, shiny paper, but a soft white that glowed in the dark. In the centre of the ceiling, from the iron hook meant for the ceiling fan – the fan we had deferred buying until summer – she had installed a mobile of fishes and birds, each bird ringed by a tiny blue circle that shimmered like water, each fish with gills that looked like tiny wings. Fish that flew, birds that swam.

Perhaps my entry into the room, the fall of my feet, had disturbed the static air inside or I had brought some winter air with me through the doors that had so far remained closed because the birds and the fishes began to move in slow circles above my head, casting shadows on the walls and the ceiling, in and out, between the stars. This was meant to entertain a child, these fishes and birds. And as I stood there, in the centre of the room, underneath my wife's handmade heaven for our baby, I saw, one by one, the objects lying there, all kept with love and hope, and not one of any use for Ithim. For example:

In one corner of the room was a baby cot, white in colour, with handrails that Ithim would, could never use. He had no arms.

Next to the cot, on the floor, was a play mat for the baby to crawl on, which Ithim could never do. He had no knees.

There were rattles for him to grasp. He had no fingers.

There were a range of stuffed toys for him to hold, chew, walk, play with. Of no use at all.

There was a kangaroo, a mouse, a duck, a fish, a bear, a green pillow in the shape of a turtle (these were toys my wife had bought without my knowing), even a tiny walker with wheels, a transparent plastic pool, inflatable, with a tube for fixing it to a tap and filling it with water, for the baby to splash around in. (Maybe Ithim could use that one.) There were two tiny cushions, each the size of my palm, for the baby to put its legs and its hands on while it was asleep, their covers inlaid with tiny mirrors and threadwork to reflect the starlight from above.

But what use was all this? Could Ithim ever stand up or sit straight in his life? What would these terms mean for him, *standing up*? *Sitting straight*? Even the most fundamental question I couldn't even start imagining the answer to: How would he grow? Which part of which section of his body would grow? Was something so deformed even meant to grow? Would Nature, looking at him every moment, put an end to this baby, this creature that, by the mere act of his blinking and breathing, was defying it like few ever had? Would Ithim die even before he had lived? And instead of answers, these questions brought tears.

The tears flowed as I stood there, in the middle of the room, the toys all staring at me as if they had come to life in the dark and conspired to snuggle up against each other, joining hands to look at this man who had just walked in, his baby lying on the bed. I cried, not so much for myself or even for Ithim but for my wife and her dreams. I cried for her imagination on display, right there, in front of me, now collapsed into useless artefacts. I cried for her sky-coloured ceiling, her handmade heaven, her safety cot with its handrails, her family of toys and how all of this added up to her idea of the world she wanted our child to walk into when he came home from the hospital. And how that idea now lay dead, if not dying.

Had my wife been there by my side, my tears would have been shared with hers. Perhaps the feel of her body pressed against mine, even in fear and despair, would have lent me, both of us, a certain solidity, prevented me from buckling at the knees, falling over, but there I was, all alone, the ground heaving beneath my feet. And when I found myself, after a while, shivering, I did not know what to do other than to lean against the wall and let the trembling die down.

Through my tears, the stars on the ceiling had become streaks, the fish and the birds moved in circles casting shadows, cold and dark.

BEHIND the toys, lined up on a wooden shelf fixed to the wall, my wife had put the feeding bottles, all Made in China, along with a sterilizer and baby formula. The formula tin had a picture of a baby's head, its torso missing, but it was a happy baby nonetheless, well fed, its lips parted in a smile, the hair on his head curled into a tiny wisp over his forehead. The Farex Baby. As I reached up to the shelf to bring the bottles down, I suddenly realized it had been a while, quite a while, since I had checked on Ithim.

Leaving everything aside, I rushed out, into the room where Ithim lay, almost ran, tripped, and when I reached his bed, there it was: a tiny wet patch on the bed sheet just below his face, that, when I looked close and touched, was warm. It was his tears.

Ithim had been crying.

And because he could make no noise, he had cried and he had cried, cried so much that the tears had silently fallen and collected into that wet smudge, almost the size of a rupee coin, on the bed. His eyes were closed now and when I touched them with my fingers, they quivered slightly. I can't describe the relief, the elation that swept over me, sure in the belief that Ithim was safe, that Ithim was alive, because from what the doctors had told me, from what Head Nurse had told me, I knew every moment Ithim lived was borrowed time that would run out any second now whereupon his eyes would close never to open again.

Yes, his death wasn't a thought so far away. Indeed, at one level – what level I can't tell you right now and please don't ask because how can a father wish for the death of his newborn? – something inside me wanted that to happen, wanted the whole thing to end rather than grow into what I could only imagine as a cycle of nightmares never ending.

For what would I do tomorrow, the day after, the next week, the fortnight, the end of the month?

How would we talk, Ithim and I? How would I tell him stories? He would never crawl, never learn to walk. He wouldn't sleep on my shoulder, he had no little hand to rest on my back. He wouldn't stumble, would never falter, he wouldn't hold my hands, let his fingers hold mine. Maybe he would be able to read given his eyes but would someone else have to turn his pages? How would I teach him a language? A few years ago, in the papers, I read about a French journalist who suffered a stroke that paralysed all his speech, all his motion, miraculously leaving just one eye intact. He used this eye to write an entire book, by blinking. He devised a special alphabet which was recited to him and he blinked every time he selected a letter, that's how he blinked words, sentences, paragraphs, pages and chapters, until his eye closed for ever. But then he wasn't always like that, he knew the letters, he had lived his life, how would Ithim do it? How would he laugh? Could he, in fact, laugh? Could I take him out of the house? I could put him in a wheelchair but his feet were not there, neither were his hands. Would he scare the other children, would I always have to keep him covered? This was winter so no one would notice if I covered his face or bought a cap with a brim large enough to shelter him but what about May and June? With his perfect eyes, Ithim would see everything but what difference would that make, what would his world be like without the reference frames of the other four senses?

These questions came in a big wave of darkness and chill, like someone made of ice, from head to toe, had walked into the room and was now standing just inches behind me, looking over my shoulder, at me and at Ithim. Forcing me to think of only one thing: *Better that Ithim die.*

Die, did I just say *die*?

I take that word back, kill that word, *die*, just three letters, easy to rub.

(Put your finger on the word on this page and scratch it out with your nails. You can also scratch it out with a pen but the ink will stay, will mark the page, so the best thing is to pierce a hole in the page, in the middle of the word, *die*, where the letter *i* is, and then put pressure on either side so the hole grows, swallows the *d* and the *e*, makes the word disappear.)

Kill it, kill it.

I didn't mean it.

I was the father, he was my son.

The telephone rang.

Once.

Twice.

In the silence, each ring was a scream setting my teeth on edge as if it had torn down the door to rush inside. Fearing for Ithim, I almost ran, tripping over the shoes I had just taken off, to pick up the phone before the third ring.

And it was only in that infinitesimal moment of silence that preceded it, the truth hit me: Ithim couldn't hear.

There was no hurry, therefore, to pick up the phone.

So I stopped, breathed deep, let my heart slow down, let the phone ring, four, five, six.

On the seventh, I picked up.

It was a woman's voice.

◆◆◆

◆◆◆

I am Taxidriver, I was sixty-four years old, for more than thirty years I worked in this city with the state government as a driver until I retired two years ago and then to supplement my pension and to keep myself busy, I went to the taxi stand in my neighbourhood for I knew the owner and he hired me right away although I told him I was not like his young drivers, I could not do sixteen-hour shifts, I was slow but I was safe and steady, so he put me on the hospital beat and said better that you stay parked there, drive patients home, they need a taxi that is safe and steady, you don't have to go out of the city, this didn't pay as much as the other routes but I was grateful that I had a job, although, strictly speaking, I didn't need it because I lived alone, my wife died three years ago, I have three sons and two daughters, I have ten grandchildren in all, and all of them are comfortably placed, my children kept telling me to come and stay with them but I said, no, I couldn't leave the house where my wife and I lived for more than forty years, I told them I would die there and, true to my word, they killed me just ten steps away from my house, I had parked the taxi at the stand and was returning home when the mob came, I ran into a grocery shop just next to my house, the owner is a friend, and as I waited there, someone called the police and they were very prompt, their jeeps arrived within minutes, even the riot vans, the ones with cages, making us think we were safe now and so I came out of the shop and began walking home but by then the police had begun firing and the mob had run away, frightened, a police bullet hit me in the head, it must not have been meant for me, I am sure of that, because I didn't do anything, I was only walking but the police bullet, it seems, had my name written on it that day, it entered my head, right between my eyes, I didn't even feel the pain, I just remember falling down, the smell of the tar on the street, the sound of feet running by, I don't have many complaints, I was too old, all my children and grandchildren are safe, in fact, I can now be reunited with my wife again but I hope my children sell my house and move out of this city now that I am gone, the city wants them out and when a city wants you out and you have a life to live, better to find another place, there is always a place in this country of one billion people where no one can get you however hard they may try.

5. *Miss Glass Talks, Yes to a Journey*

'IS this the residence of the husband of Patient Number 110742?'

The construction of the sentence was so odd, with the two awkward *ofs*, *the residence of* and *the husband of*, that its delivery should have been faltering, even clumsy. But no, it wasn't. Instead, it was calm and confident, seemed to assume more than a passing sense of familiarity, the question asked with no hesitation as if the caller were someone I knew and had put on this formal air merely as a prank and, in a moment or two, would break into laughter, assured, not only of a response but of an entire, animated conversation with a close acquaintance, a dear friend.

All I could say, in reply, was: 'Yes, I am speaking.'

'Mr Jay, I am the woman from the hospital. From Holy Angel.'

She knew my name.

'Is my wife all right?' My first question.

'Your wife is stable, in pretty much the same condition she was in when you left her a few hours ago. You don't have to worry. But I'm not calling you about your wife, Mr Jay.'

'Who is this?'

'I told you, I am the woman from the hospital.'

'I don't know, I don't know any woman from the hospital.'

'Yes, you do, Mr Jay. You visited my room looking for something. I'm sorry I couldn't leave anything behind except the picture you saw, of the pavement.'

'What picture? I didn't see any picture, I have no idea what you are talking about.'

What else should I have said?

Here was a total stranger, a voice forcing its way through the night into my house, into my ears, without any warning.

(And, as you may have guessed by now, I am not exactly one for phone conversations, I find them hurried, the response time so short that in my case even pausing for a breath, a natural pause, is seen as tying of the tongue, at best, indecisiveness and, at worst, a suspicious reluctance to reply. That's why at work, I have come to be known as the silent fact-finder, the quiet fact-checker. I am the one called upon, at short notice, to supply numbers for pie charts and bar graphs: 61 per cent employment in the country is in the agriculture sector, 22 per cent in services, 17 per cent in industry; domestic air traffic is up by almost a quarter every year, international by 18 per cent; 246 million people live below the poverty line and this number is falling. I am not the one asked to 'seal deals' on the telephone or take calls from clients to clarify their doubts.)

So, yes, while I was taken aback by her reference to the picture, I decided I was not going to admit to any of this. At least, not until I had a better idea of who I was talking to.

*

'Sorry,' she said, 'I thought you had seen the picture, but maybe I am mistaken.'

'Maybe,' I said. I could feel the picture still in my pocket, its hard edges.

'Let's forget about that, I called you to say that we should meet.'

'Why, what for?'

'That I can't tell you over the phone. We have to meet. And you may bring him along.'

'Bring whom?'

'The baby, the boy. I want to see him.'

'How do you know it's a boy?'

'I found out.'

'Who are you?'

'I told you, I am the woman from the hospital.'

I am tempted, as I report this, to explain simultaneously, perhaps in the margins, what I felt as I heard her, as it became clear to me, with each passing word, each sentence she spoke, that here was a woman who was no ordinary caller, who spoke like no stranger I had ever spoken to. And who, in less than a minute, had established herself as the one who held most, if not all, of the threads in the fabric of this conversation. Who was pulling the strings while I, at the other end, was reduced to a mere listener, passive and jerked around.

'You have a name?' I asked.

'Give me a name,' she said.

'Listen, please. Don't joke, I don't understand why you called me.'

'I told you twice, we should meet; we have to meet.'

'I can't.'

'Why, why can't you? There's nothing pressing, urgent for you to attend to, is there?'

'What do you mean, nothing urgent? My wife is in hospital, unconscious, you seem to know that already. The baby needs my help. I have taken a few days off from work but I have to stay here, take care of my child until my wife comes home.'

'The responsible husband, are we, Mr Jay, the responsible father?' she laughed, the mocking clear in her voice. 'No one would guess that if they knew what you have been through today.'

'I don't know what you are talking about,' I said. 'Where are you calling from?'

'I am in the city, the same city as you, I used to live here until this evening. I can't tell you exactly where I am, all I can tell you is that I am safe, no one can get to me now, others aren't so lucky.'

'What does that mean?'

'Mr Jay, you must be the only person in this city who doesn't know what's been happening the whole day, what's been happening right through the evening and the night. Surely, you have heard the city is on fire?'

'Yes, the guard at the hospital mentioned something and the nurse told me to be careful because of the fires but I haven't seen them yet.'

'The fires are all around, you just have to look. That's

what I have been doing the whole day, looking, even taking some pictures.'

'Where are you, how did you get my number?'

'How did you enter my hospital room? Burns Ward, fifth floor, thirteenth door from the corner?'

'I am sorry, I have to go now, the baby is crying.'

I looked at Ithim, his eyes were closed, he must have cried himself to sleep.

'I can help you,' she said.

'Help? Me?'

'Until your wife returns, Mr Jay, I can help you take care of the baby. Men can't handle such a condition.'

Did she know what condition Ithim was in? It seemed she did, given what she had said so far. For, if she knew I had been to her room, if she knew the baby was a boy, if she knew my phone number, surely, her sources for these details, whoever they may have been, would have also known about Ithim. But if she knew about Ithim, she wasn't giving even the tiniest hint away. On the contrary, it seemed, or she made it seem, that she wasn't aware of what kind of a baby he was.

'No, I can take care of the baby, thank you. But tell me who are you? Tell me right now or else I hang up.'

*

I thought this threat, deliberately not veiled, would rattle her, that it would help me take the reins of this conversation back into my own hands – but it had just the opposite effect.

'If you hang up, I will call again, and then I will call again,' she said. 'I will call and I will call until you have to keep the phone off the hook, which, of course, you won't do since you are waiting to hear from the hospital. In case something happens to your wife. You wouldn't like to miss that call, would you?'

'What do you want from me?'

'I want nothing, Mr Jay.'

'Then why are you calling me? Why did you choose me from among so many at the hospital, so many in this city?'

'Now we are getting into things more complex and now isn't the time to deal with such questions. Let's, for the time being, leave it at that. That you, Mr Jay, are the chosen one.'

'I am tired, you are calling very late, it's not even morning.'

'Well, that's good, isn't it? This is the time when everyone's sleeping across the city, when blankets are drawn tight, when the windows and doors are all closed so the wind doesn't enter. Not that there is a wind blowing tonight, in fact, it's very calm. I wish there were a wind; some of the fog would have cleared, along with the smoke from the fire, and I would have been able to see through the window. Anyway, because it's so late, it's quiet and we can hear each other clearly. But the main reason I'm calling, Mr Jay, and as I told you earlier, is that I need to meet you, I have to tell you something. Let's meet, I will tell you in detail, I will tell you everything, there isn't much time to waste.'

'You can email me.'

'I know that, Mr Jay, I know your email address, I plan to send you a message in the morning, a follow-up to this conversation. But I wouldn't have called you so late in the night, I wouldn't have disturbed you, if that message would serve the purpose.'

'I am sorry, I am hanging up now. I see no point in this conversation.'

'No you won't, Mr Jay. I know you won't. You won't admit this, even to yourself, but you like this, don't you? A woman calling you, asking you to meet her? A woman you have vaguely seen, at a hospital window, from a distance. Tell me, what did you see, did you see my face?'

I heard the sound of laughing from her end, I heard the sound of quite a few people laughing.

'What was that?' I asked. 'Is there anyone else there with you?'

'That's nothing,' she said, 'just the sound of laughing. Could be a late-night show on television. Or people talking in the upstairs flat; it could be something on the radio, static on the phone, disturbance, it could even be a sound in your head, or from the street where they have set the house on fire. Now answer my question, please. Did you see my face?'

'I guess so.'

'Describe it, I want to know how well you recall, how well you see.'

'No, it wasn't so clear, nothing was clear, I just remember your hair, it was short, up to your shoulders.'

'That's pretty good. What was I wearing?'

'Something in white.'

'That's better. Where is your baby? They say you should never leave a newborn out of sight, even for a second, because children at birth are as vulnerable, as defenceless, as puppies or kittens, they can choke on anything, even their own breath.'

'Yes, I see him, he's right there, he's all right. He's in front of me, on the bed. Now will you tell me your name, please?'

What good that would have done, I had no idea. How would knowing her name help? Perhaps it was just my half-hearted attempt to fill in the blanks, to hold my end up in what was clearly a losing battle of words and nerves and will, that made me ask this question. Whatever, it didn't work since, in answer, she turned the question around.

'My name? Why don't you give me one?'

'Is this some sort of a crank call?'

'Give me a name, an unusual name, I know you can come up with interesting names, like the one you did for the baby. Ithim, I like that name.'

'How do you know he's Ithim?'

'I know the Head Nurse, I know the doctors, we all

know each other. They told me, they showed me the form you filled in, the discharge slip. So give me a name.'

'I don't know, I can't think of anything,' I said, 'I just saw your face through the glass.'

'Well, then,' she said, 'that's it, you just gave me a name, Glass. How about Glass? Yes, call me Glass, you saw me through glass the first time and I like the sound, *glass*. It's an unusual name, it makes me stand out in the crowd.'

'OK, Miss Glass.'

'See, we have progressed. Already you are on first-name terms with me.'

'Where do you live?' I asked.

'Mr Jay, you keep asking the same question over and over again. I have told you I can't give answers on the phone. Do I have to say it again, Mr Jay? I can say it ten thousand times if that helps you but why are you being so stubborn? Why haven't you asked the most obvious question yet?'

'What's the most obvious question?'

'It's staring at you, it stared at you earlier today, think of the evening, you should get it.'

'I don't.'

'Think. What made you look at me?'

'It was an accident, I was standing in the hallway, looking out and then my eyes travelled across the lawn, to the building where you were, rose above all those floors and stopped at your window. I saw you there. It was pure accident.'

'No, it was no accident, but forget that for a moment, you didn't see me. You saw something else first that drew your attention, that kept it fixed, fixed so hard that later in the night you had to get into that building, visit my room.'

'Yes, you had written two words on the windowpane. You wrote help me.'

'Use my name, please.'

'Miss Glass, you wrote help me.'

'There, it wasn't difficult at all, see?'

'Why did you write that?'

'You forgot my name again.'

'Why did you write that, Miss Glass?'

'I like that, I like being addressed as Miss Glass. I stood there, looking out, my gaze travelled too, just like yours. And I saw you standing there across the lawn, in front, at that window. I was with someone who knew you, who had seen you earlier in the day.'

'Where, who? Who was this someone?'

'Again, you are asking questions that we should be discussing face to face, not on the phone. So let's meet, Mr Jay.'

'Where?' I said.

Trust me, I wanted to take that word right back. Right then and there, I wanted to squeeze myself into the phone if that was the only way out, swim down the telephone line, go underneath the road or fly through the sky to wherever these telephone signals go, catch up with that word, *Where*, grab it, do anything, not allow it to reach her. But, of course, I couldn't. The word was out. She had heard it.

With that one word *Where* and the sense of the question mark at the end of it (*Where?* spoken in a manner that begged an answer, an answer I knew would inexorably push me towards something I had no idea of) I had crossed the line. The line that divides what-is-safe-and-tested-and-trusted from what is not. I shivered.

Why had I said it? Where had that word *Where* come from? All along, I had been holding myself, refusing to bite this bait that had been thrown at me from somewhere in the city somewhere in the night. I had switched subjects, had settled for the inane and the trite, even the stupid, and then suddenly, even without my knowing it, I had said what I had been trying all the while to avoid.

And given Miss Glass what she wanted.

'I knew you would say yes,' she said. 'It's far away but not that far, we have to take the train, it will take a few hours.'

'Train? I am not taking any train. I can't leave the city.'

'Yes, you can, I have checked. Your wife will remain in the hospital for at least one more day. You will return before that. In time to see her wake up. It also gives us time to be away until the fires die down, until the city is safe.'

'What makes you think I will do something as stupid as go on a train journey with you?'

'I know you will go.'

'And where do you plan to go?'

'Why do you want to know everything?'

'I have a baby, I will have to bring him along, I need to know where we are going. I don't want any harm coming to the child. Forget it.'

'You know what? My mouth hurts talking to you, my ears hurt listening to you say the same thing over and over again. I may very well forget it and never call you back, never ever. Anyone listening in on our conversation, anyone with even the slightest, most basic intelligence, can make out how horribly unbalanced this whole thing is, as if I am involved in a dialogue of the deaf. As if I am the one who's desperate, who's throwing herself at your feet. When the fact is that it's *you* who are. You have a baby who frightens you. So far, I have not raised this subject but now you have left me with no choice. I know all about the baby, I have even seen it. You have a wife, a caring wife who loves you, who perhaps is the only one who loves you, not because she has no choice but because she has decided to love you and her decision has been made, it's irreversible. You are lucky, Mr Jay. And yet when she's lying there, still not having held her baby as new mothers usually do, you don't realize what difference you can make. You can bring the baby with you, come with me to a place where I know they will help you and your baby, maybe even set him right. I can't guarantee anything but it's worth trying. And what are you doing instead? You are trying to be this man who is not moved, who is seeing all of this as a mere distraction, who doesn't remember anything. Who is listening to me, and perhaps thinking, here's this strange woman who has nothing better to do at this time of the night than make calls to men. Are you there? Hello, are you there? Say something, breathe, shout at me but don't just stand there holding the phone. Silent and mute.'

'What do you want me to say?'

'What do you want to say?'

'I want to say just leave me alone.'

'No, I can't leave you alone, I will not leave you alone.

This is very important for me, too. It's taken a lot of work to track you down. Listen – and I am saying this for the last time – listen carefully. I am going to say this very slowly so that you don't miss a word. Come and see me, I have booked two tickets on the train at five thirty this evening; that's rush hour, too, the station will be very crowded at that time. And given what's happening in this city, everyone will be trying to get away. So the earlier you are there, the better.'

'Where?'

'At the station. In a few hours, I will send you an email with the details. It should be with you in the morning. So there, it's all set now. We are ready to meet.'

'What did you mean when you said we will go to a place where they can set him right, the baby? Set him right.'

'I meant what I said, they can set him right.'

'How can you say that when you don't know what's wrong with him?'

'I know, Mr Jay, I know what's wrong with the baby. Everything, almost everything, isn't it? There's nothing right about him other than his eyes and his eyelashes and his eyebrows?'

'Yes.'

'But look at it this way, he is alive. You can't say that for quite a few children in this city tonight.'

'When you say he can be set right, does this mean he will become normal? That he will grow arms and legs, ears?'

'I told you I can't give you any guarantees, the one assurance I can give you is that he can't get any worse. And let's talk, you need to know a few things, too.'

'What do I need to know?'

'We are meeting tomorrow, Mr Jay, when everything will be clear. Just one more day. Don't forget to check your mail. See you, Mr Jay, have a good night's sleep.'

'OK,' that's all I could say.

'And one last thing, start early. You never know which roads will be blocked, the city is on fire.'

Miss Glass hung up.

I heard the phone click.

Click and bring to an end, abrupt and sudden, this conversation in the course of which the colour of the sky had changed, from the black of the night to the pale blue of its dying, during which the silence from the street outside had begun to break, like glass, into shards of noise, jagged and grating. Someone coughing, someone waking up on the street below, the sound of the water tap on the street, someone washing his or her face, someone who had woken up before the sun. My ear hurt from pressing the phone to it. The handset itself was warm, almost hot to the touch, where I had gripped it for so long; when I put it back on the cradle, I could see my fingerprints, marked in sweat on the dust. Ithim lay still, the tears on his face had dried. He hadn't cried again. Not once. Through this conversation between me and Miss Glass, between his father and this woman who seemed to know much more about him than his mother.

This woman who until a few hours ago was The Face in the window, a scrawl on the glass, an empty room, and who of course was only in my imagination, tired and fevered and whatever was there of it. But with that call, an entire world had gaped open; now she had not only a voice but a certain character as well, a hard-edged confidence, almost arrogance, and a sense of proprietorship over me and my baby.

She had talked to me in the disquieting manner of one who makes you feel she knows you better than you do yourself, who will always be several steps ahead of wherever you are. Who was this woman, where had she come from? She had called me stubborn, she had said that talking to me was like a dialogue of the deaf, but she was the one who had built a wall around herself and every time I had tried to chip away at it she kept adding another layer, word by word, sentence by sentence, so by the time the conversation had ended, all I knew about her was that she was hidden behind a fortress of her own making. And from that safe perch, she had not only disarmed me, she had forced me to surrender, lose the battle.

But before I could think through what she had said and what I had heard, before I could try to look beyond those walls around her, I knew I was fighting another battle, this one more immediate: a battle with sleep that came like water rising, rushing upwards, in a wave. Beginning with my feet, rippling in and out between my toes, rising to my ankles, then to my chest, lapping against my shoulders, climbing over my jacket, gurgling as I breathed through my nose, reaching my eyes, filling them both.

I slept.

◆◆◆

I am a member of the Audience, I am going to appear right at the end, I will be sitting in a gallery, the lights switched off, I was nineteen years old, they stopped me on the street, they said you killed the people on the train yesterday morning and I said no, I wasn't there, but that didn't matter, they said, tell us where you were between six and eight in the morning yesterday, that's the time when the train was attacked, tell us in detail so I told them I was sleeping at six, I told them I slept until seven, seven thirty, and then I got up, washed and I prayed, then my mother said we don't have flour in the house so I went out to buy some, when I returned I was still feeling sleepy so I lay down on the bed for about half an hour or an hour, I watched the smoke from the oven, I could smell the cooking, my mother got angry because I don't have a job, she said I just sit at home and eat, I sleep too much, when I finally got off the bed it was about ten in the morning so there you are, I said, I was nowhere near the train between six and eight but that didn't matter, they said, why don't you cry, why don't you feel sad, as sad as we feel, at the fact that fifty-nine people have been burnt alive, I said I don't know how sad I should feel, they said, don't try to be funny, and then they stabbed me, once in the back, then in the front, they said you may have been asleep but why were your people near the train and before I could tell them that I don't know anybody who was near the train I had already begun to bleed, I felt the air rushing out of me, my eyes swim, I didn't feel the pain at all, I saw the blood draining out, they had turned, they had begun to walk away and the last thing I remember is hating myself for making such a mistake, I think I should have told them yes, yes, yes, I burnt the train, I was so happy when I heard the news that I told mother, I will get not only flour but milk and honey as well, I should have told them that my family attacked the train, my mother was there, my father, my two sisters, my uncle, my cousin, my aunt, my grandmother, all of them were there, even my future wife and my future children, and all of them lit the fire, one by one, and that we would do it again if we got the chance, I should have told them that, if only to see what would they have done different, would they have killed me still?

6. *Falling asleep, awake in dreams*

HOW long I slept I am not sure but what I remember distinctly is that no sooner had my eyes closed than my mind began to give Miss Glass flesh and blood, size and shape. And the Miss Glass I saw, with my closed eyes, was tall. She wore a red sweater, long-sleeved, that hugged her thin frame and outlined her small, high breasts and her arms, the sleeves of the sweater falling a few inches short of her wrists and her palms, showing long, slender fingers.

She was sitting in a chair, just a few feet away from me and Ithim. Her back was turned to us, her hands rested on a table, a study table of sorts, as if she was reading something, her red sweater riding above the waistband of her trousers, showing a strip of skin, a soft pale pink, almost translucent, offset by the hard red. Her trousers were black, close-fitting, so they sharply defined her legs, her knees. The ends of her trousers, because she was sitting, rode a few inches above her ankles, showing off two red socks and a bit of each calf, each sock had a white line skirting its edge. She had shoes with laces. There was a headband tied in her short hair, also red, like her sweater, but speckled with white and blue dots, one end falling over the nape of her neck.

Because her back was turned, I couldn't see her face. I

could have leaned forward, craned my neck to look, but that neither occurred to me nor seemed possible given the state I was in – it was as if I was rooted where I sat and I could alter neither my angle of vision nor my field of view – so all I could see was just one side of her face, in profile. Her sharp nose was pierced; I saw the glint of a ring, white and dull, rusted steel or blackened silver. Her lips were pale red, parted, as if a word had escaped, or just formed, unsaid, in the space in between. She was tapping one foot, measured and in step with perhaps a song or a tune she could hear that I couldn't.

How old was she?

Her face only about a quarter visible, I couldn't be sure, but her frame, tall and thin, the almost flawless strip of skin above the waistband of her trousers, her ankles, whatever of her face I could see, the way she had tied her hair, the way she was moving her foot, the socks she wore, all suggested she was young, both in spirit and flesh. Yes, I did see the grey line of her underwear near the waistband, running above her trousers, I did see the arrangement of fabric and skin, of colour and texture, the black trousers, their half-swell over her bottom, the strip of pink flesh and the red of her sweater. Yes (why should I hide it) I did imagine what was beneath, I did imagine her breasts, my chin in the hollows behind her knees, her lips, my lips, her tongue, my tongue, the roof of her mouth, the ears, their lobes between my teeth, the taste of her toes.

And yet at the same time, I felt – how do I say it – I felt protective.

For, sitting in that imaginary chair at that imaginary table, her face turned away from me, perhaps it was her thin frame or her slender wrists and fingers, but there was no mistaking her vulnerability. Or maybe the whole time I was looking at her, that scene from the hospital earlier that afternoon was playing in some part of my head: her writing on the glass, the two words *HELP ME*, before the lights switched off in her room. Followed by the manner in which she kept avoiding that in her conversation on the phone, betraying at some level a desperate need to put up a brave face, hide her weakness.

Whatever, I kept waiting for the Imagined Miss Glass, the Just Conjured Miss Glass to get up from the chair, give me a fuller view of herself, maybe walk over to me, even have a second conversation, this time face to virtual face, answer the questions I had not yet asked. But instead, she faded away as the light inside my eyes dimmed and darkened, my lids grew leaden and heavy dragging me down to the depths where other dreams lay in wait.

This, initially, seems more like a memory than a dream.

I am a child playing cricket in the apartment building I grew up in. The expensive bat we are playing with belongs to the kid whose father exports steel rods used in construction. We play with a rubber ball, the agreement being that the kid who owns the bat doesn't have to buy the ball – ever. Others have to take turns: it costs half a rupee. We lose a ball at least once a week, to either the traffic on the street or the toilet at the end of the passageway.

It's my turn today. So I pray extra hard that the ball doesn't get hit onto the street, run over under the wheels of a bus or a tram because Father says he can't afford half a rupee for a cricket ball if I have to buy one every month. 'I am not a businessman selling steel rods,' he says, 'I am a schoolteacher. I can pay only once every *two* months for a cricket ball. Tell me if there is a book you need and I will get it for you but not a ball.' How do I tell him that under the wheels of the traffic on the street there isn't much room for his logic, that his probity is almost brutal.

The toilet, I can handle.

It's a 'public-service' toilet, with no doors, just a shoulder-high wall for privacy, a tap that's usually out of order and a bucket that's almost never used. At least twice, during a game, the ball takes the top-edge, gets deflected, bounces off the wall, finds its way into the toilet. Into the sludge of piss and shit of countless strangers. As it does today.

The stench I cannot smell since I am holding my breath. I bend down, use my left hand to reach out for the ball and just when I am only a few inches and seconds away from it, an arm shoots up from within the toilet bowl, grabs me, pulls me down. Whose arm is it I do not know.

I scream.

But because I am holding my breath, the noise is muffled. I am now inside the toilet bowl, all my four feet ten inches or so fitting magically into that confined space that is the hole, the shit entering my eyes, my ears, my mouth. Bitter, sour and sweet. I retch a greenish fluid, remnants of the late lunch I had when I returned from school, and it mixes with the sludge around me, I am pulled deeper and deeper down. I see bubbles forming near my nose, in rapid succession, as the trapped air rushes forth. And although I should not be able to see anything since the filth has entered my eyes, I can see clearly.

I am now inside a giant tunnel, swimming with the tide of the sewage, being carried along like a paper boat in the flood, and all this while the ball is a couple of inches in front of me, racing ahead. I lunge forward to reach it but it's moving faster than I am. As if it has a life of its own, mocking me as it darts, swings, curves, pirouettes. Sometimes it brushes against my outstretched fingers, teasing; at other times, it moves so quickly, almost leaping, bouncing so far ahead I can only see it as a distant speck in the onrushing waste, thick and heavy, foetid and fierce.

Through the tunnel's ceiling barely inches above my head, I can hear the traffic, the rumble, the whine, of wheels and feet. The loud hum and chatter of my friends, calling out to me to hurry up, the light is failing and the innings isn't over yet, the game has to be completed this evening, someone has to win and someone has to lose.

The sewage has entered my mouth, caked my tongue, I spit it out but it keeps entering so fast that my breathing can't keep pace. I can hear the boys shouting, every nerve, every muscle in my body aches as I am buffeted by the slurry, increasingly viscous, dragging me behind one time, pushing me forward at another, increasing the distance between me and the ball with every passing second.

Then, almost as suddenly as it all started, I see the ball slow down, closer to my grasp.

But it's not a ball any more. It's a different size now, it grows as I look at it, not radially, but in length. With each stroke of my arm as I move towards it, fighting for every breath, the ball gets bigger and bigger, slower and slower, and by the time I reach it, it's almost like a little tube, made of rubber, a slight circular bulge at one end reminding me of the shape that it once was. Covered with the sludge, it's also brown in colour and when my fingers brush against it, get a hold, some sort of a grasp, I know what I'm holding: this is no cricket ball, this is Ithim.

I am screaming.

Can Ithim survive this? This headlong fall, this onward rush? Can he swim through the filth, Ithim who has only eyes and neither arms nor legs to propel himself? I reach out to grab him and the moment my fingers touch Ithim, he turns over, and there they are again, looking at me, his perfect eyes, his perfect eyebrows and his eyelashes. Not one of them touched by this ordeal, they are as clean as when I first saw them.

Ithim is now in my arms and we are both swimming; the water is crystal clear, like a mountain stream. We can see the night above, the ceiling of the tunnel has long gone, there are brightly coloured fish navigating us, guided by the gleam of the stars. When we reach the surface, there is a boat waiting for us, shaped like a taxi, its black frame and yellow canvas top, polished, sparkling in the night. Ithim and I get into it and the moment we are seated it takes off, noiselessly, without the usual rev and stutter, and within minutes, it has lifted above the surface of the water into the air and we are now flying over the city, Ithim and I.

The wind whistles past us drying the water on our bodies. The sky is cloudless, the moon bright, and below us we can see the lights of the city, winking, returning my child's blinks from above, as if the city and Ithim were communicating a coded message to each other. The boat steadily gains in altitude until we are so high that my head begins to reel. I close my eyes, I clasp Ithim closer to me, my hands on his face and my fingers can feel his eyelashes rustle, as if I have trapped a firefly in my palms in the dark.

I am naked.

And I am pregnant, with Ithim.

I stand in the bathroom, looking in the mirror, and I can see Ithim inside me, the outline of his shape marking itself beneath my skin. His head by my chest, the entire length of his body running like a furrowed bulge, in one almost straight line, down to my navel, as if someone has inserted a tube into my throat, a tube made of rubber and blown air through one end. I try to cover this bulge by wearing a vest, a second vest, a striped shirt, a thick blue jacket, a wind-cheater, but it doesn't go away. Instead, it grows and grows, pushing at my lungs and my heart, causing an excruciating pain that begins in my stomach and stretches up to my chest. I can feel Ithim's eyes blinking inside me, so hard they make a noise that echoes my own heartbeat.

My clothes get tighter, the buttons start to pop. I take them off, hurriedly. Ithim has begun to move.

His head, so far just below my chest, is now pressing against my neck. His body has also moved higher up, my collarbones twist under his pressure, I can hear them crack, the muscles inside stretch, making a sound like a door creaking. Soon he may reach my mouth, push himself up my throat, claw at my tongue, my lips. And then I hear it, what I have been dreading all along: I hear the sound of something tearing, like fabric coming apart at its seams, not properly stitched.

It's my chest, it's splitting open.

Beginning right in the middle, halfway between my neck and my navel, just below my nipples, in one horizontal line, like a zip being unfastened. The skin is giving way to the pressure from within, I can see the outer layer peel away first, the epidermis, with the hair, the pink of the dermis, I can see my veins and arteries intertwined in the yellow-white fat and the tissue. Ithim's head appears through this widening crack, the charred skin below his forehead and his eyes, his eyelashes and the eyebrows, all drenched with my blood. My chest is wide open now, the floor red with blood I have lost, but I feel neither any pain nor any weakness. Just a growing lightness, of pressure pent up being released, my breathing now faster, but certainly much easier.

I look like a kangaroo, my chest a pouch formed by the two ends that have given way and which now frame Ithim's head. He's peering out, it seems, he's blinking. I gently hold him, feel the bones inside his skull, just underneath his scalp move, twist and turn. I try to prise him out, he closes his eyes. I pull hard and my opened chest opens further, Ithim emerges, and with each centimetre of his body that I am able to extricate from my chest, blood flows, thick and fast, running all the way down my stomach, matting my hair, over the penis, before running down my legs, and then onto the floor. It collects in a pool near my ankles, it clots as the fibrinogen meets the cold winter air.

Ithim is now out of my body, I place him on the counter of the bathroom sink, my blood dripping from his body, a huge red blotch on the white ceramic. I open the drawer in a small cupboard, my wife's stitching set is there, the one I picked up from a hotel room. A small packet of translucent plastic in which lie a needle, two buttons, a safety pin, threads in three colours, white, black and sky blue, wound on three rectangular cardboard strips.

And I grit my teeth, brace myself, start stitching my chest up. Each stitch is surprisingly painless and as soon as it's done the thread changes colour, from white to the brown of my skin; it merges with the skin, becomes the skin itself. So much so that once the stitches are in place, strands of hair begin to sprout, almost instantaneously, covering the stitches so there's nothing to show what happened except for a faint line across my chest and, of course, the blood on the floor. So much blood I wonder how we can ever mop all this up, wash it away without a flood, a deluge.

WHEN I woke up, my entire body was aching, my shoulders were stiff, as were my neck and my legs. Both my feet, propped up on the bed next to Ithim, had gone to sleep and waiting for the blood to rush back so I could move them, I saw, in the shadows of the night that draped Ithim, that his cheeks were wet. So wet that the tears had even seeped into the bed sheet leaving two stains. Dark and tiny. He must have cried several times when I was asleep, he must have cried himself awake, he then must have cried himself back to sleep again. No noise, of course, to wake me up.

I left the chair to walk to the bed, sit down next to Ithim. When I leaned close, my head just a few inches away from his, I could see his chest rise and fall.

And I could smell.

A stench from Ithim like thick smoke from a fire, black and noxious but invisible. It made my eyes smart and I had to hold my breath as it churned my insides, pushed the bile from last night into my mouth (because I hadn't eaten anything for hours, only drunk a few glasses of water, the bile was bitter but weak, it didn't burn my throat, just mixed with the taste of sleep and my dreams and scalded my tongue). Ithim had soiled himself.

And because Head Nurse had only wrapped him in the towel, leaving the diapers to me, I knew I had to change him.

It was back to the printouts.

The thumb rule is that you have to always, always, make no mistake about it, you have to first clean your hands. And cleaning your hands means not wiping them in a towel but scrubbing them hard, the palms, the fingers, between the fingers, up to the wrists. Because the germs that your hands carry are worse than what live in a baby's soiled bottom. Unwashed hands, with the germs still very much there, can damage the baby's tender and sensitive skin. So, let me repeat, wash your hands thoroughly before you begin cleaning the baby up.

Settle the baby down on a changing table, or any soft, warm, clean and dry area. You can even place your baby down on a blanketed floor. Peel off the old diaper or the wrapping but before you remove it completely, use one end of it to wipe out any of the excess pee or shit. If your baby is a boy, it's a good idea to cover his penis with a clean piece of cloth. This way, while you are cleaning him up and he decides to go again, you need not get your face drenched by the sudden spray.

Gently grasp the baby's ankles together with one hand and lift his bottom off the table, floor or the plastic mat you may have draped on the bed. Use baby wipes or a soft, wet cloth to wipe the baby's genitals.

At this stage, some people apply baby talc to the bottom but you need to check with the doctor about what you are using. Baby powders are more or less safe but then given that your baby's skin hasn't had much contact with anything in the world except maybe his mother's, it's always a good idea to avoid any substance which has unnatural compounds and chemicals in it.

I washed my hands, thoroughly, I peeled off the hospital towel and set to work, looking at Ithim, naked for the first time.

The flesh-tube that lay in front of me on the bed just needed to be wiped gently, no complex movements of the arms and the legs, I only had to lift the flaps of skin that covered his penis and his anus. I used Head Nurse's towel, drenched in the hospital's antiseptic, to clean the mess Ithim had made. It was watery brown in colour with some scraps of white, maybe from the baby formula I had fed him hours ago. When I took the towel to the bathroom, dropped it below the sink, for a moment, in a flash, I could see the congealed blood on the floor of my dreams.

My wife had bought diapers but when I brought one of them out it soon became clear it wouldn't work, it was too large. So I used more tissue paper, rolling it out to prepare a pad, placed the pad over the anus, adjusted it so that the tiny penis flopped on it and then I put one of my wife's sanitary napkins around it. The entire package now seemed to overwhelm him, a big bulk of white over the tiny, deformed brown – but Ithim looked clean and fresh, protected and safe. I fetched a fresh towel from his nursery, a towel my wife had bought, its price tag still stuck on, and wrapped Ithim again.

The dreams I had just had, of retrieving Ithim from that tunnel of sludge, then flying over the city, of Ithim tearing me up, drenched in my blood, the physical exhaustion of the previous evening and the night, the endless questions that had assailed me about my child's uncertain future, Miss Glass and her mystery phone call, perhaps all these had piled up, one on top of the other, adding to a crushing weight and the only way for me to relieve it was to get up and walk out of the room.

And as if my feet were dragging me, fleeing in that primitive instinct of self-preservation, I found myself leaving Ithim asleep on the bed, walking away from him. Yes, I knew I had to feed him again before we set out, maybe clean him once more, wrap him up, make arrangements to carry him on the journey that Miss Glass had planned for us. But all that could wait.

Right now, I needed to be alone, I needed space away from Ithim.

⬩◆⬩

FIREPROOF

I am Doctor 1, I was forty-four years old, I have a wife and three children, two sons, fifteen and thirteen, and a daughter, ten years old, both my sons were born in Oman where my wife and I lived for eight years, where I worked as an Emergency Room specialist, the salary and the benefits were very attractive, almost five times what I make here, tax-free, so when we returned – because my wife said, let's go back home, we have made enough money – I used my savings to buy an apartment in this city, a very well-constructed apartment, there was no damage to it during the earthquake although it's on the sixth floor of a ten-storey building and many houses next to it were cracked in so many places that they had to be abandoned, we survived the quake and I would have survived the fire, too, had it not been for the driver of the van, they stopped him, they asked him who we were, what our names were, and he told them, if he had lied, if he had made up two Hindu names for us, they would have let us go, I doubt they would have forced two doctors in uniform to undress, Doctor 2 and Head Nurse were sitting next to me, Doctor 2 did try to open the van so we could get out but there were so many people pressing against the doors that it was impossible, maybe the van driver just got frightened and didn't have the presence of mind to lie, anyway now it's all over, my wife should sell the house and, with our children, leave the city, she has relatives in Dubai who are fairly well established, they are rich, one of them has a house near the Creek, I am sure they will all help her and the children, find a way out, maybe even get her a job, she has a BA degree in history, she used to take private tuition, she can do a BEd through correspondence and get a job as a teacher in the international school there, affiliated to the Delhi Board, the children then won't have to pay any fees, they are doing very well in school, I never thought this would happen to me, usually those killed in such situations are the poor who live in slums and have no security, of all the patients I treated in this city almost ninety-nine per cent were Hindu but then these things don't matter, a mob doesn't think, you can't argue with a thousand people at one time, in fact, Doctor 2, I remember, did tell them we had treated many injured people in the hospital, but that just made them more angry, one of them laughed and said, now we will send you to the hospital, don't you worry, let's see who takes care of you, they said, and then the flames slipped in through the window, I heard Head Nurse scream, her face the last thing I saw through the smoke, she trying to cover it with her shawl.

7. *News on TV, Man From Ukraine*

AND guess who came rushing in to fill that space which I had just carved out of the night for myself, away from Ithim? A man from Ukraine, a large man in red Spandex shorts and a Nike T-shirt with no sleeves. A woman from South Korea and another woman from the Czech Republic, all in a television studio in some place called Burbank, California, under bright lights that washed over the studio audience, reflected off the blue-glass backdrop, rode on canned music travelling across the world, through space, to reach me that thinning night when I switched on the TV in the living room, Ithim fast asleep. One hour, I told myself, at the most, just an hour, I will start with Channel 0 and then work through to Channel 99.

Why do I recall what was being broadcast that night? What's its relevance now? For one, the noise from the TV, its shadows and its flickers, the faces and voices of strangers, filled the room, bringing for the first time since the previous evening a sense of the predictable and the normal into my life and my home. It took me away, temporarily, from what lay in the next room, from the dreams I had just had, away from the unknown cold fears that had slipped into the house after Miss Glass had hung up. And, then, of course, there was the man from Ukraine, the women from South Korea and the Czech Republic. But let's go in sequence, from Channel 0 up.

CHANNEL Zero on TV was *Business News*, a rerun of the late-night bulletin, the fresh Friday programming yet to begin. In her studio, lit blue, Anchorwoman sat at her sweeping glass table, pale white, translucent and glowing, like glass bathed in hidden lights. She wore a red top and a purple blazer, her hair was straight. There was a laptop on her table, its screen opened out, she was talking about the Budget tabled in Parliament that morning. She shrank in size, reduced to about a tenth, looking out of a window on the screen's top right-hand corner, while to her right scrolled numbers and charts, white in bands of blue. The Finance Minister, she said, had set up a Rs 15,000-crore fund for states to use if they reformed faster, especially in the agriculture sector, if they opened up their markets. There was a five per cent surcharge to fight terrorism, money was needed to keep the country safe from fear, taxes were up, the deficit had gone out of the window, foreign banks had reasons to celebrate, they could set up new branches, non-resident Indians could fully repatriate their earnings in India. Facts, figures, facts, figures until all I could make out was her lips moving – coloured mauve to match with her blazer. (In a few days, when I would have to return to work, these same facts and figures would be sitting on my desk, stale and cold, like a dark cloud, and it would be my job to polish its silver lining.)

'The markets gave a thumbs-down to the Budget,'

Anchorwoman said, trying to smile for the camera and yet appear suitably grim for the news, her face caught in this indecisiveness. The Mumbai Sensex closed at 3562, down almost 143 points, the Nifty down 47 points to 1142. I remember the numbers, I am good with numbers, I am the fact-checker, I am the fact-finder, 62 was my father's age when he died, 35 is what I will be in five years, when Ithim goes to school, 143 is one less than twelve dozen, 47 the year India got freedom, 11 and 42 the first and last two digits of my wife's hospital identity number.

'There is nothing in this Budget that will set the street on fire,' said a thin man, smiling, in a white shirt, a black suit and a striped tie, a fund manager from Mumbai. Anchorwoman wrapped up her segment by referring to the city on fire saying how that, too, had put 'downward pressure' on the market amid fears that it might spread to other cities across the country.

Up next was another woman, this time in Singapore, where it was already morning, and she had another man by her side, another white shirt, black suit and striped tie, this time from CLSA in Tokyo, where it was well into the trading day, talking about the Nikkei. Words and figures that floated over me as I sat there staring, waiting for the ad break. The crawl at the bottom: *Daniel Pearl already dead when throat slit on tape: US law enforcement officials; Queen arrives in Australia for Commonwealth summit, Watch out for special on Oscars and the box-office.*

Next channel.

News.

Maybe now I would get to know the details of the fire in the city, the fire that Head Nurse mentioned, that Miss Glass seemed to know a lot about. But I had caught the tail end, the least important stories, so I had to sit through them until they looped back to the lead.

A four-year-old girl in Kanpur who gouged out the eyes of her classmate, another four-year-old girl. Her left retina had been ruptured, the victim's grandmother said school authorities were to blame. 'Tell me,' she asked the reporter, 'how can we blame such a young girl? Obviously, she did not know what she was doing, they must have had a fight over something very minor. But how come a girl in a school has a kitchen knife in her hands? How did it get there? We plan to file a police complaint against the principal.' The principal, a woman with thick grey hair and thin grey glasses, her face averted, the camera showing her hands, her fingers interlocking and unlocking: 'How can you blame us? Not one of our teachers or staff was negligent. This happened during the lunch recess and the two girls were in the playground, there was a commotion and one of the senior students came rushing to my office and I wasted no time. I called for an ambulance. We rushed her to the hospital, what more could we do?' The wounded girl lay in an iron bed in a room, peeling plaster on the wall behind her. There was a huge cotton swab over her left eye and she was fast asleep, her legs sprawled across a small pillow. Next to her sat a woman, perhaps her mother, who brushed the TV microphone with one hand, gesturing that she would not say anything, that she had nothing to say. I watched a clip of endangered marine life seized near Chennai, the smiling face of the official as he stood there guiding the camera over the corals, the sea cucumbers and shells. I watched an icy expanse, the picture taken from a helicopter, the trees were tiny, the camera jerky, all the branches covered with snow, the screen white. It was down there, a voice said, below the ice, that they found the bodies of a Swedish tourist and her boyfriend who had got lost trekking twenty-three years ago. 'Even their clothes are intact,' said the voice, 'the Embassy has been contacted to send the bodies home.' There was an old photograph of the two, both with golden hair, the woman had a red scarf, a blouse with white and blue checks, the man had a leather jacket, fur-lined.

Then the lead story, the city on fire.

'In what they called revenge attacks for the killing of fifty-nine people on the train last night, hundreds of—'

A technical failure, there was no sound, only images.

This city this afternoon, a mob looking into the camera, waving, smiling, a close-up of a body on a stretcher, its face covered but the stretcher on the floor, surrounded by several women crying. (They showed this Floor Body several times.) A house on fire, a shop on fire, women and children huddled on the floor, a house on fire again, another shop on fire, a rubber tyre on fire, a car on fire, Floor Body again, a policeman speaking, a woman screaming. Floor Body again. The sound was back. Screaming Woman was loud, her hair across her face, several strands splayed across her lips, blowing in the air she breathed out as she screamed.

'. . . reports of deaths have come from Ahmedabad, Godhra, Vadodara, Bhavnagar, Sabarkantha, Rajkot, Panchmahals, Anand and Kheda.' Again, the sound went off.

The Prime Minister walked into the frame, his eyes closed, shuffling out of the frame, soft and cautious given his reconstructed knee. The Law Minister, looking as if he had just stepped out of the shower, fresh and wet, the ash scrubbed away, his hair brushed back. The Chief Minister smiling. Sonia Gandhi, her daughter by her side. (It must have been very cold in New Delhi, much colder than here, since both mother and daughter were wrapped in shawls, ash grey, like the sky above. Mother raised her arm to adjust her hair, there were sweat stains under her armpits.) On the TV now was a house on fire, a shop on fire, a city on fire. Smoke, thick and black; flames, red and yellow. Empty streets littered with stones, iron rods, a child on a stretcher. Floor Body now being picked up, moved out of the frame. Screaming Woman again, this time noiseless, the camera closing in on her tears, the gash of her parted lips, her teeth, her tongue.

In the ad break, they promised a special Oscar package for March: thirty-two movies in thirty days, beginning with *Jaws*, *An Officer and a Gentleman*, *Spartacus*, *Top Gun* and *Babe*.

The TV still on, I walked back to the bedroom to check on Ithim. Gone was the stench, he now smelled clean, fresh and dry. He hadn't moved one bit. His eyes were closed and when I brought my ears close to his slit-lips, to hear his breath, I could hear them move. Very faint, like the sound a fly makes when it walks on glass. I returned to the TV, safe in the belief that Ithim, for now, didn't need my attention; I would feed him later.

*

AND then came the man from Ukraine. This was *The Guinness Book of World Records*, broadcast from Burbank, California. On stage, next to the host, was the man from Ukraine. Short and squat, his flaming red shorts and red T-shirt seemed to have been painted on his body, outlining his chest, the slight bulge of his abdomen near the waist, a bigger swell of the crotch. He was the insect-eater, the insect-swallower. He picked them up from a huge glass aquarium in which they writhed, squirmed, crawled – two young women stood by his side, in white skirts, browned legs; their job was to poke the insects back into the glass case with a stick if they crawled too near to the edge. Beetles, crickets, flies, cockroaches, ladybugs, spiders, dragonflies, caterpillars, insects I couldn't name, red, white, green, yellow, black, monochrome, dichromatic, spotted, speckled, striped, banded, the man from Ukraine would pick one up, toss his head back, arch his body in a brilliant red curve on the blue stage, open his mouth wide as if he was about to scream, then drop the insect in. Wings and tentacles and legs and antennae rustled against his lips, his tongue, the last desperate flurry before his teeth came down, as if the creatures knew the end was near and there was no flying away, the microphone thrust so close it recorded every crunch, magnified into a sound I had never heard before. Whenever the man from Ukraine closed his lips, his face filled the screen, and I could see the twitch of his chin, the ripples on the surface of his cheeks as the insects flew inside his mouth, their blood, red, white and green, dribbled out, one of the women on the stage ready with a napkin.

Next came the woman from South Korea, her feast: razor blades. She swallowed them twelve at a time, tickled her throat with a straw (provided once again by one of the insect women) and threw up. The screen filled with a dozen razor blades in a pool of her phlegm, she wiping her lips. Another woman, this one from Prague, wore a blouse that bared her back. She looked like a ballerina, she walked like one, on her toes, each step filled with so much grace that I thought she would dance. But a man followed her with a bundle of darts in his hand, each black and glinting, with a knife-edge tip. She stood still while he began throwing the darts on her bare back, each dart getting embedded in her skin, marking its tip with a thin stream of blood that trickled down to her waist. Within minutes, so many darts had been thrown that everyone had lost count and her back was a river of blood – not one but countless tributaries mapping out a red pattern, not the faintest flicker of movement on her face.

I switched the TV off but on the blank screen I could now see Ithim in the studio, raised on a pedestal moved by pulleys and ropes and cranks, tiny Ithim, each part of him exposed to the camera's gaze, the charred skin on his forehead, the funnel-ear, the fused chin, the fold of flesh that covers his anus, the congealed mass near his waist, the child who is both It and Him, the camera then zooming in on his eyes, capturing the rustle of their blink, merging with the hollow claps of strangers. And it was at this precise moment when I sat in my chair, the TV humming although switched off, the three performers still in my head, that I realized the importance of Miss Glass's message and made my decision: yes, I would take that journey.

I would go wherever I needed to go if that could set Ithim right.

After Miss Glass had hung up, I had been weighing the options, balancing her promise against my fears, but now the scales had tilted. All the doubts and the uncertainties had melted away, like the night outside, leaving me not only more determined but stronger as well. As if the Ukrainian man, the insects fluttering in his mouth, the Korean woman allowing razor blades to travel down into and inside her body, the Prague woman with the red blood-map on her back, all these had cried out to me in their silence. No, I would never let that happen. I would never let Ithim perform, be the object of curiosity, I wouldn't allow a single person in this city, in this world, to look at him and pity him, no, never.

So relieved was I that for the first time, I felt hunger, my first selfish impulse, I heard my stomach churn and growl, and I saw this as yet another sign of order finally creeping into the chaos. I took two heaped spoons of Ithim's baby formula, washed it down with cold water, then prepared his feed, sterilized the dropper.

Once, while I was feeding him, he glanced up, his eyes looked into mine for more than a minute or so, I smiled at him, I caressed the skin on his forehead. He liked it, I think, because his eyes grew heavy and they began to droop, to close.

IF you were a stranger who had not heard a word of what I have said so far, if you were looking in through the window at me that morning preparing Ithim for the journey that I was now resolved to take, you would have thought I was packing up an object, certainly not a child and certainly not my child, not my newborn baby. While preparing Ithim for the journey, there were three things on my mind. One, I had to carry him close to me so I missed not the slightest movement. Two, he had to breathe (although I was still not sure whether the air found its way through his slit-lips or the two holes in the centre of his face, nor what route it took, how it travelled to his lungs, how it cleaned his blood, sent it to every corner of his body. But he had to breathe, I was sure of that). And, three, his eyes; they had to be free so he could watch, he could see, if only because that was the only thing he could do.

The rest was easy.

Because he had no arms or legs, no neck, no joints to manoeuvre delicately, no twists and turns to be careful of, the rest of him I saw as a frail object. Like a china bowl that had to be wrapped. I had seen my wife do that, wrapping gifts. She would sit on the bed, the coloured paper all around her, as if she were in the middle of a garden strewn with flowers, and her fingers, long and slender, would seem to acquire a life of their own, a dance, a beat to a rhythm I never heard but only saw, rapt with admiration. I tried to recall those moves, that sequence of movement of her fingers, how she folded the paper, how she prepared the extra layering, what she used first, what she used second and what she did last, as I picked up Ithim, very carefully, afraid I would drop him onto the cement floor.

I clothed Ithim in a tiny white shirt my wife had bought, a shirt complete with collars and sleeves and slit at the bottom on each side, adult-like. (I spread the shirt out, placed Ithim in the centre and then wrapped the two sides over him, one on top of the other. Its sleeves flopped on either side, I buttoned just a few buttons and to make sure that their plastic didn't scrape his skin, I layered the inside of the shirt with several handkerchiefs I had. The shirt reached a few inches below his waist, which helped, since I turned that over and used it to cover his bottom.)

Then a bag. Of course I couldn't carry Ithim, even if he was swaddled, like other fathers do. Not only was he too frail, I couldn't run the slightest risk of him being seen by someone on the street. At the same time, his comfort was important and so was my freedom of movement when I carried him. Therefore, the bag. A cloth bag that could take any shape and so would be softer on Ithim's frame. I lined it with towels and tissue. It had a flap at its mouth that could be closed to prevent dust from entering his eyes and yet its cotton fabric was porous so that air and light could enter. Its strap was sturdy, it would grip my shoulder. And allow me to hold it from below with one hand, keep my other hand free.

So Ithim all covered, with tissue and towels and fabric, safe and snuggled, I slid him into the bag, his face up, and kept it free, uncovered.

How did he look?

The most beautiful baby in the world.

As if he had been given to me by angels who had come down to the city. My Ithim was ready. And with help from Miss Glass, we would set him right.

From outside, I heard someone wake up in the dawn.

END OF PART ONE

I am Miss Glass, I was twenty-three, I was thirty-three, I was forty-three, I was fifty-three, I was sixty-three, I was a hundred and three, you choose any number you wish because, sorry, you aren't going to get me to say who I was, who I left behind, I am not going to give you a personal profile of my grief in about 350 words, in small type, single spaced, I am not going to tell you what happened to me, I am not going to tell you the last thing I remember, I am not going to tell you anything because I have a lot of work to do, I will see you later, towards the end.

PART TWO

THE DAY AFTER

8. *The First Light, Bodies Rain*

IF seeing is believing, then maybe not seeing is not believing. How I wish, therefore, I had an image, like the photograph of the pavement I took from Miss Glass's hospital room. Better still, a series of images, maybe video plus audio, but I don't and even if I had, I doubt it would make much of a difference because you would watch, you would hear and, in the end, you would dismiss it as doctored, you would say they can do these things these days, they can split, they can splice, morph and manipulate, they can pull anything out of thin air so why not bodies from the sky?

So how do I say this without straining credibility? Well, I will do two things. One, I will tell it like it is, and two, I will describe everything else in a fashion, absolutely matter of fact, just like I did with Ithim in the beginning, switching off the adjectival lights, using terms cold and clinical, black and white.

It rained corpses that morning.

For a full five minutes.

I checked my watch, I saw, I heard.

Yes, bodies fell from the sky.

But we will come to that in a short while because I need to begin with Ithim and me stepping out of our house. The child fed, cleaned, safe in the bag slung across my shoulder, in the first light of day. That's when we saw the fires. Not fires exactly but I saw what the flames had left behind, the remainders and the reminders of the night gone by.

I had missed them in the dark when I had brought Ithim home from the hospital in the taxi but I saw them now on either side of our street, I saw them now in the row of shops, tightly squeezed against each other: black rectangles, gaping hollows, their edges twisted and bent.

Three such holes I could make out, without much effort: Ahmed Meat Shop; Rehman, the tailor's; and the shoe store. The rest – the majority – of the shops were closed, shutters down, untouched. Streaked with dew, not with fire, guarded by a police van, blue and white. Two policemen sat in the front seat, their legs propped up on the dashboard beneath the misted windscreen where the cold vapour met the warm glass. There was nothing for them to police, maybe that's why they were fast asleep.

I wanted to walk right up to one of those holes and look inside, see what had been burnt and what had been left behind but there was no wasting time. Ithim and I had to go to the hospital, check in on my wife, wait there for a while, for Head Nurse to look at him. And then we had to, as Miss Glass had said, head for the railway station. Before that, of course, I needed to stop by at Mr Meeko's cybercafe to check the email Miss Glass had said she would send. With 'detailed instructions', that was the phrase she had used.

But this was Ithim's first day out and the only way I can do justice to that occasion is to mark the route we took.

In fact, I have a diagram to show you, a simple line diagram in black and white with no room for grey. Our L-shaped route, starting from the steps that lead from my apartment building to the pavement. Ending with our destination, the bus stop on the other side.

For me, the father, a short walk on the surface of this city, a walk I have taken a million times, but for my son that morning, almost a trip to the moon. I have put it down on paper for another reason, self-serving though it may sound. To impress upon you that my recollection isn't merely impressionistic, it's based on facts. So that later, when I tell you about the bodies falling, you don't brush it away as my momentary lapse of reason:

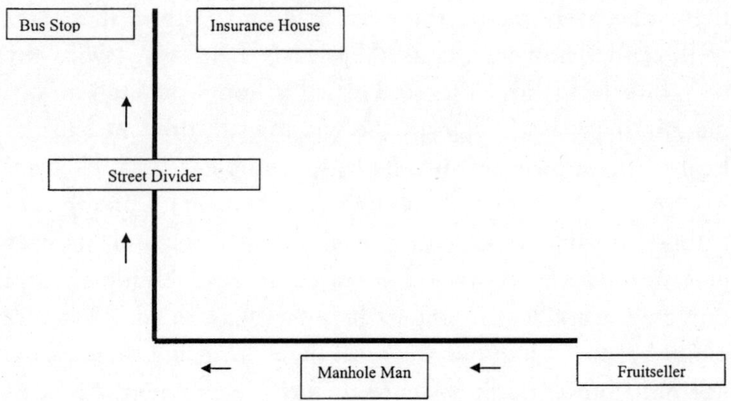

Fruitseller

He is among the first to come in every morning and set up his mobile shop on the pavement. That day, he had rigged up two wooden planks propped on upturned wicker baskets for his display cart. I see him every day when I go to work, he sells bananas, mostly. He supplements, complements, depending on the season. If it's May and June, he keeps cucumbers which he peels and slits, uses the knife to pat some salt on the slices; if it's after the rains, he has mangoes; if it's winter, as that morning was, he has some apples and oranges, sometimes grapes, too. But bananas, every day of the year.

There are always flies on the bananas. Buzzing, flying in circles, triangles, straight lines, ellipses.

I like flies.

I like their whirring sound, their furry feel, their tickle when they come to rest on my arm. I become still, I watch them delicately probe the surface of my skin, I like their frail, tender movements as they wash their legs. (Once my wife killed a fly and I looked at it for hours through an old magnifying glass. It lay on the windowsill, drenched in the heat of the afternoon sun, its legs, crumpled and tucked in, its tiny chest distended, perhaps the last of its breath still trapped inside, waiting to exit along with its soul, its eyes glassy and grey as if it had cried in fear, trembled and quivered in the last moments before it was killed. That was a pity because I like playing with them, swatting them away, not hard but enough to scare them for a moment. Most of all, I like watching them dare me.

These little creatures, not one bit afraid of me, of someone more than a hundred times their size, or is it five hundred or is it a thousand? We need to calculate, come up with, of course, an estimate. Let me do a simple exercise, if only for Ithim. If Ithim is one day able to hear, to understand, this is how I shall explain it to him: the courage of the flies.

If I am covered with flies from head to toe, my entire body, my fingers, my nails, in between the ridges of my elbows, behind my knees, on my anklebones, in every twist and turn, in my armpits, in between the toes, how many flies would that be? I am about five feet ten inches; if you approximate me as a cylinder, my area is two multiplied by π multiplied by my radius – which given my waist size of 31 will approximate 10 inches – multiplied by my height which works out to roughly seventy inches so the surface area works out to about 4544.8 something square inches and if you divide that by the area covered by one fly resting on my body, which will be roughly about point zero three square inches assuming an average fly is a quarter of an inch long and about half as wide, it works out to 150,000 flies. So, there you have it, it's amazing, the fly isn't scared of me. Me, who is about one hundred and fifty thousand times its size. Show me a man with that kind of courage.)

That's why I stopped at the Fruitseller that morning, that's why I adjusted Ithim in the bag – there was no way I would bring him out – so his eyes faced the flies, so he could watch through the fabric of the bag.

A father wants to share things with his son.

Manhole Man

Not more than ten steps away from Fruitseller, I saw the manhole cover of the drain. A thick circular plate made of iron, the colour of cement and concrete, ash and black and grey, a number engraved on its surface (the number the Corporation gives to each manhole in the city, as an identifier). That morning, the cover was placed on the street, in such a way that half of it was on the pavement, the other half in the drain, the edge of the cover in a pool of black water. We walked close to the manhole, Ithim and I, and there he was, Manhole Man.

Just his head, shiny black hair, not a single grey fleck, no, never – since they only use young men to do this job – his head rose out of the manhole. Like a swimmer emerging from a pool to catch his breath, to acknowledge the applause. I saw his bare torso, his legs bare, his feet bare, a small red towel wrapped around his waist to cover his nakedness. He climbed out, black sewage sticking to his body as if he had come to the surface from inside the shaft of a mine and coal dust from its walls had rubbed off on his skin.

In one of his hands, there was a bucket, made of aluminium, a small bucket, the kind I have in the bathroom to store water. This bucket was full of wet sewage, overflowing, so much so that it had formed a tiny black hill on top, the sewage water, brown, muddy, flowing down the side of its walls.

Still half inside, I saw Manhole Man place the bucket out on the street and then pull himself out, using his two free hands to lever himself up. Once he was out, he retrieved the bucket, walked to the drain where he emptied it. He must have started early on in the day, since at the edge of the drain, where he tipped the bucket, there was already a little hillock of black sewage.

Looking at Manhole Man, the dream I'd had that night,

of the cricket ball and Ithim in the drain, carried along by the current of sewage, suddenly seemed to appear softer, less threatening. The open cover of the manhole, the first light of day, the calmness, the grace with which Manhole Man was going about his job, made me think of that swim in the dream tunnel, of the river meeting the sea and the ocean, merging with water from across the world, waves from the Bay of Bengal and the Arabian Sea heading for the Atlantic thousands of miles to one side and the Australian coast thousands of miles to the other. (One day, I will go there with Ithim, maybe on board a ship; we will take a room with portholes through which he can see the water. At night, I will take him to the deck, remove the covering over his eyes and hold him face upwards, so he can see the stars and the moon. Then I will tilt him gently, show him how they reflect in the waves.

A father has dreams for his son.)

Street Divider

Past Fruitseller and his bananas, past the flies, past Manhole Man, the growing hillock of sewage, Ithim and I began to cross the street. Midway we stopped at the divider. The divider is, in essence, a long cement garden, a narrow rectangular strip that bisects the street, about four feet wide and a few inches above street level, running as far as your eyes can see on either side.

It was recently constructed, part of the city's plan to widen this road. Grass was planted there in the first week of June to mark Earth Day. (My wife, newly pregnant, and I stood in the balcony and watched the day's ceremonies. Boys and girls, men and women had reached here early morning, in shorts and trousers and white T-shirts with caps saying Save the Earth. The state Minister for Forests and Environment was the Chief Guest. A bureaucrat, dressed in a suit and tie, did the digging with a shovel, planted a sapling and the Minister poured water.

My wife said she would use that plant as a marker for the growth of our own child. However, in the six months since that morning, my wife swelled but the sapling died, the grass grew only in patches.)

The divider has a railing on either side to prevent pedestrians from jaywalking but the railing is broken in several places, some through neglect, some by intention, so it's stopped serving the purpose for which it was set up. While crossing the road, you can squeeze yourself through one of the gaps, step onto the grassy patch on the divider. This is used as a pit stop by many people. A temporary resting place.

Which is what we, Ithim and I, did that morning. We crossed one half of the street and then waited at the divider. We saw the posters up close, posters on billboards attached to the street lamps that sprout from the divider like tall trees planted at regular intervals. That morning, all the billboards on the divider were taken up by a cellphone company advertising its special roaming service across the country.

The ad featured a dog following a boy wherever he goes, the dog, a little pug, obviously standing in for cellular signals and the boy, about seven or eight years old. (I have seen the ad on TV as well.)

Boy and dog running across an empty field, low-lying hills as the backdrop, boy always in front, dog behind.

Boy and dog running along a train track, trees on either side.

Boy at his study desk, perhaps doing his homework, dog sitting at his feet, its ears flopped down, one eye closed.

Boy in a marble bathtub, his little head propped up on the rim, dog on the floor, its head between its two front paws.

And so on. Boy and dog, always together. Like Ithim and I.

A father and son, never to be separated.

Insurance House

Once we had stepped off the divider and crossed the street, we were at the tip of the vertical rule of the L, just where the bend begins for the walk to the bus stop. Ahead was Insurance House, the new office building that sells life insurance and pension plans to this city. Walls made of red sandstone and its windows made of thick stained glass, it's a new building completely out of place in our neighbourhood. In fact, one side, the building's wall, is entirely formed of glass. Black, shining and opaque. I like looking at this glass facade not only because of how it catches the glint of the sunshine during the day, the bounce of the yellow neons at night, the huge poster of a happy, insured family (father, mother, son and daughter, all sitting on a wooden floor, watching TV, a golden retriever in the middle), but also because of how the glass distorts my reflection, so I become almost ten or twelve feet tall, my face more than two feet long. The glass widens my forehead, stretches the chin below the lips so much that even I can't recognize myself, my legs become almost as long as the lamp post on the divider.

That morning, with Ithim, I was tempted to take him out of the bag, remove the towel that wrapped him, and see what he looked like in that glass. Because he was deformed, I wanted to see how he would look de-deformed and magnified, would the glass, by some freak of optics, give him some semblance of the normal? Of course, I did no such thing; and, instead, headed for the cybercafe to check Miss Glass's email.

That's when the bodies rained.

IT began with a sound of something falling, something large and heavy, the sound dull, deadweight. In the shuffle of feet, in the noise of vehicle horns, and brakes, sudden and slow, the clink of the bucket of the Manhole Man and the creak of a wooden door opening somewhere, closing somewhere else, Fruitseller shouting at the flies, a radio blaring an old song, scratchy and loud, this specific sound would have gone unheard. But that morning, it seemed, just for the very moment when it happened, silence had stretched taut, tight across the entire block. And this sound had neatly punctured it, torn it open.

So loud it was.

It came from across the street, that I was sure of, and from near the burnt butcher's shop, but when I looked, I saw nothing. Maybe, I thought, it had come from the shop itself, some overhanging beam that had been charred to its foundation and suddenly fallen off, its joints coming unhinged a fraction of an inch every hour or so until its entire weight had given way.

And then there was the second sound.

In the space of a few minutes. And this was closer; it seemed to be coming from right behind me. So close, in fact, that it made me jump. When I turned to look, it wasn't actually that close – it was well beyond the bus stop – but this time I could see the source of the noise. On the same side of the street that I stood on, it lay half sprawled over the pavement, half on the drain.

It was a body.

Maybe it had been lying on the roof of the shop nearest to us, had rolled off, pulled by gravity down the incline of the asbestos roofing. It was a man's body, neither tall nor short, a head of thinning grey hair, dressed in a white shirt now smudged in several places, grey and brown and grey trousers that had slipped from the waist revealing a bit of his stomach. He wore a red half-sleeved sweater, frayed at the V-neck. Both his feet were bare, one leg flung over the other as if he had been sitting in a chair with his legs crossed when he had died, and then rigor mortis had set in locking the legs in that position when he fell. His neck twisted, I couldn't see his face clearly, just the back of his head, the stab wound in his chest that had drenched his shirt with blood that had by now dried to a crust so hard it didn't even look like blood, just thick brown paint. On his left wrist, I saw a pale white band on the brown skin. Perhaps that marked out where his watch should have been.

And then it struck me, how no one had noticed this

except me; how people were walking past the body as if it were a discarded bag or a pile of clothes. Certainly, I could have walked up to him, could have turned him over, or just circled around him to see, Ithim pressed to my side in the bag. But before I could think anything of this, another body fell.

This time, it landed across the street from me, a few feet in front of the manhole. This body was different, it was black in colour, so black that it didn't even seem human. And small, just about the size of both my palms, cupped. Once my eyes had adjusted, once the thud had died into silence again, I could clearly make out its limbs, all four of them, tiny, like four little fingers pointing upwards. I walked across to the divider to have a better look and only then did I realize it was a body all right, but it seemed to be the body of a baby – a boy or girl I had no idea – and it was charred. So intense the fire was, I guessed, that the entire body had warped and twisted, its limbs pointed to the sky. Like this was no child but a calf-puppet milkmen make, of sticks and cowhide and thatch, colour it black, to fool the cow into lactating, a black cow that has lost her baby.

In the next minute or so, other bodies fell, all within my field of view, marking out – almost – the circumference of a circle where I was the centre. As if someone invisible were hovering right above me, someone as big as the sky, draped over the entire neighbourhood, sealing all the cracks in and between buildings, filling all the empty spaces. And this someone was dropping these bodies. (For me to see, for Ithim to see. I reached inside the bag and pulled the edge of the towel across to cover Ithim's eyes; I felt his eyelashes close against the back of my palm. He couldn't see, he wouldn't see, that I was now sure of.)

I heard the bodies fall, the bones snap, I heard the crunch, even the sound of dead flesh hitting the cement, concrete, I heard the light wind that had begun to blow, adding to the morning chill, the rustle of the clothes the bodies wore as they caught this wind. And when I turned and walked to the bus stop, the body of the old man was still there and the charred child was in front but there was also a woman now, dressed in a blue sari hitched to her knees, her legs splayed, her hair loose, black and dry, falling to her waist. She lay on the divider, her torso hunched, as if she were sitting against the wire cage around a sapling, her head twisted at an impossible angle. Her left earring had been wrenched from her earlobe and blood had crusted there, the skin sliced as if her ears were made of paper or rubber, easily torn and shredded. There was dirt in her toenails polished red; I counted and there were four nails where the polish had chipped leaving behind just a hint of colour.

The last two bodies were far away, almost where the street seemed to end and from where the bus would emerge any moment now so I couldn't make out who they were, I just saw dark, hulking shapes, two bundles, one on either side, one curled up, thicker and smaller, the other sprawled so distant that the only part of it I could see was an arm, outstretched.

But I saw three of the five bodies clearly.

FIVE minutes passed, then ten, fifteen, sixteen and seventeen, no more bodies rained. It had been a drizzle and the drizzle had now stopped. I did call to the Fruitseller, 'Did you see that?' I gestured to the charred child, Fruitseller looked once, smiled at me, and then continued waving the flies off the bananas.

Had he not seen it? Could he not see it? Was I the only one who could see the bodies?

I wanted to rush back to the safety of my house, lock the doors and windows, look through the slats for the scene outside to shift, for the first signs of the crowd noticing, for more men and women to gather, wait for the safety of numbers.

I was frightened both for myself and for Ithim because what did this portend, this happening right in front of my eyes? Whose bodies were these, where had they come from and why had they fallen, as if from the sky? Why did they all bear marks of murder, of killing? Who were these victims, who were the culprits, were there more wherever they came from? Were they linked to the fires that I had not seen for myself but had heard about? And why wasn't a single person on the street noticing the bodies were right there in the middle, in the way of the traffic?

Eventually, though, it was this, the very fact that no one else had noticed these bodies, that began to quieten down my own fear. I was too tired and maybe I was seeing things, I thought.

I found myself crossing the street, past the charred child, past the hunched woman, to the cybercafe. A welcome wave of relief swept over me when I saw the shutter had been rolled up; the glass door was closed but through it I could see the light glowing. Yes, I could check my message from Miss Glass.

At the same time, there was Ithim.

All along, he had been quiet in the bag, not even moving. (Or if he had, I hadn't felt anything.) I lowered my right hand into the bag, gently brushed my fingers around his head, I touched one finger against his eyes, I could feel him blink. He was awake. Through the fabric of the bag, the dappled light of the morning that filtered in, had he seen what I had seen? Certainly not, how could he? And even if he had, he would surely not be able to make sense of what he saw. I hoped that at Holy Angel, while I went to the recovery room to see my wife, the nurses would take care of Ithim, clean him up, medicate, feed, check, fortify him so that he would be ready for the journey.

Obviously, I wasn't going to tell them I was taking Ithim on a train. You can't do that, I was sure they would say, since when have you heard of any newborn – and one too who needs all the help he can get, one who has arrived in the world, with all the odds and evens stacked against him – being taken away from his mother when he's not even a day old, put in a bag, howsoever gently or tenderly, have you heard of such a baby being taken on a train journey?

'He will not survive it,' that would be the Holy Angel's verdict, 'you cannot take him, it's like taking him to his death. It's a crime. Are you out of your mind? Mr Jay, what do you think you are doing? Here, please sign the consent form, the release form, some form or the other. He is in no shape to board a train today. What will you feed him? What about infections? The shudders, the jolts, the cold air?'

To which I would have said: 'He's my child. Bring out any piece of paper you need me to sign because I am taking him this afternoon. I want to set him right.' Well, if it came down to it.

I pulled the cybercafe's glass door open and stepped inside. It was empty but all the terminals were switched on, they glowed blue and green. I saw the back of Mr Meeko's head as he sat at his own terminal, keying in something.

◆◆◆

FIREPROOF

I am Fruitseller, I was twenty-seven years old, I was born in Gaya in Bihar, I had a wife and four children, I lived in the slum under the bridge, my father was also a fruitseller but I started off making bidis in a godown for almost two years, I worked from 9 am to 8 pm with a lunch break at 1 pm but I got tired sitting in a closed room the whole day on the floor, cross-legged, and working only with my hands because I like walking, I like being in the open so I left that job, pushed a handcart for six months, ferrying supplies to and from a furniture shop but when I got married and the children came, my father said I needed something more steady and one morning he said he was very tired and could I take the fruitbasket out that day, I liked it, moving from one neighbourhood to the other, setting up shop on the pavement, and although the income wasn't steady, day by day, I got to know most of the roads and the lanes until I realized that I could remember places just after one visit, I could recall landmarks big and small, like a garbage heap, a broken lamp post, in fact if I were alive, I would eventually have become an auto-rickshaw driver, I know one in the neighbourhood and he makes good money but then came the mob, I remember that all of us were at home, sitting on the floor, in a circle, we had locked the door and the window, we heard them outside, it was afternoon, I hadn't gone out that day because the schoolteacher who lived with us in the slum, he is the only one who reads a newspaper, had gone around telling everybody to be careful since after the train attack there was fear that we would be targeted, so I wanted to be at home in case something happened but I could do little when the mob set our house on fire, I opened a window to let the air come in but instead there was more smoke and more fire, I thought the fire couldn't be so strong it would take all seven of us but it did, I was the last one to go, I am not going to describe to you how my wife and children died, I cannot describe that, all I can say is that I was the last one to go, I have a brother who is still in Gaya, once a month I would call him from the phone booth near the police station but I am sure he will hear what happened here, he won't wait for the call, he will take the next train to come and look for all of us, there must be some people in our slum who got away, they will watch as he searches for us, as he looks at our house, they will then tell him what happened to all of us, he will then go back and will never have to visit this city.

9. *Mr Saxel Meeko, My Only Friend*

JUST in case you accuse me of letting emotion cloud my reason, I need to come clean, I need to tell you that when I talk about a man called Saxel Meeko, you will detect in my voice a tone of admiration, maybe even some adulation. Allow me this temporary indulgence, for Mr Meeko is a friend – you will soon see why, and, if I may be so bold as to suggest, I think you will like him, too – and therefore it was only appropriate that I take Ithim inside, that he get to see the man, the one man his father admires in this city.

That the cybercafe was empty when I walked in came as little surprise because its main business is at night, in the last hour before midnight. It's then, Mr Meeko knows, that the women in his neighbourhood, wives daughters, mothers aunts, have cleared the dining tables, are preparing to sleep, some combing their hair, all assured in their assumption that their men, who have worked hard the whole day, need to take a walk, work off their stress, meet other men, discuss the day and its end.

It's then that Mr Meeko knows they will come.

The men walk into his cybercafe, put the money on his desk, fifty rupees an hour for broadband, including tissue paper and a glass of Coke or Pepsi. No stuttering dial-up.

Instead, welcome to Uninterrupted Access, Streaming Audio Video. To watch porn. Almost always, white. Once in a while, inter-racial, black on white, Asian, white on yellow, Indian, brown on brown, mix and match, keep the raw material the same, please. That's what matters, the rest is just detail. As long as no one's looking over your shoulder.

Which, Mr Meeko, as a professional, has worked hard to ensure.

So even when Internet costs have crashed, even these days when they offer PCs at slash-down prices, he knows they will come because these are images and sounds best seen and heard alone or in the company of strangers. Trisha, Jemma, Angie, Sylvia, undressing and moving, oceans and continents away, only for these men at this time in this city.

Therefore, Mr Meeko has carefully designed his fourteen cubicles for privacy, with a partition between each, a glass slab double-plated to muffle noise. And a pair of headphones. The customers, too, are discreet. Careful of what they do. Mindful of each other as they work on their coming, the boxes of tissue paper close at hand. Once in a while Mr Meeko gets up to walk around, unobtrusively, quietly, in bare feet, so his customers don't even know he's there. (He does that ever since the night he saw a customer masturbating to what looked like a naked child on the screen, barely three or four years old. It had filled him more with dread than revulsion, a fear he couldn't place and he had to assure himself over and over again that this was no reason to close down his business and as long as he laid down the ground rules – in fact only one ground rule, no children, please – things would be fine. But rather than put that rule on paper or tell his customers about it – Mr Meeko never talks to them, even to make polite conversation – at least once a night, he gets up, on the pretext of going to the bathroom or drinking a glass of water, and walks between the cubicles. Like a schoolteacher supervising a class test, walking in and out of the rows and columns of chairs and tables to ensure that no one's cheating.)

Sure, there are laws, the Indian Information Technology Act 2000, under which his business at night (child or no child on the screen) is illegal; his cybercafe should be closed down. But Mr Meeko is practical and The Practical Mr Meeko has found a way out: a monthly payoff of five thousand and one rupees to the station house officer of the local police station, a man called Rakesh Sharma (the same name as the country's first astronaut who went into space with the Russians). And Sharma gets three hours of free surfing every week. And surfing not on a terminal in one of the cubicles but on Mr Meeko's terminal, the best of them all: a 17-inch Samsung screen, an optical i-ball mouse that glows in the dark, red beneath its surface, an ergonomic keyboard from the black market, split in the middle, so the wrist doesn't strain. Specially padded earphones, too, so that Mr Sharma can listen to the audio as he comes to the video without hurting his ears, walk away after wiping himself with a paper towel and dropping it onto the floor.

It's tough. It makes Mr Meeko grit his teeth, the crumpled balls of tissue paper, stained with the semen of these men, but he slips on rubber gloves to clean up, putting each ball into a plastic bag which he then takes out, at the end of every night, and sets ablaze near the drain.

It helps him feel clean, purified.

*

HOW do I know all this? Well, trust me, I know. I have to admit I cannot vouch for the veracity of each detail but my information is based on several conversations with Mr Meeko. We have talked about work, his and mine, about the cybercafe, the neighbourhood, the city, the world – more so when my wife was pregnant and we began using his services regularly, at least twice or thrice every week. (It was during one of those meetings that he first showed me the webcam mounted outside his cybercafe looking down on the street below, permanent and unchanging, except for one click every hour, when it captures the scene in its rectangular frame and relays the image to Mr Meeko's desktop. He would sit and watch, right through the day and night, the angle of the shadow change on the street, the ripples in the stagnant water in the drain caused by the vibration of a passing truck. Someone dropping a cigarette butt, a shred of paper caught in a sudden wind, a pair of feet passing by, all these, on his screen, imbued with a sense of the majestic and the wondrous.

But if this was Mr Meeko's unique *virtual* window to the world, he has a unique *real* window, too, in the basement where he lived, just below the cybercafe. So unusually positioned is this window that it serves as a peephole to the street outside, a vantage point through which Mr Meeko can see without being seen. He sits in the chair and watches feet passing him by. Once in a while, he will see a face, and that too, just a glance when someone on the street outside bends down. To tie his or her shoelaces or pick up something they have dropped.

From the outside, if you stand on the street, even if you bend down, so unobtrusive is the window, covered by a brick ledge that juts out of the wall, you won't remotely suspect someone could be watching you.)

SUCH is Mr Saxcl Meeko. As I said earlier, forgive my excitement, my awe, but I see in him a combination of the practical and the ideal that live, in most of us, only in opposition but in him have merged so effortlessly and gracefully. Here is a man who has cut himself off from this city but at the same time is watching it every waking moment. And, watching, not as we do, with our eyes always moving on, but by securing an extra pair of eyes and directing their gaze at something no one looks at, a tiny patch of pavement. And by not sharing it with others – as so many people do on the Net these days – he has added a permanent exclusivity to it that makes it more special, unique. And then the fact that he lives in the basement.

Once again unseen, unheard, below the surface, plumbing the depths and like his webcam giving him a vantage point that no one else in this city has. Both webcam and basement keep him indissolubly tied to the city, the pavement above and the ground underneath, and yet both give him a sense of immeasurable distance, of living his life in a space and a time that are his own. Perhaps that's where he gets his strength from, the grit to pick up the balls of crumpled tissue, stained with semen every night, then burn it outside on the pavement. Also he knows his power, that he holds all the strings in his hand, that he is the one who gets men to walk into his cybercafe every night and strike pitiful, sorry figures, their penises in their hands, their squirt and their groans.

In a way, I sensed this the first time he introduced himself to me, in his formal, odd manner of speaking. 'Myself, Mr Saxel Meeko.'

'Yes, I saw,' I said, pointing out to the printout on the wall where he had typed out his name in different fonts.

'Where are you from?' I asked, because of a name like that in a city like this, because his face gave nothing away, so ordinary and nondescript it was, with not one feature, neither hair nor eyes, or colour of skin, or weight to single him out from anyone else in this city – or this country, for that matter.

'I am from a family. Just like you, just like all,' he said, smiling, and then pulled me closer, taking me aback with this sudden, disquieting physical contact. 'Mr Jay, in this city, Saxel Meeko is the best name. Safest name, they will never be able to guess who I am.'

Now you know why I felt so comfortable that morning when I opened the door to his cybercafe and walked in. Because if there was any place that seemed safe, that seemed like a haven after the bodies falling from the sky, from my fears about the journey ahead, it was this.

Mr Meeko, however, didn't notice me as I entered the cubicle in the farthest corner to check if Miss Glass had sent her message.

⬩◆⬩

I am Body 3, I was five years old, that is what my mother told me, I want to go to my mother, it was very hot, there was fire, I want to go to my mother.

10. *One Message, Three Names*

SO odd was Miss Glass's message that whatever idea I had of her until then, beginning with The Face by the window, the strands of hair on her forehead, the strap of her nightdress, her writing on the glass, the picture in her room and now in my pocket, followed by her phone call at night, her confidence and her arrogance, her form in my dream, the red sweater, the strip of pink skin above her waist, her nose ring, the tapping of her feet, all were put to the test as if they were bricks I had placed one on top of the other, one next to the other, to build an edifice called Miss Glass, I then saw them crumbling, falling to the ground, raising dust when I first opened my mailbox and saw:

Sender: Miss Glass, the Subject line: Our Conversation.

From: Miss Glass
Reply to: 'Miss Glass'
To: Mr Jay, Husband of Patient No 110742
Subject: Our Conversation

At the railway station,
As we discussed last night,

Meet at five in the evening,
We will set the baby right.

Don't worry about a thing,
I will remain by your side,
Yours loving Miss Glass,
She who knows where to hide.

And in case you don't see me
In the maddening crowd,
There will be someone there
To call out, clear and loud.

SO, that was the message? These were the 'detailed instructions' she said she would send me, to prepare us for the journey?

Rage.

My first reaction was rage.

What did she take me to be, a wooden duck, a cardboard train being pulled along at the end of a string?

What did all of this add up to? Was this someone pulling a fast one? Was Miss Glass a fraud? Someone who had seen me at the hospital, who may have known someone working there, some nurse, some guard, some doctor, maybe Head Nurse, and had bribed someone (just as I had bribed Old Bird) to get my details, my number, my wife's condition, details about my Ithim, and made a prank call last night? And then, put the phone on speaker mode, got friends to sit around, laughing at how gullible I was – and, yes, I *did hear* the sound of laughter on the phone last night, a sound that Miss Glass had dismissed straight away, brushed aside – so, at this moment, they were slapping each other on the back, as they imagined this scene, of a man made a fool of, his baby by his side. Early in the morning, in a city on fire, sitting in a cybercafe, the first customer, reading junk?

No, it couldn't be. How could it be?

Because one thing I was sure of: I had *seen* the woman by that window, *I* had *seen* her write those two words on the glass. I had picked up a picture from that room and Miss Glass had referred to it in our conversation. Also, to be fair, yes, I had detected arrogance, confidence, an unusual familiarity in Miss Glass's tone, but no, I hadn't heard a single false note in whatever she had told me last night. But then why had she done this, sent me a message that was of no help at all? When she knew I had taken, solely at her insistence, a leap in the dark. When I had put Ithim in a bag – while he should have been in a bed in the hospital under expert medical care or pressed to his mother's breasts, feeling their rise and fall – and set out on a journey she had promised to map out, to lead, to guide.

Let me print this message out for whatever it's worth, I thought.

And just as I was about to do that, I noticed it: there were three attachments, each with a name I had never heard of: **Tariq.Doc, Shabnam.Doc, Abba.Doc.** And beyond those three paragraphs of silly rhyme, her message went on.

Dear Mr Jay:

I tried my hand at rhyme, I thought let's bring a light tone, that's what we need after our conversation last night. Anyway, let me make one thing very clear, maybe it didn't come across last night, I will never, never mislead you. Trust me, I am only doing what I have to do . . . It's for your own good.

The station this evening will be crowded . . . I don't know if you know . . . the fires across the city have taken their toll, they say that almost two hundred have been killed so far, and not all deaths have even been counted. Bodies are showing up in all kinds of places and as the day progresses, in the sunlight we shall see more . . . some people have said they have seen bodies fall from the sky . . . I think that's an exaggeration but you get the drift . . . those lucky to have survived have decided to leave the city, go to other places . . . where their friends or relatives live, where they feel safer, where there won't be a knock in the middle of the night, or a flaming rag thrown into the house in the middle of the day . . . some have decided to return once the fires die down, once they know that the killers have got tired . . . which they will, I hope, given how hard they have been working. But then many may never return because there is nothing in this city now for them, their homes are gone, their places of work too . . . you must have seen three of them on your street itself, the tailor, the shoe store and the butcher shop. I doubt if any one of the three will come back. There are countless such cases. I am telling you all this to assure you that I am not stringing you along . . . these are hard times in the city . . . these are fearful times when people do not admit, even to themselves, what they may have seen, what they may have done . . . so please do not panic if you don't see me at the railway station . . . I have work to do, unfinished business to attend to . . . maybe it will never be finished . . . but I have to keep trying, now that I seem to have all the time in the world . . . Yes, I am concerned about your baby, about Ithim (did I tell you what a nice name that is?) . . . the baby is the most important thing on my mind right now and I want to help and hence this message . . .

That's why I have arranged for someone trusted, someone you will like, someone to be there at the station when you arrive . . . he may act a bit funny, strange, but don't mind, he was always like that, he has a kind heart and he is one of us . . . I will try my best to be there myself but, to be honest, I can't give you any guarantees . . . given that the city is on fire, I don't even know what will happen by the time you reach the railway station, how many more will have died by then. As you may have noticed, I have attached three files with this message . . . please read them carefully, they need time and concentration. It will help you and it will help me if you read them before you reach the station . . . they are about three people from last night who were not so lucky . . . I mention their stories hoping that you will get a better sense of what's happening in the city . . . did I tell you last night that I took some pictures? I have sent them as well. These pages have been written at great risk, with great effort . . . Mr Jay, I know that if there were questions in your mind before you started reading this second message, there must be now many, many more. Rather than providing answers, I think I have added to the questions you must have, I have multiplied and magnified your fears, your doubts . . . But, as I said earlier, all this is for the better, trust me. It's for you, it's for the baby and it's for me as well. By writing on the glass that night, I wanted to help you because by doing that, you would help me. If all this sounds convoluted, don't worry, everything will be clear in due course but that course is still due, there are questions that cannot be answered before their time has come. I wish you the very best and I look forward to meeting you very very soon. Go ahead with the journey, Mr Jay, there's nothing to fear, there's nothing to lose and that you are reading this means that you are well into your mission. In fact, your journey began the moment you saw my letters on the window. A journey, I promise, you will never forget. You will meet some of my friends too, they have been waiting for this. Please take care of yourself, this is a city on fire. And, by the way, my friends love my new name, they say it sounds mysterious. That it suits me. Thank you for it. You have a way with names. Take care of yourself and take care of the child the way I am sure you have been doing . . . I will see you soon.

I will always remain,
Yes,
Yours loving,
Miss Glass.

FIRST things first, I needed to download the attachments, which I did, printing them out right away lest there be a power cut or some virus in the system and I lose them. (And while they were printing, I checked on Ithim as it had been quite a while.)

The printer stopped; all three attachments were there, on warm, crisp, A4 paper. There were some pictures too, in black and white. I checked for any missing or blank pages, found none. Miss Glass had marked the End on each one of the three files. She was meticulous.

I shall not summarize anything, will not read between the lines, until you have read them, for yourself, all three files and seen the three pictures. (You can come back to them when you have the time, read them again, read them as many times as you need.) All I want to say before I take you to the attachments is only one thing: it was with the receipt of this message and Miss Glass's note that I realized, as Miss Glass had put it, my journey had already begun.

That she had kept her word and although I was still

clueless as to where I was going, I had inclined myself to believe her when she said there was nothing to fear, nothing to lose. That it was for my own good, for Ithim's good. That the baby was the most important thing on her mind.

Trust me, she had said twice.

I did.

Once again, how wrong I was.

⬩◆⬩

◆◆◆

I am Body 2, I have nothing to say.

◆◆◆

11. *Tariq*

(The First Attachment)

OUR first eyewitness is a boy. Name is Tariq, he is ten, or, at the most, eleven years old. He wears shorts and a T-shirt although this is February and it is cold, and if you look close enough, you will see his elbows and his knees are bare. The skin covering them is cracked and dry. A boy with not enough clothes in this city – he shouldn't stand out in any crowd. Still, they got to him.

That's his house in the picture.

A simple frame. Simpler than the house a child would draw when told to draw a house. Just a long rectangular box, the windows cut out as an afterthought. The house built, as if, not to defy the elements (the rain, the sun, the dank or the chill), but instead to surrender itself to them, its plaster to be streaked, its corners to be shadowed, its walls to be eroded. Unprepared, totally, for fire, for men intending to kill and burn. That's why the door's gone, the windows and the ceiling, all shattered into countless pieces scattered inside and out. There are some clouds in the sky but no evidence of smoke, it's bright, it's clear.

We will come back to this house later. Now let's return to last night.

Through the drift of the fog and the smoke from fires far away, through the yellow haze of the neons in front, through the black-white exhaust of vehicles that streak past his house, through his tears that bend, refract everything he sees, Tariq witnesses the woman lying on the street. She is his mother.

Tariq's eyes also witness four men.

A, B, C and D.

They look like educated men, not like the men he sees in his neighbourhood in frayed clothes, stained and unwashed, dust in their hair, dirt in their fingernails. They are not men who shout and who scream when talking will do, they are not the hangers-on who sit for hours at the iron gate of the former Member of Parliament's house down the street, they are not men Tariq sees in the crowd during election time, men who go from door to door with coloured flags and handbills. They are men he sees only one at a time. In a car, talking on a phone, taking out a pen from their pocket to take down something. Men his mother points out saying he has to be like them. Confident and educated. All in their late twenties, maybe early thirties, young but not so young, old but not so old.

Tariq hears them say things to his mother, he sees them do things to his mother, he hears words and he sees action.

And behind all this, there must be some rhyme and there must be some reason. But forget reason for a second. Let's get the rhyme over with first. Even though it's silly, even though it's stupid. But that's the way it is. Rhyme, different schemes. This one is *abcb, defe.*

A wears glasses,
B, a striped shirt.
C ties his shoes
And D means to hurt.

A pulls her hair,
C gives a shout,
B just watches
As D lashes out.

Tariq watches her falter, stumble, he watches her hand reach out to C, more by instinct, desperate and blind, than any deliberate thought.

C takes several steps back as if Tariq's mother is the predator and he is the prey. She slips again, her ankle twists, one of her slippers comes off.

C brushes her hand away, kicks the slipper across the street.

B watches as D does the same to the other.

A laughs, the frame of his glasses glinting in the street light and he begins to unbuckle his belt.

B keeps watching.

His mother's blue-and-white rubber slipper, the Hawaii chappal, white sole, blue straps, one of them loose. (Straps you fix by greasing the hole with a lubricant and sliding the rubber in.) If the men are observant, they will see white flecks on the straps. This is because she always keeps her slippers inside the bathroom, near the bucket, near the tap, when she goes in for a bath. Tariq knows. He knows that soapsuds fall on the straps and dry. That his mother has had these slippers for more than four, five years, which works out to over eighteen hundred soapsuds. That's the number if you assume that only one, at least one sud falls from her hands or her hair, while she is bathing, to land on the strap. The result: the blue gets paler by the day.

That's why this night the blue slipper is almost white, like the sky is in the morning. In the picture.

Kicked, her first slipper comes to rest against the cement divider on the street at the foot of the lamp, below a billboard advertising cellphones. (The poster has the picture of a little boy and a dog, a pug, which follows him wherever he goes, across the park, up the hills, down the slope, up the stairs, into the house. It's an ad for a cellphone service, national roaming, Rs 99 a month, good deal.

You and I, we go wherever you do.

The boy and the dog are looking straight ahead into the hills, across the river and the meadow, the flowers and the grass; they are not looking at what's happening below them, on the street.)

The second slipper doesn't travel far although it is kicked as hard as the first. It lands right in the centre of the street, waiting for the night's traffic to run it over.

Sit Tariq, this eyewitness, this kid, down, give him time, a day, a week, a month, a year, and maybe he can describe everything but right now there are only a few things he can remember:

1 The end of his mother's sari tearing. Sound like paper being ripped, shredded, in the middle of the night.
2 Laughter and talk, talk and laughter. From all four: A, B, C and D. Mixed up, jumbled, so that he can't make out whose laugh is whose, whose voice is whose.
3 Their teeth. White. They take care of their teeth.
4 Their shoulders. Rising and falling with their laughs.
5 Mother saying something, words in a language he has never heard before. Or maybe the words are not her own, are being pushed from somewhere inside her, without her even knowing.
6 A's hand. On her head.
7 Her head snapping back, A pulling her hair so hard it leaves her forehead bare, washed by the yellow light.

8 Her eyes opening, closing, then opening again.

Two more things he needs to make it ten. Three for eleven.

(For a list of eleven appears more complete, more valuable. Can be presented as evidence, as details that add up to something bigger. Otherwise who knows, they will say he's making everything up, that nothing happened, that he wants our tears because his own don't quench his thirst for pity.)

So, here goes:

9 There's a noise his mother makes when she is dragged along the street. It's the sound of her skin scraping, being peeled off. It's the sound of her legs against the tar, of her sari against the tar, of one hand, which flops to one side, against the tar.

10 Bare legs, theirs and hers. Naked.

And, how can he forget

11 The cars.

Two cars pass by.

A 3rd, then a 4th. Then a 5th, 6th, 7th. It's the 7th car that runs over the second slipper.

Tariq watches the street light, the insects at this time of the year fluttering against the halogen to keep themselves warm, undeterred by the sight of their friends dying, falling down onto the street below. Black, like the sky, like her hair.

Tariq hears their words, their laughter, the cars.

And her crying.

Drowned out by the radio from one car, the 8th (or is it the 9th?), which slows but doesn't stop. Its windows are rolled down, both in the front and in the rear, despite the cold, so he hears the radio loud and clear. A woman's voice, singing a song.

The car's engine keeps running, fogging where the exhaust fumes meet the cold air. The driver gets out and runs into the shadows, they get in, all four of them, B and C in the rear, A and D in front.

Then they all drive away.

They don't see the boy.

Other cars come, Numbers 10, 11, 12, 13, all pass her by (one even swerves to avoid her as she lies, half across the divider, half on the street). Tariq sees her mouth open, the lips part, the flash of red on her forehead, it's blood. White, her teeth. He sees her mouth move, as if she were gulping the night down, chewing it, drinking it, as if she had been emptied and needs the darkness to fill her up once again.

She must have heard him walking, his footsteps, over the noise of distant traffic. Lying on the street, she must have seen him coming because when Tariq is near, just a few feet away, without her eyes meeting his, she stretches out an arm, her right hand, to hold his, this time not a desperate lunge but more confident and measured. And she gets up and, together, they walk to where her slippers lie. The son picks them up one, two, and then, hand in hand, they walk home. Son and mother, mother and son.

He can make out, distinctly, the tread marks of the car on one slipper, the hard black bands on the soft white platform, the tyres stamping their imprint on what is meant for her feet.

She limps. Tariq helps her cross the street, the second time in his life he has done this, the second time in his life that he has led his mother home. (The first was when his father died, two years ago, and when the neighbourhood women, after their crying, left the house, he had helped his mother get up from the floor and walk to her room.)

The blood, by now, has trickled down from her forehead. In a thin red line that jumps over her left eyebrow, skirts her eye, ends in a pale smudge on her cheek, near her lips. She wipes it with one hand and then she wipes it again with the corner of her torn sari.

'I wish I had some warm water,' she says when they enter the house. It's cold in the kitchen, the gas has almost run out. (The man from the gas company had promised to come in the morning with a refill but he couldn't. The city was already on fire, roads were blocked and all the shops had been forced to close.)

Because the cylinder is almost empty, it's easier for Tariq to move it. Otherwise, he can barely make it budge: twenty-five kilograms of the gas plus the weight of the cylinder. More than Tariq's own body weight.

Tariq clicks the automatic lighter in the burner, as he has seen his mother do. The flame flickers, more yellow than blue, a sign the gas is running out, she has taught him. It sputters for a couple of minutes, long enough to warm the water in the steel bowl, then it dies down.

And while he watches the water heat, the tiny air bubbles forming at the bottom, rising up to the surface to break into the winter air, he hears, over their gentle pop and hiss, he hears her in the bathroom, hears the water fall. He hears her remove the slippers.

Minutes later, she walks into the living room where Tariq stands with the warm bowl of water. Her hair is wet, sticking to her head, one strand across her forehead, the water dripping onto her neck, down her blue blouse and the blue sari that she has changed into. There is some cotton wool sticking to her forehead with a Band-Aid and the red line is gone. She has washed the blood away.

She sits down in a wrought-iron chair, he puts the bowl on the glass table in front (the glass table that had come with the chair had the same wrought-iron carving, its legs matching those of the chair, its frame that held the glass in place arranged in the same pattern as the chair's backrest, the iron strips hammered into leaves and flowers and petals and stems).

The son turns to leave but his mother stops him, pulls him towards her.

Then she dips both her hands in the water and keeps them there. He puts one finger in the water and runs it over her knuckles, cold in the warm.

Her eyes are closed, he can see and feel her shiver, her hands tremble, as if underneath the water, what he can see is not her hand or her fingers but only their reflections and ripples. He can smell the soap in her hair when he rests his head on her shoulder, his cheeks feel the dampness of the fabric on her arm.

Mother and son find comfort in the warm water in the night of a city on fire.

'Did you watch?' Mother asks Tariq.

He can see her words hover in the air, near her lips, slide

down her neck, curve left across her shoulder and then reach his ear, cold to the touch.

Tariq shakes his head.

'No,' he says, his voice so low even he can't hear.

'Then let's go,' she says, 'we have some work to do.'

She gets up, wipes her hands on her sari and tells him to go wait outside, at the door. Once again, Tariq can see the cement divider, the boy and the dog in the poster, the street lights and the insects, the cars passing by.

She is back with a can of kerosene in one hand and in the other, a bundle, the sari and the blouse, the clothes she wore when she was with A, B, C and D on the street.

'Be careful,' she says. 'Don't stand so close to me.'

She sits on her haunches, her knees click, she lights a match, sets the bundle of her clothes on fire.

The wind at this time is light so she bends her face forward and blows on the flames. (Like she did with the coal oven before they had a gas cylinder.) The fire begins to lick the ends of the sari. She then steps back and comes to where the boy is standing. She puts one hand on his head, wet, he can feel the water, still warm, getting warmer as the flames grow.

They stand there for over half an hour, forty minutes, no one notices the small fire outside the house. They stand there until the flames are so high they cast shadows on the wall of the house.

Funny shadows.

In which Tariq looks like a giant, she double his size, her shoulders so wide it seems she could carry the whole neighbourhood. Even the entire city, if she wished to.

And then when nothing is left, other than ash, bits and

pieces of fabric, charred, when the nylon in her sari has left a tiny oil-like slick that streaks the pavement, a tendril of smoke coiling up, she says it is over.

'That's it,' she says, 'now go to sleep.'

The son doesn't sleep that night, he can't sleep that night.

Neither does she, that he is sure of.

Because he hears her crying, he smells the smoke drifting in from outside, he hears her walk to the bathroom again, pour water over herself, twice, thrice, four times, come back to the bedroom and cry again.

IT'S a few hours later. Unable to sleep, Tariq gets up, takes out his books from the schoolbag. There's some homework to do, not due until a week's time but he wants to do it now; he switches on the ceiling fan, hopes it will blow away the smoke from the balcony, clear the air. He lies on the floor, his face resting on both his wrists as he tries to read, the pencil kept in between the pages of his book, the pages that flap in the breeze from the fan. Once he gets up to stand at the window, pulls the curtain to one side and looks into the dark. Then he comes back, falls in and out of sleep until they return.

They have come back before the city wakes up, before it washes its eyes, still crusted with broken sleep, its face, still smeared with the ash of last night.

There are A, B, C and D, the ones who were there last night. But this time they are joined by E, F, G, H, I, J, K, L, M, N, O, P, Q all the way to X, Y, Z and then again from A (keep reading out the alphabet, listing the letters one by one, five times, make it six, and you will still run out of letters, so many of them are there).

But the same four are leading the mob, A, B, C and D. They know their way around. The rest wait outside on the street. With their torches and their mops soaked in kerosene, waiting to be lit.

D is the one who gets to work this time.

He breaks down the door, it isn't difficult, the wood has already given way, the bolt that holds it is an iron chain, rusted and bent, kept in place by a wooden peg that itself is so worn down it holds on to the door by a sliver and a prayer. Both give way to D's blow. He then tears the blue curtain off.

She sees it all, the breaking, the entering, she sees it standing in the middle of the living room, without a flicker on her face; she tells Tariq to go hide in the bathroom, lock it from the inside. As if nothing has happened, as if only a strong breeze has entered the house and will soon go away, after toppling, harmlessly, a few glasses, after rattling a few windows, whipping a few curtains.

Inside the bathroom, the water from her bath last night hasn't dried yet, her slippers are still there, the soapsuds still fresh and wet.

The wood in the bathroom door, just like in the main door, is chipped where the latch is. This creates a chink small enough to go unnoticed from the outside but large enough for Tariq to bring his left eye to and see everything.

See the shapes, the arms and the legs, the faces, the lips, the eyes as the mob squeezes into this tiny aperture, its blur made sharper and more focused so that he sees everything more clearly, the edges hard and defined. He sees them first stand in a circle, he sees one of them piss in the centre of the room, he sees the others stand around and laugh, he sees them empty out cupboards and shelves, he sees them throwing down cups, plates, spoons, kick in the small television set Mother bought just last month, reach inside, through the smoking glass, and wrench the wires out, he sees them walk to his study table, turn it over, pull the drawers out, fling everything inside, one by one, into the centre of the room. His pencils, his geometry box, his eraser, his schoolbag, his tiffin-box, his exercise books (the one where his mother has written, the one where his teacher has written); he sees them tear the books, page by page, until they get tired, he sees them pull the curtains down, fling them into the centre, into the pool of piss, he sees them spit on the bed, stamp on the sheet with their shoes, like little boys playing. Like angry little boys fighting.

And then Tariq sees everything they do to his mother.

A, C and D.

B watches.

But they haven't seen him yet, they think there is no one else there, that this woman was alone last night and is alone this morning.

He hears D say: 'You live alone,' and he can't hear her reply, all he can see is a bit of her forehead, on the floor. Her bare legs, her knees, his mother's knees. This is the first time he sees his mother's knees.

He can scream:

'So what if the police didn't come and if they did, they only watched from the street outside, I don't need the police, Mother isn't alone, I am Tariq, I am her son, I will be the police, I will break open the door and I will rush out and before you can even move, before you can even understand what's happening, I will pick up my mother, I will pick up all my books, all my school things, my mother and I will then crack open the floor, together we will fall down, the earth shall part for us, before you can even say your name, we will be in the tunnel below the surface of the earth, we will travel fast, far away from any one of you, into cities and towns and villages that you can not see, that you will never see, where you will never be able to reach us, the earth shall close as soon as we have dropped inside and the ground shall move beneath your feet but you won't be able to do anything, it will be too late, if you want to get to us, you will have to crack the earth open again, maybe hope for an earthquake like the one that came to this city last year or if the earth doesn't open there is the sky, I will lift her and we will fly out of the window and above the street, over and above all of you, leaving you standing down there and turning your heads to look but all you will see is my mother and I against the sky, rising higher and higher, on TV, they will show it too, we will be so far away that all you can see is the morning sky above this city, smoke, a few crows flying, dust, the last patches of fog melting in the sunlight. And my mother and I, safe.'

But that is reason, he can hear only rhyme. He can see them pour the kerosene, light the match. He sees the curtains catch alight first.

Ma, don't you worry,
You won't feel the pain.
The fire will be gone,
Then will come the rain.

Its drops will be cold,
Its tears will be wet,
But I'm not going to cry
At least, not yet.

Rhyme's over, now can we have some reason?

No, reason can wait. Who cares for reason? Why doesn't Reason, the right, honourable Reason, come out and reveal itself to all of us? Why does it, instead, slink into the shadows behind the burnt houses, bury itself deep in the pile of ash, in the heap of embers? Why does it dive below the bed, in between sheets, into the hem of pillowcases? Why does it slither into books, like silverfish? Worm itself into the page, the paragraph, the middle of a sentence? Then into a word? And even if you trap it there, close the covers hard, press Reason flat against the page, why does it burrow into the letters, hide between their curves and their loops, inside the dots of the *i*s, below the dashes of the *t*s? Why the hell doesn't it burst forth from wherever it's concealed itself, dazzle us all in this darkness, blind us with its flash? So that we can all see what Reason has to say to Tariq.

(When that happens, let the boy know. Until then, he will live with rhyme. It's silly. But that's the way it is.

Because what do you want the kid to do?

You want him to scream, 'I am an eyewitness to the city on fire'? You want him to write it out, in letters, each as big as a building, I AM AN EYEWITNESS TO THE CITY ON FIRE, you want him to etch these in shining silk, onto a banner so huge he can drape the entire city with it? Maybe then everyone can read it, from above and below, even passengers inside aircraft on their way to Delhi or Mumbai, pedestrians on the street, walking, all forced to look up, notice this shimmering curtain, newly installed in the sky above their city. Maybe then, this curtain hovering above, every day every night, will cause someone to sit with the child, record his complaint. Maybe then some judge, who doesn't like the curtain blocking the sun, the moon or the rain, will take note. His Lordship will neither smirk nor sneer just because the eyewitness's skin is cracked and dry, just because the eyewitness breaks into verse conjured up then and there. He will listen carefully, he will ask the right questions, will push and prod, cajole and encourage, will wake up the sleeping prosecutors, frame charges, hold hearings.

Get A, B, C, D, E, all the way to Z, to come and defend themselves. And then when the judge is done with Tariq, maybe he will move on to the next one, to the second eyewitness. Who will appear a little while later.)

Meanwhile, what does Tariq do after they all have left?

He sits on the floor where what was home is now at his feet. He watches over his mother's body, he looks at what's left, at the smashed television set, the wires, the tube and the screen, the glass panes gone, the curtains ripped, his schoolbook out on the street, all burning, the flames, red, blue and yellow. He sits there as night slips into morning slips into midday into afternoon, as the police come and go, as they take her away, as photographers arrive to take pictures, as the TV woman fakes a tear while she speaks to the camera, and he hides from all of them because he knows the places in the house to hide. Then he sits, waiting for the shadows to loom again, for the street lights to be switched on, the insects to reappear, and then he will go out, stand where he stood last night and look at his life, just ten or eleven years gone, the rest stretching ahead.

Like the long, littered road in front that leads to a place he's never been to, alone, without his mother.

END OF FIRST ATTACHMENT

12. *Shabnam*

(The Second Attachment)

THIS is her father's auto-rickshaw, her father who has been killed, her mother, too. This is a city on fire. And she's running, she's running, she's running, this second eye-witness.

Name is Shabnam.

Age sixteen, plus or minus one. This daughter this girl this woman this child, in black salwar kameez, her shoes with shoelaces, melting and dropping off, their soles, their straps, their rubber, their leather, their plastic, their everything. In the heat, the black tar on the street has cracked and blistered, its surface molten extruding into countless spikes that stick to her feet, scrape her soles. As if a giant brush has suddenly emerged from the earth, with its bristles of black grass, hard and metallic, spreading itself out beneath every step she takes. And this brush is wiping, licking, stripping her feet, her heels too, both her insteps, all her ten toes, even the skin in between so that the fire can rage without any resistance, so the flames can slip underneath her salwar legs, singe whatever fuzz remains on her calves, dart to lick the inside of her knees, char her skin, push it to peeling. Make the brown pink, make her nails glisten, her eyes water.

And Shabnam isn't used to running so hard, running so long, Father would have never allowed it. Father, who ferries the city through the day and through the night in the auto-rickshaw he bought three months ago, using his life's savings as down-payment for a loan. No, Father would have never allowed it.

'My daughter should never have to run on the street,' he told her, 'when I am there.' The day he got the auto-rickshaw, it was a Friday. The bank had given him a watch as a gift with the loan. 'Cars come with clocks on the dashboard,' the loan officer had told him, 'auto-rickshaws don't, so here, take this watch, it's automatic. You only need to replace the batteries.' Her father had slipped the watch on, taken the auto-rickshaw to the mosque for his prayers and returned home. Mother and Shabnam were waiting. The vehicle came home on a Friday, he told them, it is special, it would run faster, it would weave in and out of traffic better than the others, it would not tilt if there were too many passengers. It was sturdy, even if a bus grazed it no harm would come to anybody. And now he had his watch, Shabnam would never be late.

'I will drop my Shabnam to school every day,' Father said, 'every day we shall take a different route. And if there are no passengers, I shall come to pick you up as well. In a few months, she will go to college, the first girl in my family, the first girl in this neighbourhood, to go to college.'

At night, when Father slept, and Mother cleared the kitchen, washing the dishes so she didn't have to do them first thing when she woke up in the morning, Shabnam, her schoolwork completed, would clean the auto-rickshaw. She knew its every corner, the hollow beneath the passenger seat, the ridges on the floor, in the footrest, the *No Entry* board nailed on the right side, Father's driver seat that curved just the right amount for him to rest his weak back. Taking a mop, a clean handkerchief, one of hers, Shabnam would wipe the rubber grip of the handrest in front so that Father's palms remained clean when he reached out to help her get inside. She would wipe the windscreen, sometimes even breathing into the glass (to fog it, use the moisture) to make it sparkle.

'Shabnam, you clean it so well that in the morning it seems there is no windscreen, I can see everything,' Father told her.

Now there is no windscreen; the auto-rickshaw is there, Father isn't. Mother isn't. And Shabnam is running as if her feet have wings and these wings are on fire and she's looking for a place to hide. Cold, preferably. Wet, it will help.

The heat from the fire in the house and now from below, from above, from the left and from the right has blackened her face, brought out the sweat from inside her, matting her hair that falls almost to her waist and sticks to her forehead, like bars in a cage. Just looking at Shabnam running, you can't tell, nobody can tell, whether she is child or adult. Whether her skin is wrinkled because of the fire or because of her age. Just looking at her, from head to toe, sizing up her height, you won't know a thing because she is neither short nor tall. When the smoke enters her eyes, she cries like she's eight, without making any noise, like a little girl who's fallen off a swing in the playground, into a sandpit, and is not hurt, only shocked. When she breathes the smoke in, she coughs like she's eighty, as if her insides are ancient and tired, as if they want to get out, uncoil themselves and pull the rest of her down the street. When she jumps over a brick, or a tyre burning or a manhole cover opened, it's as if she's thirteen, nimble and quick, as if she knows every step she is taking. (The men who came crashing into her house, A, B, C and D, had looked at her, screaming in one corner, and they had laughed. C had pointed to the dark fabric of her kameez, crumpled and stained, and asked her about her breasts: 'Are those full-grown, are they new, are they old, are they small or are they just crumpled balls of paper you are hiding in the pockets of your shirt? Want me to check?')

Shabnam is running. To a place she doesn't know.

Her eyes fixed in front, frozen, as if that place were only a few yards away, as if, in the middle of this city on fire, she has seen something that you haven't, as if she has seen a lake, placid, cold and blue, with patches of warmth and green because of the hyacinth, the lotuses and fallen leaves. She has seen the water, knee-deep, right in front where the street ends, and she's running into it. So that within minutes, no, make it seconds, there will be a splash. And Shabnam will enter that pool.

There will be a hiss that you can hear above the sound of her running footsteps, the gasp of her breath. The fire will fight with the water and the fire will lose, leaving behind only smoke that will rise into the night like creepers hug a black wall. Shabnam will then slow down because of the water's drag; she will rest, maybe. In this lake which is not deep, a lake that's safe, where you don't need to swim, where she doesn't have to be afraid that she will drown. Shabnam will run into this lake, she may even sit down in the water, let it flow all around, over her head, her face, enter her ears, her nose, her eyes, wash the grime and the soot and the dirt and the sweat and the bruises and the cuts and the blood, wet her shirt, cool her body. She will lower herself farther down so that even her head is under water, her hair will float, like black reeds, she will sit there and she will sit there. When she opens her eyes, she will see what lies beneath. Tiny fish, brightly coloured, swimming in shoals around her, welcoming her with little quivers of their gills and their tails, lighting the darkness with their eyes, glassy, and their scales, glinting. She will see big flowers, their petals wet and floating in between the tall, thin plants that grow only under water, only in this lake and nowhere else in the world, white in the green and blue. She will see water-fairies riding on seahorses she has seen so far only in books and pictures, she will see children who live under water in houses made of coral. She will see them play on swings that move in the water, she will see bubbles of air from their mouths, brightly coloured. And although it's night, although there is a moon above the lake, shrouded by the smoke from the fire, she will see a soft sunlight, yellow and orange and green, bathing the entire floor of the lake, making the children's houses sparkle and get reflected in the children's eyes, making their pupils gleam like points of silver.

Of course, nothing of this happens, because Shabnam is alive, because there's no pool, because this is a city on fire and she is running.

SHE runs past trees, trees that don't help, trees that cannot provide shade when the city is on fire. (For their leaves are small, razor-thin, tilted, so that during the day, their shadows are just thin black lines on the street below. And at night when you don't need the shade, it's then that these leaves open up, they block light from the streetlamps, they add to the darkness.) These trees watch her run.

She runs past a giant poster for sanitary napkins, the kind with wings on either side. She used them once, borrowed from a friend, a classmate, who, at this time, must be fast asleep in her bed, safe. (Her periods, the bleeding is about one week away, she shivers at that thought, at the napkin, a white bird in her hands, a bird that instead of flying got trapped between her legs and died, drenched with her own blood.) She runs past a billboard advertising ovens, the kind Mother wanted to buy and Father said, wait, let me start paying off the auto-rickshaw loan, four or five months at the most, and then we will get that oven for Id-ul-Fitr.

Shabnam keeps running.

She runs past auto-rickshaws that have not been burnt, parked on either side of the road, their steel rims glinting, their owners asleep, sprawled on the seats, their heads resting in the laps of Aishwarya Rai and Sushmita Sen and Preity Zinta, whose film-star lips smile over the sleeping faces. (Shabnam remembers the argument she had with Father: she had wanted him to put Tabu's picture in the auto-rickshaw. On the backrest of the seat. 'Passengers will like to look at her,' Shabnam had said, 'she is the most beautiful, the most intelligent of them all.' Father had frowned: 'No, I drive an auto-rickshaw, I don't run a cinema hall.' Shabnam had then gone to Mother who said: 'Don't be impatient. Now he is stubborn but after a few months he will agree, I am sure of that. Doesn't he always say yes to whatever you want?' Father had overheard this from the next room and he had smiled, without Shabnam's knowing.)

She runs past houses, apartment buildings named after Hindu gods and goddesses, the idols painted in cement, garlanded with marigold flowers made of plaster coloured red or orange, gods staring at her saying you are not welcome here, keep running. She runs past policemen fast asleep, policemen laughing, policemen sifting the debris with their sticks, the tips of their shoes. She runs past shops, their shutters closed, and because she's looking straight ahead, she can't read all their names although, once in a while, she can't avoid looking through the corner of an eye, right or left.

Gallery Touchwood, Imported Furniture from Italy. *Intact.*

Baby Palace, your one-stop shop for baby needs, from bottles to cots, playmats to dining chairs. *Intact.*

Ahmed Meat Shop. *Charred, black shutters, the signboard half-melted in the heat of the fire.*

Insurance House. *Intact.*

Nokia dealer, exchange offer. *Intact.*

Sweet Tooth, chocolates and cakes. *Intact.*

Designer Designs, women's Western clothes. *Display window broken, shards of glass, clothes half-burnt.*

Metropolitan Shoes. *Burnt to the ground, shoes melted, the smell of leather.*

Patel Stockists and Sellers of Books, Class X and Class XII Boards. *Intact.*

Ganesh Electronics, TV repair, rent, sale and purchase. *Intact.*

Rehman Tailoring. *Burnt to ash, a black hole where the shop would have been.*

After a while, Shabnam can't even make out the names so fast she is running, she can only see what's intact, what's burnt, what's intact, what's burnt charred, what's intact, what's black, what's intact, what's shrouded with smoke, what's intact intact intact what's shattered, broken, what's intact.

In between some of the shops, she sees houses again, all windows and doors closed. In one, she sees a curtain pulled aside, the shape of someone talking on the phone. She can stop, she can scream at him or her, 'Who are you talking to, safe inside your house, why don't you come down and look at me?'

'Look, look,' she can say, 'look here, here and here.'

And she can point to the bit of flesh, her father's flesh sticking to her shirt, just above where her heart is. She can point to the blood staining the thread in two of her buttons, no, three, even the one in her collar. Her mother's blood. (For if she doesn't point that out to you, you will think the tailor, while stitching her buttons, ran out of thread and so he used some red and he used some white.) And if he or she still doesn't listen, she should stand there, right in the middle of that street, catch her breath, wait for her heart to slow down, gather all she left unsaid the whole evening, pack it into a scream until the entire neighbourhood, the block, the city wakes up and they all come out and stand at their doors and their windows, men, women and children, shivering in the cold, their blankets trailing behind them, and they all listen to her.

And she should scream:

'I am here to tell you what A, B, C and D did to Father and Mother. I am here to tell you what they did to the auto-rickshaw, to our house, I am here to tell you not to be fooled into believing that just because I am running away I am running away from it all. That I am frightened. I am not, I am not frightened, I will use magic to take revenge.

'Black magic, white magic,
Brown magic, blue.
Whatever the colour,
I will still get you.

And in the very end
It will all be the same.
The colour you choose
Is the colour of the flame.

'Magic means I will thrust my hand into the cold winter air, through the smoke and the fog, I will pluck out a gun. An automatic, unlimited round of bullets. Not just an AK-47, but an ABCDEFGHIJKLMNOPQRSTUVWXYZ forty-seven thousand, forty-seven million, billion, trillion. And I will fire it, keep firing it, right between your eyes.

'Magic means I will breathe in, I will swell my chest, rise on my toes, and you will watch me grow until I am double my size, triple, quadruple, five times, six times, seven, eight, nine, ten. Until I, Shabnam, am so big that my eyes full of tears will become as huge as water-tanks, hot and steaming, the water mixed with the fire, the heat gurgling, the vapour fierce and hot. Ready to drench all of you.

'And then I will start walking towards you, I will be so large that your doors and windows will scrape my ankles, your terrace won't even reach my knees. I will be so tall that clouds will wet my dry hair, the wind will comb it back into its place and shape, into its flowing form, the moon will make it gleam, the stars sparkle.

'And I will walk all over you and yours, your loved ones, your next of kin, your house, your living rooms, the marble floors, the granite counters in the kitchen, your wind chimes in the window.

'I will then do what I saw A do to Father, C and D to Mother, I will prise your mouths open, pull your tongues out, slit them, one by one, drop the tongues, pink and black and brown and yellow, drop them into the sewer pipes that overflow by the side of the street.

'I will watch, like B did – he stood there and watched – I will watch your tongues slither down, with the water, through the iron grille of the drain, squeezing through the pipes until they float all the way to the river that meets the sea like they were shoals of fish with neither fins nor eyes nor scales. While, back in your homes, you will stand and sit, weep and laugh, without your tongues you won't be able to talk, you won't be able to tell your friends and your family what A, B, C and D did to Shabnam and her father and her mother.

'How they held my head straight, forced me to look at my parents, naked. They said you haven't seen them like this before, thank us for this. Then A pulled Father's watch off, saying you don't need to look at the time any more, you don't have the tongue to speak, threw it out of the window, where the rest of them stood, around the auto-rickshaw that was burning by then, the heat and the smoke streaming inside in waves. They laughed, I saw their tongues, I saw how they ran them over their lips, I saw them piss into Father's and Mother's open mouths. I heard them say their piss was yellow since they had no time to drink water that morning and look, look, they said, see what colour it becomes when it mixes with the blood. See how yellow and red turn into brown.'

But, of course, Shabnam doesn't say anything, she doesn't have the words to say all this, all she has are her feet and her arms, her knees and her elbows clawing through the fire and the fog. She's breathing short, hard, the noise echoing around the walls of the buildings on either side. Once in a while she lets out a scream (but then how can you scream when you have run so long and so hard?), more like a whimper: it only helps to clear her throat, allowing the cold air to rush in, cushioning her laboured breaths, giving her more oxygen. Letting her live.

Keep running.

She should rest, she has to rest, because she can't go on like this.

It was her father who had told her, 'Run.'

(Through gesture, not words, because they had taken his tongue out, because blood was flowing down his lips, his chin, drenching his stubble, falling on to his chest. Streaking his white shirt, his grey trousers that he had reached out to cover himself with, to cover his shame in front of his daughter. She saw his red half-sleeved sweater, frayed at the neck, a dying animal bleeding on the floor. When they had forced Father to undress, Shabnam in front, he kept shaking his head no no no no no no no, Shabnam can't see this, and they kept laughing, Shabnam has to see this, Shabnam can't ride in her father's auto-rickshaw any more, Shabnam can't go anywhere, Shabnam has to see this, Shabnam has to see her father and her mother naked, because wasn't this how she was born? Or did they do it all dressed up? Shabnam has to see this. If she closes her eyes, we will kill her too.

And Shabnam saw.

Father kept shaking his head, telling her with his eyes run away, run away, you have a life to live, don't let them take it. Telling her with his eyes, the fire is near, they have already set the curtains alight, the flames from the auto-rickshaw are now creeping up the window frame, they will soon reach the walls and the doors, the chairs and the table, they will enter the kitchen, make the gas cylinder explode, they will feed on the fuel, then spread to the bedroom where they will lick the sheets clean, take the cot as well. They will then travel to the door where you stand, they will enter your hair first, your beautiful hair. So, Shabnam, run.

They just want us, it seems, so let them take us, you run, use whatever you can of the kindness of these strangers.

And she turned to look at Father and Mother for the last time, she saw the auto-rickshaw burning, the windscreen long gone, she saw A, B, C and D turning away, their job done, she saw them locking the door from the outside so Father and Mother couldn't get out, naked and tongueless. And then Shabnam closed her eyes, climbed on a chair, out through the window, the flames singed, she felt the skin curl, and she ran.)

She had first run to the public phone booth down the street; she knew the man in charge, he would smile at her every day on her way to school. 'Go ahead and make your call,' he said. Father was right, use whatever you can of the kindness of strangers.

All lines busy, her hands trembling, she dialled and she dialled. She got through to the father of a classmate, and he said: 'I can't come, the city is on fire.'

She couldn't reply and when he heard her cry, he said, 'Shabnam, call me in half an hour, I will see what I can do.' She couldn't wait half an hour, she couldn't let them get to her, because they don't need eighteen hundred seconds.

And so Shabnam ran.

The man closed the phone booth and went home.

SHABNAM is slowing down, she has seen a sheltered patch of black on the side of the road, a lane between two houses. There doesn't seem to be any one there. She enters. Once in the lane, once she's draped in the darkness, once she is sure the light from the neons on the street won't reach her, she stops, sits down, leans her head against the wall. She can hear her heart, she has to wait for it to slow down, she is sweating in the cold, she can feel the ring of perspiration on her neck, her face. Shabnam closes her eyes, cups her palms over them to keep them closed.

And her eyes, which had been forced open, not even blinking as they had taken in the flames and the smoke and Father and Mother and A, B, C and D, and the day and the night, the street and the city, those eyes, once closed, opened up.

And Shabnam cries.

Her palms still covering her face, her eyes closed, the tears flow, she feels the water on her thumbs on either cheek. The tips of her fingers, cold, on her forehead, hot. She can hear her breath, noisy, wheezing, as it tries to get out to meet and mix with the air of the city, but trapped, for now, between her hands and her face. The tears still flowing, she opens her eyes, sees in front, just beyond the fringe where the shadows of the lane end and the lights of the street begin, a divider, a narrow strip of concrete with saplings planted in a neat row, each ringed with an iron cage. Cars drive by, she moves closer against the wall, she doesn't want to be seen.

Where will Shabnam go,
This girl in the lane,
What can you tell her
To ease her pain?

There's nothing, nothing,
Nothing you can do,
Except point to Tariq,
Say who's just like you.

SO all you can say then is Shabnam, not far from where you live – in fact just down the street – there will, at some point in the night, today or tomorrow, appear from the shadows, from across the way, a child, a boy, ten or eleven years old, in a T-shirt and shorts. He will carry his mother's slippers in his hands, it will look like he's searching for something. Don't draw yourself deeper into the shadows, Shabnam, don't be afraid since he is not enemy, he is friend. (They got his mother before they got yours.) Friendship is when both of you watch the fire burn, when both of you watch the ones you love get killed, friendship is when you are both alone and afraid in the city. So watch him as he climbs onto the divider, squeezes himself through the iron railings, and stands at the foot of the lamp post. Watch him as he looks at the cars go by, count them along with him.

And then, after this, what do you tell Shabnam? Because she will keep looking at you, she will keep listening, she has no words of her own right now, she is empty, she is like the burnt shell of her house.

What do you tell her?

Wait until the night clears, wait for the smoke to clear, you are intelligent, you are not six or seven, surely you can find your way home.

The police will be there by now because while you were running, the Prime Minister spoke in New Delhi, his eyes closed in anguish, so now there is no fear, they won't come back to kill the dead, you can't burn what has been charred.

Be careful, walk into your house, search for what's left behind. There must be something there, not everything burns.

Your neighbours will be there as well, your neighbours who closed their doors and windows and didn't hear Father and Mother scream, your neighbours who all came to look at Father's auto-rickshaw, ask him for a ride to the station, to the market, to the cinema hall.

And now they will come again, now you are alone, one of them will ask you inside his house, will warm some water for you in a bucket, ask you to take a bath, give you a brand-new cake of soap, sandalwood, your favourite, the wrapping waiting for you to remove it. To wash the sweat and the tears away, the charred scales on the soles of your feet. They will give you a blue detergent soap to wash your clothes, your father's flesh sticking to your kameez, the city's dirt on your black salwar.

They will spread out for you, on a freshly made bed, a soft quilt, a fresh set of clothes, smelling of warm water and soap. They will tell you to join them for lunch, you have nothing to worry about, we will take care of you. Here, take some more rice, don't be shy, think of this as your own home. Then they will give you dinner at night.

And then what?

What should Shabnam do then?

Get into the bed, pull the quilt over herself, close her eyes and go to sleep?

Forget Father, Mother?

Forget Mother and Father naked?

Forget the Friday Father got the auto-rickshaw?

Forget the windscreen she cleaned every evening, forget Father's watch they threw away?

Forget the fire, forget the smoke, forget the tongues being slit?

Forget all, the past has been burnt. So start remembering from today because you haven't been raped, you haven't been killed, you haven't been burnt alive?

Well, that's the only way out, but who will tell her that? As Shabnam sits in the lane, her tears flowing, cooling the memory of the fire.

Someone should tell her, sooner rather than later.

END OF SECOND ATTACHMENT

13. *Abba*

(The Third Attachment)

'YOU are like my students,' Abba says and he keeps repeating it, this man who is seventy-six years old, our third and last eyewitness, so thin that his mere standing straight seems to be a defiance of the wind and the elements. He's tall, unusually straight-backed for a man his age; his hair's white, flowing, his beard too; he repeats it like a chant, he shouts, he begs, he implores, he pleads, 'You are like my students you are like my students you are like my students you are like my students you are like my students.'

They don't listen, A, B, C and D.

A chews his lip,
B blows some air,
C looks around,
And D fixes his hair.

'You are like my students,' he says, 'you are more well off than my students, I can see that in the way you dress, in the way you talk to each other, you are educated. Your parents must be kind. You should be in college, in the university, you should be studying science, commerce, these days everyone wants an MBA, you should be studying that. There are many private management colleges now. You have a very bright future, all of you. My students aren't so lucky, it's a government school and you know what we have, what we don't have, but I keep telling my students, don't waste your future. All four of you should be working, if you need help, please come to me any time, day, night, morning evening, I am usually free, I retired long ago. Although I don't know if I can teach you, I teach boys and girls, in junior classes. I now teach only two days a week in the school, they haven't hired new teachers yet, you must have seen the school on your way here. I have difficulty sleeping, I don't have any children here, the only one lives far away, he got married last year. His wife, my daughter-in-law, is here with me now. She is about your age, she is like your sister, she is pregnant with my grandchild, four to five more months before the birth, she has come to stay with me for a few days because my son is away, he didn't want to leave her alone, he will be back tomorrow and until then she is staying with me. Her own parents are no more but I told her, don't you worry, I am here. And it doesn't matter, son or daughter, let your child be safe, healthy, let you be safe and healthy. My wife died thirteen years ago. So besides being a grandfather, telling the child stories at night, I will have to be the grandmother as well, make the child eat, take him out in the sun, play with him, oil him, his hands and his legs, so that his muscles and bones grow. How much can the mother do? She takes care of me, she is busy cooking and cleaning the whole day. As we are talking, I am talking, you people don't even say a word, she is working in the kitchen now, making dinner.'

They don't listen.

A clenches his fist,
C sizes up the man,
B just watches,
D chalks out the plan.

'You are like my students,' he says, 'take all my books, all of them, there are about a hundred, the only valuables I have. Help yourself, take whatever you want. But they are old books, I don't know if they will be of any use. Many of them are in Urdu, I can read them to you. There are some books in English as well, mathematics and history, that's what I teach, some adventures, some pocketbooks in Hindi I buy at the railway station whenever I go to pick up my son and my daughter-in-law. I always go to the station, they keep telling me, Abba, you are old, you should not be waiting there in the crowd, I told them if I can teach twice a week, I can go to the station. You can take these books with you, I will buy more. Anyways, I have to go out tomorrow,

I have to collect my pension from the school, if it's open. Tomorrow, I have to sign the life certificate, proof that I am alive so that they can release my pension. You are four young men, I will help you, give me your addresses and I will come, right on time; I won't charge anything because I like teaching. I taught for thirty years.'

They don't listen.

Maybe we need some wood,
Maybe we need some oil.
Then we could light the flame,
And watch the thing boil.

'You are like my students,' he says, 'some of them are like you, very headstrong, impatient, angry but that's because you are young and young people get angry, should get angry. Especially young people in this country. Once I wrote a letter to the editor of the paper, they published it but they cut it, only published about five or six lines when I had sent them two full pages. I told them the Prime Minister, when he refers to the common man, should talk about the common young man and common young woman like my students, they are common, everything in the country should be for them. Don't do anything special for us, the elderly, we just want to live peacefully. One day, and that day isn't far away, we will die, so please don't waste your time or money on old people like us, please take care of the young. Because the young are the future, we are old, can't do anything other than teach a few children and sit in our houses, think of what has gone by, wait for our grandchildren to grow up, maybe drop them off to school.'

They don't listen.

Do we get him first?
Or do we spare him?
Go for the woman,
And then come for him?

'You are like my students,' he says, 'they feared me, yes, but they always respected me. Everyone in this neighbourhood respects me because I am the teacher, this is why I am still here, why I didn't move out of this neighbourhood although my son kept saying, come here, you should live with us in a safer city, in a safer state. I laughed at him, I said, no one will kill me here, they all respect me, it doesn't matter which religion I am. Even now, after retirement, when I get off the bus and walk home from school, the children, boys and girls, come running to me and say, Abba Abba, let us carry your bag, your books, they are heavy. But I tell them, no, as long as I have two hands and two legs and as long as I can carry this weight, I will do it. Thank you very much. But my son says, Abba, this has nothing to do with how honest you are, that you called your students home and you taught them for free. It doesn't matter that you did not miss a single day at school, that you were the only teacher who had a hundred per cent attendance even if you had a fever. They will come for you if they wish to. But I told him, no, you are just angry. They all respect me because of the kind of teacher I was. That's why I will always be safe.'

They don't listen.

When will he stop
This silly, stupid chatter?
His son is dead right
That it doesn't matter.

'You are like my students,' he says, 'if you are hungry, tell me, I have something in the kitchen. When my wife was alive, many of my students would come for help with their homework and stay for dinner. Some of them were from poor families so I thought, why not, let them eat here, I don't have ten people to feed. Now my daughter-in-law is here, dinner will take her just about half an hour or so. She's a very good cook, makes some Chinese too, where she learned all this I don't know. If you want to eat in separate dishes, I can arrange that, too. I won't mind at all, I have paper plates and paper cups. If you can't wait, I think we have biscuits, she can make you some tea. Sit down, have some tea and biscuits, it's cold tonight. Tell me about yourself, one by one. But you know you don't have to tell me if you don't want to. In my class, I never forced my students to answer questions and that's why I think I was one of their most respected teachers. I never singled them out, I never told them to stand up and answer, I would ask a question and say, whoever among you wants to answer, please answer, and I never took it seriously because I know some of the best students are those who are shy, who don't want to get up and talk. And I was proved right, there was this one student who never got up to answer a single question but is now teaching in America. That, too, history.'

They don't listen.

Did any one see
The woman perchance?
What does she look like?
Worth a second glance?

'TAKE whatever you want,' he says, 'as I told you, the only valuables I have are my books. If you don't want to read them, you can sell them, you will get good money since many of these books are books out of print, special editions you may not find anymore. Or you can even sell them as scrap, there is a dealer, five minutes from here, where I go with my month's newspapers. If you don't want the books, take the furniture that I have. There are two chairs I bought thirty years ago when my wife first came from the village to the city, when she didn't know the language of the city and used to stay at home all twenty-four hours. The chairs are of teak or mahogany, I am not sure which, they haven't splintered once in thirty years. Solid, now they don't use wood like this, now they have things called board, plywood. But in my house you won't find even one centimetre, one inch of that.'

They don't listen.

Doesn't this man know
That it's not about wood?
It's about fixing him
And his brothers for good.

'Take whatever you want,' he said, 'there is also a TV set, about a year old, my daughter-in-law got it for me when she came the last time. She saw me sitting in my room with the radio on and I told her I don't need a TV set but she got it and went to the cable operator, paid him a year's cable charge and installed it here. Three thousand rupees for just the cable. I watch it sometimes for the news, sometimes for cricket, my daughter-in-law watches it more when she is here, she has all these shows that she likes to watch, beginning in the afternoon. I told her it's better to read books but then I know, given how hard she works the whole day and especially now that she's pregnant, this relaxes her so I let her do what she wants. But you can take the TV set. She can always go to the neighbour's. And anyways, she will go back to her own house tomorrow. They have a TV there with a bigger screen.'

They don't listen.

Let's get it over with,
Just as we did,
The auto-rickshaw man,
And the woman who hid.

'Take whatever you want,' he says, 'if you don't want the TV, there's some jewellery, which my wife left behind for my daughter-in-law. It's gold; one bracelet, four bangles, two anklets, a few necklaces and three pairs of earrings she got from me during her marriage and some she brought from her father's home. Some I was keeping for my grand-daughter or my grandson when he gets married. If I live that long. But take it, you will get a good price. I don't know how long I will live anyway, my father died when he was sixty-four so I have outlived him by twelve years. Many days, I sit and wonder what I am living for, and then the only thing that comes to mind is that my grandson, or my granddaughter, will be born in the summer, four more months, the doctor has said. I would like to see him grow, learn to walk, maybe even go to school but no, I am not that selfish. Once I see him walk and go to school for the first time, that's enough, anything over and top of it is a bonus. So that's four years at the most, I will be eighty by then, a good time to go, eighty.'

They don't listen.

A hits the man,
C kicks his shin,
B just watches,
D has gone in.

'Why do you want to kill me,' he says, 'please go and ask everyone in this neighbourhood, please go to my school and ask my students. Ask about me, ask what I have taught them. I have never taught hate; I am not lying, please look at the exercise books, please see the homework, please see my notes. Read my diaries, the essays I asked my students to write. Yesterday, when I heard about the fire in the train, ask everyone here, I said, this cannot be explained or pardoned, how can you kill passengers in a train? I said the same thing last year when that attack happened in America, I asked how could you kill men, women and children like that and not feel sad. Imagine if one of my students was there in that building, with an old father, just like me; what would happen to him? Every August 15, Independence Day, I sit with my students and tell them how proud and privileged we are to live in this country. I have the National Flag with me, it's kept very carefully, I can ask my daughter-in-law to show it to you. It's made of silk, in the cupboard, on the same shelf as my wife's jewellery. They call me for the flag-hoisting in the school because they say, Abba, you are the only one who has seen Nehru and Gandhi. If all of this means nothing, if you aren't listening, if you have to kill, just as you have the others in this neighbourhood, if you have come here with your mind made up, then please let my daughter-in-law go, please kill me instead. She is like your sister, she has a baby inside her. Kill me, I am already very old, I have finished my time in this world. Yes, I will not be able to see my grandchild but that's all right.'

They don't listen.
They brush him aside,
He falls to the floor,
They then walk inside.

And then they rape the daughter-in-law

They strangle her with a towel.

They slit her throat.

They wait for her to die.

They slit her stomach, all the way down. From her breasts to her pubic bone.

They take her baby out.

They throw up, at the sight of unborn flesh.

And, of course, the blood.

They throw up on the kitchen countertop, over the vegetables she was peeling.

Then they set the house on fire, they burn the dining table.

The gas cylinder explodes, the ceiling caves in, the pillar holding it comes crashing down, they sprinkle kerosene, they throw flaming rags.

The fire licks the floor, spares two dish racks on the wall, as if it had mercy at the end.

That's the picture of the kitchen at the top of the page.

On their way out, they wipe their hands on a small hand-towel and throw it onto the street.

They kick Abba, the talkative old schoolteacher, in his stomach, they spit on him but they leave him alive.

So he can collect his pension tomorrow, can keep talking. So that he can live the last few years of his life with a fear he has never felt before. So he can sit down when his son comes and they can both cry and he can tell the son all that happened, all that he told A, B, C and D, and his son can say, 'I told you so, Abba, I told you so. It has nothing to do with your honesty and your respect and probably nothing to do with the silk flag lying in your cupboard. Let's leave this city.'

And what will they do then?

Should Abba sit with Shabnam and Tariq and teach them history? Or should he tell his son to go and remarry, to forget his wife, forget the kitchen, to father another child so that the child can play with Abba, Abba can take him to the market, to school, and maybe one day tell him what happened?

Look at Abba, he is hurt, he is bleeding, he is alive. He who told them that he had finished his life in the world, he will get up later in the morning and wait for his son. Because

Abba has to carry on. He can't kill himself, can he? Imagine what people would say: this man committed suicide when the city was on fire, when there were already enough people on the streets being killed, when there were already enough people who wanted to kill.

END OF THIRD ATTACHMENT AND END OF THE MESSAGE

14. *A Dot and a Streak*

MISS Glass had said, please read them carefully, please give them time and concentration. Well, I did give them time, I did give them concentration. Forty-five minutes, a full forty-five minutes minimum – it might have been more, up to an hour, I wasn't checking my watch – that's how long it took me to read all three attachments, Tariq, Shabnam and Abba, the ten thousand words or thereabouts, the thirty-five or so pages. And to look at the three pictures, not very sharp but, yes, I did concentrate on the details. Like the fire's scorch marks on the wall of Tariq's house, below the windows, beside the doors. I saw the ridges in the floor of the burnt auto-rickshaw, the *No Entry* sign, the ripped-out roof, the shreds of canvas, the iron frame that had withstood the blaze. And in Abba's kitchen, the steel kettle was safe, the teacups behind it (three I counted, there could be more), the plates, dishes. All left untouched. And, of course, I read about the four killings. A mother, two parents, a daughter-in-law.

Five, if you add her unborn child.

And didn't Miss Glass say, in her message, they had already killed hundreds, perhaps even a thousand.

So shall we, for a moment, ignore those thousand, look at only these five?

5 out of 1000, that's 0.5 per cent. I am good with numbers.

If you prefer metaphor instead of mathematics, words and full stops instead of digits and decimal points, consider this: point five per cent means that if all the murdered, the men and the women, the boys and the girls, the children and the foetuses – not one bird or beast was killed – were crushed to fit into the palm of your hand, a mother, two parents, a daughter-in-law and an unborn child, all of them taken together, would be little more than a speck on one fingernail.

A dot.

Easy to see, easy to erase.

That's why, sitting in the cybercafe, I didn't dwell on them for long. Having read the attachments, after giving them my time and concentration, I folded the pages carefully – sure, I would read them again, look at the pictures again – and put them in Ithim's bag, behind his back, as a support, as a cushion.

'THAT'S one big message.' Mr Meeko was standing behind me, looking over my shoulder just as I had finished adjusting the straps of the bag.

'From a friend,' I said, 'he has a lot of things to say.'

'I am sure,' Mr Meeko smiled.

Had he seen Ithim? It seemed unlikely because the bag was in front of me and I was clearly obstructing Mr Meeko's line of vision.

'You don't have to pay for the printouts, you know, Mr Jay,' he said, 'you are the first customer of the day, very auspicious, I charge only for the time.'

'Thanks.'

'How's the Mrs? When is the big day?'

'She is in the hospital, any day now.'

It was the first time I had lied to Mr Meeko, who I had always thought of as a friend, but at that moment it seemed to be the most natural thing to do. It didn't require any effort, it seemed harmless and it seemed practical: my wife hadn't seen her child, so why should I show Ithim to anyone else? Also (and perhaps this was the real reason), I was on my way to set Ithim right, which meant that Ithim wasn't ready yet.

So did I feel embarrassed showing him to people? Did I see his physical form as some sort of a personal slur? I would be lying if I said no but then again, that wasn't the issue. Ithim was my child and it would be unfair, I thought, to let people see him like this, to make a first impression when I had been assured of a second, improved version.

I had already spent far too long a time at the cybercafe but I wasn't too concerned. I needed to be at the railway station by five and it was still early morning, not even seven, seven-thirty, at least eight or nine hours still to go for the train.

I followed Mr Meeko to his terminal as he began writing out the receipt, I could feel Ithim pressed to my chest, the bag now heavier, weighed down by Miss Glass's pages. Mr Meeko wrote slowly, stretching each letter out, the curl of the J, the angle of the A, the downward stroke of the Y, as if he wanted to keep me there for a little while, opening a gap for maybe a conversation.

And as if compensating for the lie I had just told him, I rushed to fill in the gap: 'Mr Meeko, you heard about the fires in the city, the killings?'

Without looking up from the receipt book, he said: 'Yes, very strange, I saw something on my webcam, on this terminal.' And he glanced up at me once, then reached out, the pen still in his hand, and patted his terminal. The screen on his computer was blank. 'I saw it here on my desktop.'

'What did you see?' I asked.

'Why don't you sit down for a while?' Mr Meeko said. 'Are you in a hurry?'

'No, I was just going to the hospital,' I said.

'Well, then I wouldn't like to delay you. Hospital hours are very strict but if you have some time, join me for a cup of tea.' He pointed to a chair next to him, behind the counter, on which sat a kettle and two cups. Not very different from what I saw in the Abba attachment.

My silence had perhaps given him the answer. The receipt ready, he gently tore it off and after he had handed it to me, taken my money, counted out my change, he got off his chair, pushed it aside and then began pouring out the tea.

A cup of tea, why not? I needed it.

'I didn't have my morning tea today,' Mr Meeko said, 'the webcam kept me very busy, very disturbed.'

'THE sun wasn't up, Mr Jay,' Mr Meeko said, 'when I came in this morning and the image on my desktop was exactly as I have shown you so many times. The same pavement, that same tiny strip, but then this morning there was a streak, almost a diagonal, white in some places, black in others, grey in between. As if someone had taken a chalk and drawn a line over the lens of the webcam outside. Or on the screen itself. A fingerprint, perhaps, maybe mine.

'But then I looked hard.' Here Mr Meeko began to act it out, turning in his chair, bringing his face close to the terminal, the teacup in one hand, the pen in the other. 'I tore off some tissue paper, moistened it with warm water and rubbed the screen, wiped it with the sleeve of my shirt. But the smudge was still there.

'And then, Mr Jay, suddenly it hit me, it couldn't be removed because the streak wasn't on the screen, it was in the picture. And it was smoke. Smoke carried up by the warm air in the cold of the night, smoke outside. And just now I saw on the Net that the city is on fire, that hundreds have been killed.'

He moved to the door. 'I have kept you long, Mr Jay, I am sorry.'

I had listened to Mr Meeko without saying a word. I was tempted, very strongly, to show him my message from Miss Glass, the three pictures, maybe even ask him to read the attachments. (For, so far, in all our conversations, it had always been Mr Meeko who had the interesting tales, and I was the one adding my bit to each but now, it seemed, I had a better story in my bag than Mr Meeko could ever have imagined.)

But no, I decided against it. Because that would have surely opened the floodgates: if I were to show him the message, I would then have to tell him about Miss Glass, about her phone call, the hospital, about Ithim, about this journey; I would have to admit that I had lied to him. I couldn't resist one question, however.

'You saw the bodies? Where have they come from?'

'What bodies?' Mr Meeko asked, looking bewildered. 'I haven't seen any bodies.'

'You can see them now,' I said, pointing to the one nearest to him, on the street near Fruitseller, the small one, blackened and charred.

Mr Meeko's gaze followed my arm and he shook his head. 'No, Mr Jay, there is nothing there,' he said, 'and don't joke with me about serious matters like these.'

I could have dragged him there by the arm; we could have gone down on our knees and stared at the body, up close. But, no, I could see the bus across the street and if Mr Meeko, my friend, couldn't see the bodies, well, then there was little I could do.

Must have been the sun that got into his eyes.

◆◆◆

FIREPROOF

I am Floor Body they showed on the news on TV, I was twenty-six years old, I don't have much to say, my friend just had her birthday, I am alive, she said, you are dead, so I should send you a gift on my birthday, it will make you feel better, she said, and she sent me a poem she wrote:

'I have no right to fear and tears now.
I have to laugh and smile.
Eat to my stomach's content.
And have a nightful sleep.

I am still alive and unharmed.
My home, not yet looted or burnt.
Nor am I raped or roasted alive.
My family is still around.
My friends haven't written the obituary yet.

I have no right to fear and tears now.
I have to laugh and smile.

Birthday celebrations, cake and cream.
Anonymous survival, the hidden head held high,
Some more photographs for the album,
Are the only acts of Defiance.
One more day adds to Life.

I have to laugh and smile.
I have no right to fear and tears now.
I have to eat to my stomach's content.
And have a nightful sleep.'

My parents, my sister, my uncles, my nephews, my aunts, my nieces, my friends, my old schoolmates, my teachers, my neighbours, all are alive, my friend is right, they now have no right to fear and tears, that's only for people like me.

15. *On The Road, In The Mall*

CALL it coincidence: within an hour of seeing the bodies rain down on the street at the bus stop, within minutes of reading Miss Glass's message, I saw a mob, I saw some of those behind this city on fire. And I saw them, not through written words or printed pictures, not between the lines of singsong verse – with their a-rhyme-any-time kind of rhymes – but in the flesh, through the windscreen of the bus I boarded after I left the cybercafe. (No. 46 Circular, the one that goes to the hospital, then to the railway station, I would have missed it had the driver not stopped when he saw me running across the divider, holding what must have looked to anybody else like a rather bulky bundle.)

There was no one inside the bus except the driver and me (and Ithim, of course), so when it started moving, the clatter was louder than usual, the noise of its engine resonating in the emptiness inside, amplified by the trembling of the bus's decrepit, wooden frame and the jangling of its worn-out wood against tin, warped and dented in several places. I took the seat right behind Busdriver, behind the aluminium partition that set him apart from the passenger section. That the bus was empty at this time of the day and that there was no conductor – who would I pay for the ticket? – struck me as odd and unusual but once I was seated and the bus was moving I felt safe and reassured, aware that Busdriver was only a couple of feet away and, because he had stopped for me to board, had become an unsuspecting ally in my journey.

I had taken the window seat, placed the bag in my lap, and was looking out as we passed the cybercafe and the burnt shops, my chin resting on the window's wooden bars. Ever since I was a child, I have liked doing this in a bus, resting my chin in such a way that my teeth chatter, feeling the shudder of the vehicle transmitted across my entire body and thus connect my insides, my face, my lips and my teeth, through the axle and the wheels to the road below and, from there, to the entire city. And while I sat there, almost frozen in that position, and because I was there all alone, with no other passengers to look at or be looked at by, not one face in front (except the driver), or to the left or the right, I thought: Why not let Ithim feel this, too? Why not like father like son?

I brought the bag close to the edge of the seat, raised it to the window and then uncovered Ithim's face. He was asleep, the charred strip of flesh on his forehead looking softer in the morning light. Careful that the towel wrapping him didn't slip off, I lifted Ithim to the window and then, for just a moment, let his cheek touch one wooden bar. He kept sleeping, connected to the city. I tried to imagine what he would have felt, the trembling of the bus against his new skin, the wind across his face, the sunlight that he must have seen through his closed eyelids, yellow half-light in the dark.

'Where are you going?' Busdriver's voice was loud, almost

made me jump in my seat. I saw that he had slowed down the bus so I could hear him above the noise.

Hurriedly, I slid Ithim back into the bag although there was no way Busdriver could have seen him. 'Holy Angel Hospital,' I said, to which he nodded his head, noisily stepped on the gas again.

'Why is the bus so empty?' I asked.

He didn't hear me, kept driving.

'Why is there no one in the bus?' I stretched the question out, awkwardly, word by word, a pause in between:

'Why, is, there, no, one, in, the, bus?'

This time he heard. And replied without turning to glance in my direction. 'There's a curfew where we are going,' he said. 'No one is allowed on the streets.'

'Near the hospital?'

'No, on the way to the hospital.'

'So how come you are on the street?'

'I know I shouldn't have taken the bus out but I need to deposit it at the terminal where my owner's other vehicles are. If I don't, I lose one day's salary. But you don't worry, I'll drop you off right in front of the hospital.'

Busdriver's back was straight, his arms too, his hands held the steering wheel, almost too big for a man his size.

'Are the fires still burning?' I asked.

'Yes, the whole of yesterday, then last night and even now, they continue across the city. You must have seen them last night.'

'No, I was at the hospital,' I said, realizing after I had said it that I hadn't needed to tell him that. Surely, he would now ask me why I was at the hospital. But it was as if he hadn't heard.

'Many were killed last night,' he said. 'Hope your child is all right, good that you have covered him with a bag, you can never be sure.'

So then Busdriver had seen Ithim, possibly in his rear-view mirror.

'Yes, he's all right, I'm taking him to the hospital,' I said. 'He was born—'

'Get down,' Busdriver screamed, as if in reply.

'GET down,' he said, 'get down and lie there. And stay there until I tell you; don't move.' I got down, scrambling to the floor, Ithim in his bag still on the seat, the bag now slumped to one side under its weight. I was on all fours, crouching on my hands and knees; I could feel the movement of the bus course through my body and I tried to balance myself as we swayed and swerved but soon I gave up and I let myself fall, face down.

'Stay there,' came Busdriver's voice again, 'do as I tell you.'

Still lying down, I looked up to check on Ithim. Propped on the seat, he seemed safe. I reached out with one hand, crawled forward and touched the bag; I could feel him through the fabric and kept my hand there, holding him in place, afraid a sudden jerk could topple the bag down to the floor.

'OK, now get up slowly but stay low, stay crouched,' Busdriver said, 'come towards me, raise your head and look.' The bus had now slowed to a crawl; Busdriver had pulled over and was merely inching forward, the noise of the engine now a soft purring. 'Don't let them see you.'

I did exactly as told.

And I saw the mob.

Over Busdriver's head, over his oiled hair brushed back, over his white shirt collar streaked with grey, the mob appeared like a thick black line etched where the sky meets the city, stretching from one end of the street to the other, thicker than a mere line, more like a band of several lines, about ten or so, like bar codes you see on products in markets these days, each drawn behind the other, close, hardly any space in between. Each moving, all moving. Each advancing, all advancing.

Towards, so it seemed, me.

Towards the bus. And towards Ithim.

As for the noise? No words, no sentences, no paragraphs, no punctuation, the mob spoke in a language I had never heard, unintelligible, a hum, like static in a radio the size of the street, like snow flickering on a television set, the screen as wide as the sky. Rising and falling, like a wave, advancing towards us, carrying along with it scraps of voices, shouts and screams and the shuffle of feet after countless feet. The only thing I could make out clearly was that they were all men, most of them in shirts and trousers, some with handkerchiefs wrapped around their heads like scarves, the first few rows of the advancing column armed, some with steel poles, others with wooden sticks and still others with torches in their hands, flames, yellow and blue, set against the sky. And because the morning had begun to give way to the day, the flames looked weak when the torches were held high but fierce when they were lowered flickering against the faces of the mob, the yellow and the blue against skin, dark brown. Yes, I felt fear but under that fear, like water below ice, I also felt a sense of awe. There were hundreds of men and the fact that each one had temporarily switched off his mind to plug himself to something larger – this was the power of the mob, its menacing sense of order coexisting with the chaos that gave it its energy. If Ithim hadn't been there, perhaps I would have watched, standing by the side of the road, maybe even joined.

'You have to get off,' Busdriver said. 'This could get dangerous. I'll drop you off near the mall,' he said, 'Plaza, it should have just opened so you go inside, it's very safe. There are extra forces deployed there, many policemen. Stay there for a while, look around, wait for the mob to pass, then you can come out, take either the 46 or the 56 to the hospital. Or take a taxi, I would suggest.'

He was reversing, turning into a side street. The mob didn't seem to notice, or even if it had, didn't seem to care. Perhaps an empty bus with a lone driver wasn't worth the effort. (And a man with a deformed child wasn't what they were after either.) I picked up Ithim from the seat and pressed him close to me again. When I checked in the bag, I saw Ithim's eyes were open; he was blinking. His eyelashes and cheeks were dry so he hadn't cried. But what had he seen through the bag?

'Get down here, go, go,' said Busdriver, the bus having stopped in the middle of the street at the entrance to the mall. A man in blue overalls and yellow plastic boots was scrubbing the huge glass doors, his bucket of dirty water by his side. Three policemen sat on a bench, two of them fast asleep.

'Go,' Busdriver said, 'don't worry about the ticket, just go. And take care of the child.'

Before I could turn to take one last look at him, he was gone.

And I was on the street, right in front of Plaza Mall, the city's latest showpiece, safe and intact in the fire.

AND he was right. Busdriver was right. For the moment Ithim and I stepped inside, through the glass door that the man in overalls opened for us, I realized what he meant when he said you will be safe: the sheer number of doors I was facing now, all inviting me to enter, offering me places to hide, places to seek.

Doors, lined up, one next to the other, brightly lit interiors behind each as if it was morning outside but evening inside as if the mall existed in a different time zone within the city. This was certainly disorienting at first – this was my first visit to Plaza, although my wife and I had made several plans to come here, all derailed by her pregnancy – but soon it became clear it would be difficult, if not impossible, for any one to track down either Ithim or me here.

We were safe. For, look what we had, prostrate at our feet, at our beck and at our call:

> *Nirvana Fitness Studio*, lose weight the safe and healthy way, fitness solutions for the entire family under one roof, for men and women, unisex also, special yoga classes by prior appointment
>
> *Viewfinder Optique (Eye and Ear)*, reasonable,

satisfactory, well-equipped, designer frames, state of the art equipment, laser

Elegant Furnishers, specialists in sofas and curtains, Roman blinds, drapery rods, awnings, beanbags, wicker-cane baskets, seat

Smokin' Joe's, fresh pizzas with three toppings free, yummy, yum, yum

Blooms 'n' Petals, flower delivery anywhere in the city

Travelbug World Tours, special packages for couples and families, Europe, USA, Australia, New Zealand, Mauritius, Singapore, Kuala Lumpur, Dubai, complete with veg, non-veg food, special arrangements for Jain veg food without onion and garlic

The Nike Store

Tia's Treasure House for traditional wears, saris, kurtas and kurtis, for parties and marriages, engagement ceremonies

Tommy Hilfiger, pre-spring sale . . .

And these, just in one half of the ground floor, just within the first few minutes of our stepping inside. There were three other floors, all linked by escalators. So all I had to do now was to walk in and out of these stores, browse, window-shop, Ithim in my bag – there were even benches if I wanted to sit, rest my feet, take the bag off my shoulders – and the hours would go by, the mob would pass, the fires would die down, the sun would climb higher in the sky, the bodies that had fallen would be picked up in trolleys or ambulances, taken to be buried or burnt again. And then I would head for the hospital.

I doubted there would have been any change in my wife's condition – it had not even been twelve hours since I had seen her last – but if, by some miracle or accident, she had improved, I didn't want her to wake up, to ask for the child, for me and be told that neither of us was available. (Or worse, I didn't want Head Nurse, even Doctor 1 or Doctor 2 telling her what had happened, who Ithim was, what kind of a baby she had given birth to.) I wanted to be the first one she saw at her bedside when she woke up. I wanted to *prepare* her, to give her the news myself and although I had hardly given it any thought – I had no idea what I would tell her, how I would introduce her to Ithim (whether I should perhaps wait for her to get well and come home?) – I was sure of one thing: that with me by her side when she opened her eyes, everything would be easier.

('Stay by my side,' that's what she'd said to me before we rushed to Holy Angel that night when she woke up and said she'd felt her waters break.

On our way, in the taxi, her face ashen, her body cold, she kept saying she didn't feel a thing inside, that maybe the baby had died. And between telling the taxidriver to speed up and be careful I kept squeezing her hands, telling her, in the same breath, no, this was normal, that I had read somewhere – and this was a lie because I hadn't – that in the last hour before delivery, just when the waters break, the foetus is under severe trauma and shock knowing its time has come and it's this trauma that silences it, freezes it in what is, in essence, an act of survival. In short, what she felt in her womb was an expected calm, a sign of the baby's survival rather than the opposite, as she feared, its death.

Of course, in the daze of that night, with the city rushing by as the taxi darted in and out between buses and trucks, the driver blowing the horn in one continuous whine, his assistant sitting next to him, a boy hardly fifteen or sixteen years old, thrusting his left hand out and waving a red towel to warn passing vehicles that the taxi was on an emergency, I doubt if my wife heard one word of what I was saying. Her eyes were closed, she was in pain and, her hands in mine, her nails were digging into my palm; in her painfully thin arms, I could see the veins even in the dim light that entered the taxi from outside. Her veins that had first caught my eye.

By the time we had reached Holy Angel, by the time the taxi had left us in the front porch, by the time I had carried her inside, helped by the driver's assistant, his red towel-flag now a scarf he tied around his head to cover his ears against the cold, my wife was unconscious. And she had not woken up since.)

And even if – as was likely – there was no change in her condition (after all, Doctor 1 had said it would be several days), I wanted to see her before I set out with Ithim on our journey, wanted to assure myself that although I was taking him – her baby, our baby – away without her knowledge or consent, the fact that I would walk into her room, see her, maybe hold her hands, touch her forehead, watch her chest rise and fall, maybe even rest Ithim against her for a while, have his skin touch hers, would make me stronger and more confident about whatever lay ahead.

Yes, I would do that.

Definitely.

Certainly.

'Come in, sir, this side, sale, there is a sale on, trousers and shirts, just your size.' The voice behind me was insistent.

It was a security guard, dressed in uniform, a blue shirt and blue trousers, a badge stitched onto his pocket, a white badge with four letters threaded, h a n g – the same as the hospital, Holy Angel and Nursing Graduate – but spelled out on the brim of his hat: *Housekeeping and Guarding*.

He was guarding the store. And, evidently, playing salesman, too.

I walked in.

'You have to leave the bag at the counter,' Plaza Guard said, 'I will give you a token.'

'I can't leave the bag,' I said.

'Don't worry, I am here, nothing will happen.'

'No, I can't leave the bag.' There was no way I was going to be separated from Ithim, even if for a few minutes.

I looked around, there was no one in the shop except a young woman in a red jacket, sitting behind the cash counter to my left, who hadn't noticed this exchange between me and the guard. She was reading something. Shirts and trousers hung from steel rods arranged in rows in the centre; women's clothes were to the side against the wall. There was a wooden case near the entrance, built like a bookshelf except that the shelves were taller, deeper; this was where Plaza Guard stood and where customers had to deposit their bags.

But, no, I wasn't doing anything like that.

'You want me to enter your shop?' I told Plaza Guard, more as a statement than a question. 'You let me get in with the bag.'

'Sir, I have to check with Madam,' he said. Madam was evidently the woman in the red jacket, maybe the manager or the owner or the owner's daughter.

'Please wait here for a second,' said the guard.

I knew that Madam would look at me so I brought out one of the sheets of paper from the bag and began to read it, I had to appear calm, I had to make it look that this was just another bag that I was carrying, with some important papers inside, papers I couldn't afford to leave.

I could have turned and walked out of the shop but at that moment, it didn't seem to be the practical option. I had already walked several steps into the store and I needed to put on this act because I didn't want to create a scene, make a fuss about the bag I was carrying. What if that aroused suspicion?

What if Plaza Guard said, *There is a man who's entered the store and he won't let go of his bag, Madam, we have told him he has to keep it outside for security reasons but he says, no, he won't, he even walked out of the shop over this, will you please tell the police, the city is on fire and there is a suspicious man here with a suspicious bag*? I had seen the policemen at the entrance and the last thing I needed was for them to start asking questions. What would I have said if Ithim had been discovered? If they had asked, why have you stuffed this newborn in a bag? They would have accused me of stealing him. Or even worse, they would have said look at this heartless father who plans to dump this baby somewhere, maybe in the huge garbage dump behind the mall, just because it is deformed. On a day like this, when the city is on fire.

So I stood there, staring intently at a page of Miss Glass's message. Trying to look as if the bag was least of my concerns.

The act worked.

'Please go in,' Plaza Guard said, 'the Trial Room is in the corner.'

I picked up two pairs of trousers, draped them over my bag to cover it and headed for the Trial Room. Madam was still reading, not once had she raised her head, even when talking to the guard.

As if she were a mannequin.

◆◆◆

I am Head Nurse, sorry for coming in so late, I was forty-three years old, I had worked in Holy Angel for almost fifteen years attached to the Maternity Ward, I have two daughters, sixteen and thirteen years old, the elder one has her Board exams next month and she wants to be a doctor so to help her prepare for the entrance exam I got her enrolled in a special correspondence course, I told her she should not be a nurse if she can be a doctor and I was lucky since both Doctor 1 and Doctor 2, the two doctors I work for, told me I could bring her to the hospital on some days if she needed help with her studies, both the doctors are kind and we have got to know each other over the years, who knew that all three of us would die together, that afternoon, I got to know of the mob pretty early, around the time my children come home from school, someone who lives near our neighbourhood had brought a patient to the hospital and he talked about a crowd that had blocked the road, was setting shops and homes on fire so immediately, I got Doctor 1's permission, took a taxi from near the hospital gate, I know Taxidriver, he's been a regular at the hospital for a while now, no one wanted to drive me there but because I know this driver – in fact, I refer many patients to him, it helps his business – he said, no problem, I will take you home but I will not wait, so please don't take much time, which was fine by me and when I reached home, I found my children were already back from school, the mob had been dispersed, the police had come so I told them to stay inside, their father, my husband, was not in town, he was supposed to return next week, I returned to the hospital since it was a busy day, many of the injured and the dead were being brought in and in the evening, the hospital gave us a van to go home, that's when it happened, the van was stopped and although Doctor 1 and Doctor 2 both tried to reason with the mob, no one heard in all that noise, the fire spread too swiftly, I couldn't even tell them that I am a Christian, I am from Kerala, my identity card was in my purse with my name but I doubt it would have helped because two years ago they were after Christians, too, I am happy that both my daughters are safe and if they don't have their mother, they at least have their father and in a way it was good that I didn't tell the mob about my religion, it would have been very selfish of me given that Doctor 1 and Doctor 2 were also in the van because if they had let me go, I would have died every day with guilt.

16. *Father and son, 5 minutes in the Trial Room*

FIVE minutes in the Trial Room, at the most, six, that's all I had, that's all most of us have, anything over and above that would have surely raised suspicions. Just one thing, please indulge me, if you will, I have a little request: let me slip into the third person as I tell you what happened in the Trial Room. For a while, just a while, let me banish the *I*, bring on the *He*.

Yes, I know it's somewhat odd, coming as it does at this time, and it may strike you as unusual but, as you shall see, it's wholly appropriate.

This man likes Trial Rooms in garment stores, especially in this city, right in the middle of the crowd: it's the Private in the glare of the Public. He likes this tiny space cordoned off, a space he can enter and where, without one second thought, he can begin to undress. He can shed the old, the present, hang it on the wall, let it fall to the floor and see how he will look in the new, in the future. For example, when he is inside, not once does he pause to consider who before him has tried this particular piece of clothing, a shirt or a pair of trousers, that he has just slipped into. Whose skin has it touched? Which part of the body, bare, has it rustled against? Whose sweat has it soaked up, whose smell has it absorbed? Questions that would usually make his skin crawl but here in the Trial Room it doesn't matter. How he wishes he had a Trial Room for everything, for every thought, every feeling, so he could shed the old, slip into the new, if only for a moment, look into the mirror, see how it fits, before deciding. But this morning, he's not entering the Trial Room for any of this, he's walking in for only that space, that gift of solitude in the middle of this city. Away from the mob that walks the street outside. The father needs to spend time with his son. So let the countdown begin. In minutes and in seconds.

00.00: He walks in, he looks around, he sizes up the Trial Room. It's barely five feet by five feet, seven feet high, there are mirrors on all its four walls and there is a small leather sofa in one corner. The ceiling has two sunken lights, one yellow, the other white, both dim, forming a curious cone of light over his head but leaving much of the room in shadow. There are four pegs in a line on one wall by the door. The door itself is flush with the floor so no one outside can look in once it's locked, even if they were to lie down on the floor, press their cheeks against the floor and try to peer in. (This makes him comfortable.) There's a small poster stuck onto one mirror, with tape; it shows a woman, a blonde in a black turtleneck, her breasts visible through the sheer fabric. Poster Woman wears a skirt slit near the knee, a wrap-around skirt that softly clings to her legs. She is sitting on what looks like a park bench, there are trees in the back-ground, blurred, and a cobbled pathway that leads from the bench into the blur of the trees. The man closes the door behind him, slides its bolt into place, looks into the mirror, brings his face closer for a better look. He has stubble, is dishevelled as if he had been running against some wind. He wears a striped shirt, a blue blazer and dark trousers. Below the pegs on the wall, there is a switch for a tiny fan perched in one corner of the ceiling. It's cool inside, the man doesn't need the fan, so he looks at it once, looks away. Then he changes his mind, switches the fan on. Perhaps he needs the noise, needs the whirring to fill the room. The man removes a bulky bag from his shoulder and places it on the leather sofa. There are two new trousers that he walked in with, both draped over the bag. He picks them up, lets them drop to the floor, at his feet. He isn't interested in new clothes. He presses his ear to the door to check if anyone is on the other side, if there's anyone listening. The fan, the sound of the trousers falling to the floor. He can hear no one.

00.48: The man sits on the sofa, near its edge, away from the bag as if he's careful about not touching it, not causing the slightest disturbance. One leg propped on the other knee, he begins to take off his shoes. These are layered with dust and ash. Black. He runs a finger over it, wipes it on his trousers. The shoes fall from his feet, their thud muffled by the noise from the electric fan. He is now in his socks. He wiggles his toes, stands up, leans against one mirror-wall as he removes his trousers, hangs them on the first peg, looks at himself in the mirror again. He can see the pale white marks of his dry skin, the hair on his calves, his knees. He cuts an ordinary figure. Then, instead of bending down, picking up a new pair of trousers (as we would expect), he takes off his blazer, hangs that up as well. Now he's standing, in his striped shirt, his underwear and his socks. The shirt was tucked in because we can now see the creases at the bottom, where it covers his thighs. Now he removes his shirt, lets it fall to the floor. He has a vest on, a cotton vest, close-fitting, there are ridges on the fabric. He's thin, it looks like the vest has been draped over his collarbones. He takes that off, too, he slips off the socks, smells each one of them before he lets them drop.

Now he's naked. The man, the father.

01.51: Naked, he sits on the sofa, reaches into the bag and, very carefully, as if he is reaching in for the most precious, the most fragile object in the world, he takes out a bundle. Emptied of Bundle, the bag folds over itself, slides to one side, its mouth open. (There is a sheaf of papers still in the bag. Neat, white.) Bundle in his hands, the man stands and looks into the mirror, looks at his infinite reflections in the four walls. Tries to count how many he can see but soon gives up. He presses Bundle against his chest, raises it to his left shoulder, holds it, both arms around it. A man holding a child. Standing straight, he looks at himself and Bundle in the mirror again. He transfers Bundle to the right shoulder and as he is doing this, he also turns to the right so he faces the second mirror. Then transfers Bundle to the left shoulder and turns again. And a fourth time so that he's back to where he started, has completed a full circle, a 360-degree turn.

02.46: The man places Bundle on the sofa, then switches the fan off. In the silence that fills the tiny room, he can hear himself move. He checks the bolt on the door, it's still securely in place, the door is locked. There's nothing to worry about. He presses his ears to the door again to check if there's anyone there: nothing. He returns to the sofa and once seated, begins to unwrap Bundle, layer by layer. Towels, small and big, tissue paper, a tiny white shirt. All removed, Bundle is now his son, naked. The man takes one end of a towel and begins cleaning him, wiping his son, near his penis and his anus, then he crumples the towel and puts it into the bag, next to the paper. He gets up, unhooks his trousers from the peg, takes out a handkerchief from the pocket. There is a small heap of talcum powder within the folds; he daubs his fingers with it, applies it to the son's face, chest, waist. He feeds the son out of a bottle, with a dropper, wipes his son's mouth and his face, then cradles him in both arms all the time looking into the mirror.

03.50: Still holding his son, the man pushes the bag to the floor, lies down on the sofa. The sofa is much smaller than him so the man has to keep his knees bent; he presses himself hard against the back of the sofa so he doesn't fall. Lying there, away from the cone of light, in the shadows, the man holds his son high, his palms around the baby's chest. Then he brings the baby to his face, kisses him on the black strip of charred skin that is the baby's forehead, kisses him on the eyes, on the mound of his nose, the knife-cut of his lips, kisses him on the funnel-flap of his left ear, on the right where there is none, just skin stretched taut. He lifts him up, lowers him again, lifts him up, lowers him, looking at him, at his son, and then into the mirrors as well. To see how they reflect, father playing with son. His hands hurt, he lets his son rest on his chest. He closes his eyes; the room floods with a dazzling white light that hangs over him and his son for one moment and then fades into black; he opens his eyes. Both father and son are naked, skin against skin, newborn against old and tired. And he stays still, waiting to hear the beat of the heart inside his son against his own.

Father and son, son and father.

04.50: Still holding his son, he bends down. Suddenly, there, in the mirror, he can see it. His son is looking. At himself, at Father. His perfect eyes have opened, they are blinking. Father brings him closer to the mirror, he can see his perfect eyelashes, the perfect eyebrows. Son won't sleep now, he's just woken up, thinks Father, so let me take him to the park for a walk, the park in the poster on the mirror, behind Poster Woman, where the trees have begun to grow fresh leaves. It's the first day of March, it's spring in the park. The poster peels off under the weight of the new leaves and the sway of the branches. Without making any noise, the mirror cracks, its shards of glass falling to the floor. Poster almost gone, Poster Woman has a puzzled look on her face. She gets up and walks away, along a narrow path between the trees, the new leaves brushing her shoulders, the grass green against the black of her skirt that clings closer than ever. Poster Woman gone, the cobbled path clear, the park now in full bloom, Father is walking, watching his son, teaching his son to ride a blue-and-red bicycle. It wobbles, the son laughs, his hands and legs outstretched to balance his tiny frame. Father runs after him, holds the bicycle seat so that the child doesn't fall, the son turns his face to look at Father. 'Don't look at me,' says Father, 'don't look at me, look straight ahead, keep the bicycle steady.' The son smiles, blinks at his Father, the bicycle moves forward and Father can see, in the light of the park, dappled by the leaves and the branches of the trees, the bicycle's handlebars and pedals disappearing. Fading, dissolving into the air. And his son, legless and armless, still moving forward, the soft crunch of the bicycle wheels against the leaves. Then the seat begins to disappear and, with it, both wheels until Ithim is floating in the air.

05.45: Plaza Guard knocks at the door. 'Sir, you are done?'

No answer.

'You take your time, there's no hurry, sir, there's no one in the shop yet, no one's waiting.'

'I am done, I will be out,' the man coughs.

'You want me to bring you any more trousers, any more colours?'

'No, it's OK,' the man says, 'we are done.' Then he realizes what he has just said. 'I am done,' he corrects.

And in movements he has by now mastered, Father wraps his son in the layers again, puts him in the bag, gets into his own clothes, his socks and his shoes, leaves the two new pairs of trousers on the floor, walks out.

*

WHEN I came out of the Trial Room, Madam was standing in one corner of the store, arranging a stack of clothes in the women's section.

'Nothing you liked?' Plaza Guard asked.

'No, it's good but not the right fit.'

'We do alterations, Madam has some very good tailors and you can pick it up later in the evening.'

'No, I'm just looking around, I'm leaving the city today,' I said.

Why did I say that? There was no need for me to say that.

'You don't live here?' he asked.

'No, I'm just leaving the city for a few days.'

While talking to Plaza Guard, I saw Madam near the shelf – what she was arranging I wasn't sure of since everything looked arranged and there had been no customers so far – and then she turned, her eyes caught mine, she smiled: 'Anything else you wish to see?'

'No, it's OK, thank you,' I said.

'From next month, we will have an infants' section,' she said, moving to stand right next to me.

What did that mean? Had she seen Ithim?

'That's great,' was all I could think to say, trying not to betray any panic or the tension that was tying little knots in my stomach, making my heart race. 'My wife and I will be here then, thank you.'

As I walked out of the shop, Plaza Guard called to me from behind. 'Sir,' he said, 'if you are looking around the mall, there is a new cinema hall upstairs, you can go and spend some time there.'

'Thank you,' I said.

I walked towards the escalator that would take Ithim and me to the third floor, where the Multiplex was. Yes, why not, why shouldn't Ithim's first day out also include his first day at the movies? In a cinema hall, dark, with velvet curtains and a flickering screen. It was only later that I realized this was a mistake, that Ithim's cover was about to be blown.

◆ ◆ ◆

I am Window Curtain, I was just three months old, look at the window in the picture of Tariq's house, the first from the left, next to Main Door, I was the curtain in that window, I was blue in colour, Tariq's mother got me stitched three months ago from an old bedspread she had which was torn so she could get only two curtains out of it, one was me, for the window, the other for the main door so we never felt we were separated, both of us curtains in the same house, same room, we would talk to each other at night, Main Door Curtain kept complaining how he was always being pushed around more often than me and I told him, well, you are the big one, you have to be the tough one but, to be frank, neither of us, tough or gentle, stood a chance against the fire, although Main Door Curtain lived, he was ripped up, thrown into a heap outside the house, they did that while breaking the door down, they did that to me as well, me, who liked being in the window more than on the bed, the glass pane I faced was broken so I would always get the breeze even on still and hot days, when Tariq's father was alive he bought his son a toy car, Tariq doesn't play with it any more, it was kept on my windowsill and because I was longer than the window, at least a couple of inches more, sometimes when the wind blew hard, Tariq would fold my edge and put the car on top of me, on the sill, as a weight so I didn't flap, he didn't know that I liked flapping in the breeze but I didn't mind, the car and I became friends, the car also burnt that night, there was a lot of plastic in it, I can't help feeling guilty, though, because I was the first to catch the fire, I was the one to pass it on, see the charred streaks below my window, these were formed by the flames that began with me, I am now scattered all across the pavement, across the neighbourhood, my ash sticks to people's shoes and slippers when they walk by and so one day I will be spread across the city and as for Main Door Curtain, I saw someone come at night, take him away, maybe he will go back to being a bedspread in a house that escaped the fire.

17. *At The Movies, Good Girl & Nice Boy*

WE were carried, Ithim and I, up, up and up, smooth, we were gliding, riding the sparkling metal teeth, black and yellow, of the newly installed escalators, up from the ground floor to the first where the restaurants were, all closed, the chairs still upturned on the tables, too early for lunch. From the first floor to the second, where the beauty salons and the hairdressers and the luggage shops and the music shops and the cellphone shops and the TV shops were, all open, bright and early, waiting for customers. To the third where Ithim and I got off, the floor with seven screens, the Plaza Multiplex.

Of the seven halls, there was only one movie showing at this time of day, due to start in fifteen minutes: an English film called *For the Icy Nite*, its poster showing several men in combat fatigues, sitting atop a tank, guns blazing all around, their faces grim. Not exactly a movie I would have chosen but it would do.

The Multiplex ticket counter was a glass cubicle in which I saw two young men, in ties, in uniform, each behind a computer flatscreen, both of them framed by a large HBO poster for March 8, International Women's Day Special, *The Power of Womanhood, HBO knows what women want.*

In the line were just two people, a young woman and a young man – a couple, in their early twenties, attractive. Maybe college students who had bunked their classes.

Good Girl and Nice Boy.

I waited behind them.

Nice Boy and Good Girl took their tickets and when they turned, Good Girl's eyes caught mine.

I stepped up to the counter.

'Fifth row, thirteenth seat, please,' I said. Miss Glass's coordinates.

'The hall is empty, sir,' Ticket Boy said, 'you can sit anywhere you want to.' He handed me the ticket and the change and pointed to the carpeted hallway that led to the entrance of the theatre.

Ticket Boy was very polite, just like Madam.

I was still counting the change he had given me and walking in the direction he had pointed, my eyes lowered, maybe I didn't look, but I brushed against Good Girl. I didn't see her, I had no idea she was so close behind me.

'Mind your step, mister,' said Nice Boy, 'can't you see where you're going?'

I mumbled a sorry. Yes, it was my mistake.

Good Girl had seen my bag and I don't know how but she must have caught a glimpse of Ithim. (I had covered him carefully in the Trial Room, so carefully that even Madam, standing right next to me, hadn't noticed a thing, but maybe when I brushed against Good Girl, the mouth of the bag had opened without my knowing, Ithim's cover had slipped.)

'Look, what's he got inside the bag, look, look,' Good Girl was shouting, stepping back, 'it's some kind of an animal.'

Then she pinched her nose with her fingers, made a face. 'It stinks,' she said, 'and it looks like a monkey.'

Nice Boy laughed, 'Is he the monkey man?'

Ticket Boy was looking in our direction but hadn't heard a word through the glass.

'Tell him, ask him.' Good Girl was now laughing so hard she was stumbling over her words: 'Ask him, ask the Monkey Man . . . can he get the monkey to dance, we will pay.'

Although there was nobody else around, I felt heat rising from my feet all the way to my face. Anger, shame, even fear. In a move that must have appeared clumsy and awkward, I pressed the bag closer to my chest and hurried, almost ran, down the hallway, towards the entrance to the movie theatre, desperate to get in, to be in the dark, Good Girl's laughter licking my ears like fire.

'Don't hurry, the show hasn't started yet,' said Usher, who didn't even ask me about the bag as I walked in and sat down in E13, fifth row from the screen, thirteenth seat from the corner.

There was no one in the theatre.

I was trembling. Yes, I was angry at Nice Boy and Good Girl, the anger making even my breathing difficult, but more paralysing than that was my sense of helplessness, an impotence that made me burn and freeze at the same time. With everything I had, I'd been trying to protect Ithim ever since they had handed him to me at Holy Angel. I had embarked on this journey at great risk and on a vague promise that he could be set right, and I was not going to let anyone judge him before I had finished the journey. But, then this. This was the outside world's first view of Ithim and it had been a sneer and a laugh, revulsion and disgust. And I, the father, was the Monkey Man.

'Ask him if he can get the monkey to dance, we will pay,' she had said.

Once seated in the theatre, darkness came like a blanket that I let slip over me. There was music playing, the screen was blank, the red velvet curtains still drawn. The solitude helped calm my anger, helped the shiver to pass. I put Ithim in the seat next to mine, adjusted his bag so it couldn't be seen by anyone else sitting behind us. Thus settled, I closed my eyes and felt the soft chill of the air-conditioning fan my face.

The ads began; I kept my eyes closed right through, ads for motorcycles, for Coke and Pepsi, kept them closed through previews of coming attractions, closed as they demonstrated their Dolby-enhanced system with the surround sound of rain, of water drops travelling from one end of the theatre to another. I kept my eyes closed even as the movie started. I had shut myself off, closed all the doors and windows through which the world could enter.

When my eyes opened, the movie had been playing for a while. I checked on Ithim, reaching into the bag, he was still. When I turned to look around, I saw two people sitting way in the back, several rows behind me, perhaps Good Girl and Nice Boy, both quietly watching.

Good Girl and Nice Boy.

My eyes closed again.

*

I AM at My Most Charming Self, gems roll off my tongue, uncut yet sparkling, brightly coloured, catching the light of the shuttered storefronts, their display windows. There's hardly anyone in Plaza Mall now; it's well after midnight. The policemen have gone home, the last Multiplex show is over, there is only an old woman sweeping the floor in one corner, her back turned towards us. My gems bounce as they fall from my tongue, making Good Girl and Nice Boy fall to their knees, like little children, scrambling to pick up the jewels as they slide on the freshly scrubbed marble floor.

Let me drive you home, I tell them.

Good Girl giggles. (Nice Boy doesn't listen, he's chasing after the gems that have now rolled into the metal teeth of the escalator.)

We will call a taxi, says Good Girl and I say, no, the city is on fire, there will be a curfew so let me drive you home. You are a Good Girl and he's a Nice Boy. How can I leave you alone?

She runs to Nice Boy, tugs at his arm, tells him to get up, tries to explain to him, like a mother to a child, that he can't get the gems because they are stuck in the escalator which has been switched off and maybe next morning, when the Plaza maintenance men come, they will get them out for him.

Nice Boy stumbles; I steady him with one arm, avoiding any touch with Good Girl, I am the gentleman, she smiles at me, touches my shoulder, near the strap of Ithim's bag. (It's not the cloth bag I stepped out of the house with this morning. It's a superior bag, far superior, made of fine leather, hide, with soft, warm lining.)

Good Girl, Nice Boy and I get into the car and I drive

them home – to my home. It's a new, luxury car I have bought, automatic transmission, specially imported. I drive it through this burnt-out city, past the bodies fallen from the sky during the day, rolling the windows up so that the smell doesn't enter. I drive past shops and homes now black, smouldering rectangles, visible in the night only through the smoke that marks them out; these were ugly buildings, illegally erected, more like slums and now the city will clean them up. I drive down dead streets – the city looks so much better when everyone is at home – passing sleeping police vans supposed to be on vigil, driving over the assorted debris, the car's shock absorbers making sure we don't feel a thing. I see some people crying by the side of the road, I let them be.

I let them wash the streets with their tears.

Let the wretched do something useful for this city.

Good Girl and Nice Boy find my house unfamiliar yet inviting; they explore while I go put Ithim in his cot in the nursery my wife has set up, under the mobile with flying fish and swimming birds. When I return, they are both standing at a window, pointing to the cement divider on the street, to the people sleeping on the pavement, men, women and children, the bundles in rows and columns, one stacked above the other, the heaps I cannot do anything about. Good Girl and Nice Boy are playing a game, whoever can guess which bundle will move first, gets a point. It's a silly game but they are just college kids. I watch them play for a while, even join in. (I start winning because I know these bundles better than anybody.)

Then I tell them both to undress.

Good Girl laughs, says I will do no such thing, are you joking, mister.

I want to see a change of heart, I want to tell her, but I don't say the words, let it come as a surprise.

Nice Boy thinks I am joking, too, because he laughs, his eyes are closing and he seems to be falling asleep. It's against the law to drink in this city but then maybe he had a bottle with him, maybe he is drunk, although I can't smell anything. He allows me to tie him to the chair.

What are you doing? asks Good Girl, let my friend go.

I tell her not to worry about her friend, I will take care of him. I have a knife in my hand – I picked it up after putting Ithim in his cot. It's a kitchen knife and it looks crude, I should have something more sophisticated.

But it will do.

At the knife's point, I get Good Girl to lie on the bed, where Ithim slept last night. She begins to scream but there is no one awake at this hour to hear. Even if there were, there are too many people screaming across the city tonight for her to be noticed. I tell her to let me tie her up, both her feet and her hands. Then I realize it will be difficult to undress her if she is tied up, difficult to remove her jeans and her shirt and her underwear unless I cut them off which is quite complicated so I tell her to undress first and then I tie her up. Don't rape me, she says, she thinks I want sex.

Does a father, on his first day with his newborn child, a child that needs all the help he can get, does this father want sex?

She is a college kid, she doesn't know.

I have never done this before, I have only seen it done at the Ahmed Meat Shop (now burnt down), so I try to remember and I begin with an indiscriminate stab in her stomach. She screams, pointlessly. I don't want to take any chances so, the knife still in her stomach, I gag her with her shirt and while I am doing that, she begins to jerk her head violently. I feel her hair against my hands, between my fingers, I can feel its soft, smooth rustle. I place one hand on her head (no, it's quiet, there's no fluttering like with Ithim). My second stab is harder and although I am not very strong, I see the knife has entered deeper this time which comes as a huge relief. The knife still in place, I put all my weight behind it and drag the blade down to her waist, below her navel, then drag it up again, right to her breasts, the knife blade moving silently, smoothly except for a noisy break where it hits her ribcage.

Nice Boy is fast asleep in the chair. I will wake him up later.

From where I am, I can see the door to Ithim's room and although I cannot see him – he must be fast asleep in his cot, unaware of what Father is doing – I know that Ithim is my Model Baby, that I have to make an Ithim out of her, as close as possible.

No, he isn't a monkey, he's a beautiful little child.

So covered with Good Girl's blood, just as I had in the dream last night, I walk to the kitchen, I fetch the pestle my wife sometimes uses for spices – most of the stuff she grinds in an electric mixer but she says some things you need to do by hand, to keep the natural flavours intact – and begin to pound Good Girl's head and face. Over the gag of her shirt. Once, twice, thrice, four times. Five, six, seven, eight, nine, ten, eleven until I hear the crunch of her teeth, her lips, her nose. Until my fingers hurt along with my hands, and my arms, from wrist to elbow all the way to my shoulders, until the gag is red and even the pestle has begun to drip.

I sit on top of Good Girl, I straddle her, I start working the knife again. This time, I begin peeling her skin off, pink skin, soft skin, smooth skin. For a second, for just a fraction of a second, in fact, a fraction of a fraction of a second, I want to fuck her with each layer of her skin that I peel back, I want to enter her through the slit in her stomach that the knife has just created, I want to move inside her insides but I check myself.

The change of heart? I almost forgot.

In all the pounding, the cutting, the stabbing, I have forgotten Good Girl's heart. So back to the knife that's now almost twice, thrice its weight, covered with blood and flesh and skin.

I carve under her breasts; it's slow going, as muscle and bone impede the blade's path. Her blood gushes out as if on tap and I let it run over both my hands, flow over the wooden handle of the knife, trickle down her chest, onto the bed sheet. (I should be afraid but I have gone through this with Ithim in the dream so it's a familiar sight, I am not worried except for the fact that there will be a lot of washing, cleaning up, to do, maybe I will get Nice Boy to help me with that.)

I can see her heart now, a red-brown mass inside her body, a lump, a growth, trembling like an animal, triangular and deformed. No nose or ears, no arms or legs, just a torso, somewhat like my Ithim. But, no, Ithim has perfect eyes, Ithim can see; there is no comparison with him. Using both hands, I hold her heart and pull. Good Girl twitches but I can't see her face, everything is mangled, I use the knife to cut the cords that bind her heart, I wrench all the heart-strings away.

I have a towel by the side of the bed, a soft towel, like the ones they have in fancy hotels, white, absorbent, the kind they fold and drape over heated steel rods near the bathtub. Or fold and place in warm wicker baskets, along with green, white and blue translucent plastic bottles of oil, shampoo, conditioner and moisturizer. I think this will do, Good Girl deserves the best. I roll the towel into a ball, mop up the blood that's spilled over her breasts, and then insert the sodden bundle into the cavity I have just carved out, that I have created. Immediately, more blood begins to soak into the towel, red staining the white until all I can see is one tiny white speck and I know then that Good Girl has had a change of heart.

I have not spoken a word during this, not a whisper has passed my lips. I tell her that she will be all right after I am done, she just got a change of heart, the old, hard one is gone, and now she has one that's softer, she's now Better Girl, not just Good Girl. She will look at my Ithim and not see a monkey but a beautiful child.

She doesn't listen.

Nice Boy has woken up, he is staring at me.

He is staring at my hard work. He is lazy.

Still sitting in his chair, his hands tied behind his back, he begins to scream. I want to tell him to stop but I am coughing, I am retching, my phlegm grey and green, speckled with the soot of this ugly city. I am sorry, I tell Nice Boy, let's clean her up, then I need to take a shower, to feel fresh, I haven't had a change of clothes for almost two days and two nights now, I have been through the fire, the hospital, the bus, the mall and now all this, I need to stand under water.

But he says no no no no, don't make me do it, he is shaking his head. (He looks like one of those brown toy dogs people hang in their cars, from the rear-view mirror, and because this city has so many potholes, these toy dogs keep wagging their heads all the time.)

Sir, says Nice Boy, and he can't get his words out, he is stuttering. Sir, let me go, he says.

Not yet, I say, we have to clean this up.

So we both get up on the bed, Nice Boy and I (he is tall, taller than I am and he has to crouch so his head doesn't hit the ceiling). Nice Boy is very helpful – I am surprised – he is efficient, better than I am, stronger than The Monkey Man. I wrap the bed sheet around Good Girl, the bedcover too. The mattress is stained in several places, I will need to change that, the pillows as well. (Maybe I will buy a new set, surprise my wife when she returns.) With a heave, Nice Boy hoists the bundle down from the bed, onto the floor.

He is crying, he is saying something I can't make out between his whimpers and his toy-dog shake of the head.

I love her, he says.

Which makes me very angry.

If you do, I say, why didn't you once open your eyes when I was at her? You could have stopped me.

He can't answer, Nice Boy has no answer, he just keeps crying, like a child, stammering, shivering.

You know why this happened? I ask him, and once again he stares at me. I take him by the arm and lead him to Ithim's room, to Ithim's cot and while he stands there, I remove the towel that's draped over my baby. I show him that this isn't a monkey. This is my child and he's the most beautiful child in the world.

Yes, sir, Nice Boy says.

And I make him lean forward and gently touch Ithim on his forehead, just above his eyes.

I am tempted to let him go. But, no, I am sure his father, Good Girl's father, too, I am sure they are VIPs, not auto-rickshaw drivers, retired schoolteachers or ordinary mothers, I am sure they live in bungalows with gardens in front, or apartment buildings with power generators, they can pull strings with telephone calls, they can trace it back although no one saw me bring them home. (At least, I don't think the old woman sweeping the corner of the mall saw anything but why take any chances?)

So I tell Nice Boy, Sorry.

And I get working on him as well and now I have done it once, it's easier; in fact, I never thought it would be this easy although there is no doubt that fire is better, fire is faster once it gets going, flames lick everything clean, leaving nothing except smoke and ash that the sun and the wind can clear. Now there are two bodies on the floor and through the window I can see the bundles on the pavement are still there, not one of them has moved. Ithim is fast asleep, too. And looking around the room, at the bed, the floor, the blood, the flesh, the skin, at Nice Boy and Good Girl, at what I have just done, I feel the warmth of anger in the city on fire, a glow I think I have felt before.

'WAKE up.' Usher was standing next to me, shaking me by the shoulder. 'Ten minutes the show got over,' he said, 'we have to clean up for the next. If you want to stay, go get another ticket.'

The lights had come on but these were small lights set into the ceiling, like the stars in Ithim's unused nursery at home. The hall was still dark, the screen blank. Ithim's bag was where I had put it, on the adjacent seat. Safe, intact, unmoved. Sweat ran down my back, my neck, my arms, even my legs making my trousers stick.

'Just a minute,' I said, but Usher had already walked away.

I sat there, waiting for the cool breeze from the fans and the air-conditioner to dry my sweat. When I looked into the bag, Ithim was fast asleep but I could get his smell. He must have soiled himself again.

From the direction of the door I could hear the buzz of a crowd, waiting to get into the cinema. That meant the mall was busy, perhaps the street had returned to normal, the mob must have passed by, scattered or dispersed, which meant I could finally leave Plaza Mall.

It was almost 1 pm, more than three hours had slipped by since I was in the Trial Room. I had four hours before the train, enough to take a trip to the hospital, check on my wife and then leave for the station. To meet Miss Glass.

The dream about Good Girl and Nice Boy had left me drained and it was only when I saw them in the crowd again, just outside the theatre, looking at the Nike display window, laughing and talking to each other, Good Girl pressing herself against Nice Boy, that I felt some of that exhaustion slowly lifting.

◆◆◆

I am Screaming Woman from the TV news, I was twenty-six years old, or thereabouts, I am not so sure, I had one daughter, I lived in a large family with fifteen other people, aunts and uncles, brothers and sisters, we lived in a village two hours from this city, all our homes linked to each other, we would have our fights but then we also felt safe because there were so many of us living under one roof, my father-in-law has lived here for twenty-five years and everyone knew us in the village, I was known as the athletic one since, as a girl, I was always climbing up and down the stairs, running in the fields, even when I was pregnant with my daughter and if someone had to bring down a box, a suitcase from a high shelf on the wall, they would tell me to climb up and get it, my husband worked in a factory making plastic bags, he told me he wanted to move out of the village and go to the city to make some more money and he said he wanted a son but now it makes no difference, that night when we heard the mob coming, we decided to run to the neighbouring village where there were more of us, it would have taken us only ten minutes, there was no moon in the sky which was a good thing because it was dark and we knew the route, a narrow road running through the fields, but they got us within five minutes of our leaving, they raped me, they raped my aunt, they raped my sister-in-law, my mother-in-law, they killed all of us, my daughter first, we were slit with knives, they raped my sister as well, they killed her three-year-old child and they left her for dead but my sister tricked them by lying still, by getting them to believe she was dead when she wasn't and in the morning, the police came and took our bodies away, sprinkled a lot of salt on us and then buried some of us, others they set on fire, I was among the buried, the next morning my sister came looking, with a man from the village, they asked the police where we were and they said, sorry, we could not keep the bodies in the police station because it was warm and there was no ice, they did not tell her about the salt, about how it made our skin melt faster so that we began to smell and they buried us, one by one, they removed our bodies of evidence, now my husband is alive and I am gone, I will start searching for my daughter and everyone else since all of us are now together, in the land of the dead.

18. *Skipping Holy Angel, Ithim misses the meeting*

ITHIM and I left Plaza Mall and walked into the blazing sun. The street was strewn with slippers, stones and broken glass where the mob must have fought with the police while we were in the Multiplex, for the area was quiet now, the air shimmering in the heat that had wiped off any reminder of last night's cold. Right by the exit, in front of the mall's glass doors, I saw a private taxi, a white car parked behind the police vans, its rear door partly open as if it was waiting for me and Ithim. For Father and Son.

Without even checking with the driver, I got in and said: 'Holy Angel. I need to spend about ten, fifteen minutes there, then we will go to the railway station. Please be careful.' I couldn't take chances with Ithim in my bag.

Through the taxi's window I could see evidence of the fires, some still smouldering. I saw burnt-out shops – shop after shop; unlike my neighbourhood, where I had seen only three, here there were rows and rows of black rectangles, so that after a while I lost count, I couldn't make out where one shop ended and the next began. In one place, it seemed, the fire had swallowed the entire block, the neighbourhood, erased all divisions and partitions.

I saw men and women sifting through the rubble, the

shop owners and their families who had had to run away last night and now returned, in the light of the sun, to search for what the fire didn't take. Sirens screeching, red lights blinking, a convoy of cars, led by a fleet of police vehicles, sped by, forcing the taxi to pull over to let them through. They were, I guessed, VIPs from New Delhi who had come to inspect the damage, to see what had happened last night and what had not.

And even as they passed us, I saw a black cloud staining the horizon, the smoke darkest near the ground and growing lighter and lighter as it met more of the white-blue of the sky, hard and unbroken.

'Is that another fire?' I asked.

'Yes, sir, don't know when this will stop,' Taxidriver said. 'About two hours ago, there was police firing near the Plaza. And now, it seems closer to Holy Angel.'

'Is the road clear to the hospital?'

'Sir, when is your train?'

'Four,' I said, giving myself a one-hour cushion.

'Let me see, I will try to make it to the hospital but if the road is blocked, it's better to go straight to the railway station taking the bridge.'

How could I tell him what I had pictured in my head, what I wanted to do.

To walk into my wife's room, to place Ithim, in his bag, on top of her. Between her ankles and her knees. I wanted to take my time looking at her, at her hands on either side, the marks on her wrist where the tubes were inserted, where the skin was punctured. I wanted to look at her fingers frozen in a curl, just like they were last night. I wanted to slip one hand into that curl and wait for her fingers to move. With my free hand, I would have touched her lips, dry and chapped; with my fingers, I wanted to mark the outline of her chin, of her nose, her cheeks, the holes in her earlobes where they had removed the rings when they wheeled her into the Operating Theatre. I would have looked down, at her sheet rise and fall, each movement perfectly matching the breath I could feel against my face. I wanted affirmation, definitive evidence that my wife was alive. For then I would have got the son to meet his mother.

I wanted to take Ithim out of the bag, remove all his clumsy covers, until he was bare – I didn't care who saw him, who didn't – and then I wanted to bring his face to hers, to let his forehead, the charred strip of skin, touch her nose, lips, cheeks, eyes. I wanted my wife to take in all of Ithim's smells, the baby formula, the talcum powder, his day-old skin. I wanted to press his lips, the knife-cut slit, against hers, press his left funnel-ear against her lips so that he could hear if she wanted to whisper anything to him. I wanted to place Ithim on her breasts, above her hospital gown, so his heart was right above hers and each could hear the other beat.

'Sir, I don't think we should go to Holy Angel.' Taxidriver had stopped the vehicle.

Up ahead, I saw the narrow road leading to the hospital, sealed off at the entrance with several police vehicles and ambulances.

There was splintered glass on the ground. One

ambulance had its doors open, through which I saw stretchers stacked, one on top of the other, each one with a body, sheets so hurriedly pulled over each that in many, I could see toes, feet, the glimpse of hair on a head.

'What happened here?' I drew Ithim closer to me.

'Must have been another mob, it's gone now but they aren't allowing anyone to pass. Maybe you could walk from here, I will wait for you if they let me do that. Otherwise, you have to take another taxi.'

There was a phone booth just across the street from where we were. I decided to call the hospital and check on my wife rather than walk there with Ithim. What if the police stopped me, asked me to open the bag? With Plaza Guard I had been lucky, but for a second time slipping past without being detected didn't seem plausible. And I was taking no chances letting go of this taxi.

Here's my side of the conversation, from the phone booth, as I can recall it now. This is for the record. (The other side is irrelevant.)

'HELLO, Holy Angel and Nursing? This is the husband of Patient Number 110742.

'I am calling to check on her condition, she is in the Maternity Ward.

'OK, I will hold.

'Maternity Ward, Maternity Ward, sixth floor. Last night was the birth.

'So who has the records?

'Well, I am telling you the birth was last night.

'No, I was supposed to call.

'Doctor 1 told me to call him today, he said someone at the hospital would page him. And he would tell me how she is.

'I want to know when she can be discharged, when I can take her home.

'Last night. She was admitted last night.

'I brought her to the hospital. I'm not sure of the exact time.

'Number 110742.

'Yes, how many times do you want me to give you the number?

'Mrs Jay. Yes, J, A, Y. OK, I will hold.'

I heard the phone being put down on the table. I heard coughing, I heard someone shout.

In the phone booth, through the glass door, I saw another police van driving towards the hospital, I saw the taxi driver looking at me. Just a little while, I gestured to him.

'When will Doctor 1 be there?

'Can't you page him?

'He said he had a pager. He told me that last night.

'Switched off? Can you then get me Head Nurse, please?

'Head Nurse.

'She filled out the baby's discharge slip.

'I-t-h-i-m. Ithim.

'When does her shift begin?

'Can't you find out?

'But Head Nurse will come in today?

'Is there any other doctor I could speak to?

'OK, I will hold.

'Yes?

'I said, can you please check the room?

'What do you mean that won't help?

'Isn't there an extension you can transfer the call to?

'No, I can't come this evening, I won't be here, I will be out of town.

'It's personal.

'Do you have Doctor 1's home phone number?

'It's urgent.

'He said she will be under observation for a few days.

'You have a list?

'Yes?

'OK, I will hold.

'Yes?

'Mrs Jay, I told you.

'She's not in that list?

'I will call later.'

So it had come to this: they couldn't help; Head Nurse and Doctor 1 couldn't be traced; there was no one to go and check how my wife was. If I wanted specific information, I would have to go after six in the evening, when the nurses' night shift began. Maybe Head Nurse would be there, too. And, no, they couldn't tell me if she was on duty or not. No, they couldn't contact her. They hadn't been able to contact her since last night. But, yes, there was a current list of casualties at Holy Angel this morning. And, no, my wife wasn't on it. Patient Number 110742 was not on the list. Means she was alive, she must still be under observation. Just like what Doctor 1 had said last night.

'WE are almost near the bridge,' said Taxidriver. 'Let's hope it's clear.'

The bridge, my wife and I had stood there one night the week after I had proposed to her and she had said yes.

It was a scorching summer, there was fear that the city would hit fifty degrees. So hot it was that even at night it seemed the sun was still in the sky, just blackened, rendered invisible by the heat. Walking was forbidden on the bridge – it had no pavement as such but there was a four-foot strip of concrete that flanked both sides, possibly for maintenance workers as and when they needed access. Traffic was thin, a couple of trucks carrying cargo, and I asked the autorickshaw driver to stop. He seemed unsure until I offered to pay him extra.

We had walked on the bridge, my wife and I, had looked at the giant metal plates and the joints that kept the beams in place, held together by rivets, each the size of our feet. We had looked at the broad arches that swept across the sky, the trusses that cut the clouds with iron. The riverbed below was dry, just patches of stagnant water that caught the shimmering lights of the city. My wife had held my arm. 'The bridge is moving,' she had noticed with a touch of fear and surprise. And it was.

Moving, that colossus swaying like a child's toy, made of rope, slung between two trees. 'I think they build it like that,' I had said, 'to absorb the vibrations of the traffic. It swings because that's the way it stays safe.'

'We should come here again,' my wife had said.

'It's clear,' said Taxidriver, 'the bridge is clear. We are lucky today.'

As the taxi had picked up speed, I turned in my seat to see if I could identify the place where we had stood, my wife and I, that night. And there it was, clearly visible. So I raised Ithim's bag. Let him have a look, too.

I pointed the spot out to him and for the first time since I got him home, I found myself talking to him, to my child. 'That's where your mother and I once stood,' I said.

He couldn't hear but just in case he was watching, filing away the image in some corner of his mind that he might one day recall, even act on, once they set him right – now that we had entered the last lap of our journey.

END OF PART TWO

PART THREE

THE NIGHT AFTER

19. *Bright Shirt At Railway Station*

IT was as if the city itself, or the part of it that was on the run, had hurriedly packed whatever it could gather and had come to the railway station, ready to leave along with Ithim and me as we got out of the taxi. A sea of children, women and men, their luggage afloat like countless pieces of wreckage. Tied with plastic strings or jute ropes, bundles and briefcases balanced on shoulders, trunks dragged along, some on wheels, some without. Bed sheets and quilts folded, trussed up in holdalls. Cups and plates and jars and tins squeezed into bags. And all these buffeted by wave after human wave, so unpredictable its crest and its trough that I didn't have to wade or swim, much less offer any resistance. Clearly visible in that ceaselessly shifting wave, were faces swathed in bandages, some even on stretchers, some limping, crushed arms and legs in casts, men, women and children with a flash of hard plaster white on their feet or their arms. All sitting, walking, limping, embellishing their pity with signs and symbols. Ithim and I found ourselves being swept in, carried along with other passengers until I found myself in front of the Arrival/Departure Display Board, its green and red lights flashing like beacons to those still adrift.

I read through the list: there were Express trains and Passenger trains, there were the Superfast Expresses and the Galloping Locals, going to and coming from, with their platform numbers and their schedules. And only then, standing there, afraid to move, did I realize I was marooned with neither a map nor a compass. I had no idea where Ithim and I were heading.

On the phone, Miss Glass had said not very far. I checked her message again in case she had mentioned the train, the time, the place, maybe between the lines, somewhere that I had missed. But, no, just those three verses stared at me, almost mocking me with their vagueness.

At the railway station, as we discussed last night, meet at five in the evening, we will set the baby right . . . and in case you don't see me, in the maddening crowd, there will be someone there to call out, clear and loud.

Some comfort came from the huge clock on the wall that showed it was close to three – the journey from Plaza to here had taken more than an hour and a half, a journey that on any other day would have taken only half as much. The train, Miss Glass had said, was at five so Ithim and I had time, enough time, I thought, for Miss Glass – or the someone she had sent – to find us here, even if by accident.

'Miss Glass told me
You will certainly be here,
With the child by your side
And a little bit of fear.'

More than forty minutes of waiting later, this high-pitched singsong whine, nasal, almost metallic, like the soundtrack in TV cartoons. The words rattled off so fast that each one fused with the other, withthechildbyyourside, littlebitoffear, childbyyoursideanda, into a glorious garble and only when the lines were repeated, over and over again, could I make them out.

The voice was coming from down below, from somewhere near my feet, where I suddenly felt someone pulling at my trousers, pressing against my shoes, making me think it must be a child but when I looked, no, this wasn't a child, when I looked, I almost jumped back in both horror and disbelief.

This was a man, a dwarf, a midget.

Balding, his hair a thin white frizz around his head, his face almost overpowered by his thick glasses, two to three sizes too big, which kept slipping down to the tip of his nose so he kept, in what seemed a totally futile effort, pushing them back into place. He was in costume. As if he had come straight from some kind of a show. His yellow trousers hugged his legs in a drainpipe fit all the way to his ankles where they suddenly opened up and flared out, almost covering his disproportionately large shoes, their laces dragging along the floor.

His face was fair, almost white – whether this was his actual complexion or whether this was face paint I had no way to tell – but the paleness was accentuated by his shirt done right up to his chin, its collars so large that their corners fell over his shoulders. And what a shirt it was. A profusion of not only fabric, a fabric that shone like silk and velvet, but also of wild colour and twisted asymmetry: blue and red and green and yellow and white and black, stripes, checks, triangles, circles, swirls, ellipses, straight lines, curls.

And as if this weren't loud enough to make whatever statement he was trying to make, there was a scarf, too, around his neck. A black-and-white-chequered woollen scarf that was obviously not made to measure since its edges trailed on the floor behind his back so that he seemed to stand in a large coloured puddle of his trousers, his shoelaces, the scarf and his shoes, all mixed together, and all, it seemed, ready to trip him up at any moment.

But he didn't seem to care less.

Instead, he was running, on the spot, stomping and stamping in this puddle, his clothes flapping like giant tropical birds perched on his body. He was jumping up and down, his elbows and knees jerking back and forth, restless, impatient, like a player limbering up before a game. But the oddest thing of all was how he appeared so natural in whatever he did, how he made his perpetual motion appear smooth and graceful, almost at one with all the chaotic swirl around him in the railway station. And how not one person passing by even stopped to take a second look when a man, of his appearance and mannerisms, would normally have attracted quite a crowd in this city.

'Myself, Bright Shirt,' he said, 'very obvious as you can see. You can call me Shirt, you can call me Bright, you can call me Joker, Clown, anything that suits you, depending on the time of the day or night, use Hindi, use English, sometimes Hindi sometimes English, mix it up. Call me names.' He finally paused for breath. And offered his hand to me.

So suddenly had Bright Shirt appeared and so out of the ordinary was his presence that it took me a while to recover from the shock. He must have sensed my unease, however, as I realized that to shake hands with him I would have to stoop, almost go down on one knee, because he thrust a hand into the pocket of his trousers, and still whistling, fished out a red plastic rectangle that he then unfolded into a table, barely a foot high. He placed this on the floor, right next to where I stood, climbed onto it and then again offered his hand, this time almost level with me.

'No need to bend, Mr Jay, when I am ready to stand up to someone like you,' he laughed, showing off two rows of yellowing teeth.

'I am at your service,' he said, 'for you are the father, you are the one who took care of Ithim, follow me, sir.' And as quickly as he had clambered up there, he jumped down from his makeshift lectern, folded it back into his pocket, and broke into verse again:

'Forgive my looks, for
I am just a clown,
My job is to cheer you up,
Whenever you are down.

You look very tired, sir,
You look quite beat,
So let's sit down for a while,
And get something to eat?'

Then he turned, with a flick of his heel, a stamp of his foot, like a soldier in a parade, and was off.

He walked as if there was no crowd, barging right into people, banging against their suitcases and their bundles, almost knocking his head against their knees. This strategy of his seemed to work, though. For the crowd was parting for him, easily and spontaneously, and he was walking, running, jogging, as if this were a playground and he were a child.

In fact, from a distance, he *did* look like a child if you, for a moment, ignored the white hair on his head, his baldness, his girth – and at first I tried to maintain this distance, to signal to whoever was looking (although no one was, I have to admit) that I had nothing to do with this strange character. Several times, I lost him in the moving thicket and tangle of the crowd's legs but then he would resurface, within seconds, his shirt blooming with colour, his trousers slapping against his shoes, his scarf trailing, causing passers-by to sidestep lest they trip. And so purposefully did he move, unmindful of any obstacle that came his way, that I had to run finally to catch up. 'Where are we going?' I asked.

He stopped, seemed to freeze as if he had been hit in the back, a hard blow. And, then in an exaggerated gesture (he must have been a performer, I had little doubt about that), he raised himself on his toes, swivelled until he was facing me, brought one finger to his lips and said in a loud whisper: 'You are with Bright Shirt, you are happy, you are safe, don't worry.' And then added, this time louder: 'Here, give me your bag, sir, you have been carrying it all day. Rest, let me take the burden for a while.'

He leapt up, right from where he was standing, in one loop, so quickly that before I could move (before even instinct kicked in to make me duck) the bag was with him; how he had managed to get the strap over my head I had no idea. Realizing the bag was almost as tall as him and would touch the floor if he carried it the way I had, he shortened its strap by tying a double knot, his fingers moving so fast they were almost a blur. And all along he kept whistling, looking inside the bag, cooing baby prattle: 'Beautiful baby, beautiful baby, just as I had thought. Sir, we are indebted and grateful to you for taking care of this child. I can't wait to play with him. Baby, baby, beautiful baby, our baby.'

I reached out to snatch the bag away from him but it was too late, he had turned and was off again, the bag swinging, the crowd rushing in, like water, to fill the distance between him and me.

What the hell was this, who the hell was this?

Who had Miss Glass sent?

This clown, this outrageous buffoon, this two-bit jokester, what did he know about Ithim and where was he leading me to?

Was Ithim safe with him? What did he mean, 'our baby'?

What if he gave me the slip right now? Deformed Baby Kidnapped by a Dwarf; guess how that would make me look if I had to complain to anybody.

But then watching him in the crowd – he had now slowed down as he kept checking on Ithim, looking inside the bag, making baby faces – made me, for the time being, at least, suspend my concerns. For he was the first person in this city who had looked at Ithim and displayed neither disbelief nor pity, who had reacted as if there was nothing wrong, as if this was only a baby like any other in the station in the city that day, or even more than that perhaps – a special baby, a child he had been looking forward to meeting. And this, together with the fact I had recovered from my initial shock, helped me take a more charitable view of this clown, as I saw him enter the railway cafeteria.

Here again, another surprise.

Bright Shirt made a grand entry, strutting in, then stopping, holding on to Ithim's bag, he performed a jig, twirled around on his toes. 'Special guests, today,' he shouted, 'there is my table, let's go.'

And no one noticed.

Not one of the customers, not one of the men behind the counter, the waiters clearing the dishes, the boys sweeping the floor, walking in and out of the tables and the chairs, not one of them stopped to look as Bright Shirt strode across the huge dining hall in a blur of movement and noise, making his way to one corner where I saw *his* table.

It had to be his table. It was split into two levels, one at least a foot lower than the other, with two chairs corresponding, one tall, the other short, all made of a rich, dark wood that seemed freshly varnished. This odd arrangement had been set up evidently with more care and luxury than any other seating in the hall because a white lace cover was spread across the table and the chairs had matching cushions.

'I have a baby with me,' Bright Shirt shouted to no one in particular, sliding past the lower leg of the table, 'so first, get me some boiled water and milk for him and then get us your special of the day. For Sir and for me.'

I didn't realize how hungry I was until the food arrived; it was my first meal in so many hours I had lost count. It was railway-station food, bland and tasteless – served in a steaming steel plate with compartments marked out for rice, dal, vegetable curry, a piece of chicken, curd, pickle, salad, in its journey from the counter to our table in the hands of an impatient, clumsy waiter, all these items had merged into each other, the compartments serving no purpose – but that didn't matter at all. And so unabashed was I in attacking what lay in front of me, it was only when I was halfway through that I realized I hadn't even bothered to check on Ithim, far less, Bright Shirt.

I looked up from my plate, looked down across the table, there was no reason to worry.

For Bright Shirt had cradled Ithim in his lap and was feeding him, his own plate untouched on the table. While I had been busy eating, he had unwrapped and cleaned Ithim, taken out the baby formula, got the cafeteria staff to sterilize a cup in boiling water, had prepared the feed, taken the dropper out of the bag, settled Ithim in his lap and was now feeding him. And Ithim?

His eyes blinking, Ithim stared at Bright Shirt, swallowing every drop, not one rolling off his slit-lip. Every half a minute or so, Bright Shirt would lean forward and kiss Ithim on his head, his brow, his ear. To any one looking it would have seemed that Bright Shirt was the father and I, just another customer sharing the table. That I was there by accident. So natural he appeared, so calm and composed, patient and efficient, so caring that it seemed Bright Shirt and Ithim had made their acquaintance long before I had ever met my child.

ONCE Ithim had been fed, cleaned up again and was resting, in Bright Shirt's arms – he had said let him stay outside for a while, get some air, he's been in the bag the whole day, logic to which I had no counter-argument – I waited for Bright Shirt to finish his lunch and then I began with the first few of the countless questions that I had: Where are we going? Which train are we taking? How long is the journey? Where is Miss Glass? Who is she, what is her real name? Who are you? What will happen to Ithim?

Without raising his head from his plate, Bright Shirt listened to all this, paused, drank some water, glanced at Ithim in his lap and then returned to his food.

So I pushed it.

'Give me my Ithim, and we will go back,' I said, my voice rising, 'if you don't start giving me some answers. I have had enough of this, I have been strung along all this while.'

Bright Shirt looked at me, right into my eyes, not a hint of sheepishness or defensiveness on his face. 'Go on, Mr Jay, go on,' he said, 'let it all come out, anything else you need to ask, or say? And don't worry if you want to shout, shout as loud as you wish, no one here will even hear. Just remember that I am here on Miss Glass's instructions.'

He returned to his food.

The tone of his reply surprised me, so different was it from what I had heard and come to expect all this while; his voice had acquired a more serious, heavy edge as if suddenly, behind that crude exterior, that outlandish attire, the joking and the kidding, there lurked a maturity, even a certain sophistication.

'How do I know you are who you say you are, that you aren't lying to me?'

'Ask me a question,' he said, without looking up from his plate.

'What question? I just asked you several.'

'No, not those questions.' He pushed the plate to one side, wiped his hands in a towel the waiter had brought him. 'Ask me about the call you got last night, I know about that. I know what Miss Glass told you, I know about the message she sent you, the pictures, I know about Tariq, about Shabnam, about Abba. I know you are carrying that message in this bag, what more do you want to know?'

He got up from the table, still cradling Ithim, gone was the cloying smile on his face, in its place a determined, almost triumphant look as if he had silenced me, had just proved his credentials, once and for all.

'But I didn't imagine meeting someone like you.'

'What do you mean, someone like me, Mr Jay?'

I tried to be polite: 'Just the way you are, Mr Shirt, your clothes, the way you talk, the way you walk. I can't figure this out.'

'I'm sorry, sir, I can't change that, can I, the way I look? I am not like Ithim, unfinished. I am old, I am finished, I am over. I am the way I am and I know that when I don't make you laugh, I make you cringe. And if I am not the person you imagined, wait until you see where we are going, wait until you meet the others.'

'That's what I have been asking you all this while: where are we going?'

'I am Miss Glass's humble servant, she leads, I follow. She orders, I obey. And, sir, I didn't even know her until last night but now I can't think of my life without her. Isn't that something?'

'Where did both of you meet?'

'We met in the city, in the smoke and in the fire. I will say no more, I will only add that everyone is waiting for you, for you and Ithim.'

'Who's everyone?'

'Sir, I told you my lips are sealed. I think I have already spoken more than I should, my job is straight and simple, I just fetch and carry. I was told to pick you up here, drop you off there.'

'Where?'

'You will soon see. Not very far, it's a beautiful place about six hours away by train. I have booked the best, Air-conditioned First Class, for ourselves, two berths, Upper and Lower, and a sliding door we can close so no one will disturb us. You must be tired. After the late lunch, you could do with some sleep. I will look after Ithim. Both of you are in very safe hands now.'

Well aware that I wasn't going to make any headway with my fruitless interrogation, I decided it was better that I let go, that I reconcile myself to the fact I would have to continue in the same uncertain vein – lots of hope and of blind faith – that had brought me thus far. And so resigned, I got up from the table and was about to start walking towards the cafeteria door, when Bright Shirt muttered under his breath,

'Look at this child,
So sweet and so strong
What's the problem? I
can't find any wrong.

Look at this child,
Like a star in the night,
Tell me, sir, seriously,
Want to set him right?'

'What do you mean?' I asked. 'What did you just say? That there's no need to set him right?'

'I am sorry, I didn't mean it that way,' said Bright Shirt.

'What way, then? Even you, look at you, you have arms and legs, you can walk and talk. My Ithim has nothing, Miss Glass said she will set Ithim right and that's the only reason I came all the way here, carrying him with me.'

'No, Mr Jay, I was only expressing a thought, my humble, personal view. What happened between you and Miss Glass is none of my business, sir. Whatever Miss Glass told you that's for you and Miss Glass to discuss, not for me. My job, as I said, is just to fetch and to carry. Fetch and carry, fetchandcarry.'

And with a gleam in his eye, Bright Shirt pointed to the display board in the distance:

'The train's here,
the train's here,
the time has come
To go, my dear.'

Freeze this moment.

Call it absurd, farcical, even poignant, call it whatever you wish. If you were looking at the crowd from above, if your eyes had swept across the station, they would certainly have stopped at this dwarf, at this splash of colour, this dwarf carrying a baby in a bag, not even a day old. And the baby's father following him, as if he were a child himself, afraid that he might lose his way in the crowd. Bright Shirt had told me nothing I didn't know, he had made me appear distrustful, suspicious, he had acted as if it was a crime to ask him questions, he had taken me for granted, he had assumed I had no right to ask him anything, that I had no options, that I was at his mercy now and I couldn't do a thing to change this. Well, the fact was that Bright Shirt was right.

I had no options, I had to board the train now I had come this far. Because wasn't this what Ithim and I had been waiting for all this while?

◆◆◆

We will all be quiet now, no more distractions, no more whispering in these footnotes, let Mr Jay's story move towards its end, smooth and unhindered.

20. *Night of the Scorpion, Jump from the Train*

MY mother, my father and the night of the scorpion, all three slipped into the train from some place far, far away, many, many years ago. Unmindful of the train's sway and jerk, they must have moved, on tiptoe, unseen and unheard, put one foot on the lower berth where Bright Shirt and Ithim were and then climbed onto the upper berth where I lay, resting my head on the bag, rolled up to serve as a pillow. It had been more than an hour since we had pulled out of the station. The train's rhythmic clatter, the soft padding of the berth under my back, the dim light in the coach, my legs stretched straight, my stomach heavy after the meal I had so ravenously eaten, the load lifting from my head – that, finally, I was on board – and the hushed sounds from below, of Bright Shirt humming what seemed like a lullaby to Ithim: these together had the same effect as someone gently closing my eyes. And opening to let slip in a dream. Of my mother, my father, the night of the scorpion and, of course, the rain.

I am about nine, ten years old, I have to stand on my toes to reach the light switch on the wall. It's very early in the morning (or it could be very late at night), because it's still dark. It's raining very heavily.

The night had been still and hot, there was a power cut as we went to sleep, Mother, Father and I, so we all slept on the bedroom floor rather than our beds, because the floor was cement and cooler to the touch. The rain must have begun later in the night, after we had fallen asleep.

I woke up to its noise: its drumming on the asbestos sheets of the slum outside, its gurgling down the pipes that hugged the wall of our flat and ran all the way from the terrace to the yard where we played cricket.

Rain is distilled water, my geography teacher said, it's pure, condensed vapour, it's only when it falls down, through the air, that it picks up dirt, the smoke of the city, and once it touches the ground, it picks up everything else. So if you can trap the raindrops the moment they begin their downward journey, not allow them to fall through the sky, if you can put a giant cup or plate right where the clouds are, you will get water purer than you get from any filter in the world.

At this time of night, there is no smoke in the city and less dirt in the air, so I imagine the rain falling cleanly in the yard below. I close my eyes and wait for sleep to drag me back into its folds.

It's then that I hear voices.

Mother and Father are awake. Father is saying something, his words unclear above the noise of the rain. I open my eyes and slowly, like fog in the winter sun, the night clears to show Father sitting on the floor. I hear Mother crying. Power hasn't been restored and I can see the blades of the ceiling fan, flat and unmoving.

'It will be morning in one hour or so,' Father says, 'I will get the doctor.' At first, I think Mother is running a temperature and she is weak but then Mother doesn't cry when she has a fever. Her eyes are closed, her face is drawn as if she is in pain, a lot of pain.

'What happened?' I ask.

I was supposed to be asleep, my question is unexpected, it makes Father turn with a start. 'What are you doing up so late? You go to sleep, it's not morning yet.'

'Why is Mother crying?' I ask.

Mother reaches out with her left hand and holds my hand, I am awake now, I am sitting on the floor, so that Mother is now the only one lying down, between Father and son.

'You go back to sleep,' she says, 'Father is right, you have to go to school tomorrow.'

I want to tell her, no, I want to know what has happened, because I have never seen Mother cry like this. (Only once have I seen her cry but then she was in the kitchen and when I asked, she said it was the smoke.)

'Something bit her, some insect,' says Father, 'if you don't want to sleep now, then sit beside her, hold your mother's hand, near the wrist, and keep pressing hard. Something bit her finger, the poison mustn't spread. I will go light the lantern.'

He gets up and walks out of the room. When he opens the door, the sound of the rain comes gushing in, louder, bringing with it a spray of water drops that shower my face with a million tiny points of cold and wet. 'Close the door,' Mother tells Father, 'he will fall ill if he catches the rain.'

And I sit there, holding Mother's hand, her fingers

covered with their own shadows. In the dark, I can't see any swelling, any bruise, but I keep pressing her wrist with everything I have.

'Not so hard,' she says, and I relax my grip, ease the pressure, but I am still holding, afraid, the task is too much for me, the responsibility immense. Even the slightest wavering and Mother might die. For if I am not careful, the poison will spread from her wrist, run into her veins and her arteries, travel along her arms, her shoulders, her neck, then down again, to her heart and her stomach to her legs to her face to her head her fingers and her toes – the pus, the black blue yellow green.

So I keep pressing her wrist without the courage to look at her, outside it's still raining, harder now, the asbestos sheets clap loudly in the wind and the rain, a section must have come off, slapping the wall that separates our cricket pitch from the slum.

Father is back, with a lantern and some warm water in a bowl. He sits down and in the yellow light I see Mother's face drawn in pain, her eyes closed. 'Keep pressing on the wrist,' Father says, as he dips the end of a towel in the warm water, wrings it nearly dry, and then places it on top of her hand. Now I can see what's causing her so much pain, her thumb is swollen, it's blue and yellow, as if something has entered her, some creature with a yellow tongue and blue eyes and black teeth and is sitting there, refusing to come out, and is breathing poison inside her, waiting for its breath to travel all through her before it decides what to do next.

How long we sit there I am not sure, me holding Mother's hand and Father daubing her fingers and her forehead with the warm towel, but the night begins to fade.

When the water in the bowl has gone cold, Father gets up, leaves, comes back dressed in a shirt and trousers. He takes an umbrella, and, telling me to sit beside Mother, to keep watch, keep pressing, he says he is going to get the doctor.

Mother has fallen asleep by then and I sit there, the thin morning light seeping in through the crack in the door, like the rain itself. I listen to the rain, I look at the light, my fingers on her wrist, in a vicelike grip, I am determined not to let one drop of the poison slip into her body. When my fingers hurt I switch hands, but I do this so fast and in such a manner that her wrist never once goes unattended. I am her son. To save her life is my duty.

My eyes feel as if stones have been tied to each eyelash but I have to keep them open until Father returns. Now that Mother is sleeping, I have to be more careful. I am afraid that if I let my eyes close, even just to blink, the poison will rush in. And so I sit and wait, my legs hurting now, the floor cold, the rain howling outside, the only comfort the rasping sound of Mother breathing, as if it's taking a considerable effort: Mother is alive.

Doctor comes carrying a leather bag, his hair wet from the rain. Father closes the umbrella and props it against the wall; in the lantern light it looks like a huge, wet crow, resting in a puddle. Doctor sits beside Mother, asks me to let go. 'Good job, you have done well,' he says, and I watch him prepare an injection, I turn my eyes away. Father tells me to leave the room. From the veranda, I can hear Mother scream.

I stand near the door, my ears pressed to the wall, my heart racing, one half of my body drenched in the rain that shows no signs of letting up. 'There, it's done,' Doctor tells Father, 'the danger is gone, I have written out a prescription for some ointment you must get when the shops open. And I brought some tablets she should take right away.'

'What was it?' I ask, coming in.

'I told your father,' says Doctor, 'it looks like it was a scorpion. It could have been dangerous but good that your father fetched me; even one more hour and I don't know what would have happened. The scorpion must have died by now, though. Look for it when it's light.'

I stay at home that day, skip school. Father does too.

The power comes back with the rain-soaked sun and once the ceiling fan is switched on, blowing the dank air out of the room, and Mother is fast asleep sedated after the injection, her hand draped in a white bandage, double its size, I fall asleep too. I get up several times during the day as the rain continues, to keep vigil beside Mother, and then once to the balcony to watch the yard below, now under almost a foot of water. (There won't be any cricket today.)

Later in the afternoon, when the maid comes to do the dishes, she finds the scorpion in the drain, just outside the bedroom. After stinging Mother, it must have crawled back there and died. (She calls me to come and look and what strikes me is how small it is. I had seen pictures in books and had always imagined the scorpion to be a monster, with huge poison sacs touching the floor. But here it is, a tiny insect, no longer than my little finger.)

The maid brings a hammer from the kitchen and hits the scorpion. A greenish liquid squirts out. 'That's the poison,' she says, 'you need to do this so that other scorpions can see and don't come to this house.'

I believe it.

It seems the most logical thing in the world. That hitting this creature and hitting it ruthlessly, with no mercy, with a hammer, even when it's dead, is what you need to do, to teach the others a lesson.

So I take the hammer from the maid and I pound the scorpion, I keep hammering away until a bit of the cement chips off the floor, I keep hammering away until the greenish slime dries into a crust, until the scorpion's body turns into paste, until the maid comes running and says, stop it, you will wake up Mother, I keep killing the scorpion until my hands hurt, until I am sure that all the scorpions in the city have seen what I have just done. There is sweat running down my back.

In the evening, Mother wakes up; the maid has cooked dinner, soup and some rice and some fish. Mother sits on the bed and I watch her eat. She reaches out with her bandaged hand and places it on my head. 'I am so lucky,' she says, 'that the scorpion did not get you.'

A few years later, in school, I got a new poetry textbook that had a poem, right at the beginning, called 'The Night of the Scorpion', by Nissim Ezekiel. And to this day, I can recall the lines by heart. *I remember the night my mother was stung by a scorpion. Ten hours of steady rain had driven him to crawl beneath a sack of rice. Parting with his poison – flash of diabolic tail in the dark room – he risked the rain again.* And the poem then described how local farmers came searching for the creature and *buzzed the Name of God a hundred times to paralyse the Evil One.* How their candles and their lanterns threw *giant scorpion shadows on the sun-baked walls.* The father in the poem, *sceptic, rationalist, tried every curse and blessing*, even poured paraffin on the mother's toes and set it on fire. *I watched the flame feeding on my mother,* the poem ended, *I watched the holy man perform his rites to tame the poison with incantation. After twenty hours it lost its sting. My mother only said: Thank God the scorpion picked on me and spared my children.*

I remember that afternoon rushing home with the poem, reading it to my mother, who listened, then asked me to read it again. This was the first time in my life I had read a poem that was about something I didn't need to imagine, something that had happened and had happened to me. I asked Mother how the poet's mother said the same exact thing as she, my mother, had said that night. She smiled in reply: 'Mothers are the same everywhere; they always think about their children first.'

'ARE you OK, Mr Jay? You were talking in your sleep, you were almost shouting.' It was Bright Shirt, standing on the lower berth, his face staring up at me, I could smell his sweat, I could see the colours on his clothes, muted in the dim light from the electric bulb in the coach.

'How much longer?'

'Just a couple of hours,' he said, swinging up, to sit on the berth, at my feet. 'And don't worry about Ithim, he's fast asleep. I have already cleaned him and given him another feed so now there's nothing to worry until tomorrow morning. I covered him with a blanket, I wanted them to reduce the air-conditioning but they said it can't be done.'

'Where are we?' I asked, propping myself on my elbows,

straining to look through the window below my berth. All I could see was a black rectangle, streaks of light, maybe some village, some station where the train wasn't supposed to stop. I also saw lines of water on the window, from outside. Maybe it was the water condensing, or maybe rain.

'I told you, sir, about two hours to go. I will wake you up when it's time, you can go back to sleep now.' And then he added, almost as an afterthought: 'Just one thing I wanted to tell you. We aren't getting off at a station, we are going to get off in between two stations.'

'What do you mean, between two stations?'

'To save time. I will pull the chain, then jump out of the window.'

'But the windows are sealed.'

'No, I have found a way out, in the next coach, there's a window that can be opened and no one will see me there while everyone is fast asleep. I'm going to pull the chain and jump with Ithim in the bag. Not to worry, I can do that, given my size. But you should be at the entrance. The moment I pull the chain, the train will begin to slow down; don't wait for it to come to a dead stop, but when it slows down enough, to a pace you think you can handle, jump. I will be waiting and then you can follow me. We will have to walk fast, we may even have to run the first few minutes.'

'But why? Why can't we get off at a station and then take a bus or something, go from there? This is too risky.'

'It's not, this is the tenth time today I will be doing this. This way, we save more than three hours, since the closest stop is at least a hundred miles away from where we have to go. Also, it will be dark, no one will see us, no one from inside the coaches will even know the train has stopped. And by the time the guard wakes up, finds out it was our coach where the chain was pulled, it will be too late, we will be far away. At the most, he will curse us, call us all sorts of names. But it's late in the night, he will wave the green flag for the driver, return to his coach and fall asleep.'

At any other time (in fact, until a couple of hours ago, before I had met Bright Shirt), if someone had proposed this, I would have put my foot down, said no way, are you crazy? But I had decided, back at the station itself, that if I was going to let myself be led, I shouldn't let myself be weighed down with doubts and apprehensions. Yes, in deciding this, I knew I was taking a gigantic leap of faith, but then hadn't I already taken that leap in the morning, stepping out of the house with Ithim in a bag? (The problem was that I had taken the leap and was still in midair, the earth rushing up to meet me, and I wasn't letting go. Well, now I would do it, I would let myself land wherever the gravity of the earth or the wings in my feet took me.)

So I smiled at Bright Shirt and said: 'Anything you say.'

'That's the spirit, sir,' he said, not showing the slightest surprise over my ready acquiescence, as he clambered down to his berth. 'You try to catch some sleep now. I will wake you up when it's time.'

But sleep didn't come.

I sat up on the berth, my head almost touching the ceiling. To my left, I could see a display board, the letters painted in red, the paint uneven, congealed into lumpy drops at the tips of the letters. *Secure luggage with wire ropes provided under the seat*, *To Stop Train Pull Chain, Penalty for Use Without Reasonable and Sufficient Cause, Fine up to Rs 1000 and/or Imprisonment up to One Year.* Bright Shirt, of course, knew all this and I was ready to go to prison for one year.

Wide awake, I closed my eyes, covered them with the back of my right palm. Once again, I saw Mother sleeping on the cold cement floor, I heard the rain pouring in the dark outside, I saw the scorpion lying dead, its pincers mangled under the weight of the hammer. This wasn't a dream, I was sure of that – it was definitely a memory but why had I remembered it now? What could have been the trigger? Try hard as I did, I couldn't place it at all.

(When my mother died, I remember coming back home after the funeral, after setting her on fire – all the while standing in front, instead of tears I had been gripped with fear, afraid the logs of wood stacked on top of her would fall and I would be then forced to watch her burn – and seeing friends and relatives filling the house and hoping that by doing this they could crowd out my grief. They told me what a responsible son I had been, how I had taken care of my mother once Father had died, how strong I was and how perfectly capable I was of doing justice to her memory. And once they had left, once their words had slid down my body and collected in tired little heaps on the floor along with the dust from their shoes and the petals of the flowers that had decked Mother's body, more than the grief, I had felt a crushing, permanent sense of loss: gone was the only person in the world who, every time she looked at me, however old I may have been or would become, would see a child, someone no one else would or could ever see. I haven't been able to fill that loss and I don't think I ever will, although I wonder what makes me want to be seen still as a child when I am now a father. So, perhaps, the prospect of losing my wife, of Ithim losing his mother, had taken me back to that night when a boy sat on the floor in the rain trying to save his mother's life. Or maybe it was the other way around, maybe because I had not heard my wife talk about Ithim yet, this had prompted me to recall Mother's words on that night of the scorpion, that *mothers are the same everywhere, they always think of their children first*.)

Or maybe I was just playing around.

With my thoughts. Letting my heightened anticipation of what lay ahead make my mind mirror the train. Hurtling in the dark, careening, swaying, threatening to switch tracks, get derailed, fly off. Land on the ground in a heap of twisted metal and debris. I had to rein it in, bring it back on track. I would do this by reading Miss Glass's message again. That sheaf of papers in the bag.

MISS Glass's message. Yes, that was it, would focus my thoughts, push this clutter away. I took the pages out from the bag, let the bag hang on the hook below the display board, let it swing in arcs with the train. And I read Miss Glass's message again.

'Please read them carefully,' she had written, 'they need time and concentration. It will help you and it will help me if you read them before you reach the station . . .' Sitting in Mr Meeko's cybercafe, I had read these pages once but then the details had been drowned in the swirl of events that had followed. Now I was captive – there were at least two hours to go before I had to jump off the train (I couldn't believe I had said yes to Bright Shirt's Bright Idea) – why not read the three messages again? And I decided that this time, I would read them as if I were at work, in my office, making sense of research reports. With a clear head for facts and figures, numbers and data.

I began with the first attachment, about Tariq and his mother, and I looked at the picture that prefaced the text, the charred house, the burnt windows and the missing ceiling. And there it was, staring at me, it didn't take me even a minute to notice it: the pavement.

I was looking at something I had seen earlier, long before Miss Glass had sent me the message, in fact, even before Miss Glass had made the telephone call that night. It was the image I had found in her room in the Burns Ward.

This was the complete picture.

So did this mean that what I had seen in the hospital was a foreshadow of things to come?

My eyes raced through the pages and over the words, over the description of Shabnam running, her feet on fire, past Ahmed's Meat Shop, past the shoe shop and Rehman Tailoring, the three shops that I had seen that morning, charred and burnt. So she was in my neighbourhood last night?

And then the poems.

The four-line stanzas, the second and the fourth lines rhyming, simple sentences, in Miss Glass's message, in all the three attachments. In Tariq: *Ma don't you worry, you won't feel the pain, the fire will be gone, now will come the rain.* In Shabnam: *Black magic, white magic, brown magic, blue, whatever the colour, I will still get you.* And throughout the third attachment. *Let's get it over with, just as we did, the auto-rickshaw man, and the woman who hid.*

And it was this rhyming that Bright Shirt used too when I met him at the railway station. His silly poems about *you look quite beat, So let's sit down for a while, and get something to eat* and about Ithim being *like a star in the night*, and did I really *want to fix him right*? The same scheme, the same trivial tone. Who was the author then of the three messages?

Miss Glass hadn't mentioned anything about that, she said she had taken some pictures. Maybe it was Bright Shirt himself. Bright Shirt, this jokester, this buffoon who was now sleeping soundly?

What had started out as an attempt to unravel everything had now ended up tying me further and further into knots, throwing up questions that generated more questions, until I had to close my eyes again in what seemed to be a futile effort to escape the confusing circle in which I found myself hopelessly trapped.

I tried to think it through, bring logic to the equation, but even assuming my hunch was on the right track, even if I were to go along with the hypothesis that there had to be some link between the three incidents, the three killings, what did any of that have to do with Miss Glass and her message? Other than the fact I lived in the neighbourhood that Shabnam – possibly – ran across late in the night when I was asleep with Ithim? And what did this all have to do with Ithim? And this journey? And setting him right?

'The time has come
To jump off the train,
You go to the door
While I pull the chain.

Don't you worry, sir,
Very safe is your Ithim,
Wherever we go,
You'll always be with him.'

That infuriating, singsong voice again, that nasal whine, that rhyme, Bright Shirt was now standing, smoothing his shirt, his hair, adjusting his glasses, smiling at me.

'You didn't sleep a wink,' he said.

'No, I was reading Miss Glass's message. Tell me one thing, Bright Shirt, did you write it?'

No, he wasn't going to give anything away, this clown.

'Give me that bag,
Let me put Ithim inside.
Just look what unfolds
And keep those questions aside.'

And he climbed onto my berth, to pull the chain.
Everything went exactly as per plan.

On the way to the entrance of the coach, I passed an old woman returning to her berth from the toilet. She turned sideways to let me pass, our eyes didn't even meet. And it became clear to me that Bright Shirt had, indeed, done his homework. As he had pointed out, almost everyone was fast asleep; it was almost midnight and being an air-conditioned coach, all the passengers were concealed behind curtains, thick and heavy, fastened by loops made of cloth that ensured they stayed in place despite the movement of the train. The safe passage these curtains provided was made safer by the dim blue-green of the nightlights overhead.

When I reached the end of the coach and opened the door, all I could see was the blackness rushing by, the shapes of trees, telegraph poles, and what looked like distant hills set against the sky. A narrow strip of light, from inside the coach, raced over the stone-chipped bank outside; we must have been passing through empty fields because I couldn't see a single street lamp or a village lantern. How did Bright Shirt know where to stop the train? There was no obvious landmark.

But, almost as if on cue, there was a piercing, hissing noise, like steam being released under extreme pressure from some monster hydraulic machine. Brakes squealing, the train's clatter began to quieten slowly and steadily until it became a creak and a whine and the train slowed down.

I peered out, the air slapped me hard on the face, tore at my hair. I could see Bright Shirt and Ithim now halfway out of the window, Bright Shirt waving at me, gesturing to me to jump. But how could I? The train was still moving too fast. Then I saw him jump, a blur of bright colour in the black.

So I followed.

The train was still moving when I hit the air.

It was still moving when I hit the ground.

◆◆◆

21. *Water and Canvas*

AND I landed in water although on first impact, it felt nothing like water; there was neither a splash nor a ripple, no wetness, no drag. But it was water, there was no doubt about it. Water that reached up to my knees, water that stretched as far as my eye could see, on either side, in front and behind, the surface stretched out like glass, black, glinting and endless.

'Don't look back, keep moving forward,' Bright Shirt said, standing a few feet away, his vivid colours glowing in the dark, the water up to his chest, inches away from Ithim in his bag.

But I had already turned to look. The train had by now slowed down to a stop and I saw its reflection in the surface of the water, a panoramic view of the train, above and below, its windows, the frosted in the first-class coaches, the barred in the others, a row of lights, dim and yellow, tiny rectangles all arranged in a straight line. Its blue coaches now black rectangles silhouetted against the sky. So placid was the water and along with it the reflection of the train that it seemed I was looking at a painting, perhaps *Still Life, Train at Night*, the black canvas stretched tight, taut from one end of the sky to the other. Adding to this effect was the silence and the odd colour of the sky, not black as in the city, but more a deep shade of purple like an over-ripe plum, the stars sprayed like flecks of powdered sugar. Even the low-hanging moon sparkled, as if someone had climbed up and scrubbed it clean; it had not one dark smudge.

'Where are we?' I asked Bright Shirt, my voice so magnified by the silence that I was surprised by its loudness.

'Let's go,' he said in reply, 'let's get out of here before the guard finds out. Keep walking and hurry up.'

I turned, my back to the train now, and took the first step forward. In that expanse of water, there was no sign of any trail or road I could use to navigate, but Bright Shirt was the guide and I followed. He seemed to glide, with an amphibian ease and grace, as if he knew every inch of the terrain, above and below. I have crossed through flooded streets in the city but here it took me a while before I could fall in step, before I could move forward without constantly having to look down to see where I was treading. For, one, each step I took was noiseless, making it confusing, if not impossible, to believe that I was really walking at all. And, two, the surface was so clear, so transparent, that in the soft light of the scrubbed moon and the flecked stars, I could not but keep looking at what lay below. So I was torn between looking down and looking forward, between stopping and moving.

And ironically, it was when I looked down that I realized I needed no compass, no sense of direction. Because instead of what I had expected to see – dirt tracks, grass, mud, saplings, stones – I saw below my feet a ribbon of concrete, black and smooth, streaked by broken white lines. Exactly like the new highways springing up just outside the city. This black strip was complete with road reflectors and cat's eyes that glittered in the dark like corals on a seabed I had once seen on TV.

'Where are we?' I asked Bright Shirt again, this time more sure of my footing.

'Miss Glass calls it The Hideout,' he said, stopping in his tracks and waiting, politely, for me to catch up. 'This is where they will come, we hope, those running away from the city on fire. Those who can run, those who cannot. The city has set up shelters for the living, the relief camps, but when Miss Glass went to look, she found neither relief nor a camp. Just open spaces baking in the heat, crammed with men, women and children, more women and children than men. She walked on the hard stone floor, she saw flies get trapped in her hair, she saw children playing hide and seek in portable toilets that overflowed with stench and sludge. She saw food being cooked in ovens, food that no one dared touch since it was fried on flames. She saw the fear of fire in their eyes, and she said we have to have this place, we have to have The Hideout. That's why we decided there will be water here, wherever you can see, to ensure there is no fire. Never ever. Even if someone tries, no spark will light here, no flame will burn. That's why in the dark the only glow is that provided by the people and their clothes and their skin and the things under the water themselves. The tiniest accident has to be avoided, so no house here has any electricity connection either; we can't take the slightest chance with sparks, especially when there is so much water around. Let's go a little farther ahead and then you will see what we have done, what she has done, Miss Glass. She is amazing, she is our saviour, she is our angel.'

These words came in a torrential although muted whisper as if Bright Shirt didn't want to disturb anyone in the dark. Since we had met, this was the most he had spoken in one uninterrupted stretch, and as if he was suddenly and acutely aware of this, he then lapsed into silence, turning to walk away, not waiting to see what effect these words had on me.

Just when they were sinking in, his bizarre explanation, I heard a noise from behind. It was the train, its wheels beginning to move again, along with their reflection in the water, both gathering speed until that sound, too, faded into the overwhelming silence that now draped The Hideout.

How long we walked I lost track of but what I am sure of is how another memory of my mother came back, this time with the first sight of the first house. From where I was, it looked like any ordinary dwelling in a marooned village or town, a low brick structure looming in the dark, ringed by water. Almost exactly like the house my parents had lived in, before they moved to the city. My mother had showed me its photograph and told me its story, how one monsoon it had rained non-stop for nine days, how the river had breached its banks and floodwater had inundated the entire ground floor and some of the first as well so that my parents, my mother then pregnant with me, had to live on the roof for three days and nights, scanning the skies for the sight of an army helicopter – they called it Big Bird – hovering above to drop packets of rice and sugar onto the roof. And when the packets landed in the water instead, the sound they made, my mother said, would break her heart because she knew that I – who was still inside her – would have to go hungry. ('Mothers always think about their children first,' she had said.)

'Look.' Bright Shirt was pointing to the house that had suddenly loomed out of the dark as if it had sprung up right there, right then, in front of our eyes. 'These are houses we built only last night once we knew the number of the dead would keep rising. Aren't they special?' There was no mistaking the note of admiration in his voice.

And it was not without reason.

For this was a house like nothing I had seen before. What at first glance seemed like an ordinary brick structure, the kind in Mother's photograph, was actually planned with meticulous and, if I may add, fanciful care. It was just inches above the water level so water lapped against its doors and its walls, making it seem that the house was perched on a tiny invisible island. When I walked closer, almost to its door as if to knock – 'Don't be afraid, just go and look,' Bright Shirt encouraged me – I realized that not only was there water around the house, it was inside as well.

This was a house of air and water, air outside, water within, water that made its walls quiver, as if the house were a living creature that had just come to the surface to breathe before diving back into the depths.

'They are so happy here,' Bright Shirt said, standing behind me, so close that I could feel the breath of his words.

They were three people, a family: a mother, a father and a child, son or daughter I couldn't see, as I looked through the window. The windowpanes were made of pale blue glass through which I could see a soft yellow light filling the space inside. It was like a tank or a huge pool in which they were swimming, bathed by the glow and the silent ripples of the water. I saw the graceful strokes of their legs, their arms, powering them forward, their hair billowing behind perfectly, like in movies, little bubbles of air breaking free from their lips.

'Who are they?' I asked and Bright Shirt shrugged his shoulders, glided away into the distance. 'We are losing count,' he said, 'we can't keep track of the names, of the details. We are getting them by the hour, by the minute. These three were killed last night, all of them sleeping when the house was set ablaze. The fire spread so fast the child didn't even wake up.'

He ended the sentence and the second house appeared, making me stop in my tracks suddenly. I faltered, almost fell face down into the water, tripping over something unseen, unfelt. For the first time since I had been told about the city on fire, I could feel a chill creeping from my toes up, so strong and so deep that it made even the water around me colder to the touch, on my knees and around my calves. There it was, in a house identical to the previous one, a house lit inside and full of water, just in front of me the kitchen I had seen, just hours ago on the train, in the message about the old schoolteacher, in the third attachment Miss Glass had sent.

This was Abba's kitchen.

Except that the kitchen here was arranged almost to perfection, with the same objects as the one in the picture, the same cups and plates, the same dishes, the same kettle, the same clothes on one wall, the two dish racks on two walls, one with the tiny two-shelf cupboard with a white frame, the walking stick on the floor, a charred log of wood in the centre but everything was suffused with a back-lit radiance of the kind they have in magazine photographs of model kitchens. And, of course, everything was under water. As I stared into this room, cold with disbelief, a woman swam in, a young woman whose face I could not see. She swam, she glided, she flitted from one end of one wall to the other, picking up items from the shelves, arranging them, rearranging, as if she were working in the kitchen but, surprisingly, leaving the items lying on the floor untouched.

'That look familiar, Mr Jay?' Bright Shirt was smiling and his eyes had a gleam I had not seen before. 'Look into the other room,' he said, and gestured towards the next room in the same house where there was another woman, older and heavier, also arranging things, what looked like a schoolbag and books on a table. She was wearing a blue sari and her long black hair unfurled behind her in the water. Was she the woman in the first attachment, was she Tariq's mother? Bright Shirt had reached into the bag and pulled out the sheets of paper, Miss Glass's message. 'You want to read these again?' I tore the pages away from him; I didn't need to read them, yes these were the pictures I had seen on the train.

And here, in The Hideout, these pictures had taken a life of their own.

It's at this point that I should have stopped, that any man, any woman, with any sense of what is real and what is not would have stopped.

*

I SHOULD have let my head clear, I should have taken a step back, seen through the absurdity of it all, I should have told Bright Shirt that no, I wasn't buying any of this, that it wasn't happening, that this construction, apparition, whatever you may call it, had to be little more than a dream. (Perhaps I was still on board the train, fast asleep.) It's at this point that I should have told him to give me my Ithim back. And I should have turned, walked back to the railway tracks, followed them to the next station and there I should have waited for the next train to the city and returned home. Six hours coming, six hours going, I would have been back in my room in the morning, Ithim on the bed, safe and sound.

But I did none of these things.

We had already moved away from the two houses and those rooms I had just seen seemed to dissolve in the water so quickly and so effortlessly that I didn't have time to dwell on them at all, my eyes being pulled now by what lay ahead, a setting of such singular beauty that, instead of letting my reason come to the fore, I pushed it back as far as I could and asked Bright Shirt to let Ithim see what I was seeing. I wanted to share it with my child.

Bright Shirt said Ithim was wide awake and he was, indeed, watching the night, the water, the houses of air and water and the people swimming inside. Maybe this was it, I thought, this was the place where Ithim would be set right, in this place called The Hideout, where the water was so special people could live under it. Where pictures, still, and black and white, transform into the scenes they depict, of resplendent colour. It was this belief, anchoring itself as a conviction, that my son's perfect eyes were watching this wondrous spectacle unfold and soon he would be set right that prompted me – instead of turning back as I should have done – to take the next step, the next step, and the next step. Allowing the water to close in, open up, close in, open up and around my feet.

What reinforced this belief was what I saw beyond the houses: children playing under the water. Five, six, seven years old, some even younger, two or three, one was almost a baby, a few months older than Ithim, I think, their faces blurred through the water, their clothes of a material that shone in the dark. They were in a park, there was a playground. There were children on brightly coloured swings that cut smoothly through the water with each arc they took, there were some on slides that shifted gently yet ceaselessly. The children were all swimming, equipped with what seemed like gills on either side of their heads, tiny, wafer-thin shimmering translucent ears that trembled in the water and propelled them forward. If these children had grown gills and taken to the water, maybe the water did have some magical powers, powers that could, as Miss Glass had said, set Ithim right.

As I saw the children, I also saw the scene below the surface shift. Either side of the black concrete strip where I was walking, there opened up a landscape of trees and plants, ferns and sea shells of dazzling colours. Fish that swam in and out of the leaves once in a while, coming to the surface where they would turn into birds and then fly away into the dark, leaving a trail of sparkling water drops in the air. Under the purple-plum sky.

'Miss Glass is the one behind all that you see,' said Bright Shirt. 'She chose this place because it's not far from the city and yet no one there knows about it. In fact, in the daytime if you come here, there's nothing; the water dries up and it's like any other landscape seen from the window of a railway train. The kind of place you pass by, not worth a second glance.'

'What happens to all these people, these houses, the children during the day?' I asked, knowing very well that whatever answer I got would defy logic and reason just as the scene in front of me did.

'They go all around, wherever they want. Some of them rest in the trees, the children dance on the tips of the leaves or hide under blades of grass. Some of the adults roam the city trying to see if anything has been left behind in houses that are now burnt down. They sift through debris, they pick up, they leave behind. Maybe you saw some of them on your way from the mall to the station this afternoon.'

'Give me my Ithim,' I shouted – screamed – making Bright Shirt stop, a puzzled look on his face at this sudden outburst, completely unconnected with what he had just been telling me.

Or was it?

For hours now, since the afternoon in the railway station when he had taken Ithim from me – you rest for a while, he had said, let me carry him – I had not held my son. Even in the train, I had climbed onto the upper berth and dozed off, secure in the belief that Bright Shirt was taking good care of Ithim. (Which he was, there was no doubt about that. In fact, it had struck me, watching both of them on several occasions, that Bright Shirt displayed an unusual tenderness in his affection, almost a sense of familiarity that I doubt even I had. Perhaps this was the very reason that I wanted Ithim with me. For if there was one thing the events of the last few hours – or were they last few minutes? I can never be sure – had done to me, it was to make me doubt every thing that I had so far taken for granted, including the fact that Ithim was mine and would remain with me. So when I saw my child with Bright Shirt, it fuelled a fear that I could be losing my grip not only on myself but over my child as well.)

'Here, take him,' Bright Shirt said, 'yes, I think it's now your turn, I have been lugging this young man for a while now.'

The bag still covering Ithim, since I didn't want even an accidental splash of a water drop on him, I showed him the playground below the water, I showed him fishes, the black concrete, the white broken line marking the lanes. I stopped at a window and showed him the inside of a house, the nursery there, a cot and walls brightly coloured, toys that floated and swam. I showed him a mother who was sitting in a rocking chair, swaying, like mothers in English storybooks, a child in her lap, I knew Ithim couldn't hear but still I told him his mother was waiting for him in the hospital and she would do that too and tell him stories. And I told him he had the best story of them all. He had seen what no child ever sees, except in movies or comic books; he had seen a fairy-tale land and he was the one now who knew all its tales.

Ithim blinked at me and I saw the drops glittering on his eyelashes and I knew they were tears of joy, of amazement. Maybe he realized too, in his one-day-old head, not fully formed, the bones still moving underneath the skin, that the time had come for him to be set right.

*

FROM the seemingly sublime to the obviously ridiculous, there's no other way to describe what happened next. The Hideout soon gave way to The Tent, the water ending as abruptly as it had begun, petering out into a ring of slush and mud that spattered the edges of a sprawling canvas tent, not unlike one of thousands of such tents that sprout in lawns and parks during the wedding season in the city. But this one had no such pretensions. It was a tent, plain and simple and makeshift, with naked light bulbs fastened with electric wiring on bamboo poles, one more indication that we had left The Hideout behind, we had left the world with no fires, not even a spark.

There was no denying, though, that this semblance of normalcy, in the setting, if not the circumstances, came as a great comfort after The Hideout. But when Bright Shirt lifted the canvas flap at the entrance and Ithim and I walked in, I saw this was no tent for a gathering; it was more like a venue for a performance, a show: there were rows and rows of seats, all plastic chairs with armrests, facing a stage.

The red chairs were closest to the stage, set in seven concentric rows. Behind them was the blue section, another set of concentric circles, this time about ten or eleven or even a dozen, and behind the blue was the white – the same chairs in all three sections, just different colours – and it was in the rear, where the last row of white chairs ended, that the gallery began. Wooden planks arranged in steps, empty spaces in between, like a tiered arena, almost a dozen or so tiers. And while the chairs were empty, red, blue and white, I could see the gallery was crowded, almost crammed. When we entered, the lights inside had been switched off leaving just the stage lights on. The red section, therefore, was the only one that was lit, the gallery was in shadow.

'We will be here.' Bright Shirt pointed to a chair in the very first row. 'These are special seats, you can see everything clearly.

'Please bear with this, sir, please.' Bright Shirt's tone was back to being cloying and apologetic, just as it was at the railway station when he had first met me. 'Except for Miss Glass and myself, no one here knows anything about you, or Ithim, or that you are here with me. Before we begin, there is this little thing that we need to do for the audience, to keep them entertained.'

I couldn't say a word; I didn't know what word to say.

'Don't you worry,' said Bright Shirt. 'Mr Jay, it will be for about five minutes or so, just a little juggling act. And then a short play in which all your questions will be answered. Here, let me take Ithim. I think he needs a feed and cleaning up. I will get him right back, we will let him watch the show as well.'

So comfortable and reassuring his tone was that I didn't even think twice. That I, who had just retrieved Ithim from him, afraid I was losing control, now just sat back in the red chair and handed over my child, let him go. From behind, from the gallery, I could hear noises, claps, laughs, a hushed roar like the sound of a radio cricket commentary.

At first, I thought the show hadn't begun because I saw several people on stage and none of them seemed to be performers, no one in any costume – in fact, Bright Shirt seemed to be the only one dressed for the occasion – all men and women, young and old and poor, their clothes torn, their faces drawn, some sweeping the floor, some pulling at a thick nylon cord that activated a pulley high above the ground, some dragging tables and chairs on or off the stage.

Others were pointing to the band above, in a balcony above the stage: four men, one with a guitar, another at a synthesizer, the third on the drums and the fourth, a flute, and they were tuning their instruments, adjusting their speakers and the lights. And all this was going on right in front of the audience, in their full view, the curtains raised, the stage being set, the props being put in place.

Where had Bright Shirt taken Ithim?

Suddenly I was seized by a fear that Ithim would be put on display, maybe that's why the pulleys were there, to hoist him atop a platform that would move around giving everyone a ringside view of his blinking, his perfect eyes and his deformed form. Like the Ukrainian man and the Korean woman.

(I had heard that in some villages near the city they did hold such shows, and perhaps I had been trapped into bringing Ithim here so that they could take him away from me, for ever. And, yes, Ithim was such that people would come from far and wide to look at him, even if they had to pay ten–fifteen rupees per ticket. They would come and point at him and say, look, look at this boy, can he shout and scream? see if it twitches, can he feel? touch him, run your fingers down his charred forehead, check if he can smell, bring a lighted match to his face, see if he can smell the burning, see if the heat makes him draw back, look at his eyes and his eyelashes and his eyebrows, he looks like a monkey, can he jump, can he make faces, can he cry through those eyes, let's hit him on the face and see if the monkey-face gets wet.)

Bright Shirt was nowhere to be seen; all I could see were the shapes in the gallery, heads and arms and legs, no face in the audience visible in the dark. Bright Shirt had said no one was aware of me but they must have seen me enter, sit in the first row where the lights were. But, no, that seemed unlikely since I was now in the dark, not visible and no one, either in the gallery or the stage, showed even the faintest sign of any acknowledgement of my presence.

Applause broke my train of thought, the wave of cheers came from behind me, from my left and my right, even from my front, meeting in a swirl where I was seated, breaking up into eddies and currents, churning, the froth and the foam drowning whatever doubts I might have had. The stage lights dimmed and the first performer walked in to an announcement on the microphone, so scratchy and loud, whining with the feedback from the machine, that I couldn't make out a single word.

A thin wiry man, his eyes narrow, his hair straight, he was wearing a white shirt and black trousers and a long white overcoat complete with a bowler hat, he had a Charlie Chaplin moustache and even his trousers had that loose, ill-fitting feel, crinkled at the knees and bunched near the toes. Face deadpan, his moustache kept twitching as if it had a life of its own. His feet doing a continuous trot, jump, shuffle, he took a bow and, to a drum roll, four clowns came onto the stage, all dwarves, reaching barely to the man's knees. They circled him, kept pointing to him and laughing.

From where I sat, right in front, I could see the colour of the costumes the clowns wore had faded, the paint on their face was rough and cracked, light in some places and dark in others. One clown turned his back to the audience, made a gesture as if he would pull his trousers down, sending the crowd again into rapturous applause.

Then, from his trouser pockets, one in front and one behind, Clown 1 took out four coloured balls and tossed them at the man, who lurched forward and began to juggle them in the air. Within minutes, a second clown, Clown 2, tossed another ball at Juggler who thus had to deal with five and then Clown 3 joined in, then Clown 4 and Clown 5 until Juggler was moving fast and furious, the music loud from the balcony, Juggler keeping eight balls in the air, his moustache twitching all along, when suddenly everything slowed down including the tempo of the music and a hush fell over the audience at the sight of another clown, Clown 6, walking onto the stage holding a blazing torch – a piece of cloth soaked in kerosene tied around what looked like a short bamboo pole – in one hand and a stack of giant steel rings on his other arm.

The Juggler, too, had slowed down, the balls still in the air but now moving perceptibly slower as if the air itself had become thicker, more viscous. Clowns 1 to 5 were now sitting in a ring on the stage around Juggler, making faces of worry, arching their eyebrows, nodding their heads, pulling their lips, resting their chins on their palms, as if they were thinking, as if they were contemplating what Clown 6 would do. This mock concern made the crowd titter but there was no mistaking a certain tension in the air.

Clown 6 started to hurl one ring after another at Juggler, each ring about four feet in diameter, each ring so accurately thrown that it fell over Juggler's head, slid down his chest, and the moment it reached his waist Juggler began to sway faster and faster to keep the ring from sliding down to his feet, all this while still balancing the eight balls in the air.

Clowns 1 to 5 now stared at Juggler with exagger-ated amazement, as he twirled his waist to keep the rings in the air, twirled his arms to keep the balls from falling to the floor, tilted his head to balance both, shuffled his feet, until he became a blur of movement, his face, his head, his neck, his shoulders, his chest, his waist, his legs, his knees. The crowd was on its feet now, cheering the man who could juggle horizontal, vertical, circular, sideways, up and down. And when some people from the gallery began shouting to him to stop because just watching him was making them giddy, Clown 6 walked up to the front of the stage, sneaked up from behind Juggler, thrust the flaming torch to his feet, and set his trousers alight.

At first it was a tiny flame that licked the end of Juggler's trousers, almost dancing over his shoes as if in step with him and then it spread. Over his calves, hugging his trouser legs, up his thighs to his overcoat, catching his shirtsleeves until Juggler himself was on fire, the flames engulfing his entire body. Juggler screamed but the applause was now so deafening that no one heard him, Clown 6 was dancing, repeatedly pointing to the fire, Clowns 1 to 5 sat in the ring, staring at Juggler with their mouths wide open.

One by one, the balls fell to the floor, as did the steel rings, with a clatter, and Juggler was now running from one end of the stage to the other, blazing, still shuffling his feet, performing his trot and his jig as if the flames weren't there. There was a smell of burnt rubber in the air as Juggler fell down, playing dead, the clowns began crying, their tears mixing with the paint on their faces as they lifted one of his hands, still burning, and then let it fall as if it belonged to a corpse.

They dragged his fiery, inert frame across the stage, over the sawdust, they dragged him like he was a gunny bag, his arms flopping by his sides, one of them stepped onto his face and pounded it with his shoes and all this while the crowd kept laughing, the fire kept burning.

Clown 6, who had slunk into a corner of the stage, was now back in action, but this time he came on empty-handed, stood beside the burning Juggler and then went down on his knees and began licking the flames. Clown 6 had become the Fire-Eater.

Like a dog sniffing or nibbling at a bag lying on the street, Clown 6 started from Juggler's feet. His tongue darting in and out, his face stretched tight with the paint, drenched with sweat and his eyes glowing, Clown 6 was eating the fire, swallowing the flames. By now, the crowd in the gallery behind me was on its feet cheering him and the other clowns stood in a line, clapping, as Clown 6 moved up the legs over the knees over the waist the coat the shirt the neck the hair. And his lips and his tongue left in their wake wisps of smoke on Juggler's frame until the last flame had been licked clean.

Juggler got up, his clothes charred, his face surprisingly untouched, hugged Clown 6 and, together, they walked off the stage in a cloud of blue-black smoke. Clown 6 threw his head back, began to blow smoke rings from the fire he had just eaten.

More applause.

*

'You didn't want Ithim to see this, did you?'

In all the excitement, I hadn't even noticed that Bright Shirt was back, sitting next to me, without Ithim.

'He's sleeping, Mr Jay, don't worry, I didn't want to bring him here in all this noise. He has had a long day,' Bright Shirt said.

He smiled. 'Sorry, Mr Jay, I told them it was a silly idea but Miss Glass said let them do it, at least it will serve as a distraction, just to keep these people entertained, to let them know that they shouldn't be afraid of fire. It's the next act where you come in, Mr Jay, that's where all your questions, the questions you have been carrying all along, will be answered. So listen carefully. And you have to excuse me, since I am involved in it, too. I will meet you backstage once the whole thing is over. And don't worry about Ithim, he's absolutely safe.'

Bright Shirt got up, stopped after he had taken a few steps, turned back and said: 'And Miss Glass is in this, Mr Jay, Miss Glass, our Angel you named last night.' And then he vanished into the dark.

What followed next, I shall not describe, I shall only report.

I shall not comment lest you charge me later with deception.

I shall not do anything to influence you. That's why I have to change the narrative itself, present events just as they were. The last act, so to speak, in this drama of the absurd.

A play, in two short acts.

◆◆◆

22. *The Last Act – I*

AS the curtains begin to go up, they reveal a stage draped in darkness. The audience is silent, you can hear only the rustle of the curtains and the sound of water lapping, sloshing, flowing, gurgling. Soft at one time, loud at another. Clowns 1, 2, and 3 glide noiselessly through the water, each holding a high chair, with a small backrest. They leave the chairs and walk off the stage. You can see there's something on each chair, although what those things are you can't see. The curtains are fully drawn, the lights come on, bright and harsh, three overhead spotlights trained below, one on each chair. And then the lights move. They move across to show that the entire stage is flooded, the water almost knee-deep; just like in The Hideout, it laps against the legs of the chairs, against the low wall that skirts the edge of the stage to prevent the water from spilling over. The lights then travel behind the chairs, up above the wall, where the water cannot reach, where you can see three pictures, the pictures we saw earlier in the attachments: Tariq's burnt house, the burnt auto-rickshaw belonging to Shabnam's father and Father's burnt kitchen. But each picture now has been blown up, to almost life size, so you can see details that until now were invisible. Like the number of leaves in the sapling on the pavement outside the house, 17; the red and yellow lines on the No-Entry plate of the auto-rickshaw; in Abba's house, the ceiling fan burnt, its three blades twisted and drooped, like grey trousers left out to dry and the number of steel dishes, 9; the number of small white china plates, 8. After your eyes have registered these three pictures, you can now see clearly what lies on each chair. There is BOOK *on the first chair from the left,* WATCH *in the middle and* TOWEL *on the last chair, the legs of each chair submerged in the water which reflects the lights in its ripples.*

From off stage, a voice speaks.

It belongs to a woman and it's clearly MISS GLASS.

She remains off stage throughout.

MISS GLASS Forgive the flooding; we had to do this to make everyone here feel safe, just like we have done in The Hideout. Because everyone here said we aren't walking anywhere, we aren't sitting anywhere until we are sure that there's water, at least up to our knees. So that we feel the cold, so that we feel the wet. (*Sound of splashing.*) Because we have never heard of any one setting water on fire. (*For one moment, the splashing gets louder, there is a murmur in the audience before silence descends again.*)

BOOK (*Flaps a few of its pages, speaks in a boy's voice.*) Miss Glass, I don't need water, my pages take too long to dry. As for fire, when I am closed, air can't reach my pages, can't feed the flames. You can char my edges, of course. As they did last night.

WATCH (*Speaks in a man's voice.*) Fire melts my straps but water fogs my dial. Best to leave me high, best to leave me dry.

(*They both look at* TOWEL, *who is silent.*)

MISS GLASS Just look at Towel, she knows when to speak, when not to disturb. Let me finish. We begin tonight with three characters who are special, special because of what they endured before we picked them up. Look at the pictures on the wall, the charred house, the charred auto-rickshaw, the charred kitchen, these three survived it all. Well, almost. If you don't count Book's charred ears, Watch's cracked dial and the hole in Towel. A little bit of trimming and binding, some polishing and fixing, some stitching and washing and these three will be back in action. They are here because they are eyewitnesses and they are earwitnesses. And unlike us, people who were killed, these three are objects. That's why their story will be objective. And their words will, therefore, carry more weight. Book shall begin. Watch will follow and then Towel.

(*The stage falls dark again, there is now the sound of a wind blowing. One spotlight is switched on, its beam lights up* BOOK, *the other two are switched off. The water is now still.* BOOK *catches a bit of the wind, lifts its cover, then lets it fall, begins to speak.*)

BOOK My name is Learning to Communicate, I was edited and illustrated in New Delhi, many of my 124 pages were originally written in London, I was packed in Mumbai, I came to this city in a cardboard box, on a train, there were 500 of us. It was raining and they had wrapped us in plastic and canvas so that water couldn't seep in. When we reached the city, at the station, there was a man from the school who had come to pick us up. We all went our different ways, I reached the house of a boy called Tariq. That's my introduction. Now to that night. It was, in fact, early in the morning, very early. (*The sound of the wind gets louder, the water is still.*) Tariq had opened me to page 43, he had homework to do. He switched the fan on and to keep my pages from flapping, he put a pencil on my spine, my favourite pencil. Tariq never studies at the table, he lies down on the floor, props his face on one elbow, like he did that morning as he began writing the answers on my page. The chapter he was working on was called *Fire in a Hotel*. It was about a man called John Brown and a dog called Chum.

John Brown is a blind man, Chum is his dog, his seeing-eye dog. One day, Mr Brown decided he needed a vacation and so he and Chum took the train to the village. As I told you, this chapter was written in London, so this is an English village with rolling hills and forests and meadows and a narrow country road, smooth, no potholes, no dirt, like in this city . . .

WATCH We get it, we get it, an English village. We have seen it on TV. There was a similar picture in an ad for me once, the picture of a woman at the door, looking at her watch, waiting for the school bus. She was a British woman.

BOOK I don't know about that but I have a picture right here of the village, on page 45, maybe someone can turn me to that later. Well, to cut a long story short, after a day of relaxation, Mr Brown sat in a chair and enjoyed the breeze on his face, the smell of the grass. Chum chased rabbits, sheep, butterflies. And they both were very tired.

WATCH Aren't we all?

(*A voice once again, from off stage, it's* MISS GLASS.)

MISS GLASS (*Clearly admonishing.*) Please, Watch, let him finish. Too many interruptions. You will get your turn, too. Book, continue, please.

BOOK That night, a tired Mr Brown and Chum went to sleep. Being a dog, Chum smelled it first, the smoke, and began barking. The hotel was on fire. (*The wind gets louder, ripples begin to disturb the surface of the water.*) Chum barked and barked until Mr Brown woke up, struck with fear. He had been blinded when he was only five or six years old and had therefore never seen a fire in his life. It was late night, the hotel staff were fast asleep. None of them had heard the fire or smelled the smoke. Helped by Chum, who kept pushing him in the leg with his wet snout, Mr Brown walked to the windows, opened them wide for the fresh air to enter. But the fire was in the hallway, smoke came in through the gap beneath the door. Any other dog would have hidden under the bed but Chum was Chum. All that mattered to him was his master's well-being so he jumped onto the bed and began pawing at the bed sheet. When Mr Brown reached out his hand to stroke the dog, his fingers felt the bed sheet and he realized what Chum was doing. He walked to the bathroom, Chum by his side, wet the bed sheet and jammed it in the gap at the bottom of the door. Fire couldn't cross the water in the towel and the sheets. Smoke couldn't enter and fresh air from the windows ensured that Mr Brown was safe. Chum wagged his tail. By this time, the Fire Brigade had arrived.

WATCH That was a good children's story, Book.

BOOK (*Ignores this interruption.*) Tariq had read this story over and over again, he had learnt the lines by heart. For his homework, he had to answer three questions. Where did Mr Brown and Chum go on their vacation? What did they do with the towels and the bed sheet? And describe Chum in fifty words. The boy knew all these answers. In fact, if the wind tonight is strong, I will let the pages flap and you can see that his teacher has always marked Very Good in all his homework lessons, he was a bright boy. But before he could answer these questions, they came.

WATCH Who came, who came, who, who who? Tell us, Book.

BOOK If you keep butting in, I can never tell.

TOWEL (*Speaks for the first time; hers is the softest voice.*) Watch, unlike you, I can't hear very clearly, I am all folded up, I'm also the farthest away from Book, I have to strain to catch every word. Let Book finish and then you can ask your questions.

BOOK Thank you, Towel, I will try to speak louder. I heard Tariq scream, I heard him run, I heard the mother call out to him to go and hide. The pencil rolled out, the one Tariq had placed in my pages to keep them from flapping. Then they walked in, I could see their feet, their legs, their trousers, their slippers, some rubber, some leather. I stood still, I held my breath so hard the pages stopped flapping. I didn't want to draw attention to myself because they would have seen me on the floor, opened, they would have known that there was a boy in the house. I felt something wet and cold touch me, it was the kerosene they had poured onto the floor. I saw the flames. (*The water rises up the legs of the chair on which* BOOK *sits.*) I heard one of them laugh, kick me hard, to the edge of the door from where he kicked me again, out into the street. By then, my ears had caught fire, from page 74 on. But once I was outside, it helped, the wind wasn't so strong, the flames died leaving my edges only scorched. I don't know how to say it, it sounds so selfish, but you know what went through my head at that time?

MISS GLASS (*From off stage.*) You are among friends, Book, just say what's on your mind, don't bother how it makes you look. We are not here to judge.

BOOK Thank you, Miss Glass. When the smoke filled the room, when I heard Tariq scream, when I heard his mother scream, when I saw the flames, when I saw the men, I thought of only one thing, I thought of the little pencil. I thought of the wood in the pencil catching fire. (Maybe the lead would not have burnt, who knows?) I wish they had thrown the pencil out. The pencil, you see, was my best friend. We were always together. Even when I was in Tariq's bag and he was in his box, we were always close.

(BOOK *falls silent. Once again, you hear the sound of water on the stage.*)

WATCH Are you there, Book?

BOOK Where was I? Yes, I was out on the street. And by late that evening, when both of you, Watch and Towel, had joined me, along with the others, the curtain, the slippers, all of us lying in that heap, Tariq came. He wasn't crying, I think he had finished up all his tears for the day. How I wish there had been a wind then so my pages would have flapped, he would have noticed me, he would have picked me up. Taken me home, to my friend, the pencil. But there was nothing. I tried my best to turn a page but I could not move even a millimetre without a wind.

WATCH You saw them? You saw their faces?

BOOK I saw them. I cannot forget their faces. D went for

the mother, B stood by his side, C started the fire, A kicked me outside.

(*The lights switch off, the stage is dark, the sound of the wind again and the water. After a pause, of about fifteen seconds, the second overhead light switches on, this time revealing* WATCH.)

MISS GLASS (*Off stage.*) Watch, it's your turn now. And, please, no interruptions.

WATCH Time is, and has always been, of the essence to me. So unlike Book, I am not going to waste it by going into my background, where I was born, which town, which machine, which watchmaker, which store room, which case, which nonsense. I am going to come straight to the hour, the minute, that second it happened, when they pulled me from Father's wrist. Even Shabnam, the daughter, who was standing there, right there, does not know the details I am about to tell you. Father had parked his auto-rickshaw and walked into the house. The whole day, sitting on his wrist, I had travelled across the city, I had trembled every time he switched gears, I was drenched with his sweat, my dial covered with dust.

BOOK This isn't about you, Watch, tell us what happened to Father.

WATCH (*Ignores this interruption.*) Father walked in, he went straight to the kitchen where Mother was and said the city was on fire. That an angry crowd had stopped his auto-rickshaw, a crowd with petrol cans, one of them was about to smash his windscreen and only when he had told them his name, that he was one of them, did they let him pass. Mother said she had heard what happened to the little boy's mother early that morning, just down the street, and she was afraid the mob would come for them, for Shabnam. Father said, don't worry, there is a very important leader who lives down the street, he was once a Member of Parliament, and they don't kill such people just like that. These people can pull strings. On his way home, Father told her, he had stopped at the entrance to Leader's house and Leader told him not to worry, just stay at home, I have told the police, I am a VIP. But Mother wasn't so sure and while Father was telling her all this, she held his hand, trembling, her hand on my dial. I could see through the gaps between her fingers; I saw her face, frightened, I saw Shabnam in the other room, pacing, her eyes closed, praying. Father said, let me go and wash now, I am hungry. But Mother didn't let go of his hand, I was counting the seconds, thirty-one, thirty-two, forty, forty-five and she held his wrist, her fingers pressed so hard to my dial, so close that the gaps were gone, I couldn't see anything, I couldn't breathe. Father then freed himself from her, took me off and put me on a side table just underneath a lamp. I don't like that, Father always did that in the evening, letting the light fall directly on my face.

BOOK Father and Mother are about to be killed and you are worried about some light falling on your stupid face.

WATCH It's very important to tell you all this in detail. Because of what happened later. Father came out of the bathroom, his hands and his face wet, and to my surprise, he picked me up, wiped me with a towel so I was fresh and clean again and he put me back on his wrist. He walked to the kitchen where Mother was kneading the flour. He walked up to her and wrapped both his arms around her; my strap was pressing against her stomach, I could see right in front the flames in the gas burner, the pressure cooker, the steam began fogging my glass. Then he put his hand on her head, her hair was all over me then, I smelled shampoo from her hair, soap from his wrist. Mother told him, careful, Shabnam is in the other room. And it's at that moment, thirty-seven minutes past seven, both my hands almost together, pressed flat, pointed south-west by south, that they came. (WATCH *stops suddenly.*)

(*A pause,* BOOK *is uncharacteristically still, so is* TOWEL, *as always. Even the wind has stopped. The glare of the overhead light falling on* WATCH *makes the ripples of the water on the stage sparkle.*)

BOOK You there, Watch? We are listening, we are waiting.

WATCH (*Still silent, a drop of something falls from its strap that hangs over the edge of the chair. It makes a noise when it drips onto the water below.*)

BOOK Come on, Watch, don't tell me you are crying.

WATCH (*Silent.*)

BOOK You, made of steel, glass, leather, you with an electronic battery, why do you cry? It's all over, we are only trying to recall now. We are among friends, we have water, we can always hide. Just get it over with. The more you delay, the more difficult it becomes.

WATCH I know, Book, I know, but the next bit is difficult. They entered the room and Father went down onto his knees, Father was praying, my dial now pressed to the floor, they forced him to get up and they asked him to undress, I felt myself against his trousers as he unbuttoned them, I closed my eyes, I prayed for my hands to move faster, so I could not see, I heard them say, yes, he is the one we are after, then they told him to get up and open his mouth and hold his tongue with his left hand and there I was, on his wrist, I was there, I was right there, inches away from Father's tongue, I was there when they brought out the knife, I was there when they cut it, I had blood all over me, and it was then that one of them pulled me off, didn't even unbuckle the strap, pulled hard, tore me away from Father's wrist and all this while I could see Shabnam standing in the room, I saw her crying, I saw her shivering as if she was sick, I heard Mother screaming from the kitchen and then they got to her, they told Mother to do that, too, to undress and to show her tongue. Then they threw me out of the window. Still in the air, I looked down, I saw Father's auto-rickshaw was already on fire, the windscreen had gone, so close was I to the flames that I thought I would land on the roof of the auto-rickshaw, that my end had come. But when I landed, I felt stone, I felt the street, it shattered my glass but yes, I was alive. Through my dial-face, shattered, I saw the fire, I saw Shabnam running. And later, much later, I saw you, Book, not far away.

BOOK Thank you for noticing me but did you see them, Watch? You saw their faces? Through the blood on your dial?

WATCH I saw them. I cannot forget their faces. B looked at me, A held the father, C fetched the knife, D went for the mother.

(*Once again, the overhead light is switched off, it's dark. This time the pause is longer, almost thirty seconds, in which you can hear the sound of water dripping – tears from* WATCH. *The third light switches on, this one over* TOWEL.)

MISS GLASS (*Off stage.*) Towel, you are our last speaker. And, Book, please listen, Towel didn't interrupt you.

TOWEL (*Speaks in a woman's voice, softer than either* BOOK *or* WATCH, *a pause in between each word as if someone was taking notes and she was dictating.*) I have been listening to both of you carefully, Book and Watch, although it has been difficult. You see, as I told you, I am folded all over, there were times when the folds muffled your voices, but I think the hole helped, the hole burnt in my middle. Through that I could hear.

BOOK Why didn't you say so, Towel? Miss Glass could have raised the level of the wind, that could have carried our voices better. But you have been unusually quiet. Even on the street, when we were all lying in a heap, you were the one quietly crumpled in one corner.

TOWEL Because unlike you, Book and Watch, I didn't just watch, I helped them kill. I am a murderer, I have blood on me, the blood of a woman, of a young mother, of Abba's daughter-in-law. (*The water splashes.*)

BOOK You are being too dramatic now, just tell us your story and we shall decide.

TOWEL I was lying on the floor, in the kitchen, just beside Daughter-in-law as she was peeling the potatoes when they walked in. They hadn't seen her but Daughter-in-law could hear everything. She got up, walked to the kitchen door and without stepping out, of course, she listened. They were talking to Abba. In fact, he was the one doing most of the talking. She heard him beg, she heard him plead, implore. Abba is a proud man and never talks like that so she knew something terrible was about to happen. And all that she could do was to pick me up, tie and untie me in knots, wrap me around her fingers, unwrap me, run to the window to see if there was anyone she could call for help but there was no one. And she would run back to the door to listen some more. When she realized they wouldn't listen, she tried to hide in the kitchen, but as you can see in the picture, there was no place to hide. So she pressed herself against the wall, near the dish rack, and watched two men walk in. Next to them, Daughter-in-law looked like a child, little more than a girl. One man said, let's get it over with before the fire spreads. The other man laughed and said, I don't think you can last longer than that. One man picked me up from the kitchen floor, the other grabbed Daughter-in-law. Yes, she fought, Daughter-in-law fought, she tried to get away but she was very weak, she had a baby inside her. I saw Daughter-in-law slide down the wall to the floor and the man going down with her, I saw her close her eyes and the man unfasten his trousers with one hand while holding the other over her mouth. But she didn't scream, she didn't even bite, she just closed her eyes. The other man took me to her, sat down at her head. As the man holding her down removed his hand from her mouth, I was the one who replaced it. It was my job to muffle her scream, I was pressed flat against her face and then I was pushed inside her mouth, I felt her lips, her tongue, her teeth. After the first man was done, it was the other's turn. Then they both used me to wipe themselves.

(TOWEL *stops.* BOOK *listens, all his pages closed, still.*)

WATCH (*Softly, so softly that those in the audience have to strain their ears to hear.*) You don't have to tell us everything if you don't want to, you know.

BOOK Are you stupid, Watch? If you can't take it, slip down from the chair into the water. Continue, Towel, yes, you are right, yours seems to be the most difficult story to tell, but we are here to speak the unspeakable.

We aren't humans, we are objects, we don't have to follow their rules.

TOWEL I helped kill Daughter-in-law. (*Loud and clear, a distinct pause between each word. The wind is now blowing hard making* BOOK*'s pages flap,* TOWEL *shudder, the water is rising up the legs of all three chairs.*)

BOOK You were used as a gag, Towel, no one died because of you, no one dies because a little hand towel is stuffed inside their mouths.

TOWEL I helped kill Daughter-in-law, Book, I helped kill her. Trust me, I know what I'm talking about. Because I wasn't just used as a gag, I was then used as a noose. Because when they were done with the rape, when they had wiped themselves in my folds, they got down on the floor again. Daughter-in-law's sari was bunched near her waist, there wasn't a word from her, no scream, no cry and then they tied me around her neck, both of them, they used me to strangle her, to bang her head on the floor. Then they took a knife and cut her open, they wiped the knife in my folds, they then slit her womb, took the baby out, the baby still not formed, not ready to emerge, they cut almost everything the baby had grown so far, even its tiny arms and legs. It didn't take long. By this time, another man had walked into the room and when he saw what had happened, when he saw the blood, when he saw the flesh, he threw up, they laughed at him, gave me to him to wipe his face but he took one look at me, saw the blood, dropped me on the floor.

(The water on the stage is now moving, in ripples that start from around the chairs and reach the end of the stage. As if someone has dropped a huge invisible boulder into the water without making the slightest of noises.)

BOOK You saw them, Towel? You saw the faces?

TOWEL I saw them. I cannot forget their faces. A chewed his lip, B blows into the air, C looks around and D fixes his hair. But, wait, I haven't told you the most important thing in this, about the baby. The baby was alive.

BOOK You just said they slit Daughter-in-law open, they took the baby out.

TOWEL I told you, the baby was alive. I saw it.

WATCH Come on, Towel, it's like me saying I am still running tick tock tick tock. How could the baby live in all that fire, after all that blood?

TOWEL The baby was alive.

BOOK Towel, sorry, I didn't want to have to say this but you are making me say this. I am the one with the stories written inside me, I am the one with questions and answers, I know reason better than any one of you here. Watch is right, how could the baby have lived?

TOWEL The baby was alive. The baby was alive, the baby was alive, the baby was alive.

BOOK OK, Towel, so if the baby was alive (let's assume it was, let's take you for your word), what did it look like? Did it look like the Farex Baby, its soft hands wrapped around the baby-formula tin? Or did it look like the baby in my book, with a pink face and blue eyes, a London baby?

TOWEL This was a baby like I have never seen before. I told you it wasn't fully formed, its time had not yet come, it was not supposed to be brought out into the world. I couldn't see the details except for a black strip of flesh running around its tiny forehead and waist, as if it had caught the heat from the fire. And, this you won't believe but I saw it, it had eyes and these were blinking. Blinking through the murder, the smoke, the men throwing up in the kitchen.

(TOWEL *pauses, the wind is now silent, the water calm, hardly any ripples. The overhead light falling on* TOWEL *is now softer, more yellow and orange than white.* BOOK *is uncharacteristically quiet, stunned into disbelief.* WATCH *breaks the silence, softly.*)

WATCH And?

BOOK Yes, and? Now you will say that the baby had wings and it flew? You are making things up, Towel, I think the fire's got to you. (*Flaps his pages.*)

TOWEL I understand, Book, I perfectly understand, I would have reacted the same way. What happened later I don't know, I was kicked by someone, just like you and Watch, kicked repeatedly until I was out of the house on the pavement not far from both of you. By then, though, I had caught some of the flames, you can see what that did to me. And until Bright Shirt came and picked me up, I lay there just thinking of the baby. The baby was alive. I am sure of that.

WATCH So what happened to the baby? Did they take it away? Did you see them take it away?

BOOK Or did this baby crawl away on its own? I won't be surprised if it did, you have made it sound like a Superbaby.

TOWEL I don't know, Book, I don't know. I told you I was out on the street by then, with all of you. But Miss Glass knows, she will tell us what happened to the baby.

(*The overhead light begins to dim, the noise of the wind is now loud enough to be distracting, there are murmurs in the audience. Someone is crying. The stage is dark again, just as it was when the curtains went up, the chairs visible only in their outlines. There's a stir in the audience, the sound of people getting up, promptly silenced by a familiar voice, again off stage.*)

MISS GLASS Thank you, Towel, for that story. And, yes, I know what happened next. That's for the last act, ladies and gentlemen. Once again, please join me in thanking all of these three special characters.

(*There is loud applause; the stage is now pitch dark except for a pale flood of light in the wings. The water is still again, I sit in wait, Ithim no longer by my side. It's so quiet that I can't even hear the faintest sound from behind me, from the gallery, it's as if all of the people there have frozen, turned to stone.*)

⬥◆⬥

23. *The Last Act – II*

THIS beam of light is so weak, diffused, that at first it seems not to be a part of the show. Perhaps there's a room in the wings where a door has opened and the light's coming from there. By accident, not design. It's enough to reveal the water, though. And you can see that while all the three objects were talking, its level has risen until with each ripple, some of the water now spills over the wall that skirts the edge of the stage. BOOK, WATCH *and* TOWEL *are still seated, silent just as they were when the curtains first came up. The light beam then gets brighter and brighter until it's a dazzling, shining arc spanning the two ends of the stage. Like a rainbow spanning the three chairs and the black water. Someone claps in the audience. This rainbow, from wing to wing, stays on for the rest of the act.*

MISS GLASS Towel is right, the baby was alive. And to tell us about this, we have our last speaker of the night, Bright Shirt. Thank you for filling in most of the blanks, Book, Watch and Towel. Now Bright Shirt will take it from here, he will do the rest. I know all of us want to get back to The Hideout before the sun rises. That's why

I have told him to take it easy with his rhyme, just stick to reason.

(*At one end of the stage where the bright, white arc of light begins, there is a commotion.* BRIGHT SHIRT *appears with a loud splash of water and colour. Just as he had in the railway station, he walks onto the stage, prancing and twirling, waist-deep in the water.*)

BRIGHT SHIRT (*Stands next to the chair, to the left of* TOWEL, *so all four are in a straight line. His movements stop, he stands as if to attention.*) Just like the three of you, Book, Watch and Towel, we too were together last night after we were killed. We, the people. There were many of us, I am losing count. And just like you on the pavement, we were piled up as well. In heaps in hospitals. I found myself in the Burns Ward of Holy Angel. Miss Glass was there, too, what a privilege. A nurse was there, along with two doctors, all of whom once worked in the hospital before they were killed, there were some guards, there was Abba's daughter-in-law with her baby. There was the newborn, there were the newdead. As for Tariq's mother and Shabnam's parents – we are still looking, they must have been sent somewhere else. We were all shaken but Abba's daughter-in-law kept crying and crying saying she was sure her baby was alive.

TOWEL See, I told you so. Thank you, Bright Shirt.

BRIGHT SHIRT You are welcome. So there we were, all of us at Holy Angel, lying on the floor, trying to see through the white cotton sheets that covered our bodies (brand-new white sheets, by the way). And here was this young woman crying. She kept saying she wanted her baby to experience the world of the living. Even if just for a day, an hour, even five minutes. She wanted someone to hold him, just as she would. She said it was very unfair that he would come into our world straight from the world of the unborn. She said her baby had to know what it was like to be the living. And then the strangest thing happened. You won't believe it. Even you, Book, with all your stories and your pages, you haven't heard this one yet.

BOOK (*Evidently thrilled that the attention is back on him.*) Surprise me, Bright Shirt, I have been waiting. In fact, I'm a bit tired of children's stories set in London.

BRIGHT SHIRT Through the white sheet that covered her face, I saw Daughter-in-law shiver and tremble. At first, I thought she was crying about her baby again but when the shivering didn't stop, I asked her what was wrong and she said she was frightened, she was very frightened. I told her there was nothing to be afraid of, it was all over. And she said, no, it wasn't, because when they were carrying her up the stairs, she had seen a gentleman walk into the hospital with his pregnant wife. She said she was sure he was one of the four who had come to her house earlier that evening.

BOOK, WATCH, TOWEL (*All together, in one shout, almost*

a scream.) Who was it? A? B? C? D? Tell us, tell us, we need to know, we remember the faces. Each one of them.

BRIGHT SHIRT Please, let me finish. I mentioned this to Miss Glass. Miss Glass, Miss Glass, Miss Glass. The angel, the saviour, the one with the dazzling intelligence, the flashing brilliance, the one with grace, the one with kindness . . .

MISS GLASS (*From off stage.*) Enough, Bright Shirt, continue. If you wish, you can praise me later; we have all the time in the world. How many times do I have to tell you that?

BRIGHT SHIRT Sorry, Miss Glass, I had to get that off my chest given it will soon be submerged; the water's rising. Well, I told Miss Glass what Daughter-in-law had just said and right there, that very moment, in a second, she didn't even stop to think, the brilliant Miss Glass, she and the nurse and the doctors went into a huddle after which she called out to me: 'We have some work to do, are you ready?' I said I am honoured, I am at your service, I couldn't be more blessed, I . . .

BOOK (*Shouts.*) Careful, I see a rhyme coming, I can see a rhyme coming. Stick to reason, Mr Shirt.

BRIGHT SHIRT Sorry about that. Well, Miss Glass had a brainwave. The doctors had said that the baby didn't have even a day to live – each blink, in fact, was a miracle. And the woman who had just been admitted to the Maternity Ward would be in labour for at least a day or two. So Miss Glass said why not see if the gentleman takes this baby as his own. Let's not tell him anything, just approach him with the bundle. Let's see if we can fulfil a young mother's dead wish. Let the baby be held, be loved, let the baby be in the world of the living. And who better to do this than the gentleman himself? He is ideal, he watched over our deaths, now he waits for birth. Such fearful, graceful symmetry, she said.

TOWEL How could you be so sure such a man would take care of this baby?

BRIGHT SHIRT That's a very good question, Towel. But trust Miss Glass to have worked it out. On her instructions, the nurse and the doctors took the baby and walked away. This was their hospital, they knew their way. Don't ask me what they did next but they returned in a few hours to say that there was nothing to worry about. That the gentleman had taken the baby as his own and would be a loving father. They were sure of that.

BOOK Strange are the ways of the living, if you ask me.

WATCH No one asked you, Book. Let him finish.

BRIGHT SHIRT Well, once the baby was with the gentleman, all of us had to get to work.

TOWEL What kind of work? What did you do?

BRIGHT SHIRT That I can't say, my lips are sealed. But I am happy to announce that it has gone as per plan. Perfect. And all because of Miss Glass. The baby is back with us now, with his mother. He came into our world just a few moments ago, delivered to us by the gentleman himself. The baby lived for almost a day. He saw the night, he saw the morning, he saw the afternoon, he saw the city. He was even named and he was loved. There was nothing more his mother had asked for.

BOOK But how did the baby come here? What happened when the gentleman took the baby home? Why did he take care of this baby? Why didn't he just kill the baby as he killed the mother?

BRIGHT SHIRT That we shall never know until the gentleman himself tells us. If he ever does, that is.

WATCH Can you tell us who he was, describe him to us so we can know if it was A, B, C, or D?

BRIGHT SHIRT Who do you think it could be?

WATCH (*After a long silence.*) If you ask me, I will say B, the one with the striped shirt. The one who just watched. Who watched me, who watched as Tariq's mother was attacked, who watched as Abba's daughter-in-law was killed. Maybe he has some goodness still left in him and that's why he was a loving father. What do you think, Book?

BOOK I wish I could be as sure as you are. Towel, what about you?

TOWEL I don't know, I can't guess, they are all the same. Who was he, Bright Shirt?

BRIGHT SHIRT Sorry, I cannot tell. Strict orders from Miss Glass. That was the promise we made to ourselves, that if he took care of the baby, we would leave him alone.

BOOK So he gets away? He takes care of the baby for a few hours, and that too because he is made to think that the baby is his, a baby whose mother he and his friends kill. And he gets away? What about Tariq and his mother?

WATCH And Shabnam and her parents? What will you tell them?

BRIGHT SHIRT That Miss Glass will answer.

MISS GLASS (*From off stage.*) What about Tariq, Shabnam and Abba, the ones who live? If the world, as they say, is a small place, the city then should be much, much smaller. So we hope that one day the gentleman will see them in a crowd, like the one that waits on the cement divider outside his house every morning for the traffic to pass. Maybe their eyes will meet. But you were right, Book, strange are the ways of the living. We sent the gentleman several reminders of his guilt even as he took care of the baby; we sent him pictures of the three of you lying on the heap, we sent him the pictures that you see on stage. He looked and he looked but he did not see. We sent him messages detailing everything you three had told us and more. He read every word but he doesn't admit it, even to himself. I doubt he ever will. It's as if he has no memory of the three incidents, as if he went inside his own head and removed that part of his brain that recorded them.

WATCH So what purpose did the whole thing serve? Giving him the baby for a day and a night if he is never going to admit his guilt?

MISS GLASS The baby is one thing he cannot deny, he cannot forget. For one day and one night in this city on fire, he loved this baby because he thought it was his own, that he was the father. So he held it close, he took care of it, he travelled with it across the city. And now he knows who the baby is, how it was forced into the world of the living, how its mother was killed, how he had a hand in all this, whenever he thinks about that baby, he will have to think about the fire, about the killing. Every time he looks at his own baby, which we have learnt is safe in the hospital, he will remember this one. The one that was deformed, that had been burnt, whose skin around the forehead and the waist had been charred and was still fireproof. And yet he cannot talk about this to anyone; he has to carry the burden of a story he can never tell. A story of his love that carries, within it, the story of his hate. That, I guess, is justice. Not the best, not the cleanest, if you ask me, but I think it's as good as we, the dead, can get.

BOOK Well, if you say so, Miss Glass. Watch, what do you think?

WATCH I wish Miss Glass could do something similar for Shabnam's parents. And Tariq's mother. Maybe they have wishes, too. Towel, you are the lucky one.

TOWEL I don't understand many things, I am only a silly piece of fabric with a hole in the middle. But I am glad the baby got to live for a day, a mother's wish was fulfilled. I told you the baby was alive.

BOOK Well, Towel, you were right. All I hope is that the gentleman is somewhere in the audience. Don't tell us his name, keep his face in the dark, Bright Shirt, but I hope he got to hear all of us. That's all that matters.

(*The dazzling rainbow begins to dim and as it grows darker and darker, one by one,* BOOK, WATCH, TOWEL *slip off their chairs and fall into the water.* BRIGHT SHIRT *joins them, swimming in the water that's risen so high it has flooded the space between the stage and the first row of red chairs. Four splashes, the curtains begin to fall. There is scattered applause, someone says don't clap, the audience is on its feet, waiting to file out into The Hideout.*)

⬥◆⬥

24. *Curtains*

THAT'S what I told you right in the beginning, don't listen to the dead, Do Not Listen To The Dead – whatever they tell you, however they tell you, sitting on stage or speaking off it, between the lines or in the footnotes, screaming or whispering, water rising or water falling, whatever fancy name or un-name they wish to go by. Because once you lend them your ears, which I clearly did, they will swallow you whole, from your head to your toe. Because all they want is to pit themselves against me and then ask you to choose, ask you to choose between the dead and me. That's why I urged you, right in the beginning, to doubt dispute distort deny everything you hear, ninety-nine point nine nine per cent of it, bury it in the ground, cover it with gravel, dirt, dead leaves, shrivelled dry and rotting, turn away, never to look back, never ever, or pile it all in front and set it on fire, watch the flames in the night or freeze it under a glacier, white, hard and solid.

That's why I ran.

And if running away makes you an accused, so be it. I didn't care. Beginning with the night in Holy Angel, they had laid out a trap, lured me into it. They tracked me down, to my wife in the Maternity Ward, there, they say, they handed me the bundle, handed me Ithim, my penance baby, my punishment baby to take care of. For one day and one night and then to hand him back. They wrote on glass, they dragged me out of my home across a city on fire, with a false promise for a false child, they made me risk my life, they got objects to sit on chairs on a stage and talk, they even got a dead woman to pronounce me guilty, yes, a dead woman's words, they said, *I was ideal, he watched over our deaths, now he waits for birth, such fearful, graceful symmetry.* Symmetry, my foot.

No, I wasn't going to remain trapped in this any more.

No way.

That's why I ran.

The curtains were still falling, Book, Watch, Towel and Bright Shirt had just slipped into the water, when I ran.

No one stopped me, no one followed, in fact, no one saw me in the dark as I tore through the flap at the tent entrance. No one heard me over the sound of the applause. At a distance, I could see the moonbeams on the rail tracks and what had seemed such a long journey hours ago, walking through water, suddenly seemed to have shrunk, both in time and in space. Maybe the night was dying and that's why I could no longer see The Hideout; there was neither water nor those houses of air or water lit by soft lights, none of the people swimming. There were no children playing on underwater swings, no birds swimming, no fish flying. I turned back and saw no tent, no naked lights on electric poles, not even the faintest sound of a crowd, no clapping no cheering.

Instead, the ground beneath me was dry and under my feet, I could feel the hard earth, the soft soil; the moon was dirty as it always is, gone was its sparkle, the plum sky was stained with grey.

No, this didn't seem to be the place where I had landed just hours ago.

That's why I ran.

I reached the railway tracks, I followed them, their glint in the dark my only guide. I stumbled over holes in the ground I couldn't see, over boulders hiding; once or twice I fell, but with no weight on my back, with Ithim gone, with Ithim taken away, just the empty bag flapping behind me, it was as if I had wings.

I flew past villages fast asleep, past men, women and children huddled around their burnt-out huts, I heard their crying. I wanted to tell them, keep crying, collect your tears to fight the fire because there is no water, there is no Miss Glass, there is no Bright Shirt and there is no Hideout. Or if there is, go there, go play, go watch a circus, go watch Juggler, don't just sit here and cry.

I reached what looked like a railway platform, empty except for a dog asleep under a lamp post. There was an iron bench on which I sat down to catch my breath; I watched trains stampede by, headed for the city, streaks of light in the dark, not one of them stopping. I walked right up to the edge of the platform and stood there letting one train pass me in a blur of noise and wind that fanned my face, dried my sweat, the clatter filling my ears and pushing out everything I had heard just moments ago. The trains may not have stopped but the rail tracks would certainly lead back to the city, they would take me home, I was sure of that. There was no doubt in my mind, none at all.

Train tracks follow a straight line.

That's why I ran.

Following the tracks. How long I can't say now with any confidence but the tracks soon veered off at an intersection where the hard uneven surface beneath gave way to a smooth metallic stretch; this was the road. And on either side the rolling night and, in the middle, a bus standing there, its engine still running, BACK TO TH CITY written on its side in huge black letters, the E missing, but each letter ringed with countless tiny bulbs twinkling in the dark. Like Diwali lights in the shops in the city. I boarded the bus, found a seat by the window, just as I had done this morning.

The train journey with Bright Shirt had taken about six hours and I expected the bus would take longer – but then I had already run a considerable distance. I tried to do the arithmetic in my head, distance, speed, time, but I soon gave up, closed my eyes and rested my head on the bars of the window, feeling the welcome shudder, the wind in my hair.

My mother was sitting next to me.

I am all right now, she said, the doctor was good, the scorpion is dead, look my fingers are now almost back to normal, the pain has gone, you held my wrist the whole night, you saved my life.

They are after me, I told her, they are after me, they are going to get me come what may, any which way.

And she said, no, don't worry, I know them, we all live together, they can't do anything, it's just talk, you are safe.

She put her hands in mine, whispered in my ear as if I was a child again, tell me what happened that afternoon, try to remember, you always had such a good memory, remember how you came running home from school with the poem about the scorpion, how you remembered exactly what I had said those years ago (even I had forgotten it until you told me), so tell me what happened that afternoon, that evening and that night, before you went to the hospital with your wife.

With my mother back, I was a child again, seven or eight, nine or ten, unable to reach the light switch on the wall, and all I remembered was the night of the scorpion, the rain pouring, its spray on my face, Father's umbrella in the veranda, and this time, I was the one lying on the floor, Mother holding my hands, my thumb and my fingers, pressing them hard, afraid that if she let go, the poison inside me would spread, green, black and yellow, *the flash of diabolic tail in the dark room*, Father telling her to wait for the morning, then saying he would fetch the doctor, I heard his voice, I heard the pounding of the hammer, the pounding of the scorpion, my arms are hurting, Mother's pressing too hard and I hear her ask again, what about Ithim?

Yes, Ithim.

Yes, Mother, I brought him home, yes, I cleaned him up, I fed him with a dropper, I watched out for his tears, I covered him carefully, I kept him close to my chest as we travelled across the city, I played with him for about five minutes (he even sat on a bicycle in a park), but now he isn't with me. They took him away and if they meant what they said, Mother, if they are all a lie, it means there is no Ithim, which means that all the hours at home, in the bus, in the city, in the trial room, in the cinema hall, in the railway station, in the train, were just shapes and shadows. It's a good thing, Mother; now my wife and I can have a healthy child, you will have a beautiful grandchild, a Baby Sentence that makes perfect sense. No cylinder wrapped in flesh and skin, no vegetable, no insect, its legs and its antennae wrenched off. No caterpillar, no charred skin like a hat on his head. Now the nursery my wife has built will be used – everything in it, the toys will be grasped with little fingers, the handrails will be held with tiny hands and we will lift our child high above our shoulders so that he, a boy, or a she, a girl, can reach out and touch the flying fish, the swimming birds on the ceiling.

But Mother wasn't listening; she had left, I could feel the poison inside me spreading, the entire bus was empty, and through the window I saw more villages, more fires, more tears, all speeding by, rushing as if it was their backwards momentum that was pushing the bus forward towards the city.

IT was early morning when I entered Holy Angel and the hospital had barely woken up from its sleep of last night. The tubelights in the lobby and the staircase hadn't been switched off, their glare brighter than sunlight. I ran past sweepers, their eyes half open as they filled their buckets at the municipal tap in the lawn, I stood in line, I put my hand below the tap, I felt the water, this wasn't a dream, I was awake.

I ran up the stairs, all six floors, I leaned forward to touch one of the steps, I felt the layer of dust, the cold of the marble, this wasn't a dream, I was awake.

I ran past the morning-shift attendants, I brushed past them deliberately so I could smell their sweat, so I could see and touch their white smocks smudged with last night's dirt, they were alive, they were not dead, this wasn't a dream, I was awake.

I ran past a boy, about Tariq's age, walking upstairs with the morning tea for the guards, kettle in one hand, a dozen small glasses on a plate balanced in the other. I touched him on the head, he turned to look, he smiled, I smiled back, he was alive, he was not dead, I was awake. I ran my fingers along the staircase wall, I scratched the plaster with my nails, it chipped, I was awake.

No, this wasn't a dream.

I passed the man and the wife I had seen the night before, I stopped, I stood right in front of them, as if blocking their way. 'Do you remember me?' I asked. 'I was the father waiting for my child and I saw you both, I saw your white plastic bag, between your feet. I saw you leaning your head on his shoulder, you were trying to sleep.'

The man and the woman looked at each other and then, with a gesture of her hand asking me to step aside, the woman continued walking, down the stairs. I wanted to follow them all the way to the exit, to their home and, if need be, I wanted them to touch me. To tell me I was awake, that they were not dead. But they had gone and there I was, in the lobby of the Maternity Ward.

The window I had stood at was still there, unchanged, thick dust still on the frame. The building right across the lawn was still there, the Burns Ward, but all its windows now reflected the first light of the day. I tried to locate Miss Glass's room, fifth floor, thirteenth window from the corner, but all I could see was a strip of white, bright and shining.

I turned to head towards the Operating Theatre where,

in a room next door, I had last seen my wife, where I had talked to Doctors 1 and 2, where Head Nurse had filled out the discharge form, where I had written down his name: Ithim. Yes, I must have that discharge form in my pocket and I would show it to the guard or the nurse but just as I turned from the window to take the first step I was struck by the silence in the Maternity Ward.

And in that silence, I saw the bodies.

THERE were so many that I had to walk on tiptoe to avoid touching them. They were on the floor, some resting against doors, some near the elevator entrance, others on the staircase landing, lining the nurses' station. Bodies, all covered with winding sheets, factory-fresh white. (I saw the name of the mill from where this cloth had come, its blue ink imprint, its golden foil seal on the sheets, in some cases near the feet, in others near the head or right on the chest, like someone was stamping the dead: *Made from Cotton 100%, Bleached Cambric, fully combed yarn. Texmark No 22. Silver Dew. Finley's Sovereign Quality, Mohar Gold Mills (U.C.), Bombay 14. NTC, National Textiles Corporation.*)

So white were these sheets – and made whiter under the tubelights – that my eyes would have hurt had it not been for the fact that the dazzle was offset by a softer shade: there were huge blocks of ice kept in between the bodies.

No, this wasn't a dream: I touched the ice, it was cold, I used my nails to scrape some off, I saw it fall to the floor. Walking in and out of the rows of the bodies, wending their way through the blocks of ice, were the mourners. Men and women, their heads lowered, sometimes going down on their knees to lift one edge of a sheet. To see a face, to check if it was family or a stranger. The silence was breaking, I could hear it, by first the sound of their shoes and their slippers against the marble floor, the rapid drawing of their breaths, and then later by the crying.

A mother crying, a sister crying, a brother crying, a wife crying, a father crying, a husband crying, I heard their tears drop, slide down their faces, their clothes, reach the floor, touch the ice.

I wanted to tell them about Bright Shirt, I wanted to tell them about Miss Glass and how she had built houses of air and water for all of their dead, where they were safe, where they could look up at the sky and see a moon, scrubbed clean, where they could see an ocean knee-deep, even watch a circus complete with a fireproof juggler and half a dozen clowns.

For a while, I walked with them, too, drawn by the sound of their tears and the shuffle of their feet. I counted the bodies, ten, eleven, twelve, thirteen, fourteen, fifteen, sixteen, seventeen, eighteen, nineteen, I stopped counting, I lost count.

I was now at the end of the hallway, near the elevator. I looked for the Ward Guard from that night. He wasn't there; in his place, someone else, in the same uniform but without a name tag.

'I am checking on my wife, I was here the night before last, in the Maternity Ward.'

'Go check the list,' he said.

He pointed to a piece of paper stuck in one corner on the wall, near the elevator.

I checked the list, I read names and numbers, people and ages.

I read Ahmed, Muhammad, Ramesh, Imran, Shameena, Nafitullah, Qasimbhai, Ehsan, Omar, Hossain-ur, Siraj, Ibrahim, Andaleeb, Sajjad, Firoze, Dimple, Bakhtiyar, Shakeela, Babu, Bashir, Syed, Javed, Rehman, Bilkis, Ishfaq, Farooq, Jalla, Rizwan, Zahra, Yasmin, Posha. Each name had an age, single digits double digits. 26, 28, 71, 64, 44, 23, 27, 5, 26, 43, 2, 31, 9, 4, 4, 2, 19.

And so on and so on and so forth and so forth.

'My wife's name isn't there,' I told the guard.

'That's good news, you should be happy. She must be in one of the wards near the Operating Theatre.'

'Where is Ward Guard who was here the other night?' I asked.

'I don't know,' he said.

'Can I see Head Nurse? Doctors 1 and 2? They were the ones who know about my wife.'

'Head Nurse was supposed to be here but she's been missing, along with the doctors and two guards; they went home in a van that evening when the fires began and we don't know what happened, they haven't returned.'

No, it couldn't be true. I reached into my pockets, I wanted to show him the discharge slip that Head Nurse had filled out, nail his lie, I wanted to tell him that I was there in the hospital and as proof, I wanted to show him the picture I had picked up in Miss Glass's room that night, the crumpled shred of black and white, but he had turned to walk away.

'This is not visiting hours anyway,' he called, looking back at me, 'come in three hours.'

No, I wasn't going to wait any more.

I had to get into the ward next to the Operating Theatre and see my wife; I was alive, I was awake, I could not let any one, living or dead, distract me now. And so when I heard the screaming of two children, both boys, who were being brought up the stairs in one stretcher from the Emergency Ward below, I knew this was my chance.

There was a commotion ahead.

A family was tailing the two attendants who carried the boys bound for the Operating Theatre. I joined this crowd, falling into line behind the man I thought was the father. No one asked me any questions, everyone's eyes were on the two children, one writhing with pain, the other still. Both had burns over their bodies; someone had draped them with a thin cotton sheet – to keep the infection away, I guess – but each touch of the fabric was making one child scream. Through the sheet, I could see their charred flesh, I could see what the fire had done, peeling away their skin, I saw the red and the blue and the white of clotted blood, veins, muscle and fat. The stretcher stopped at the entrance to the Operating Theatre, someone opened the door and before father and the two attendants and the stretcher could enter, I slipped in.

I saw several beds lined up against the wall, all full. All the patients were covered, except for two men, both fast asleep, their foreheads swathed in bandages. Adjusting the sheet over them was a nurse, her back towards me. As she heard me approach, she turned around.

'You can't come in here,' she said.

'I need your help, please, I have been waiting for a long time. My wife is here, I have to see her.'

'Give me her name and I will check the register,' she said.

I gave her my wife's name, her number, 110742, and she wrote it down on her palm, then left the room through a small door at the back.

While I stood there waiting, I saw more people being brought in, with burns, with injuries, some covered with cotton gauze drenched red with mercurochrome, some bare. And more and more white bundles, all being lined up in the shrinking space between the blocks of ice.

'The third room from the corner, to your left,' said the nurse on her return and she smiled: 'Congratulations, Mr Jay, you are a father.'

And she pointed out the door to my wife's room.

So this was the end of the nightmare.

My wife had given birth, I was on my way to meet her, I could now walk in, hold her, hold our child. What did Miss Glass say on that stage? She had said I would never forget Ithim but here I was, moments away from meeting my wife, Ithim a memory, a shadow, a ghost, and with each second that passed and with each step I took, he receded farther and farther away.

Miss Glass was wrong.

She had said I would carry the burden of Ithim's story throughout my life, I would never be able to tell it. Wrong again. For one day, when my wife reads to our child, I think I will join in, too, I will tell them how one night a face by the window wrote on glass, how children played under water, how parents swam when the city was on fire.

There is no burden I carry, whatever the dead may say. Because I am alive, I can choose what to remember, I can choose what to forget.

I stood at the entrance to my wife's room, it was a room for two but the bed next to hers was empty. My wife lay on her side, her head facing the wall, her back towards the door, towards me. The white knot of the hospital gown clasped the nape of her neck, the sheet was drawn over her waist.

I wanted to give her a surprise so I stood still, not entering, not making the slightest noise. I could see her right arm, thin, the gown's sleeve almost reaching her elbow. I could see it rise and fall with her breaths, I could hear her voice, faint scraps of whispers; she was talking to her child, to our child, who I could not see.

Perhaps I moved without my knowing, perhaps the curtains made a noise, or my shoes scraped against the marble floor, my wife turned.

I was about seven steps from the edge of her bed.

Not even ten feet, it should take me just under a few seconds.

I saw the dirt on my shoes, the mud and water and ash. Yes, we would go home this evening; no, I wouldn't keep them in the hospital one extra minute; we would enter the nursery together, my wife and I, I would help her bring the toys down, the kangaroo, the mouse, the duck, the fish, the bear, the green pillow in the shape of a turtle.

I was walking to the bed, only three steps away from my

wife – so close that I could clearly see a speck in the back of her hospital gown, near her left shoulder – when the floor below me gaped open at my feet, like the universe itself.

Black, cold, and limitless.

But after all I had been through, this was a mere distraction, I was sure, an apparition that would soon clear. I only had to walk across and I would walk across. I had jumped off a running train in the night, I had walked through water, I had been through fire, I could certainly do this. This was only three steps, one, two and three.

So I took the first step.

And I fell.

I kept falling, I shouted out my wife's name but from below came the echo of a voice which was neither hers nor my own. It was more a humming, like a dirge from the distant edge of the darkness, muffled whispers and screams of the dead and the dying, and the only thing I had, in reply, was the hollow beating of my heart. And the only thing I could see was the onrushing blackness from beneath, to my left, to my right, below and above.

I kept falling and as my eyes began to adjust to the dark, slowly, like night clouds get scattered by the lightest of winds to show the moon and the stars, the darkness began to fade and I saw Tariq's mother, the blood on her forehead now dried, a thin broken line, her sari torn, ash caught in her long black hair, its grey making her look older than she was. I kept falling, I passed Shabnam's parents, both silent, their lips crusted red, both naked, pressed against something that looked like a wall with neither a beginning nor an end, the mother behind the father. I saw Abba's daughter-in-law, Ithim now cradled in her arms, a gaping hole where her stomach should have been, the charred strip around Ithim's forehead as big as a ring around a planet. All of them were silent, unmoving, and although there was not the faintest gleam of reproach in any of their eyes, their gaze was so burningly fierce that I had to look away.

Just when I had passed Ithim, I found myself inexplicably slowing down until I came to a sudden stop as if an invisible floor had surfaced to stop my fall. And hardly had I caught my breath when I found I was now being dragged up, carried as if being pulled by strings out of a bottomless well.

On my way up, I passed them again and this time, instead of the hum of the dead, all I could hear was a voice, it was my voice, I was sure of that, although it was not I who was doing the talking. My lips moved on their own, the words formed by themselves. One after the other, three words, words that until then I hadn't once spoken, not once even thought, words that came not in a steady rush but spread out, stretched, gaps of silence between each: *I am guilty.* I heard this as I passed Abba's daughter-in-law and Ithim, I heard this again as I passed Shabnam's parents, I heard this a third time as I passed Tariq's mother, the voice growing louder and louder as I continued to be lifted up through the darkness, higher and higher, towards the edge over which I had just fallen and where, I knew, the hospital bed was. Where my wife and my child lay.

*

I was now back in the hospital room, I stood at the foot of the bed, they were fast asleep. My child, a bundle wrapped in a white towel, its eyes closed; my wife, on her side. I bent down to look at our child; everything was there, everything was normal: eyes, nose, mouth, lips, ears, tiny eyelashes, its forehead wrinkled into a tight knot.

A Baby Sentence making perfect sense.

But I was trembling hard, as if the earth had indeed begun to move; I shivered, frozen with fear that the chasm I had just fallen into and been lifted out of would abruptly open up again and, this time, I would fall into its blackness never to return. That the people I saw in there would hold on to my feet, Abba's daughter-in-law and Ithim, Shabnam's parents, Tariq's mother, would not let me rise back to the edge. My knees buckled, I tried to steady myself by sitting on the marble floor using both my hands to clasp the iron frame of the bed, ice cold, just below the warm white sheets that covered my family. I could smell the hospital's antiseptic between the cracks in the floor, the folds in their sheets.

And as my wife and my child, fast asleep, travelled through the world of their dreams, linked together, hand in hand, my wife's finger held firmly in my baby's tiny curled-up fist, I sat there, on the floor, inches away from both, afraid to make the slightest movement.

My chest hurt from the screaming of the voice inside, even my breath seemed to have lost its way, my eyes were wide open but instead of the daylight that was now streaming through the window from the city outside, making my wife's hair gleam, drawing a yellow bar of sunlight over my baby's face, I could see little more than a blur. Over each of my eyes had spread a thin, gauzy film, my unwept tears.

I closed my eyes, hoping that this wasn't anything more than a nightmare, that when I opened my eyes, the film would be gone but the moment I had done that, the voice was back, this time as a whisper, soft and gentle, I am guilty, as if it had deliberately lowered its pitch, not to disturb my wife and child. From outside, through the half-closed door, I could hear the rustle of winding sheets being pulled over the dead, the squeak of hospital trolley wheels rolling up and down, the footsteps of patients and visitors as more and more bodies from last night were brought in, someone shouting out to clear the way. But even over these sounds and these noises, even if no one was there to hear what my voice had just said, I knew the dead had heard.

Wherever they were: in the chasm below me, outside the window in the city on fire, in the flames and in the smoke, in the Hideout far away, under the water that lapped against the railway tracks or on the stage, brightly lit, in the dark shells of their houses where ghosts flitted from door to window, window to door. I knew the dead had heard, I was sure of that, because when I opened my eyes, the sunlight in the room was bright and clear, the floor below me was as hard as it could be, my wife and my child were waking, the film over my eyes had lifted and my tears had begun to flow.

◆◆◆

EPILOGUE

(THE CLOSING STATEMENT)

We, the undersigned, do solemnly affirm in this, our closing statement to you, the reader, the following:

1. **That this is Mr Jay's story. We made no changes in his narrative, not one word. Except for his name. For if we remain unnamed, it's only fair that he should, too. But then, Miss Glass said, he is our central character, anonymity could be seen as dissembling, even disrespect. So we called him Mr Jay.**

2. That in all, they burnt down 12,000 houses where we lived, 14,000 shops where we made our living. That's a lot of empty shells, rectangles and squares. In some places, the ash has been cleared, some buildings have been painted a fresh white (with a little bit of blue put in the paint to make the white look whiter). But many are untouched.

   Left, maybe, for us to flit around, to walk through the rooms where we once lived. To look out of the windows on to the streets where we once walked. And after the rain and shine and heat and cold of so many seasons, these gaps, many now say, look as if they were caused by time and neglect, not by fire and hate.

How easy it is for the living to deceive themselves.

3 **That there are times we get tired, impatient. Let us move on, we say, let us accept that the city, the country has to forget. And that, in the end, we are and we will always remain the meek, we will inherit nothing.**

4 That, at these times, Miss Glass comes running in, says, snap out of it, stop whining. It's the living who need to move on, she says, because they don't have much time – we, the dead, have forever. There's no arguing with Miss Glass.

5 **That Miss Glass says she has unfinished business. That just as we helped Ithim's mother by getting Mr Jay to admit his guilt, we have to help Tariq's, then Shabnam's. Go after the others, she says. I will have to start with each one of you, she says, all those who could only whisper in this story, as a footnote. I will begin with Ward Guard, then go down the list. One by one, I will do all one thousand.**

12 But that will take a long time, we tell Miss Glass. Even if you keep one day and one night

for each, as you did for Ithim, and a day in between to rest, it will take nine, ten years.

'So what?' she says. 'What's the hurry, we are all dead.'

On this note, she laughs, as she climbs down the steps of the castle of clouds and, with Bright Shirt by her side, begins to fly down to the charred city below.

Like an angel, from the sky far above, from the room in the blue, fireproof.

. . . like a man who seeks to return to a beloved place
and purposely forgets a book, a basket, a pair of glasses,
so that he will have an excuse to come back to the beloved place.
in the same way we leave things here.
in the same way the dead leave us.

Yehuda Amichai
(Translated, from the Hebrew, by Leon Wieseltier)

THE END

AUTHOR'S NOTES

The events in Gujarat, in brief:

Violence began on February 27, 2002, when a train, the Sabarmati Express, was stopped and attacked near Godhra, a town about 150 km from Gujarat's capital city of Gandhinagar. The exact nature and sequence of events surrounding the attack is still not clear, with conflicting reports from conflicting inquiry commissions. While the Justices Nanavati–Shah Commission (named after two retired judges), appointed by the state government, has said there is evidence to suggest a conspiracy, another, one-judge committee, appointed by a rival government, called it an 'accident'. According to the case filed by the Gujarat police, several Muslims conspired to attack the train and set it on fire.

What is clear, however, is that fifty-nine passengers, all Hindu, were killed when fire broke out in one coach of the train, S-6. Among those killed were several 'activists' on their way back from Ayodhya (in the northern state of Uttar Pradesh), where they had been campaigning to build a temple in place of a mosque, the five-hundred-year-old Babri Masjid, that was illegally demolished in 1992. (That demolition had itself sparked off Hindu–Muslim violence across the country in which hundreds were killed.)

The Vishwa Hindu Parishad (the World Hindu Council, a forty-year-old 'religious-cultural group') called a strike to protest against the Godhra train attack the next day across the state. Endorsing the strike was the Bharatiya Janata Party (BJP), which ran the government in Gujarat and, then, the Centre as well.

Beginning February 28, 2002 – and continuing for almost a month – cities and villages across the state saw unprecedented violence targeted against Muslims, with clear evidence in many cases that police, if not complicit, looked the other way as the massacres went on. Over a thousand men, women and children were killed, more than 70 per cent of them Muslim.

Seven months after the violence, the BJP government in the state was re-elected with a landslide majority. Its government, at the Centre, however, was defeated two years later, in May 2004.

◆

The numbers, as of June 2006:

All figures are government figures, including official intelligence estimates:

Total number of killed: 784 Muslims, 258 Hindus.

Number of houses destroyed: 12,000

Number of shops looted and burnt: 14,000

Number of villages affected: 993

Number of towns affected: 151

Total number of cases filed by the police: 4,252

Cases where charges were framed: 2,019

Cases closed for what police said was 'lack of evidence': 2,032

The Supreme Court of India has played an exemplary role in prodding and pushing the state's institutions to deliver justice. On its instructions, some cases were shifted out of state to ensure a free and fair trial. And all cases, including those previously closed, have been ordered to be reviewed.

Total number of cases reviewed: 1989

Cases re-opened: 1763

Cases where trial is on: 28

Number of cases ending in convictions: 10

The trial in the train-attack case and the Gulbarga massacre are currently on hold pending the Supreme Court's instructions.

◆

All three photographs in the book are news photographs of the Gujarat violence. The context in which they have been used, however, is fiction. These were taken by the *Indian Express* photographers Javed Raja and Harsh Shah and are reprinted with permission.

◆

Some of the instructions for baby care in Chapters 4 and 6, which Jay's wife downloaded from the net, are drawn from baby-center.com.

◆

The 'birthday gift' poem in Chapter 14 is the original work of Ayesha Khan, my colleague in Gujarat. I am grateful for her permission to use it.

◆

Poet Nissim Ezekiel, whose 'The Night of the Scorpion' Jay recalls in the train, died in Mumbai on January 9, 2004. Excerpts of the poem used with permission from Oxford University Press India, New Delhi.

◆

Violence in Gujarat did begin the night the novel begins but all names of characters, products and brands, all places and incidents are imagined or used fictitiously. Any resemblance to actual persons, living or dead, events or locales, is coincidental.

◆

I am indebted to:

The *Indian Express* and my colleagues, reporters, photographers and editors, who uncovered facts of the Gujarat riots that inform this fiction.

My editor-in-chief, Shekhar Gupta – the head and the heart of the *Indian Express*.

The Corporation of Yaddo, Saratoga Springs, New York. For a gift writers dream of: time and space in a room with a view of snow falling.

Gillon Aitken, my agent, and Picador publisher Andrew Kidd, for their sustained faith.

Sam Humphreys, Picador editor. The book's beacon – had she not been there, *Fireproof* would have lost its way in the smoke.

Shruti Debi, of Picador India, for her inexhaustible energy, her constant encouragement.

Sujata Bose, for my fact, my fiction and everything in between.

◆◆◆